To Glynis,
Thank you for your support and for buying one of the first copies of my book. I hope you enjoy it. Ross

ON FIRST NAME TERMS WITH ANGELS

ROSS FRIDAY

TRAFFORD

© Copyright 2004 Ross Friday

Original cover design and concept by Ross Friday.
Original photo by Getty Images and taken by Jayme Thornton.
Portrait photo by Richard Frankland.
Graphic Design by Vinesh Pallaram.

All characters in this publication are fictitious and any resemblance to real persons, living or dead, is purely coincidental.

All rights reserved. No part of this publication may be reproduced, stored in a retrieval system, or transmitted, in any form or by any means, electronic, mechanical, photocopying, recording, or otherwise, without the written prior permission of the author.

Note for Librarians: A cataloguing record for this book is available from Library and Archives Canada at www.collectionscanada.ca/amicus/index-e.html
ISBN 1-4120-8633-7

Printed in Victoria, BC, Canada. Printed on paper with minimum 30% recycled fibre.
Trafford's print shop runs on "green energy" from solar, wind and other environmentally-friendly power sources.

Offices in Canada, USA, Ireland and UK

Book sales for North America and international:
Trafford Publishing, 6E–2333 Government St.,
Victoria, BC V8T 4P4 CANADA
phone 250 383 6864 (toll-free 1 888 232 4444)
fax 250 383 6804; email to orders@trafford.com

Book sales in Europe:
Trafford Publishing (UK) Limited, 9 Park End Street, 2nd Floor
Oxford, UK OX1 1HH UNITED KINGDOM
phone 44 (0)1865 722 113 (local rate 0845 230 9601)
facsimile 44 (0)1865 722 868; info.uk@trafford.com

Order online at:
trafford.com/06-0389

10 9 8 7 6 5 4 3 2 1

WHATEVER LIFE'S WORTH...
IT'S AT LEAST WORTH LIVING

THE AUTHOR

Ross was born in 1978 and raised in Kent, England. He grew up discovering a natural flare for art and accomplished sporting success at a national level before finishing his education. He flirted with several vocations but found a creative outlet in the form of writing songs which not only received critical acclaim, but also achieved regular radio airplay. This eventually led to him performing alongside major stars at high profile events before he was forced to establish a more conventional career.

It wasn't until he seized an opportunity reporting for a regional newspaper that his previously hidden writing ability was discovered; it made the perfect partner to his vivid imagination and he set about creating a literary work of total originality. By interweaving wonderfully flawed characters and inventive scenarios around his elaborate and highly unconventional central story, his debut as a novelist impresses on every level and stands tall as a thought provoking, emotionally complex example of fiction that can be applied to life.

For further information visit www.rossfriday.com

CHAPTER ONE

He blinked, unsure whether his eyes were even open. The darkness above was so starless and bleak in every sense it was disorientating but he daren't stare in any direction other than directly at the sky and so edged his way, scraping forward rather than stepping. He was painfully aware that anyone else would interpret his caution as indecision but it wasn't that. It wasn't that at all. He just didn't want to stumble again. This time he was going to choose his moment; it was going to happen on his terms and in his own time.

He eased forward again, testing the ground beneath him until he could feel it had run out but still he kept his gaze fixed. Without a visible moon he thought his view to be purest black until he noticed a silhouette, darker still circling silently above him. He smiled faintly; she'd been right all along... things could always be darker. It flew in widening circles until it disappeared, no doubt back to its nest and cleared his view, returning it to the flat, featureless void it had been. Here at the edge of the world, his world at least he'd hoped for a more reassuring view but he could see nothing there and worse still, no signs of it changing. Taking a long but staggered breath and holding his body rigidly straight he lifted his heels and tilted forward, his change of angle revealing a horizon of stark contrast.

The frosted rooftops opposite appeared, one at a time as gravity pulled him forward, slowly at first as if establishing its grip. The buildings loomed further into view with at least every other window glowing with anticipation and along with the lights that seemed to have engulfed the city they now seemed to stretch and rise. As the momentum gathered they streaked and blurred with the sudden acceleration as gravity found the grasp it had been searching for and now pulled violently. As he moved well beyond being able to regain his balance and into what was now an inevitable fall he didn't need a detailed knowledge of physics to know that he'd left the point of no return behind him and was going over the edge.

He had no real expectations of the sensations that awaited him. He'd never even considered anything like this before but he wondered how much more prepared he could possibly be even if he had. It wasn't like there was a book to research the subject; not by anyone who had actually experienced it anyway. But instead of meeting with the rush of undignified panic he'd suspected, he was warmly greeted with the calm and focus only experienced by those who truly no longer have a choice. It was simple; take away the decision and you take away the anguish. There were too many choices to be made in this life but here at the last sentence of the final page of his closing chapter there were no options left... and it felt amazing.

He'd almost pulled a muscle in an effort to avoid looking down but now the angle of his body prevented any other view as it arced unavoidably towards the street and the Christmas card perfect scene was his again.

From up here the chaos was almost scenic and in some strange way even comical as the crowd he'd been part of swarmed. It no longer distinguished between tarmac and pavement but spilt out across the street with no regards for the countless headlights trying, but failing to clear their path causing heavy traffic even at this late hour. The masses flooded the High Street as every vehicle imaginable divided it in two. Cars, buses, bikes and lorries all fought to escape the rising tide of panicked shoppers preparing for tomorrow as if they hadn't known it was coming. Without exception they'd sworn next year would be different but now they hurried themselves and each other as they raced the clock to closing time.

With balance now just a memory his heart was beating so hard he imagined it was trying to escape his body and pound it's way out; that it knew what was coming and didn't want to be there when it arrived. Yet whilst his breathing quickened as if to cram a life time's worth into these last few seconds his mind wasn't just clear, it was focused. He was not only still taking in observations, but forming opinions on them and even being left with time enough to find the humour in them. He smiled as a couple, so laden with shopping that they couldn't squeeze themselves through an excessively decorated shop doorway changed their approaching angle several times, trying to make the puzzle fit. They only stopped to consider setting their bags and gift wrapped boxes on the rain soaked pavement before backing up to charge the entrance, pausing briefly as they inevitably wedged in the frame before one last surge saw them explode out the other side like a Champagne cork. The irony of crushing the presents they carried to save getting them damp made him exhale in that too amusing just to smile but not quite enough to laugh out loud kind of way that people often do... he'd always thought there should be a word for it.

The speed of his descent quickened again as his bodyweight started to contribute sadistically towards its own demise. Every instinct he had screamed at him to outstretch his arms and protect himself but he held them firm knowing to do so made all the sense of a kamikaze pilot wearing a crash helmet. For the first time in far too long his brain was giving the orders, and surprisingly clearly. With nothing ahead of him now but a nineteen storey drop he understood entirely the pointlessness of attempting to break his fall. As he continued to cut a perfect arc in that unnatural, almost military stance, he remained determined to keep his last promise, if only to himself; that'd he'd keep his eyes open ... all the way down.

And what a final view it was; whilst decorated in various degrees of taste, nobody could deny that each and every shop had made the effort again this year. Lights twinkled, mechanical snowmen waved, reindeers flew like reindeers should albeit suspended by wires whilst inflatable Santa's ensured a wide berth as they continued to sway aggressively from the breeze that had been picking up until just a few moments ago. It was channelled down this relatively straight and narrow stretch by the foreboding buildings that shaped it, causing even the most warmly dressed of the colony below to at least tighten their scarves or fasten another button.

They'd all felt the temperature drop whether they were crisscrossing the parade frantically searching to fulfill endless lists or just standing, listening to, but not quite understanding the under practiced but enthusiastic group of carollers that were acting as a living, breathing roundabout at the streets narrowest point. Their voices rose towards him and they sang proudly enough that he had no doubt their cause was just, but he was equally sure that their positioning was tactical. The bottleneck in which they stood made it difficult for even the most uncharitable to walk past without emptying their pockets; Christmas had indeed come to town again, just like every other song had been promising since early November.

The clarity, not just of his senses, but of his thoughts would have come as a complete surprise had it not been for last year's accident in which he was astounded how time seemed suspended as his car spun out of control. He could remember glass shattering all around and cars bearing down on him as he careered across their path into the other lane. Yet despite the chaos and considerable threat surrounding him, he thought to counter steer and even to release the brakes slightly to prevent the car skidding any further; he even remembered to flick his indicator to the right in case he hadn't already, knowing the insurance companies would eventually be looking for someone to blame.

Whilst in so many ways, this was the opposite of that torturous memory, the way in which the world had degenerated into a slow motion and almost frame by frame vision most people only see at the movies was eerily reminiscent.

He'd now fallen so far forward that his body aligned perfectly with the rooftop momentarily like an extension of its ledge until he plummeted away so fast he felt like he'd left part of himself behind. He gasped as the sudden acceleration caught him by surprise and a sensation he'd only ever reserved for fairground rides rose up within him almost provoking the fear he'd readied himself for but it faded and died again just as quickly. Resisting the temptation to close his eyes was a battle he guessed would only get harder but by the time he'd caught his breath, the panic didn't just ease; it left all together. His jacket fluttered noisily behind him and his eyes watered as he struggled to keep them open against the rush of freezing winter air but these were the only clues as to the colossal speed at which he was now plummeting.

The bustling world and its population below carried on regardless and why wouldn't they? The competition for attention at their level left little reason to look up but he was forced to look down on them, and with good reason. He saw a couple hurry past a begging bowl pointing indiscriminately into the distance and striking their very best catalogue pose trying desperately to look interested in something... *anything* else before resuming whatever conversation they were having the very second they'd passed. It was a smooth manoeuvre that had saved them a few coins and a pitiful sight for the cost of some truly shocking acting and a small white lie. He watched them duck under a sunken banner that read 'bargain' in capital letters, unaware of the biting wit that was so obvious to him. Wrapped warmly in their ignorance they walked briskly on. Not that he was any better. But at least he knew he wasn't and that, at least was something.

He bowed his head slightly as he sighed, just enough to look back underneath himself, along his body at the building from which he'd fallen. His clothes were pulled taut by the air rushing up and over him and clearing his view. The windows were much the same as those opposite, some emanating an inviting light and others just dark, lonely shapes set against featureless brick. He couldn't help but think that within them... the image blurred, but not with the vertical streaking of his descent this time, but in every direction. This was very different; it even felt as though the distortion was within him and he shook his head from side to side with increasing force trying to stabilise and clear the picture. He regained his focus only for it to deteriorate again as if he was moving in and out of his own reception.

Whilst he'd never experienced anything like it before, he was surprised that this bothered him at all; effective eyesight was worth little or nothing where he was headed and even a complete loss of sight could be considered a blessing but he again jolted himself trying to bring it back only for it to disintegrate altogether.

He blinked, trying to bring the separating colours into focus but this just seemed to cloud them. Was it over already? He squinted in an effort to concentrate and distinguish one shape from another before a sudden blinding flash temporarily dazzled him. It must be over? Random bursts of light were less surprising at this time of year than at any other but this actually felt as if it had flared *behind* his eyes. Perhaps he had shut them, if only for a moment, but for too long none the less and what he witnessed now was nothing more than a chemical haze; the last show as the curtains closed.

But his vision returned momentarily if only to stun him with a similar burst, brighter to the point of being painful this time forcing him to turn his face away. It happened again and again with increasing intensity but each time it faded and died the images that separated them grew.

Faint outlines, almost there but not quite, flickered as if affected by static, teasing with glimpses until they eventually lasted longer than the flares which were now no more than subtle pulses but as frequent as a heartbeat.

CHAPTER TWO

Since he'd noticed this address on his schedule he'd dreaded the thought of having to deal with the same obnoxious woman who'd begrudgingly accepted delivery last year; he'd known at the time that she'd be difficult to forget but he felt sure it would be well worth the effort and so had been trying ever since. Half expecting to be instantly reminded of her air of self importance he requested entry through the yard gates.

'I'm so sorry but you'll have to wait if you'd be so kind' came the seemingly civil response. It was strange how the words themselves never dictated exactly how a sentence would be taken. The tone in which it was said could convey so much more, not only about the situation but about the person themselves. It did as far as Nick was concerned. He'd grown even more judgemental recently and now felt sure he knew the woman, or at least her particular breed, on the other end of the receiver. If he was still a gambling man he'd put his money on the fact that she adopted this approach all the time but he still couldn't help but take it personally. He never could.

The voice didn't sound particularly familiar but was so distorted through the intercom that he dare not relax yet. It could still be her. Should he, or anyone else for that matter complain regarding the way he was spoken to she would be able to say in all honesty that she had been nothing but polite. She'd be able to repeat her exact words and nobody would be able to criticise them. If she'd written them down they'd shine as a perfect example of manner and professionalism but it was the way they were delivered in which their secret ability to grate on the receiver for hours lie. They could keep irritating like an unseen parasite for hours, even days afterwards. It was like sarcasm, but not quite. It was less obvious and all the more frustrating for its cunning.

Nick squinted his eyes and leaned forward in his seat as if he genuinely believed the few inches he'd gained would be the difference between being able to see the entire way across the car park and not.

'So how long are we talking? What's my estimated delivery time? Just I was hoping to get finished up soon' enquired Nick. He spoke overly clearly and pronounced his words carefully. He didn't want to have to repeat himself. It hurt too much to be so gracious having been forced to make the delivery in the first place.

His sight was strained in the fading light, reminding him all the time of just how late in the day it was already. He hated the evenings drawing in so eagerly like they couldn't wait to end; since he'd started counting the days he'd wanted each one to last as long as possible. They'd rushed past quickly enough all summer but now he'd do anything to have those days back once more. This was the real world and he shouldn't expect much else this time of year but he'd never really been a man of easy going acceptance.

He concentrated on the signs in the comparative distance struggling to make them out but he didn't have to read them, he could see that they must surely signify the delivery point by the frequency at which they were being visited. Huge lorries that would eclipse his own waited patiently, their suspension resisting the massive load of what must be the year's last delivery of newsprint. For a centre of modern media, the building in the distance looked surprisingly old fashioned from this angle. The reception at the front of the building was of course immaculate and he imagined the offices would be the same. Yet it didn't look like the state of the factory itself had been considered for years.

Nick had already grown tired of waiting for the woman's electronic reply. He could understand if she was busy, anyone who had to be at work today must surely be genuinely overwhelmed. The yard was a hive of frantic activity but there seemed to be enough forklifts to spare and he could count at least three drivers standing idle.

They could take his delivery and be back into their cozy huddle before their coffee had even cooled and in these almost freezing conditions, that wouldn't be long at all.

His worry was that she could see him from wherever her office was, and more the point, that she could see the cargo being hauled on his open trailer. Such a nonessential delivery was unlikely to take priority but after all the apparent importance that was placed on it; his being here was made all the more frustrating. Worse still was the thought that there was no reason at all other than she was enjoying exercising her so-called authority and even took pleasure in sharing her obvious misery. If that was the case she was wasting her time and energy; he'd had enough people annoy him already today without her making the effort.

Pushing his thick glasses back up along his nose and convinced this final adjustment corrected his vision precisely he attempted to establish his bearing again. He could now make out a figure gazing out across the concrete expanse in his direction and to her credit she wasn't behind the shelter of glass at all as he had expected. The outline was of a female, of that he was sure but only after struggling to see any finer detail did the floodlights surrounding the yard take it in turns to help confirm it. As they thudded lazily to life he could see her with increasing clarity and wondered if the sudden drenching of light was automatic or if he wasn't the only one trying to see things more clearly. Perhaps her sight was as flawed as his. With visibility came his answer...

'I'm so sorry but you'll have to wait if you'd be so kind' came the almost automated sounding response. The voice seemed too piercing to have emanated from the woman glaring at him but a second shriek confirmed that indeed it had. Surely there was simply too much of her to pitch that highly? Perhaps squeezing herself into a dress that can't have fitted for a decade or more could be the reason why? Men wearing dusty suits and ladies confined in eveningwear at least a size too small was always a sure sign of an imminent office party if ever there was one. In an effort to look their best they often achieved nothing but the opposite but it was as traditional as mistletoe; he imagined she'd have her own private stash and that it wouldn't be unrelated to her attire. Nick took that as a promising sign though as at least she may be in a rush. He looked in his rearview mirror at the modest fir tree held flat on his trailer and again felt optimistic. Perhaps his delivery wasn't as irrelevant as he'd thought as it was likely to form the centre piece of their gathering so he tried again in his most likeable voice.

'I appreciate you're busy but it's probably me you're waiting for. If you could just tell me where you want this I won't need anything more than a signature to be out of your way? You've got an account so you won't even need to raise a purchase order'.

'Please be assured, we'll be with you as soon as we can'. Nick considered asking for another estimated time as it might be a wise idea to make his next drop and come back later rather than wait the wrong side of the uninviting gate that remained in its locked position in front of him but before he'd hedged his bets the woman relented, even if only so he'd switch his engine off and stop pumping his exhaust fumes over her shift as they changed over.

'We'll lift the gate in about half an hour. Then we'll get a forklift over to you if that's alright?' It wasn't a question in any sense, more a well thought out order.

For fear of what he might say Nick just sighed and turned the key in his ignition. Half an hour was longer than he wanted to wait, but not long enough to get anywhere else during rush hour. He sat back in the heavily worn driver's seat and closed his eyes. If he couldn't sleep in the comfort of his own bed, he seriously doubted he would be able to here but he was tired and the heat still blowing from his dashboard made him feel surprisingly comfortable so it was worth a try. He shut his eyes after turning the radio up as silence wasn't an option. He'd have preferred it but even the relentless onslaught of recycled Christmas songs as exhausted as he was would be preferable to the moronic, expletive antics of the masses at shift change. He remembered similar situations all too well.

The cabin continued to warm up and he settled surprisingly quickly considering his anxiousness but was disturbed by a knocking at his window. He looked out but could see nothing that hadn't been there a moment ago. In a minute or two those double doors would be thrown open and workers would spew from them towards freedom, even if it was the kind that only lasted for three days; but not yet.

Relieved and blaming his imagination he sat back again only to see a gloved hand reach up and drum against the glass. Nick readjusted himself and wound down the window that was his first and last line of defence. The same hand wrapped itself over his door and used the grip to pull himself up. As the boy to whom it was attached rose into view, Nick didn't even question what the teenager wanted, just waited for him to announce it.

'Got the time please mate?'

Nick looked confused, not at the question but at the fact that he could see a watch strapped firmly around a skinny wrist. He even started to point out the obvious but stopped, knowing it would serve no purpose other than to lengthen the conversation which he already felt sure would be anything but stimulating.

'Just a few minutes to mate' he replied but saw no acknowledgement in the face staring blankly back at him. Sighing, he realised what the problem may be. 'A few minutes to four' he concluded, blaming himself for making the assumption that he was looking for the accuracy of minutes rather than the hour itself. He hoped that was enough and was relieved that it appeared to be. Without a word the boy disappeared from view and took off across the parking lot like his life depended on it.

Nick shook his head. Just maybe there was an explanation for the watch; it could have stopped or its precision could have been under doubt. But judging by the urgency being shown now he'd obviously left it until the last possible minute to get to work and must have only stopped to ask the time as he was concerned that he was late, losing himself the few minutes it took in the process.

Again Nick shook his head and turned the heating up to replace the warmth he'd just lost out of the window and determined to make the most of the heat left in his engine before it cooled completely. He rubbed his eyes harder than can be good for him and sank back into the seat's embrace. He hadn't slept properly for months despite feeling permanently tired. Any get up and go he had simply got up and went after the first of many hospital visits and now he'd almost grown used to exhaustion. The few friends he had blamed it on emotional stress but even they were few and far between these days but it was his own fault. He'd stopped making the effort to spend time with them and whether it was due to his age or just too much time spent heaving these trees around town, the truth was his back had gone out more often than he had lately.

He stared into his rearview mirror and smiled to himself. Life had a strange sense of humour; he'd spent his childhood believing in Santa, eventually become a father and pretended to be him and now, as he approached retirement age he'd become his spitting image. He looker closer, past the obvious, almost comical features and had the smirk wiped from his face; he had yet to discover whether time was a healer but it had so far been an awful beautician.

Minutes later he was aware of being surrounded but daren't open his eyes. Workers came teeming towards him and dispersed at the bonnet of his truck. He didn't worry about the careless way they charged past; their bags and rucksacks threatening the paintwork. It was already chipped and scratched and most importantly, it wasn't his; the hood ornament was though and that gleaming silver angel was all he cared about... particularly as it was a present; it had rode with him too long to be so needlessly damaged now but it was well out of their reach. For now at least it would remain as perfect as the day it was given to him.

The swarm continued, filing past the sides and beyond its enormous trailer only to regroup behind it again. They'd left the factory but as usual had failed to leave their helpfulness behind. The knocking on the window was sharper this time and so sounded all the more urgent, but unless that gate was opening to let him through, all he wanted was to be left alone. Whoever it was couldn't be that desperate to talk to an over the hill delivery man and must surely have more important things to do. Nick didn't even flinch at their second attempt. He'd only just got the cabin temperature back up to anything that resembled comfortable and now, huddled against the door to prop himself up he actually stood some chance of drifting into a much needed sleep but it was suddenly pulled open.

Nick floundered as he tried to stop himself falling out of the cabin sideways. Steadying himself against the dashboard he looked down onto the withered, smiling and somewhat surprised face.

'You only need to request permission and they'll give you a time, just use the intercom' he offered.

Nick held his tongue. It was infuriating, but how could he speak his mind when the elderly man, who must surely be supplementing his pension had bothered to stop and offer the voice of experience... even if his advice was painfully obvious. He still wore his high visibility vest as an extra layer against the cold and that only emphasised his pointless, but well intentioned gesture. Nick smiled as genuinely as he could and thanked him with all the sincerity he could muster.

'I'll do that, much appreciated'. Nick could humour him convincingly enough, but only for so long. There appeared to be no intention of his leaving anytime soon and he just kept nodding in acceptance of Nick's gratitude. Stood there and rooted to the spot expectantly, he remained ready to assist should Nick get the process wrong in someway like miss the button completely or speak the wrong language. Nick played for time and pretended to check through his paperwork hoping the hint would be taken but he hoped in vain. Now he wished he'd just told the old man he'd already announced his arrival whether it hurt his feelings or not, but the more time that passed, the harder it got until he had no choice.

Already wincing, he pressed the intercom button down and

hesitated to repeat himself. He couldn't even apologise for it and having backed himself into a corner he'd have to proclaim his presence like it was the first they'd ever heard of it. He imagined his allotted entry time would again be delayed out of spitefulness and to punish his impatience but he looked down into the pride lit eyes that urged him on. He depressed the button and said what he had to.

'You're welcome' assured the old man looking ecstatically pleased with himself. His colleagues raised their eyes as they walked past and quickened their pace in case he tried to help them too. Nick cringed at the response that was to come and locked his jaw, ready to take the understandably abrupt intercom explosion on the chin.

Satisfied that his work was done, the charitable stranger began to walk away before turning sharply back towards his new friend for the favour he was owed.

'I don't suppose you'd have the time would you, just I'm in a rush and wasn't expecting to have to stop and help anyone out' he called. through the already half wound up window. Nick was gritting his teeth. It was the very opposite of help, it took less than a minute and surely he must know the time now if at no other point during the day as he'd have just clocked off. With all the restraint he had left he yelled 'just gone four o'clock' before closing his window tightly and incarcerating himself again.

He locked the doors knowing it would achieve nothing but it made him feel better. He often did things for no better reason than that. His frustration would build up and with no release he just had to feel like he was at least doing something to show his irritation. He had to make his point; a small act of defiance, however subtle even if he was its only audience.

Simply locking the doors was not enough. He yanked open his glove compartment and took out a delivery pad amid the bottles and containers that rattled around within; one of which was his so-called bonus for being consistently reliable, but a cheap whisky was an insult after what he'd had to put up with already. They hadn't even wrapped or boxed it; it had just been handed over unceremoniously in the plain brown bag it came in. He felt around for the marker pen he knew was there somewhere and scrawled his simple message across the pre-printed paper. The words were so thick and heavy that the finer grids and small print behind it was lost by contrast. He ripped the top sheet from its spine and slammed it against his window, the self adhesive edge holding it in place for all to see. 'I DO NOT KNOW THE TIME!' it screamed in angry red letters. Simply writing it had calmed him a little and the fact that it now hung there, declaring his wish to be left alone meant he could drop his guard again. He remained determined to make the most of the time he had left to wait.

His pulse slowed but his mind just wouldn't follow suit. It was a particularly vicious circle that he'd never really learned to live with. With the irrelevant annoyances behind him, what actually bothered him was that they affected him at all. They didn't used to. Recent and far more serious concerns should put these petty intrusions into perspective but somehow they didn't. They just enlarged everything to the point that he could never relax and the exhaustion it caused magnified them further.

He again forced his eyes closed, far more comfortable now that there were fewer passers by. His breathing returned to normal and he allowed himself to fall semiconscious, free from the worry of falling asleep and missing his opportunity. He had no doubt that even if he didn't hear the gate rise; nobody could sleep through that woman barking her commands to him when the time came.

The cabin shook and he was jolted awake as someone, and a heavy someone at that pulled on its side. He immediately thought it might have been politer to knock first but then realised that he or she probably already had. Nick unlocked the door which was immediately swung open by a suited man almost as wide as he was tall who, having ascended the driver's side of the vehicle was now worryingly out of breath.

'It's twenty-five past four' he panted. Having just woken, that simple sentence seemed strange to Nick until he remembered the glaring message that flapped against the glass. Again, he realised that in a twisted way, he was seeing another small act of kindness but he couldn't fake gratitude again. But before he could respond the gates started to rise and without a word he just slammed the door shut and drove on, watching the disgusted looking man rant about such rudeness in his rearview mirror. That'd no doubt be another complaint coming his way but he'd deal with that later.

CHAPTER THREE

Contrast crept back in from the very edges of the blinding light, gradually at first but its murky advance began finding shapes within the purest white of the most intense burst so far. Noel had yet to recover, but it was as if he'd been caught in the flash of a photo he'd not been expecting and was now waiting for the colour to slowly drain back into the world; like watching the resulting picture develop, but agonizingly slowly as the darkest parts formed first, giving only clues as to the final scene. The insipid outlines offered little help, but they were clear enough to add to his confusion. As the finer details started to take shape it was obvious that the view was very different to the fast approaching pavement upon which he'd been firmly focused a moment ago.

His imagination began to fill in the blanks as he tried to interpret the emerging shapes. To him they resembled people; and that wouldn't be unfeasible bearing in mind his ever closer proximity to the crowded street below. But as they evolved into an evermore defined human form he found himself looking up at the ghostlike figures rather than directly down towards them as he should be. It didn't take much thought to know that from his significantly elevated, birds eye position it was an impossible view. Impossible it may be; but it was irrelevant at this stage too.

He tried to force the search for an explanation out of his mind, certain that there must be something more worthy of occupying his final thoughts during these last approaching seconds. He succeeded in convincing himself that none of it mattered but he couldn't help but be disturbed by the fact that he was still considering anything at all. The moment of peace or panic that he'd predicted was defying conventional time completely. It had become so elastic; able to stretch to such an extent that the premonition of what must now be the immediate future was suddenly terrifying.

He'd prepared himself and was braced for that fleeting moment when he met with the ground but now wasn't so sure it would be over quite so quickly. Desperate to rid himself of the nightmare it could be, he returned his attention to the vision again, whatever it was.

He watched it transfixed. It was indescribable. Unlike anything he'd ever seen in his life... the latter words seemed to ricochet around the city before being reflected back towards him. He saw them hurtling back in his direction before they ploughed into him, the sudden realisation hitting him like a cannonball, decimating the remnants of any previous thoughts.

He wasn't sure whether he was relieved or afraid. Was it possible to be both? Either way it was already over. It had to be. At least it hadn't hurt. That was considerable mercy in itself but not without the cost of knowing he must have failed to keep the last promise he ever made on earth, and considering it was to himself he couldn't imagine failing more abysmally.

He could only imagine that he must have passed out as the end approached and that his body had issued its own defence, effectively shutting down under such immense stress. But the twisted logic that never failed him seemed to be in perfect tact making the images before him easier to accept. They didn't have to make sense anymore as science, facts and figures had no place here. The rules only applied in life and knowing that somehow made what he was seeing now seem far less threatening.

He tried to prepare himself for whatever he was about to confront knowing that with it he would gain a knowledge that no living person could ever possess. Something was happening around him and his eyes darted from side to side. Wherever he looked, the image appeared to have no end, no beginning and no boundaries whatsoever. It was all around him, still creeping forward out of its featureless canvas. It remained eerily transparent in places but blotches of pale colour were now growing in intensity until they reached familiar tones. The recognition filled him with confusion once more as he was met with what must surely be impossible, even in whatever dimension he was trapped.

'Sleep well'. The words were startlingly clear despite being almost whispered as they were so impossibly close. The tone in which they were delivered was virtually unrecognisable but it retained characteristics of which there was no mistaking. He must be hallucinating... hearing things then grasping for protection and familiarity.

He listened intently, unsure whether he wanted to prove himself right but there was nothing... still he waited. Then it came, so close he was sure he could feel breath against his face.

'I love you.'

He didn't and wouldn't imagine that. It was unusual for him to be so confident in his own senses but he was absolutely sure not only of what he heard, but of *who* he heard. And if he was right to trust himself, he'd also been right to be scared. Whilst there was no other voice he'd rather be greeted by whilst hovering alone in this featureless abyss, he'd left his father very much alive this morning and if that was still the case then this ordeal must be a long way from over.

The possible scenarios were few to begin with but they'd just narrowed further. He must be in hospital or at least on the way there; it was surely the only explanation left. As his next of kin, both parents would have been called and he had no doubt they'd have been at the scene within minutes. That would have been the last thing he wanted but paramedic protocol would have prevailed regardless. Nobody else would know what he'd promised his parents and therefore they'd never understand anyway.

The previously anaemic shades were dominant in places now and they bled outward, almost vein like and stopped short whenever an invisible barrier was reached, but it served to add depth and detail until the painting was complete enough.

The colours now flooded in as if they had only been waiting for the truth to arrive. His father was still nowhere to be seen but a woman leant over him. He looked up into the impossibly exaggerated smile that he hadn't seen for years. Compared to this almost theatrical grin, every other seemed half hearted by comparison but it was a simple pleasure seeing his mother so unashamedly happy again.

He'd failed her in so many ways that he probably deserved the truths she'd spat at him over the years, but the poison had began to rot him from the inside causing more damage than the concrete which had broken his fall as well as his body. He was still as sure now as when he was urged to talk about her that he'd never lived up to her expectations; he hadn't even met his own. But that didn't mean she'd ever want to see him like this although the expression on her face begged to differ and so made no sense at all.

His hurried judgments and rushed theories had been proven to be exactly that up until now, so he gave himself chance to think this through. Whilst jumping to conclusions was the only exercise he was likely to get in the near future he couldn't afford to do it again just yet. Still finding hope wherever he could, he wondered if she was simply relieved to see him still alive. It was hard to believe after all and he must have beaten all kind of odds and could possibly have broken as many records as he had bones.

He hadn't felt guilt for sometime but he recognised the feeling none the less. If she'd expected the worst, then even this must be cause for joy but what kind of son would put his own mother through that? Nobody should have to see their boy like this yet it was he who had to look away; he just couldn't face her anymore. Noel closed his eyes but it had no effect at all. He could still see her towering above but moving steadily closer. He'd be able to see his own reflection soon, growing steadily in her eyes and it didn't bear thinking about. He closed his own tighter, not daring to twist his neck but still she was there looming closer, about to inadvertently reveal the grotesque state he must surely be in. As he prepared to see his bloodied and twisted body he hoped that he wouldn't recognise himself; the detachment may make it easier to digest.

He tried to be grateful and held on tightly to the fact that he'd been saved the pain he'd deserved; the human body was truly an amazing thing. He'd often read that adrenaline ensures that the end is seldom even realised at executions. He'd always doubted the theory but now, at the later side of his own he was an entirely wiser man. Maybe he'd be able to publish a book on the subject, or an article at least. He'd be one of the few that could write from first hand experience, absolutely *knowing* it was the truth; it had to be. But even that explanation didn't account for why he wasn't even in discomfort.

They must have injected him with everything it took to numb his entire body but with the effectiveness of modern medicine that didn't mean the injuries wouldn't be frightenly severe.

But the effects of the damage were not merely being made bearable. He really couldn't feel a thing and if he'd been dosed to that extent how could his mind be so active? It was functioning as well as could be expected and his father's words, or at least his reasons for saying them continued throbbing inside his head. The edges of the letters scraped against his skull as they suddenly took on a new meaning. They were said in such a fragile manner, so totally out of character and with such sincerity that they gradually shattered any illusion that his injuries were not fatal. If they weren't, they might as well be. The safety net had fallen and he found himself coming to terms with what he'd feared the most. The numbness may not have been due to some unpronounceable medicine, it was more likely due to his broken body's total failure. He was paralysed.

CHAPTER FOUR

The force with which Evelyn was ejected caught her by surprise and was so excessive that she was lifted clear off the deep pile carpet that had always seemed so welcoming to others. Furious at the extremity, she threw an ill-judged fist behind her but, having missed her target all she achieved was to throw herself awkwardly through a half turn in midair. Now facing the garish club entrance door, she launched her half empty glass, desperate to lash out in retaliation but it merely bounced harmlessly off the closing door that had been used effectively as a shield.

With both her fists still clenched in frustration, readiness for the imminent impact and more painful still, the embarrassment of a less than graceful landing at the feet of the city's wealthier clientele, she reached out towards the solid steel banisters at the top of the stairwell in desperation. She knew they were her last chance at avoiding certain humiliation and a bruise that would show for several nights to come and so swung for them frantically, lunging in one direction and then the other but failing on both attempts to grip either rail.

Her eyes widened with sudden realization as the ground fell away from under her, step by step. It dropped beneath steeply but she remained on an even level with the pole raised banners across the street advertising reduced wrapping paper and a homemade lucky dip stand. She tried to judge and adjust her delayed landing but each time she neared the carpet it dropped further and faster than she did as she was still being propelled forwards. Her flailing body cleared a path through queues of astonished revellers waiting patiently with their tickets, each with their own stories but all staring at her, some accusingly, others sympathetically. She couldn't figure which she hated more but at least she was turning heads again even if it was for all the wrong reasons as they watched, transfixed by the dramatic exit. Some even looked concerned but obviously not enough to offer their hand.

Her glass had remained in one piece and now rolled slowly, almost politely to the edge of each return before dropping to the next step and then proceeding to make it's way again, following her like a loyal friend wanting to keep up, but not at the cost of grace. Evelyn was keeping such a pace and had already covered such a distance that to her it felt as if the buildings opposite were more likely to brake her fall than the ground, but when steps eventually ended, so did her flight.

The ground beneath her had only levelled but from her perspective it looked as though it had risen to catch her and for that she was grateful. She was even more appreciative to have landed feet first albeit far from upright after such spectacular acrobatics. She'd managed to twist and turn herself, compensating wildly for the awkward and unnatural angles she was forcing herself into to keep from toppling and stumbled out into the street on legs that did a better job of attracting glances than of keeping her stable.

Still reeling from the landing, they struggled to keep up with her body, desperate to catch it in part to maintain what little dignity was left to salvage but not least to keep the skin on her bones. Had she been dressed for a harsh winter night, the layers of clothing might limit the damage but she was dressed for work and a sequined bikini offered precious little protection against paving slabs, concrete or the over zealous doormen that had launched her towards them.

Whilst her trademark suspenders, chosen as carefully as an artist chooses his canvas seemed suddenly worthless and sleazy on this side of the club door, they did at least hold this evening's tips tightly against her thighs like it knew the value of those few notes before she did and clung to them like a miser. And now, with nowhere to stay the night, that was at least something to be thankful for. The crumpled tens and twenties remained held fast, exactly where they'd been hurriedly stuffed by husbands and fiancés who'd later claim poverty when asked for spare change on the street, no more aware than she was at the time that they were indeed already donating to the needy.

Her momentum continued to carry her forward, but having made such a spectacle of herself she'd at least alerted the crowd who still dispersed ahead of her as if she was toxic. Both legs were still playing catch up and making impressive gains but on such ridiculously oversized high heels her left foot buckled and she again fell towards the ground. It was inevitable. She knew it. And so did the horde. They regrouped behind her enveloping her in the very centre of the biggest audience she'd performed to in weeks but this was a very different show; and just as well with so many children from across the street staring at her like she's the first half naked lap dancer they'd ever seen in a Santa's hat.

She must have attracted the attention of perhaps a hundred people and it'd have only taken anyone of them to just take a step forward instead of back to prevent her fall; to reach for her instead of their partner or child but not a single person did. Regardless of age, gender, race or religion they'd retreated and watched her pass but as the gallery of faces ahead continued to part; then there he stood.

Whilst those around him sped to avoid her, he stood firm as she careered towards him, her arms and legs whirling around her so wildly it was hard to believe they were still attached but there he stood; at last.

Since she was a little girl she'd been promised this. It wasn't nearly as romantic as she'd always imagined but it had happened anyway and that was what mattered. He wasn't as tall as she'd pictured but then he wasn't wearing armour either. No sword or shield but her hero nonetheless.

He wasn't just looking straight towards her; he was smiling like he'd actually been expecting her. Maybe he had. She'd read about moments like this. Initially in picture based storybooks, then in teen magazines and more recently in lifestyle columns but the fairytales never changed and she'd never lost faith in them. She'd been waiting for him for years now and he'd been searching for her. That's the way it worked; although she imagined he might have been somewhat surprised that even at Christmas, she came quite this unwrapped, he didn't seem it at all.

She smiled coyly, battering her eyes the way she'd always pictured she would but it was an expression that didn't entirely suit a lap dancer in high heels, a thong and bra top that was hardly there as she careered across the street with all the elegance of a plane crash. She threw out her arms in anticipation as she'd have been grateful for any landing that wasn't met with concrete but she couldn't have even hoped for this. Her pace had hardly slowed and she was falling fast but she'd reach him within seconds now.

His gaze remained admiring but it didn't follow her path. It stayed fixed as she passed his line of vision and her smile faded as quickly as her balance as she began to crumble in every sense. He took a step forward but towards the club entrance where he'd agreed to meet his colleagues. He was still smiling at them but his expression turned to horror as he noticed the flurry of limbs hurtling towards him.

He paused, rooted to the spot for a moment trying to predict her course before shifting his weight alternatively from side to side, ready to react if he could only figure his best route of escape. Seizing his moment he leapt to his right in the name of self-preservation as the whirlwind passed, narrowly avoiding being swept along.

Evelyn continued along her collision course, still bowed over like an Olympic runner about to cross the finish line, but with her head now turned, an expression of disbelief on her face and her gaze fixed firmly on her 'saviour', she was now looking back over her shoulder; and not at her runway which was running out… fast. All around her, people winced, foreseeing what was coming. None would claim to be psychic but all seemed to be able to predict the immediate future as Evelyn ploughed headlong into one of the many market stands with such force that it travelled through the stalls with a domino effect knocking the vendors backwards and their merchandise sprawling across the street.

At the final stages of stumbling, she'd managed to collide at such an angle that she'd hit like a torpedo and burst through the much heralded lucky dip, wedging her between the presents that now weighed down on her. Both arms and her entire torso were inside the box and the sudden surprise of being immersed in total darkness and near silence took a few moments to interpret.

Trying to back up, she twisted her head awkwardly hoping to be released if she could just find the right angle but she only succeeded in straining her neck. With each movement the chunks of polystyrene filling cascaded down around her into her eyes, her mouth and even her ears, further muffling the world outside.

She had no idea that the reluctant sniggers had begun to spread but they were contained as nobody wanted to be the first to laugh out loud. They looked around out of the corners of their eyes at each other as if awaiting permission until just one could wait no more. Laughter must have seemed infectious as it flooded the street; even those who thought it cruel joined in rather than stand out. The sound rose and then fuelled itself until the laughter itself become funny.

And now, as she knelt on the pavement with her upper-half trapped and thrashing wildly, swallowed up to her waist with her perfectly formed but barely covered rear held awkwardly aloft it was hard for them to stop. As children's faces were turned away by conservative parents and slaps were handed out to husbands who were staring a little *too* intensely it started to fade with the exception of hormonal teenagers who'd have paid money for a lesser view. From now on they'd be more likely to recognise her from the small tattoo on her left buttock than by her face and they continued to stare whilst the crowd slowly filtered away.

Evelyn's increasing frustration built; trapped inside the box it had no release and her struggle for freedom became more aggressive ensuring she never felt the night's takings being slipped carefully from her thigh. Trying to ease herself out had only caused its contents to settle around her, effectively entombing her. Her empty glass however still embraced its rare moment of liberty and having now made it's way down the stairwell, past the queue and been kicked around the crowd, it now rolled in that same faithful, determined way towards it's companion as if to prove that diamonds aren't this girl's best friend only to be smashed to shards under her heel as Evelyn continued her blind backward march.

It could have been symbolic of the way she'd always crushed her relationships or of the manner in which she should handle her drinking habit but either way, it was unexpected and she jerked backwards so violently that she shook the entire structure, much to the despair of the vendors who were already chasing their merchandise around the street. The roasted chestnuts they'd been managing to sell for an extortionate price bounced around them, too hot to replace with their bare hands. With the exception of Evelyn, their shouts and demands to stop were heard by everyone and she again attracted their attention just in time for the banner to come loose and drop. Whilst it slipped further down one mast than the other, it stopped short, just above Evelyn who remained in the same vulnerable position, it's solid bright red arrow pointing directly towards her, slightly rippled but clearly reading 'EXCITING SURPRISE GUARANTEED, INSERT BELOW – PAY ONCE, HAVE ANOTHER GO FREE'.

As the comedians around her reached into their pockets enthusiastically and those same teenagers fought over positions in the queue forming, yet more slaps and reprimands were exchanged but nobody failed to cheer as Evelyn eventually emerged dazed and confused from her prison.

Her embarrassed smile might have been convincing were it not for her eyes welling in response to the humiliation and the various cuts and grazes that may not need stitches, but were certainly visible and looked painful enough to silence at least some of the horde. She looked at them, at her wounds and back again, then followed their gaze behind her. She tried to focus on the banner through watery eyes but couldn't make out the words. Just one blink would clear her vision but that would force a tear. She hadn't cried in years and she wasn't going to now; certainly not in front of everyone. Instead she just wiped them. Now she could read and it was all too clear. She turned to face them again, her face quivered as if in indecision. She'd have lashed out again if she only knew who to hit.

She wasn't the only one embarrassed now. It was as if the needle had been dragged across the record and in the eerie silence that prevailed people were turning away, suddenly unable to face what they couldn't take their eyes off a few moments ago. They sank into anonymity, trying to escape her accusing stare that scanned the crowd for her so-called hero, but he was now long gone. Even the vendors had stopped shouting at her not wanting to add to the damage, besides, having now counted it, the cash they slipped from her fishnets would probably cover the damage and any last few sales they may have made anyway.

Her fragile looking body shook not from the cold but from anger until she found a voice that betrayed her body;

'I'm not a whore!' seemed to reverberate off the buildings in a street too full and busy to echo. The aching cry seemed to come from nowhere and wasn't directed at anyone in particular. It was as if Evelyn was trying to convince herself rather than the crowd; she even looked shocked that it had come out at all, let alone so loud.

She collapsed on the pavement as though those four words had been all that held her up. Only the children continued to stare but their faces were again guided away as if even a glance of her would scar their innocent minds. The thought that she was considered a threat to them, physical or otherwise repulsed her and she composed herself again, crouching as far into the shadows as she could. The needle found its place again and all around returned to it's previous pace and stereo sound.

She sat there huddled against the cold, wondering how she'd make it to the end of the street dressed like this without being arrested for indecency or, if she should even try; a cell was at least a place to stay tonight. She examined the mix of blood and gravel that covered her knees and tried to stand but her high heels buckled, one even snapping off and she sank to the wet concrete. On another night she'd have found the bright side. She'd have told herself that at least being caught in the middle of winter in a thong had meant she hadn't ruined a skirt. But not tonight. Tonight she cried. She almost growled with frustration as crying was for babies and drama queens but still the tears came. Her snapped heel shifted what little balance was to be had in this dark and cobbled refuge but she offered no resistance, falling to her side and maintaining her crouched, fetal position and just lay there, ashamed but unable to move.

CHAPTER FIVE

The panic exploded within and the more Noel concentrated on sensing even a glimmer of pain anywhere in his body, the more he was convinced he'd totally lost the ability. Yet his mind was cruelly aware and his sight seemed to actually be improving. He could see with a clarity that had steadily deteriorated since his childhood. Finding courage in the knowledge it might well be for the last time, he accepted the inevitable and voluntarily looked into his mother's eyes that had become the mirror he knew they would.

He'd managed to rationalise everything so far, however inexplicable, but what he saw now defied belief of any kind. He saw his own image reflected back but it wasn't anything like what he expected and every instinct he had told him to run. It was a useless impulse as all he could do was stare, unsure of whether he was trembling or not.

She lent down towards him, closing in until she blurred and he totally lost focus of her still incomplete features. She kissed him lightly on the forehead and it took him back to the earliest days he could remember. Not before he was old enough to say the wrong things, but before he had to take responsibility for saying them. Back then each of those affectionate touches had felt like the first ever hello, but whilst identical in every other way this somehow felt like the final goodbye. He was sure he was still breathing but wasn't certain how long for as everything screamed that his time was ebbing away.

When she eventually pulled away from him, her hair had darkened and her flesh had evened in tone. The colouration of both would meet soon and once again she looked like who he knew she was.

It should have been the most peaceful and reassuring view he could imagine but it could not have hurt more. It brought another perspective to what he'd done and the selfishness of it. He'd taken the easy way out of his less than perfect existence, but those he left behind would have to live with this for the rest of theirs. With nothing to assure them they weren't responsible, they'd all hold themselves to blame in someway for things they should have done or said, or even things they shouldn't have. But not one of them had done anything to really deserve it. It was a culmination of things and he held no single person accountable apart from himself. If he could do it all again he'd have let them know that.

But hope returned and surged through him with the notion that perhaps he wasn't thinking as clearly as he thought; it wasn't too late... not quite. He'd tell them with what could well be his last lungful of breath knowing he could rely on them to ensure the words made their way to anyone else that needed to hear them; although right now he couldn't imagine exactly who that could be. He took a moment. He needed his closing verse to convey the message whilst remaining appropriate and worthy of a final confession. He steadied himself, hoping he was still capable of speech and knowing there was only one way to find out. He chose his sentences carefully then let them out only to discover that whilst he was still able to communicate, it wasn't in any recognisable language.

The shock of the unintelligible cry that emanated jolted him until it faded completely, leaving only the despair of knowing he couldn't right the hideous wrong of leaving blame and guilt in his selfish wake. He was also strangely embarrassed. The desperate and overly loud shriek was eerily childlike yet had seemed to cause his mother no alarm at all.

He watched her continue to beam, but it wasn't only that smile that had eluded her for so many years. He didn't deny that a facial expression could alter the wearer's perceived age by a decade or more, but she looked quite literally *half* her age.

It was simply too much to take in and he wanted to cry out again. He'd thought his reflection must have been imagined or an after effect of the disorientation but slowly, he actually started to accept what he'd suspected but refused to believe until now. He let go of all sense and reason; everything he thought he knew at that very moment. If he was right he could turn away without any fear of worsening his injuries... they hadn't happened yet.

He twisted his neck and proved himself right. His view was now obscured by white slats, evenly parted but thick enough to make him feel a prisoner. But it was the view between them that chilled him the most. For beyond them lay a familiar sight that he only just remembered. If he'd been asked to describe it he doubted he'd have been able to, but now it lie in front of him it didn't seem such a distant memory at all. Only this wasn't a memory; he could actually *see* it.

All rational thought he'd attributed to his previous scenarios crashed to the ground and smashed ahead of him. They fell faster than he could as he grappled with the one last explanation that was left. Was it really so impossible? Theories had surrounded it for centuries and more importantly there were variations of it in so many different cultures that maybe there was a universal truth to it.

His parents were still whispering, sometimes to him and sometimes to each other, but always about making his very first Christmas special. As if they didn't trust their memory they hauled a video camera so huge and cumbersome that it took both of them to position it above him with any steadiness. They spoke to each other in a familiar pattern that he recognised all too clearly. He'd heard it whenever he was forced to watch the resulting footage; and that was every family gathering or worse still; every time he brought a potential girlfriend home. Yet despite the repeated viewings, he'd never actually deciphered what was being said. The grainy footage he'd seen so many times had always made it seem so detached and had of course been viewed from his parents' perspective. But this viewpoint was not that of his father capturing his son's first Christmas, but was reversed completely; it was his own, staring up at the camera.

Now he could understand the words perfectly and they served to place the moment chronologically. It was without doubt twenty-four years ago to the day, probably to the minute. Whilst his parents joined forces to master the camera's controls he was given time to consider what he had heard; and it was certainly worthy of deliberation; he didn't even know his father was capable of saying some of those things, let alone to him. Until this point Noel had been convinced that they'd never actually been said, not to him anyway and it was a cruel delivery now that he could never reply. It was as amazing as it was heartbreaking. He spoke with such sincerity that it didn't deserve to be forgotten but in a way it never had been; he'd simply been too young for it to even register but now he had the chance he over analysed it the way only he could. Noel would have been little more than three months old so what would any statement of affection really mean however truthful it sounded? His father didn't even know him. There was nothing to respect or admire at all. Equally there was nothing to despise. He was just a feeble collection of skin and bones that could do nothing to amaze or offend. He wanted to be loved for his actions, his achievements and the choices he'd made? At ninety-five days old any opinion he'd provoked was no more than sentimental gesture; a new and overly emotional parent saying what he's meant to say... maybe to impress his wife or possibly just because that's what is expected.

But even now the hypocrite he sought to destroy was alive and well. Just minutes ago he was absolutely adamant that this was not only possible, but that it was actually unconditional. Not just to love a child so young and indiscriminate, but to feel the emotion so completely that you'd die, literally die for them. He'd spoken so passionately on that rooftop that it had actually reversed someone's entire belief system to the extent it changed their life completely... and now he was convinced too. He wondered whether reaching such a revelation whilst still standing on the ledge would have been enough to turn him around and back down the fire escape but if he was being honest with himself, he knew it wouldn't have been nearly enough. He had more to answer for than that could possibly resolve but it did make him wish he'd given himself time to say what needed to be said. It couldn't be a more irrelevant thought now though and it was too painful to think about any longer.

The sudden movement in front of him was a welcome distraction. Between those same, plain white slats a hurried motion could be seen. His parents moved around him ensuring every monotonous moment of his absolute lack of activity was captured from all conceivable angles before lowering the contraption to the ground. Their fascination was obvious if inexplicable and after a lingering glance they disappeared from view. They left his bedroom door open just enough to let a little light in the way they always told him they did.

The ensuing near dark seemed to last for hours with nothing to fend it off. He eventually adjusted, but only for the next searing burst of light to attack him with even more ferocity as if it had been waiting for the most unexpected time to strike. Without warning it leapt from the emptiness, catching him off guard to the point that he gasped but this time he would not have to be so patient as it faded quickly.

It was as though it had paced itself last time and revealed the truth no faster than it could be taken in. But now it had been accepted for what it was it refused to bide its time. As the space around him again became clear he was unsurprised to find himself still in his cot and continuing to be the focus of attention in a room that hadn't changed at all. Looking around it couldn't be clearer that it was the same time of year; in fact everything seemed identical except his likeness. He could just about see himself in the mirror that remained hung in the hallway to this day and he'd grown considerably.

An entire year must have passed in the time it took him to

establish that he had again escaped being blinded. All around him conversations between his parents and their many guests were held in real time; unhurried and uninterrupted as preparations were made but all Noel could think about was where a whole twelve months had gone and what any of this meant.

CHAPTER SIX

Mary slumped into her chair and rubbed her stomach. It now entered the room long before she did despite an initial phase so subtle she hadn't realised her situation for months. The near constant kicking within seemed ungrateful but gave her a bittersweet assurance that her life was about to change, even if it wasn't entirely to plan. She certainly appeared to be growing by the day now as if making up for lost time and the relatively sudden surge had been hard to adjust to.

With a hundred reasons not to, she couldn't help but smile as she lay back, holding her bloated body perfectly still whilst waiting and watching. It wouldn't be long... it never was. But the short time it was taking was too long to wait for another of the gingerbread biscuits she'd hated for decades. She reached out slowly, stretching inadvisably rather than move but she couldn't quite grasp the half eaten packet. She walked her fingers along the windowsill towards it, pinned the wrapper then carefully dragged it back towards her, snatching it as soon as it was within range. The excitement was too much and she was temporarily distracted. The first two victims were swallowed almost whole, but after the third, with her cravings satisfied for the time being she placed another just above her waist. She studied it intently and counted backwards from ten but was surprised to hear her own voice as she hadn't intended speaking out loud. She'd almost reached zero but without any event, however minor happening and so slowed her count dramatically convincing herself that delayed the passing seconds accordingly. She stretched each one for as long as necessary until the biscuit leapt into the air, kicked so hard that it left her body completely. Her previous laziness and lethargic demeanour deserted her to make way for her well honed reactions so impressive they would make athletes jealous. Her hand shot from the armrest like a viper that had been waiting to strike and caught the prize in midair. She gave out a triumphant yelp and thrust clenched fists into the air.

In a sudden moment of self-consciousness she peered over her shoulder and out of the window. Her apartment was near the very top of the building and she doubted anyone would be looking in from the opposite block but the feeling of being watched passed as quickly as it arrived. She really should get in the habit of closing the curtain when it got dark rather than when she went to bed on the odd occasion that the two times were any different. She'd do it in a moment or two, as soon as the news was finished. That's how bored she really was.

The production titles rolled and with great effort she pulled herself up, unable to actually see the television over her own body. As she did so several crumbs fell onto the sofa but it needed cleaning anyway. She might as well do the whole room tomorrow during daylight hours. She swiped at the remaining crumbling remnants without much success. Rather than brush them away she forced them further into the thick, soft wool of her colossal winter jumper. It should have been thrown out years ago, but knowing the days and weeks it took to create the multicoloured and misshapen abomination she'd never had the heart to do so. Nobody could have known that fifteen years later she would grow to fit into it with the help inside her. The jumper had more than enough room for both of them though and she felt they were safe within it. She knew why; the designer was protective and it had always transcended to everything she touched. Despite its age it still seemed to reek of her perfume. It didn't matter that it had been washed so many times its near psychedelic patterns were faded to an almost bland interweaving mass, she'd swear she could still smell her scent. She wondered exactly what kind of sadist she was to wear it so often when it constantly reminded her of everything and everyone she was trying to forget. Who could explain wanting to be surrounded by somebody they couldn't bear to visit? She couldn't actually bring herself to call for the fear that she just might no longer be at the end of the phone. She knew it was an inexcusable weakness but at times it felt like power; her ignorance could prolong life itself, in her head at least and that made her the ruler of the universe. By breaking contact with the outside world she'd effectively frozen time and granted immortality.

She'd never intended it to be this way but her condition gave her an almost endless list of feasible excuses that couldn't be disproved. She always had a reason to delay contact until another tomorrow, but with each passing day the news seemed to get worse until what would have been a simple visit became an occasion to dread. It left her waiting for the perfect day when at least one of them were stronger but as it became increasingly obvious that the day was unlikely to come, she found herself needing an excuse to actually visit rather than the other way around. But she was just days away from having the best justification she'd ever have. She wouldn't have to arrive alone and the additional visitor would mean she could avoid explaining the unexplainable; why she'd avoided the very person who needed her most. It was cowardly and she couldn't forgive herself for it but she'd backed herself into such a corner she needed to be dragged back out.

She should be stronger than this and she knew it; even without everyone telling her, but their advice had formed part of the last conversation she'd had with any of them but she'd have all the company she'd need soon.

She again patted herself gently and looked around the room for any form of distraction. Unsurprisingly nothing had changed and she looked hopefully to the phone that lay on the armrest opposite; it was never far away as the less she had to get up and down the better recently. For several minutes she just sat there willing it to ring with realistic expectation as it was already after five O'clock.

She counted down from ten again, this time in her head but had to start over several times before its screen lit mercifully. It was answered before it had even sounded.

'So are they here?' she enquired without so much as a greeting. She'd grown so familiar with her next-door neighbour over the past few months that it was no longer necessary. She'd moved in recently and had her flaws, but who didn't? And at least she didn't lecture her and that alone made her an ally at the very least, perhaps even a friend. Mary got up slowly as she answered.

'Not yet. What's the time babe?'

'Nearly ten past' she answered in a monotone voice as she checked herself in the mirror.

'Ok, what's up?' sighed the caller as if she didn't know, bracing herself to hear a different version of the same and painfully familiar story.

'Nothing, I'm fine'.

'Come on. Let's have it...'

'Well how happy would you be if you looked like this *before* dinner?' She whined whilst hitting slightly different poses and studying her reflection as if a complimentary angle might be able to hide what people were kindly calling her 'bump' in one of the most extreme understatements she'd ever heard.

'Listen to me, you've got a baby; an entire person growing inside of your stomach. This time next month you'll be your old self again'.

'Yeah, I know... it's not that. It's what's growing inside my arse that's worrying me'. She'd turned and could now see her profile. She'd grown backwards as well as forwards like her body wanted to balance and distribute her growing weight yet she still couldn't stop thinking about food. She wished she could have seen the reaction at the take away when they took her order tonight. She was fairly confident nobody had ever asked for *that* as a pizza topping, but speciality order or not, it would have to be here soon.

'I know you're right but that's my point. It's the same old me that I'm worried about. I should have had my first years ago Donna. I shouldn't be starting over now'

'Thirty-one's not a bad age at all as you well know.'

'I know, I know. Thirty-one is a great age' admitted Mary. Especially when you're thirty-four she thought to herself. It made a twisted sense to lie to the few men that she met but she wasn't entirely sure why she couldn't tell Donna the truth. She wandered over to her window and pushed her face against it hoping to be able to share Donna's view from two floors below but she couldn't quite get the angle.

There was an awkward pause in the conversation as both women tried to think of a way to steer it away from the subject but before they could, the sight Donna had been waiting for arrived.

'Dinner time' she said before killing the call. She'd watched a bike slow down hopefully until its familiar logo reassured her it was the one she'd been expecting. It circled the cramped parking area, its rider searching for a space before abandoning his bike on the pavement. He was clearly in a rush and was halfway out of the saddle before he'd even switched off the engine. His almost non-existent frame burst through the apartment block doors with the force of a man twice his size and made his way straight to the lift which, as always, was out of order. Turning back the way he came he dashed for the stairs before taking them two at a time. Having cleared the first flight of stairs in seconds he almost careered straight into the pram being delicately eased down them carefully one step at a time.

He backed up apologetically to allow the young woman to pass but still bounced on the spot like a tennis player awaiting his opponent's serve, unable to hide his eagerness to drag back every lost minute. Glancing at his watch and grinding his teeth in frustration he was slow to notice that the woman pushing the buggy must be half its weight until she groaned with effort as she tried to negotiate as smoother passage as possible.

'I'm sorry' she said noticing his obvious anguish.

'Don't be' he assured her suddenly getting things into perspective. He balanced his delivery on the corner of the banister and bounded up the steps to take the front of the pram and help her down the last few.

'Thanks so much', she sounded genuinely grateful, 'but I don't suppose you'd be kind enough?' She looked down towards the next stairwell with a hopeful expression on her unconventionally pretty face that was hard to resist. He'd already started to make his way again before she had actually finished her sentence but somehow managed to make his response sound like he'd never intended to do anything other than help her all the way down to the exit.

He didn't know how long it had taken but he was pretty sure he'd carried what was more than his share of the weight before running three steps at a time with two full size pizzas in hand to the twelfth floor. Reaching it exhausted, he leaned on the door bell as he rang it and was still gasping for breath as Mary eventually answered. She smiled awkwardly whilst taking the boxes from him.

'You should have been here at half past eight…' she looked at the boys ridiculously oversized name badge '…Rick'. As always, she was surprised at how she felt.

'Why? What did I miss?' asked the young man, completely straight-faced. His reply was unexpected and made Mary smile as she searched for a witty retort but opted for a matter of fact response instead, basically ignoring him.

'You're late by three minutes' she clarified. Rick sighed; sometimes he'd charm his way out of forfeiting payment but he could already tell that this was not one of those times. He again looked at his watch, sincerely surprised at the news but conceded without argument. He was late. It might not be by much and it might not be entirely his fault but 'a minute is a minute and a promise is a promise' as his boss would say; again and again and again.

'Then it's on the house' he declared forcing an enthusiastic smile across his face fitting of the newspaper advert that promised as much. 'But is there any chance of a glass of water? I don't like to ask but, well, your elevator's out and it's a long climb up'.

Mary looked slightly taken aback by his request but couldn't think of a plausible reason not to oblige. She disappeared expecting him to wait at the open door so was understandably startled when she came out of the kitchen to find him in her hallway making a fuss of her cat.

'Sorry' he said noticing her shock, 'couldn't help myself'.

'No, that's fine, I'm just surprised. He came from a rescue home and won't usually go near strangers'. She gave him the well deserved glass of water.

'Thanks, I'm sure I must be intruding?' he was in no rush to descend those stairs for another few minutes but was sure Mary wouldn't be eating alone in her condition and that there'd be a lucky husband in the living room. She'd have to be more than a little hungry to order two super size double crusts just for herself.

Again, Mary couldn't find an excuse to hurry him, besides she liked the way he was looking at her. He was young, too young for her to take it as genuine flattery really but she took compliments where she could get them lately, even if they weren't actually spoken. She enjoyed the way he seemed slightly nervous as he grappled to keep the conversation from ending. It was endearing in a school yard kind of way and so she helped him along.

'Well you've met my Holly so there's nobody else to introduce you to' she offered smiling coyly. She knew she shouldn't toy with him but if the suggestion that she was eating alone could keep his dirty little teenage imagination alive she'd say what he wanted to hear for a few minutes longer. Rick stopped gulping his water and began to take longer over finishing it and playfully introduced himself to the cat. Mary felt embarrassed for him and tried to save him from the awkward situation but he insisted on making it worse.

'So you like cats?' It wasn't a particularly intelligent thing to say yet he struggled to come up with anything more profound. But to ask it whilst still stroking Holly made the obvious answer seem as ridiculous as the question itself. She smiled but didn't laugh so as not to humiliate him further. She was almost certain that his awkward innocence would ensure that he repelled girls at school, college or pretty much wherever else he went. It seemed a shame that it took a woman in her thirties to find it charming. She humoured him with an answer devoid of the obvious sarcasm.

'Well they're easy to look after when you've got responsibilities yourself aren't they? They're independent, stay out all night, they don't care what I say or do and are quite happy to be left alone most of the time. She was my boyfriend's but ended up being the only one who stuck around'. Mary wondered if she was being too transparent now but she felt half her age again and that made the charade worth it. In fact she wasn't so sure that she wasn't teasing herself now rather than the boy.

'And who could blame him' replied Rick thinking that at last he'd come up with a smooth response but just a little consideration told him otherwise. Instantly wishing he'd said almost anything else and looking shocked at his own thoughtlessness he began to backpedal. 'I meant the cat; who could blame Molly for staying... not who could blame your boyfriend for leaving.' He wasn't the only one who was embarrassed now. His eagerness to impress had actually made Mary blush.

'It's Holly. Her name's Holly', she explained. 'I don't know a Molly but I knew what you meant'. She suddenly realised how self-assured she sounded and started apologising. 'I'm not being arrogant; I just meant that... well you know what I mean?' She put her head in her hands. Was she really struggling to keep the high ground over this acne infested, hormone driven teenager? She was disappointed in herself. Even she'd have to admit she needed to get out more; she'd gradually lost her ability to interact without noticing until now. Tomorrow seemed like a good day to go outside again.

'So why did he leave?' Rick didn't know he had her in retreat now. He was merely saying whatever kept him in that hallway, however tactless but whilst Mary found it surprisingly intrusive it was also refreshingly bold. She was again momentarily lost for words. In a few years time she doubted he'd be so direct having learnt the subtle art of discretion.

'Well he was independent, stayed out all night, didn't care what I said or did and basically wanted to be left alone most of the time.'

She smiled to assure him it was a joke and that he was meant to laugh. 'Seriously though, I've got to accept it. I forced him to choose between a family and that precious car of his so now I've got to live with the decision'. She corrected herself and acknowledged her figure. 'We've got to live with that'.

'Not part of the plan then?' enquired Rick seeing no reason not to. Mary just smiled. She'd have told anyone else to mind their own business but she felt he was asking out of concern rather than motive.

'It was, just not yet. If I'd have wanted to hear the patter of tiny feet I'd put shoes on her' she laughed nodding towards Holly who instantly left the room as if horrified by the thought but she'd sensed what was now only minutes away.

Now Mary didn't have the feline as the topic of conversation and she was unwilling to discuss her pregnancy in any further detail so she changed the subject completely.

'So is this a busy time of year for you or are most people eating out at restaurants?' she asked with all sincerity. Rick was suddenly very conscience of the circumstances under which they were talking and with that came a humbleness he hadn't felt until now; she was judging him on his degrading job like it was a career decision. He felt the need to inform her otherwise.

'I don't take much notice to be honest as it doesn't matter much to me. This isn't what I'm going to be, it's just what keeps me paying the bills until I become an artist. I can paint you know... better than that' he claimed whilst simultaneously insulting her taste as he pointed at the picture hanging precariously in the hall.

'Then why don't you?' came the slightly curt and aggressive response. She hadn't meant it to sound quite so aggressive but it had certainly come out that way. Even Rick could sense he'd offended her and so he tried to retract his statement.

'I didn't mean to criticise your taste, it's just that it's fairly basic. I hope you didn't pay too much for it that's all.'

'Don't worry, I didn't'.

'That's ok then.'

'Because I painted it'.

Rick just looked at her choosing to say nothing at all; at least that way it couldn't be wrong. Silence ensued until Mary broke it.

'So how come you're not busy creating your own if you're so good?' She said it as a genuine question; she was tired of meeting people who had dreams yet waited for them to happen on their own. Rick could tell exactly what she meant, partly from the tone in her voice, but also because he'd often asked himself. He wasn't sure what he was waiting for but it was simply too easy to earn enough to exist the on the back of that bike and his accommodation came with the job. The prospect of doing anything else seemed daunting after all this time. He was about to admit as much but was beaten to the next sentence.

'I dated an artist a few years back. He sacrificed his salary to work freelance and prove himself.'

'Really, did he sell much?'

'Plenty. It was fairly stable at first but then he started to sell... he had to sell his television first, then his car and on it went until he had to sell his flat.' She was aware that she must look pleased with the delivery of the line she'd so deliberately set up, but could see his enthusiasm flattened; she'd have to be gentler with him.

'But I'm sure there's plenty who make it' she added, trying not to sound too condescending. Before she had a chance to figure out how it was taken, Donna burst in through the open door pushing her pram in one hand and carrying a particularly large and convincing doll in the other.

'She does it again!' she declared holding the toy aloft like a conquering hero. 'So take me to our free...' she froze when she noticed the pizza boy was still around long after he should have been on his way but more importantly, she could see the recognition on his face. She looked at Mary, then at the pizzas and back again holding her hands up in place of asking the obvious question in acknowledgement of surrender.

Mary was the only one of the three that looked anything other than confused.

'I don't know what to say, I'm sorry?' her apology was aimed towards Donna fearing that was where the fiercest attack would come from but she didn't bother to continue with an explanation. She wouldn't expect anyone else to understand what she had done or why she had done it and judging by Rick's expression, her humble admittance was misdirected anyway. It seemed empty but he was simply saving energy for the calculations that were going on behind it. She turned her body to face him to add sincerity to her confession 'it's nothing personal, just I haven't been able to work and money's hard to find at the moment.' She wasn't sure whether he was more hurt than angry.

'Well so are jobs. We're allowed one late delivery a night and this was my second'. It was the first time tonight he'd been able to maintain eye contact with her for more than a fleeting moment but now he held it until she looked away. She pulled two crumpled notes from her pocket that she'd had ready in case the plan hadn't worked as it didn't always.

'I don't know what else to say… keep the change' she said managing to be both contradictory and patronising in a single sentence. Rick took the money without a word and ignoring her continued insistence not to, he counted the exact change. When she wouldn't take it from him he unceremoniously dumped it noisily on a nearby shelf making Holly jump no sooner had she re-entered the hall.

Mary had underestimated him. That couldn't be clearer. Now he was controlling the situation and making two fully grown women squirm with guilt and awkwardness. Aware of her own sizable part in the plot and sensing her friend's silent pleas for help Donna took her share of the blame but was ignored with the same casual disregard. He leant down to make one last fuss of Holly like she was the only one worth saying goodbye to and left without another word.

CHAPTER SEVEN

Noel couldn't even describe what was happening as dreamlike as that would mean anything could happen and he felt sure that wasn't the case. He would see absolutely nothing that hadn't occurred at some point in his life, and it was becoming increasingly likely that he'd be able to predict exactly which points they'd be.

Despite so many distractions Noel was still able to theorise; in fact he wasn't able to stop himself. This wasn't necessarily as scientifically unfeasible as he'd at first thought. Chemical reactions had explained the unexplainable before and after all, these were merely recollections. He was seeing nothing that couldn't have actually happened, even if they had occurred long before what he thought was his first memory but that wasn't the only unanswered question. Time was a reality and he couldn't change that with or without science. Gradually he was able to separate himself from the sights and sounds he was sure were within him but beyond it was the din of the street below. He had to concentrate fully to hear it at all but it was definitely there and it provided a far better measure of time than his own thoughts. Whilst he imagined that he'd have fallen the full nineteen stories before he'd had chance to consider anything at all it could still be misleading as his mind worked overtime in the face of such a threatening situation; maybe it was capable of more than he knew when self-preservation and not self-pity became it's priority. But these were the sounds of the world and he knew they worked to rules that he understood. Rhythms and beats that could be translated clearly into seconds and minutes but it was this reliable calculation that finally convinced him to accept what was happening. The carollers below hadn't only finished singing the chorus during which he'd made his decision to take his life, they'd actually started another. Time was passing slower than he could explain but it still moved, urging him not to waste what was left dwelling on the same subject for too long.

He stopped considering *how* as it seemed a lost cause and he instead concentrated on *why*. Were everyone's final thoughts those of the past and the life they'd led? Was every poor soul destined to the indignity of their own uncensored history whether they liked it or not? It was too late to learn from any mistakes and there was not time enough to enjoy reliving any successes so the phenomenon seemed pointless and nothing short of cruel.

The next white flash hurt almost as much as the last but came as less of a surprise now; there truly was little that couldn't be gotten used to. As it faded away that unmistakable and never forgotten feeling was his once more. He lay in familiar gloom again but it wasn't his surrounding he recognised first, it was the feeling in the pit of his stomach that balanced perfectly on the pivotal point between unadulterated excitement and the agony of anticipation. He'd tried to recreate it so many times but eventually conceded that only a child could feel it so purely. It couldn't be copied or manufactured; it wasn't a situation or a date... it was no more than a feeling created by absolute belief that would be chipped away every passing year from now on. If it could be bottled or packaged there would be no limit to its worth but it could not be bought.

Even though barely able to walk without stumbling, Noel understood the consequences of staying awake. It meant that none of the things he so desperately wished for would happen yet the more he tried to sleep, the more impossible it seemed. Every creak and shudder signalled the possibility of a magical approach that reopened his eyes. He lie there so still and quiet that he could hear his own heartbeat. He could even *feel* it and worried that it would give him away. He took his chances and twisted onto his front as quickly as he could and settled again instantly, faking unconsciousness almost perfectly.

His adult self reminisced and smiled. Such innocence seemed

unlikely now but he didn't doubt it existed within him once. He'd watched identical behaviour from his sister for the few years it lasted and wondered now how many hours their parents must have waited up just to be able to enter their room without shattering such precious illusions. He'd never recalled these intricate details as clearly as he could now, but in everyday life he'd always remembered back further than most of his friends seemed to be able to. It often surprised his family when he was able to join in conversations about times they were convinced he'd have no recollection of. They were certain he was cunningly regurgitating pieces of discussions he'd picked up over the years and using his questionable imagination to fill in the gaps. But when they attempted to prove themselves right by peppering their yesterday years with events that never actually happened he'd confidently corrected them. At that point they'd accepted his word and his impressive ability to recollect events exactly as they happened. But they were always viewed from his perspective and for that reason they sometimes differed enormously from the versions he had to listen to.

He didn't know if there was any particular reason but it certainly didn't appear to be genetic. For all her other perfections his sister didn't seem to have inherited what others called a blessing; a fact he'd used to his advantage since she was old enough to be lied to. It was almost cruel that he was forced to recall his exceptionally average life whilst she'd forgotten more achievements than he'd ever managed. Some blessing.

But even he had his limits and he'd never thought himself able to recall anything before he was three; possibly even four years old and as far as he knew he'd never met anyone who could honestly claim they were any different.

So was it even possible that what he was seeing was actually memories at all? Memories by their very definition were times, people and places that were actually remembered. Suffering the immense pressure he'd put himself under there could be untold ruptures in his brain unearthing the past but surely this was too accurate... too specific?

Whatever he was seeing, it was blurring again and it distracted his thoughts. Around him the walls changed colour and even morphed into different shapes but the excited atmosphere, albeit slightly forced, remained the same. His parents had made a real effort this year figuring that at four years old he would now be fully aware of what was going on around him. He had a vague understanding of why it was happening and had been told the true meaning of Christmas but possessed a thorough knowledge of the traditions it entailed; specifically, presents, chocolate and generally being made the centre of attention yet he was still hard to please.

He walked towards the piles of presents under the tree, having to raise his head the closer he got to keep their summit within view. Some of them were admittedly large in size but it was the sheer amount that ensured it was taller than he was and they kept their height most of the way around the tree they encircled. He guessed there must be everything that had been asked for, shown interest in and even glanced at. Both his mum and his dad must have felt pretty confident when asking him what he really wanted that it was already there somewhere in the heaving mass of gifts, so it must have cut deep when they realised it wasn't.

'So what, if you could have anything in the world would you be unwrapping tomorrow little man?' asked his dad with all the certainty in the world but also hedging his bets; if Noel had surprised him there were at least two hours left until the shops closed. He was confident that he had little to worry about, whatever his son replied. But if it wasn't already catered for it was unlikely he'd be unable to afford it as his building firm had seen its best year by far.

'Anything?' confirmed Noel. It made his mother's heart melt to hear him ask for something so hopefully, especially when he curled his voice up at the end of the word like that. It was so adult in its phrasing that it reminded her how quickly he'd grown recently. She wanted to make the most of these precious childhood days; there was little Noel ever went without.

'That's what I said pal, you don't always get what you ask for but if you don't let people know then you've got no chance at all.' The businessman in him came to the surface if only momentarily as he quickly added his get out clause and verbal small print to the end of his sentence in case he couldn't deliver.

'Well I want one of them then', Noel said with all the conviction of a child twice his age as he pointed his tiny hand towards the television. His parents smiled, secretly reassured and congratulating themselves and each other at having been so accurate in their choices. The flickering screen showed this year's craze being pushed through puddles and dirt. Hidden away, high in the closet upstairs was the motorised model truck that had apparently sold out in every shop this side of the country.

'But what'd we call him' continued Noel. His parents' complimentary gaze continued to find each other over their child's head, but their smiles had become a little nervous. His dad bent down so that he could see things from his son's point of view. By aligning himself behind Noel he was able to follow his pointing more accurately; it didn't lead to the truck at all, but directly towards the boy who was playing with it. It all made sense now.

'Santa doesn't deliver children Noel' he assured the confused looking youngster.

'But you said anything?'

His dad sighed under the penetrating stare of his wife. He'd brought this on himself and her look said everything just in case he wasn't reprimanding himself already. He grappled for something, anything resembling a credible and logical answer.

'Because the children suffocate in his sack' was the best he could come up with. Noel looked only slightly less horrified than his mother who appeared from the kitchen and wedged herself between them like she was trying to block the stupidity before it could reach him.

She intercepted every attempt to rectify the situation and explained the situation as best she could without getting too explicit.

With Noel's insistent questioning this took longer than she imagined but she skillfully avoided the most direct of his curiosities and managed to get to the result without the process. But it wasn't without contradiction and it didn't go unnoticed.

'So it'd be down to you?' asked Noel just wanting to confirm things.

'Exactly, but we'd need a little longer. Maybe we could sort something out by next Christmas?' She'd answered her son but it was clearly directed at her husband who nearly spat out the sneaky swig of Brandy he'd so nearly gotten away with. She always did have a strange way of suggestion but he wasn't at all ready for this one. He couldn't make out how serious she was based on her coy smile and she turned away before she gave anything else away but it would be very unlike her to say anything like that in front of Noel if she didn't mean it. Their son protested and looked disappointed enough to provoke further explanation.

'It's just complicated and takes a lot of time' chipped in his dad before he could be stopped, but satisfied that he'd realised his earlier mistake, she let him continue only for Noel to interrupt him instead. He'd heard the way his dad dealt with complicated or difficult deadlines at work and saw no reason why every problem shouldn't be solved in the same efficient way so suggested just that.

'Well can't you just put more men on the job Dad?' asked Noel with a straight face and sincere expression that would be impossible in a few years time. For the second time the carpet was nearly sprayed as his dad almost choked in response.

'I'd rather not' he said again rising to his feet and ruffling his son's hair as he did so.

Noel remembered the rest of that evening exactly as it had been but now witnessed it with wiser eyes as his parents had quiet discussions that would have gone over his head back then. But now he wondered if his misinformed and innocent request had actually been the catalyst that changed all their lives? It had crossed his mind before but he'd always dismissed it thinking it unlikely that he could have initiated something so momentous at such an early age, but now, seeing the look on their faces for an impossible second time maybe it was not so unlikely for by the same time next year he had his wish; almost.

CHAPTER EIGHT

Nick had received all the sniggering he'd expected the moment he left the shelter of his lorry but to some extent he'd grown used to it now. He was surrounded by younger men who ridiculed his less than tasteful outfit but unlike most men his age at least he knew he was dressed outrageously and that in itself meant it wasn't a delayed midlife crisis.

The woman he'd waited so long for reappeared and indulged him for a few moments to begin signing off his paperwork but still seemed in no particular hurry. Before she'd dated the final box on the form she paused as though deep in thought, made her excuses then blatantly vanished again to check his delivery and making her acceptance official. She returned quickly enough with a list of its short falls but explained that she had to see to her staff first and again disappeared from view.

Nick was left to watch the clock whilst she ensured the last work crew of the year settled into what was traditionally a difficult and riotous shift to control but he already had what he really needed; her name was written clearly enough and that was what counted; Ivy Wainsbridge. It sounded as elitist as she probably wished it was. Ideally he needed to complete the document in full and to give her a counter signed copy for reference but they were formalities that were hardly worth waiting for. He checked the time and decided that two more minutes was all she had.

Much to Nick's disappointment she arrived back twenty seconds before her deadline was up. As her left hand snatched the delivery note from him he was unsurprised to see that she definitely wasn't married. The inappropriate dress she wore had made him suspect as much… delusional singles across the country would be emerging from washroom cubicles, convinced they really had dropped a dress size just because it hadn't split at the seams and they'd all be just as convinced that it mattered. Modern culture had a lot to answer for. He considered the social pressure she must be under and almost felt sorry for her as he wondered how long it'd take her to return to her original shape if, and he really meant *if* she managed to peel the clinging material off this evening; with her attitude there wasn't likely to be anyone in the vicinity to help. If she could find so many faults with his cargo, surely no human being could stand up to her scrutiny?

In the short time he waited for her to return he'd built a complete mental picture of her life and the possible reasons for her venom. But now she stood before him again his short lived concern for her was turning to frustration but he blamed himself; in a moment of weakness he'd asked how her day had been and now he was being told with mind numbing detail. He tried to look more enthralled than he actually was but he couldn't believe how quickly he'd lost interest in his own question.

He just didn't want to hear her problems, surely he'd done enough for her already without being her psychiatrist as well but she obviously felt the need to talk and for some reason it was to him. He wondered if she was almost inventing issues with the delivery simply as an excuse for conversation but he still couldn't bring himself as far as actually being concerned. He wondered if he was being ignorant and apathetic but he didn't know and he didn't care.

Whether the goods were to her standard or not, he'd delivered the evergreen as ordered and at extremely late notice. He'd even followed her into the warehouse as instructed despite being desperate to avoid as many onlookers as possible but at least it took the attention away from her and the ill-fitting gown she modelled. By standing next to Nick she was a picture of taste and class.

Dressed in an intricately detailed, but secondhand department store Santa outfit, attention was the one thing that Nick was guaranteed. It came with oversize boots and even fake fur trim but also included accessories he didn't really need. His own beard looked more clichéd than the elasticated version he been given and he'd put on so much weight recently that he hardly saw the point in using the false stomach that had come free with the costume. He was useless when it came to counting calories and he had the figure to prove it so the last thing he wanted was to accentuate it. But when his company's research figures showed that dressing their drivers as the world's top delivery man would fill their clients with enough festive spirit that they'll choose a nineteen percent more profitable tree he'd become concerned; when he discovered that these same outfits actually cost *less* than their original uniform he knew his fate was sealed. Having learned when to debate and when to accept the inevitable he'd been the only one on the payroll not to argue about it. The younger of his peers had actually resigned over it, full of naïve bravado and that suited him just fine. With fewer drivers to deliver more trees there had never been so much overtime available and the bosses had been forced to pay triple for Sundays and holidays just to fulfill demand; and that was something he couldn't turn down. It was degrading and it was desperate. The tactic was even insultingly obvious but the facts and figures took little interpreting as far as management were concerned. And so the remaining staff would spread cheer to the sound of ringing tills rather than sleigh bells and that meant eight hours a day in what was effectively fancy dress, regardless of who you were. It didn't matter whether you used to be in a position to issue company decisions or whether you're just too long in the tooth to be pushing and pulling these trees onboard such a rickety old trailer. Nobody cared that it was impossible to move in the overly generous outfits or whether your wife is eighteen months into what was promised to be a routine check up at the hospital just a street away... everyone without exception wore the suit, polystyrene belly as well.

Trying to be there for the woman he'd do anything for had eventually cost him his high-powered job; his advancing years didn't allow him the energy to satisfy the conflicting demands so he was eventually paid off. Quite generously as it happened but the sum was quickly eaten up by the best medical treatment money could buy. Before the redundancy package ran out completely he'd gone looking for part–time consultancy positions but with so many bright-eyed graduates to choose from he'd gradually had to lower his sights. He realigned his pride and his expectations again and again until he found himself here, as Father Christmas delivering to sour women with delusions of grandeur with a rusty old lorry for a sleigh.

He wasn't sure how long he'd been forced to listen to Ivy's complaints but still she unloaded her troubles as if Nick had nothing else to do and nowhere else to go; he'd have to remind her of who he was and why he was here.

'I'm really just here about the tree, and I know you must be busy so if I could just…' He wasn't allowed to finish before Ivy cut him short. She could see he felt awkward about having to focus her and that he was probably genuinely sorry to have to do so, but it didn't stop it being humiliating. She hadn't even realised that she'd gone off on quite such an irrelevant tangent but now it had been pointed out it was embarrassing, especially with so many of her staff around to hear. Instead of defensive apology she attacked.

'The tree? You don't really want my opinion on that tree do you?' She didn't wait for an answer. 'Well I'll give you my opinion on that sorry excuse for a tree!' This time she waited briefly for a response but quickly lost her patience and continued. 'It's worthless!'

'Well tell me anyway, pretend I'm interested'. Nick looked particularly pleased with himself as he said it; even more so when the store men smirked as much as they dared. Ivy fixed him with an infuriated, wide-eyed stare before disappearing with a promise to be back.

'The tree's worthless, not my opinion'.

'Sorry my mistake' said Nick as if he really meant it. His comment had the desired effect; Ms Wainsbridge didn't want to talk anymore.

The clock's second hand had now made its way full circle more than twice since he last looked and he wasn't prepared to be detained any longer. He turned and left the building keeping a purposeful pace on his way back to the lorry but was followed. The fuming woman emerged again, calling him back. He'd only intended to draw her away from so many distractions and force her to complete signing, but now that he'd actually started walking away he began to enjoy it. And more to the point, he couldn't actually bring himself to stop and return to her because of the way he'd been *ordered* to do so. He'd never been a man to take authority well.

He elected the easiest option and simply pretended he couldn't hear her. There'd be no comeback to speak of. After all, he had her scrawl to say she'd received her order and even if she wanted a discount due to its debatable condition it was not his concern; there was little he could do about it even if he wanted to. Decisions like that were above him now and stopping to explain that to someone like her would only delay him further; he simply couldn't afford the time any longer, not today.

He'd almost strode back to his lorry and past the point where anyone could have reasonably expected him to have heard anything over the forklifts racing back and forth when the unexpected distinctive thud of a tannoy system being powered up made him flinch. It was accompanied by a squeal that made everyone in the vicinity wince before being followed by Ivy's voice, not entirely dissimilar and amplified through speakers loud enough that even the most distant workers stood to attention. To them it was something they'd learned to obey. He wondered if they'd tried a similar tactic to his own when they started their employment but he then supposed that they probably hadn't... the evidence being that they still had their jobs.

Everybody except Ivy was sniggering to themselves, exchanging knowing glances in anticipation of what was coming; even Nick thought he had some idea. He'd met her type many times before and in what now seemed like a previous life he'd dealt with them efficiently enough at disciplinary hearings but he was a long way off holding that position now; he was struggling to keep the one he had. He just wasn't that person anymore. Not officially anyway. He wasn't even convinced that he'd been promoted on his merits this time around and secretly suspected that he had his thick white beard to thank more than the reliability and drive he prided himself on all these years.

He froze rooted to the spot in annoyance. By dumping his cargo as planned then simply driving away now it would look like he was running... escaping even. Likewise, if he returned the way he came he would be embroiled in an argument he couldn't resolve let alone win, and this woman would maintain her reign of terror so he did neither, he just stood there. And so did she.

If he had to have this conversation, it would be after she'd come to him and if that happened before he succumbed to her demands, that in itself would seem like a small victory to the onlookers, all of whom had virtually ground to a fascinated but apprehensive halt.

Eventually she surged forward, powered by her pent up anger and ending the stale mate but when she moved, it was decisive and aggressive and she was upon him before he'd considered his defence. It had already been made all the more difficult due to her having a very fair point; it wasn't the best looking tree and indeed, some of the branches were not as full as they could be. But it was quite literally the second to last tree in the yard this morning and that can't come as much of a surprise? Who leaves it this late in the month to order? Surely even she'd have to take what she could get at such late notice?

Ivy retaliated to this accusation head on and explained that nobody had left the booking that late at all, but the demise of their last tree at the hands of a chain smoker who couldn't resist adjusting the tinsel had left the company with little option. The subsequent decision to ban smoking inside the building had been taken before the fire engines had even left, and for that reason the audience couldn't be greater. Office and factory workers alike shivered begrudgingly in the cold having been forced outside to light their cigarettes but they were at least grateful for the show being provided.

Nick let her have her say. It would make her look all the more insignificant when he ignored her completely. Her ranting quickly became repetitive as if she'd even stopped listening to herself. She wasn't the only one. The barrage washed over him, only odd sentences and words penetrated the sphere he found himself in. He picked up enough to piece together what was essentially a simple message littered with irrelevant opinions.

With hindsight it was clear he should have delivered in the opposite order. The perfect specimen of a fir tree was lying right next to Ivy's pitiful excuse for a tree and that wasn't making the situation any easier. As such, she was insistent that Nick was able to exchange the delivery if he wanted to and she wasn't accepting anything else. But the fact remained that it had been accounted for since July by the Grandure Hotel and Nick was becoming increasingly insistent that absolutely nothing would change that.

Without his intellect being particularly challenged he continued to tear her to shreds with limited but well chosen words whilst never really leaving his own private thoughts.... He'd worked hard today, having set out early and missed every break to get ahead of schedule he'd hoped to finish before time, but as they seemed to have done for so long now, the fates had conspired against him. Despite even breaking into what was almost a run at some points, he was late. So late in fact that if he went straight to his drop off he'd never make it back again before hospital visiting hours were over and there was no way, simply no way at all that he wasn't going see Grace today of all days.

His self-imposed schedule reminded him again that he really didn't have to listen to this. Ms Wainsbridge should never have signed before inspection. He knew it and so did she and now she could cut out the sub standard branches or cover them with baubles for all he cared. She continued with her case saying that her evergreen was going brown and whilst Nick would accept that as a problem, it only had to last her the rest of the day.

Ivy could see she was getting nowhere and so tried to appeal to his better nature. She leant in closer as she was determined that nobody else should hear her beg for mercy.

'Please, just let me have the other tree? You're making a mockery of me' she hissed under her breath. Nick didn't back off and took the opportunity to make his point clearly.

'Don't feel you need to give me the credit Ms Wainsbridge, you've achieved it all on your own' he assured her. He held her glare but she continued her argument as if she hadn't even registered his words. She couldn't have known the resonance her response would have.

'It's obviously dying. You'd have been better off just putting it out of its misery.'

She couldn't have known better than to phrase it like that but Nick had run out of understanding. It was either leave right now or do yet something else he'd no doubt regret.

He paid her the ultimate insult and turned his back on her as the air filled with promises that his boss would hear of this and that it would cost him his job faded but they fell silent with the closing of his cabin door. He took as much quiet, private satisfaction from her mortification at being ignored as he did from her stupidity. Threatening to get him sacked? How many deliveries did she think he'd make after today?

If she was more honest with herself she didn't care about the tree or his pathetic job. But she did care about the fact that she'd been made to look human in front of her minions and that was unacceptable; humans had weaknesses. As far as she was concerned if that lorry left the yard without the tree she'd so publicly sworn she'd have, her authority was over and the very fact that the forklift drivers had not already busied themselves in her presence meant it must already be slipping.

Nick felt slightly guilty as he pulled his seatbelt across his bulk as he understood the difficulty he'd caused her. She might never be able to rebuild the reputation he'd single-handedly destroyed in front of the very people she'd have to manage, but she really had brought it upon herself.

He checked his rearview mirror before pulling away as with so many low loaders around he'd be wise to be careful but it didn't hold the view he'd expected at all. Ivy's reflection startled him and, struggling to believe it he turned to look behind him as if the mirror might be lying. It wasn't. She really had climbed aboard and was now pulling on the straps securing her trophy. To her it had become the symbol of her power and nobody, especially an arrogant nobody like him was going to take it away.

There was simply no space left in his head for rational thought and without time to lose he reacted instinctively and out of spite. The woman didn't even notice the floor below her start to rise as she tore away at the buckles as if possessed without making any progress whatsoever. The tipping was slow but surprisingly smooth for such a crude mechanism allowing her plenty of time to climb back down and accept defeat before there was any real danger. But whether she was so intent on what she was attempting and simply didn't notice, or whether she was well aware and challenging Nick to give in first this time didn't matter... he couldn't. He'd regretted his action instantly and hammered the button frantically on the custom-made elevation system but it made no difference at all. It was little more than an automated ramp added as an afterthought; it was amateurishly built and wouldn't allow itself to be reversed until it had reached full tilt.

The incline steepened to such an extent that everything on board that wasn't fixed, bolted or nailed down began to slide. It was a sign that even a woman of her determination couldn't ignore and Ivy clutched at the branches themselves. The floor of the trailer was so smooth it offered nothing to grip that wasn't already slipping, but the fragile foliage was not enough to hold her weight. She was never going to suffer more than bruising and a cracked ego but he would still have expected her staff to rush to her assistance. Not that she could see who to blame as she floundered against the flat and featureless boards of the trailer floor like her life depended on it. But the only movement amongst them was to subtly manoeuvre themselves so that there was constantly at least one person in a more able position to rescue her. None of them wanted to be the main target for her wrath, but all were unable to bring themselves to intervene with what was now looking inevitable. Nick knew it too and had stopped panicking knowing that there was absolutely nothing he could do in the time available; instead he focused on events that he could change and that meant leaving here as soon as possible.

The end of the trailer closest to him had now risen so high into the air that it blocked his view completely. He had no idea where its load and its insanely resolute stowaway was and the fear of driving away with her still on board overrode the incredible urge to leave. He had no illusions that he'd have to deal with the repercussions, but it would have to be on another day. He switched tactics and watched the wing mirrors instead wondering if he was already too late as he couldn't believe she was still on board the trailer as it had reached such a steep angle now. A few seconds later she wasn't. But she must have clung on for as long as possible before whatever was holding her secure eventually gave way as she hit the ground at an angle. As she rolled pitifully along the ground and into view he at least knew she wouldn't be crushed beneath his tyres as he drove away. So that was exactly what he did.

CHAPTER NINE

By now Noel had accepted he'd never see another day that didn't fall on December the 24th but he still had no idea why. Was his whole life careering before him? Was he only able to focus on today's date or was that all he was being shown? The latter seemed to make the most sense as the comparatively short distance from the building's roof to the ground hardly allowed him the time he'd need to relive over eight thousand days; but then it shouldn't provide a period long enough to view twenty-four of them either.

If he'd chosen a taller building would he see more of his life or was that irrelevant? Perhaps everyone witnesses no more and no less than their dying day of every year they'd survived? That wasn't unthinkable but the fact that so many of the incidences that had shaped his life, and eventually his death had fallen on that specific date seemed too much of a coincidence to ignore.

These thoughts hadn't distracted him totally though and he was still aware of the subtle difference before him and what it meant. The same pictures hung on the wall and the same primitive decorations hung from the ceiling. The presents under the tree had changed shape and colour but still the tags read the same. Thinking about it now from a practical, adult point of view they probably were the same so it made him laugh to see himself crawling from gift to gift and struggling to read the recycled messages. Each time he somehow remained surprised at the standard quote and regimental three kisses in blue ink that he'd only just realised never changed. But as similar as everything appeared, his life could not have changed more and in his young head it was his own fault for wishing it. It hadn't taken much to shatter his idyllic world and she lay behind him, screaming as always. To Noel it seemed as though she reserved every barrage for each moment someone was about to acknowledge his existence. As far as he could recall, this was the first time he'd felt an emotion so cold, but it had overshadowed his life ever since. As he grew older he'd learned not to talk about it but at the time he had no such discretion. Every time he tried he was merely pointed in the direction of the mountain of presents with his name on them and told not to be so ungrateful. He was also reminded that this was what he *asked* for but he never failed to remind anyone and everyone that it wasn't; that he'd asked for a brother and all he got was a girl. He couldn't believe his parents had done that to him. He had made his opinions about the opposite sex perfectly clear since starting playschool and nothing had changed; they're ugly, can't catch and worse than that... they smell. Yet they'd gone and bought one anyway and even expected him to be happy about it. He'd wished they'd get a refund like they had when he was less than impressed with the tennis racket they gave him for his birthday but apparently it wasn't that simple. After several failed attempts to discover exactly why, he'd given up and moved onto displaying increasingly desperate acts to attract their attention. When that had little effect he'd tried the reverse and just kept quiet as at least that way he'd be asked why once in a while. Being questioned was being talked to and that was better than nothing.

His baby sister however possessed only one way to attract attention but it was all she needed; it worked every single time. If it hadn't, things might have been different for them both in later life but who needs an alternative tactic when the one you have is perfectly effective?

Noel had noticed a pattern to the outbursts. There would always be a lull; the calm before the storm. Whether this was to give everyone within the vicinity chance to brace themselves or whether the so-called bundle of joy was simply storing the energy waiting to be unleashed he wasn't entirely sure. But either way it usually lasted long enough for him to put several rooms and as many walls as possible between the two of them. And then it would rise in an ear splitting burst of torture. Its tone was not dissimilar to that of an air raid warning that he'd heard in the black and white films that Dad still watched and it received much the same urgency. The room would be invaded as the emergency was attended to by everyone except his Grandmother who would always be there, shaking her head in the same room as him. Together they would sit, equally unable to see what all the fuss was about and happy just to stay clear of the chaos while they discussed the non-events that had formed their day.

With the benefit of hindsight, her boredom must have left her craving company at any cost and the fact that she was so well taken care of meant that she had all the time in the world for him; but Noel considered none of these circumstances. He didn't see it that way; he was her favourite and that reason alone was enough to make her his. Their relationship was mutual; she was grateful to talk to someone that could still learn from her and she absorbed as much of his energy as she could. It allowed her to see Christmas through his eyes and she preferred it that way. Noel was happy to have someone show an interest in his drawings and paintings whilst everyone else failed to notice the improvements. It was easy for his young mind to believe that she really did like the music he listened to and the programmes he watched as she sat there, lying the day away. She told him untruths much the same as his parents had and for the same, caring reasons, but the difference was he believed her and for that she was honoured with the title of his best friend. It would be years until he understood just how excruciating it must have been for her to sit through endless cartoons with him but by the time he did, he wasn't only old enough to understand, he actually appreciated it. He'd even wished he'd have the patience to do the same with his grandchildren one day.

That thought brought him out of his trance momentarily. There was no chance of that now, patience or not. He'd thrown himself from nineteen stories before he'd even fathered anyone. That seemed more of a shame now than it had done standing on the roof's edge.

To combat his doubts he justified his decision by convincing himself that it would only be something else that he 'could have done better'... he'd done the right thing and at least now those particular children could be conceived by someone else, anyone else. With that sobering thought the colours again dissolved and realigned, taking him forward in time without surprise which meant he was now a little too sizable to consider what had just crossed his mind. He was of an average build for his age but it still meant he'd have to breathe in if he wanted to discover the truth; if he really had seen what he thought he'd noticed earlier, the truth was in this room and hidden behind the bed.

It was a secret place that he had never seen. Yet he was here now, standing nervously in the only room he had no excuse to be in but the answers he craved lay in darkness just a few feet away. He stood in that doorway like it marked the threshold of two different worlds. He lifted his foot but hung it in the air, thinking carefully before he stepped forward onto forbidden ground. But when he did he brought it down heavily in a simple but telling act of defiance. On the deep pile carpet his over zealous movement made no noise at all but he relished it. All over the house the floor boards announced arrival from a hundred paces into the echo of the sparsely decorated corridor halls but for the first time this wasn't acting against him; it was to his full advantage. Confident he'd be given all the warning he'd need he proceeded onward and up onto his parents' double bed but climbed back down instantly. He looked at the otherwise immaculate sheets that now bore two shallow indents where his knees had been. Knowing they would give him away he smoothed them out hastily, carefully reconsidering his tactics.

He lay down flat on the floor and crawled under the frame with all the agility that comes from being just six years old. It became more difficult when he neared the centre of the mattress as it sank lower there, but still he surged forward adopting a slither that was almost inhuman. It was difficult to maintain and the coarseness of the surface grated and burned against his shirtless torso but he was close now.

Reaching the far side came as a relief, but the tingling sensation he still felt was instantly forgotten as his eyes fully adjusted to the darkness and he took in the sight that greeted him. He twirled on the spot like the worlds shortest fashion model, trying to convince the world that bright red, polkerdot pajamas were this year's look, yet his face told a different story entirely. He was the pirate that had finally found his treasure and wide-eyed he struggled to take it all in. Not just the countless, carefully wrapped boxes of all shapes and sizes that surrounded him, but also the gravity of what this actually meant until his trail of thought was broken suddenly. He could hear voices. They weren't downstairs and they were getting closer. It was possible to navigate most of the house without triggering the creaks and groans; that much he knew from his own stealth missions to the cookie jar and back but he'd never even dreamed that Mum and Dad would know the complicated route. Why would they? They could do whatever they wanted, whenever they wanted to do it.

Looking again at the towering gifts he found the answer and so listened intently. His parents weren't only moving in his direction, they were making their way to where he stood. He dropped to the floor as a sudden burst of light glowed through the linen canopy that was now all that separated them; he'd never been more thankful for its adsorbent embrace as it hid him from view.

The material above him was snatched to one side just as he rolled back under the cover of the mattress. Peeping out he could see his parents' shadows looming, changing shape as they spoke in whispers about how to arrange the parcels this year.

'Surely at the end of their beds as always?' suggested Dad already sounding bored with the conversation.

'We could' answered a sweeter and far more thoughtful voice, 'but they'd expect that and he's a light sleeper. I don't want to get caught this year. Maybe next or even later if we can get away with it, but not this year. Besides, it'll add to the surprise... let's make them hunt for their presents, it'll last a little longer that way.'

Noel heard his father sigh heavily. It wasn't that he disagreed with the idea but he knew exactly who'd it'd be hauling every one of the ample gifts downstairs. It'd take a dozen trips at least and having sneaked a last few shots of sherry he wasn't in the mood for that, but obeying was the shortest route to where he *did* want to be; bed.

A moment of silence ensued and Noel wished the decision would fall his mother's way. If they both went downstairs now his escape would be rushed, but it'd be simple. But should his dad prevail Noel knew he was just moments away from being discovered as if they actually went into his room, the meticulously laid pillows under his duvet would not be as convincing as when it was viewed from his doorway. He didn't breathe until the battle was won but at least he'd sided with the winner.

A pair of slippered feet thudded down in front of him, startling him to the extent that he bumped his nervous head on the framework above. He froze, terrified they had heard, but as his father walked forward without a word it was obvious that they hadn't. He could only see Dad from his ankles down but he could hear him grumbling under his breath as he paced backwards and forwards, reacting to conflicting orders until those same ankles again came towards him, left the ground and disappeared out of view.

The same routine happened again and again, Noel becoming no less nervous with every repeated trip and continuing to flinch with each ungraceful landing but eventually it was over. The rustling came from behind him now so he edged forward to confirm what he already knew.

Noel looked into the forbidden view but it was much different now. Larger but emptier, darker and devoid of colour. In later life he'd look back and see that as a metaphor for life following his discovery, but right now it was just plain scary. It was the kind of dark corner in which monsters waited and he retreated back under the relative safety of the bed, choosing instead to concentrate on the continuing conversation whilst trying to judge its distance. His timing would have to be perfect if he was going to crawl out of here, dust himself off and make it back to his own room without being caught. It wasn't even like he could run as that would mean being heard for sure; that much he knew from experience.

He maneuvered himself to be able to see the doorway and his dad disappearing slowly through it, no doubt laden with gifts that hardly fitted through its frame but nobody followed. Surely she wouldn't leave him to it? He prepared himself like a sprinter on the starting blocks, ready to take his chance.

As more and more of the presents that had been stacked on the bed were transported away, the springs above him raised gradually giving Noel a little more headroom much to his relief. When Sadie could clearly be heard ascending the stairs, Noel knew his chance to make a dash was disappearing fast. Trying to get a Labrador of Sadie's temperament to settle was always the closing of the evening's ritual and Dad's last task for the day and whilst now fully grown, she seemed to have lost none of her puppy like enthusiasm. Having sensed something different had only made her harder to control and she turned immediately after she'd cleared her last step. Noel didn't know whether she'd seen, heard or more likely smelt him cowering where he would never normally be but she certainly knew where he was. She made a mad and desperate dash for her friend and paid little or no heed to the shouted commands for her to stop. She paid just as much attention to Noel's silent gestures pleading with her to turn around but within seconds her nose was pressed against his, as wet and disgusting as always but unwelcome for the first time ever.

'Get out of there!' bellowed Noel's dad, already physically exhausted from shifting what felt like several tonnes and having run bone dry on patience. He bent down to grab the dumb animal and drag her back to her own bed. It was lucky that he had always been frustrated that Sadie was the only pet he'd ever known to have it's own canine themed and extremely comfortable room, yet she always wanted to be anywhere but. It was also fortunate that she was excited by absolutely everything and that most people, especially Dad, had given up investigating what she was getting so agitated about. It was so often nothing in particular that her behaviour now raised no alarm.

Noel breathed a sigh of relief but then wondered why. He may not have been discovered but he was still trapped and as his father returned and closed the door behind him the reality of the situation started to dawn on him. The mattress above dipped lower than ever before under the full weight of two adults, one half full of brandy as the other tried to re-steer the hushed conversation her way. For what he guessed must be an hour they chatted and showed no signs of going to sleep until he at last heard Dad suggest that they use the bed for what it was made for. He then heard Mum say that it was fine with her so long as they were quiet as she didn't want to wake anyone… it was true that both of them snored but he was surprised it was ever so loud that they worried about disturbing others?

They were restless too. They must have really struggled to find a relaxed position and as they lay on such a comfortable bed it remained a mystery to Noel as the mattress, now his roof for the night rose and fell, rose and fell. As he grew older it made sense, but as with so many other mysteries he wished it hadn't.

He also wished that things wouldn't change so fast but it made no difference. Nothing was the same after that night and even after an entire year to get used to it, it appeared nothing ever would be. All he'd wanted was the truth and as soon as he got it he couldn't give it back no matter how much he wanted to. It certainly wouldn't be the only time in his life he'd make the same mistake, but as far he could remember it was the first. And even with this unearthly reminder of all his regrets and lessons learned there was nothing to dispel what he'd spent his life suspecting; that true belief lasts as long as you believe in magic, and that magic lasts until you know the truth.

An entire night spent with his head buried into the heavy carpet had given him time to do little else other than consider the connotations of his discovery. When he emerged bleary eyed the next morning he was already aware that his life had changed forever and as the sound of the opening door woke his parents at the traditional six O'clock in the morning he *knew* it had.

Years later both his mother and father would doubt his ability to act but if only they knew how hard it was for him to play an innocent angel that morning they'd have never questioned it. He'd twisted his tiny body through the now open door then re-entered just before his parents' bloodshot eyes could focus. With a convincing look of both surprise and anguish he announced that there were no presents in his room and pleaded to know if he'd been bad. As a fully grown man the thought of this charade made him sick and ashamed that his career in deception had begun so young but as time went by it only got harder to confess.

The magic of every day life started to disappear from that night on and continued to fade over the next twelve months. He found himself no longer able to take things at face value and challenging everything he was told. This not only frustrated anyone and everyone who had the misfortune to engage him in conversation but it usually resulted in the horrors of reality. He learned to hate mechanics, electricity, technology… anything and everything that more often than not seemed to shatter his beliefs and stamp on his imagination. It would appear that people never had lived in his television or the kitchen fridge and after all this time, there wasn't even anyone under his bed.

It should have been a relief when so many of the things that had scared or confused him could be rationally explained but with the fear the excitement died as well that year. Although it appeared he was the first of his class to know the truth he guarded his secret well. He would be careful not to do and say nothing to shatter their illusions and the short time they had left with them although he often wondered if they were doing exactly the same.

Being put in such a position ate away at him and altered his relationship with his parents. He now had a different reason to resent them but also more to be grateful for. He suddenly had them rather than a fictional character to thank for all the latest and greatest luxuries he'd enjoyed that had made him the envy of his class. His parents were thoughtful and generous to the extreme, but the unflinching trust he'd had in them was lost.

So here he was, only seven years old but trapped between two worlds; not of adults and children, but of those that believe and those who do not. To him that was what split society now and the two factions celebrated in very different ways, living their lives at total opposites. Yet Noel was forced to exist somewhere between both, careful to act no wiser than he'd been the previous year for fear he may have no choice but to reveal why.

Of all the emotions in the world to fake, it seemed that enthusiasm was the hardest. He doubted that all the compulsory smiles and excited repetitions in the world could ever truly convince his parents, but he tried his best anyway. He asked ridiculous questions and pretended he wanted to go to bed early so that the morning would come quicker. But before he did, he gave his parents the benefit of the doubt and one last chance. His question to them was so direct they had to swallow hard before answering. Even though they both knew and understood their reasoning there was a difference between creating an illusion and plain and simple lying. Noel fixed them both when he saw his opportunity. Little Caroline had paused to regain her strength before crying again and he knew he may not get another chance like this. He also knew that being too direct could confirm their suspicions. He'd open with sincerity; question like he didn't know the answer and word it so that it was easy for them to be truthful.

'You think I've been good this year?' he expected his mum to react more than she did and perhaps she would have had her husband not beaten her to it. The vision of his son asking like only a child can and clutching his teddy bear was too much. The apparent innocence something to be treasured; Noel knew how to hit a chord when he needed to but had been careful not to use it too often. He winced at how manipulative he'd been, even as a child but couldn't concentrate on the present for long. His father knelt down in front of him and held him firmly by the shoulders in a rare display of physical intimacy. If Noel had known at the time that this wouldn't happen again for so long he may have savoured the moment a little more.

'Noel, I couldn't hope for more and you know how hard to please I can be?' he said in an even rarer moment of self-criticism. His wife stopped what she was doing knowing that she was unlikely to hear such an admission again anytime soon. But she couldn't help taking the chance to agree with him and attacked him whilst his defence was down albeit in a lighthearted manner. It surprised her to be looked at so disapprovingly by both of them and she ceased giggling immediately realising she'd misjudged the situation and the tone.

'But you shout Dad... at me I mean.'

'I know. And I don't mean to, but when I do, just try and remember it's only because I see you doing things wrong.' He could see that Noel didn't look any happier. Perhaps he was confusing the message by diluting it so he continued. 'And being wrong isn't anything like being bad ok?'

'For things he's done wrong or for things he just doesn't know yet?' His mother couldn't help herself and again had to make her point. It was valid and with better timing it was even insightful, but right now it wasn't helping and his father left his explanation there, figuring there would be a better time soon. He looked at his wife and sighed with disappointment. It was a strange combination to be so right yet so inappropriate but Noel wasn't as happy to leave the conversation there.

'So Santa will definitely...' he struggled to pronounce the word but understood its meaning and its importance in the statement implicitly... 'come tonight with his sleigh and everything?' He wondered if he'd been too specific but apparently he hadn't.

'Definitely'. His father made the mistake of copying his son's word exactly without realising its effect. Whether it was to lighten the atmosphere as he mimicked the staggered way in which it was said didn't matter to Noel. It was a word that was as clearly defined as any. It meant 'absolutely', 'certainly', 'positively', 'unquestionably', 'without doubt' and 'undeniably'. There would be no going back or claiming he'd misunderstood. He'd hoped he could blame everything on something else, anything else and with a 'maybe' or a 'perhaps' he may have been able to do so. But for the sake of a laugh his dad had backed himself into a corner from which he might never escape and he didn't even know it.

Noel smiled and took his stocking up to bed with him. He was only an inch taller but he was infinitely wiser than he had been at the same time last year. Yet with each step he wished a little harder that he wasn't.

CHAPTER TEN

'You don't smell like one of us'. The voice sounded appropriately rough so as to suit the sentence, but not deep enough to have come from the expanse of darkness behind.

Evelyn had feared the prejudice judgment ahead of her and had backed away from it without thinking, but in doing so she had retreated into an alleyway that stretched back far further than she could see. The voice had startled her. Not just because she thought she was alone, nor because it had been so unexpected but it was the frighteningly close proximity of it. The tone wasn't particularly threatening but the situation certainly was.

It had been a subconscious decision, pure instinct to back herself into what she thought was little more than a crevice; large enough to provide shelter but confined enough that she'd only have to defend to the front. But now it was obvious that wasn't the case and that she'd be wise to be looking in the opposite direction. It hurt to do so, but without room to manoeuvre she had to twist on the spot, knowing she'd grind the dirt beneath her further into her skin but aware it was better than not knowing what lurked in the shadows. The pain and effort were in vain as she could still see nothing past the first barricade of crates and the pitch black beyond them but it was the silence she hated the most.

'And you don't look much like one of us either' the voice continued with an obvious air of satisfaction at having her at such a disadvantage. Her outline would be perfectly visible against the multicoloured and flickering backdrop of the busy High Street that for now at least might as well be a whole different world. She was in a different domain now and here the perfume in which her body was soaked would seem as alien as a kind word. But it wouldn't drift that far, not with the breeze flowing in the opposite direction, so whoever was taunting her must be as close as he sounded. The thought of him being able to reach out and touch her sent shivers even deeper. Without sight or sound in her armoury she explored different senses but this stranger either had no scent of his own or it matched their littered surroundings perfectly.

With no idea what she was facing she figured, as she always did that attack would again be the best form of defence.

'That's because I'm not one of you, I'm nothing like you'

'I'm sure you're not, I'd never be so rude as to suggest you were. I was merely making an observation your Highness' that same voice uttered, slowly so that she could digest the words. It hurt to know that even being compared to him was such an insult, but he wondered if perhaps he deserved it. From her point of view she was being challenged and it was only natural to treat the unknown as the enemy. He may have even done the same himself and he started to feel a little awkward about amusing himself in such a sadistic way. He felt edging into the light was the least he could do but he wanted an apology first. His manner didn't excuse her totally. After all, he was only guilty of not introducing himself and he'd said nothing to actually deserve such aggression.

'We are nothing alike' he continued, after all I must feel the cold more than you?' Even Evelyn would have to admit he had a point, although it was made with extreme sarcasm as he leaned towards the shaft of light pouring in from the lamp post opposite before thinking better of it. Whatever she thought she was or wanted to be, they were both sat amongst the same filth in the same alleyway but right now, at this very moment all that was different about them was that he was warmly wrapped in winter clothes and she'd swop places with him without having to think about it.

However he shifted his position, any defining features remained shrouded so she continued to imagine his face. But the very fact that she had a preconception at all made her feel worse about herself, what she'd said and the manner in which she'd said it but she couldn't manage an apology. She didn't know what to say so just stared, convinced that she'd recognised those eyes if only she could actually see them. She suspected they'd burned into her three nights a week but she'd never heard the voice that accompanied them before now. Not directed *at* her anyway.

She didn't know who he was but if her suspicions were right he wasn't a complete stranger either. He'd never been far from the club and he'd often been ushered on by its security staff, probably in a similar manner to which she was escorted out tonight but both sides had their reasons. He defended his ideal territory around the club knowing that it not only attracted the wealthy, but more specifically it was a beacon for clientele in a frivolous frame of mind, and more often than not, a sense of guilt to appease. There was nothing like a little charity to even out the scales and he must know that, but that didn't mean a place like the Heavens Gate club wanted him around. They'd be unlikely to find his a familiar face though and were far more liable to remember him by his weight as it made a difference to how far they could throw him. And even at twice the size he wouldn't have presented them with much of a problem, in fact it was with people like him that they attempted to break their own distance records.

She shouldn't feel so self-righteous though. She'd never have given him a second look except that he'd never given her much of a first. That in itself was strange. He was a man, and from having watched her comings and goings he would know what she did for a living and that fact alone would usually be enough to maintain the gaze of any male, homeless or otherwise. But couple that with his particular position and it was even more unusual. She made easy money and rarely left the club anything other than embarrassingly drunk; she didn't even arrive sober that often. Surely that made her the perfect target? Yet still he'd ignore her entirely. At first she had put it down to coincidence and unseen distractions. She remembered being grateful not to be put in an awkward position but after a while it just had to be deliberate. The only explanation she'd ever managed to concoct was that he didn't just appear to look right through her... he actually could. That he'd sat there for so long with so much importance placed on people and their reactions that he'd actually learned to see their soul; the fact that he obviously wasn't impressed with what he saw in her started to weigh on her mind.

Unable to forget it, she started to find excuses to linger around the club entrance in an undercover operation for which she wasn't entirely sure of the point, but it made her even more certain that she was right. He approached virtually every person differently and let others pass without a word. His success rate was frighteningly accurate and whilst it was rare for him to be rewarded with anything more than loose change at best, he obviously didn't believe her to be generous enough for that.

It bothered her far more than it should. Not because he was wrong, but because he was right. It might have been easy to forget if he sat in some random street but he was always there, right outside the entrance to the club that until tonight had been her home. It would be out of character for her to ask him his reasons as that would show she actually cared, but there'd never be a better time and it wasn't like she could sink any lower.

'Why do you never talk to me?' From his point of view it came from nowhere. It was true he'd never said a word to her but he was genuinely surprised she'd even noticed and that alone meant he'd misjudged her, if only slightly. But that didn't mean he was far out in his presumptions either.

'Would you? What exactly would be the point of talking to you Eve?'

She recoiled at the sound of her name, it was shocking enough that he knew it at all but nobody had known her well enough to shorten it since her father. It felt strangely reassuring to hear it said like that again, like that part of her was still alive but for it to come from the lips of a virtual stranger was almost chilling. Her unease was visible.

'Relax, I don't want anything from you.' He sank back again

sensing that she'd prefer it that way.

'I know' she uttered. He seemed to want something from everyone *except* her. 'But why?'

'You see I think it's more interesting to wonder why instead of asking my name, a perfectly natural response considering I obviously know yours, your first question, and probably your only question is why do *I* not talk to *you*. Have you never considered why you don't talk to me? Because I've wondered.'

The honest answer was that she'd never even thought about it that way before but it was hardly an appropriate response; besides he probably knew the truth anyway. She recognised a rhetorical question when she heard one and he was making his point clearly enough without her help. Despite what should remain a threatening situation Evelyn let herself stare only at the crowd still swarming past the alleyway entrance, totally unaware that they were being so closely watched. Without noticing she crossed her arms to try and warm herself but in doing so she'd also let down her guard.

'I've never seen the place so busy' she observed almost absent mindedly.

'It never changes though; I've seen it full to capacity and I've seen it absolutely deserted…' He wasn't allowed to finish his poetic metaphor before Evelyn, over compensating for his presumptions rushed to correct him.

'No you haven't. It wasn't deserted if you were here to see it.' She knew she was being a smartarse but she was tired of being presumed to have a low IQ simply because she had high sex appeal. A wry smile curled in the darkness; he really had underestimated her and he was pleased to be wrong.

A hand stretched out from the darkness but it didn't look like that of a beggar's; it was the wrong way around. The palm faced downwards in a loose fist instead of open and upwards. Instinctively Evelyn reached out assuming the missing role herself despite the humiliation of the reversal she suspected it to be. She was surprised at the trust she was putting in someone she knew so little about but the gesture was obvious and her need great enough that it seemed a risk worth taking. She closed her eyes with both relief and frustration at having judged the situation accurately; she was right that he meant her no harm but this homeless rogue, this *tramp* pitied her to the extent that he offered charity and she struggled to accept the situation. The warm, damp coins poured from a hand that should not let go into one so well manicured it was embarrassing.

'Why?' Was all that would come out from her equally cared for lips.

'You need it more than I do' was the devastatingly simple response. Evelyn swallowed hard. It was a bitter pill indeed and it stuck in her throat as he continued.

'I'd give you more but I know what it'd be spent on. Learn from tonight. Stay off it; you don't know what it's being cut with, especially around here.'

Evelyn nodded in shameful agreement. She had no idea how he'd come to learn of the habit she'd found herself dependent on; she hadn't told a single person.

'Promise?' The single word was half question, half demand but it required an answer either way. It should have been easier to lie to him but he looked directly at her as he said it and it demanded honesty.

'I never promise anything but I will try' she replied only just managing not to look away. Her answer hadn't been what he wanted to hear but it was at least sincere and that was to be respected.

'There's enough there for a bus ride home; no more and no less' his voice seemed gentler now somehow.

She looked in her hand, without counting it was anyone's guess whether he was right or not. It was going to be close either way but it might just cover the fare.

'I don't know what to say' whispered Evelyn.

'Then don't say anything, just take it, besides, it's not all I've got. I've enough left for what I need'.

'And what's that?' questioned Evelyn. The man smiled... now she was interested.

'I used to have what all those have'. He motioned to the street behind her and the shopping laden hordes that walked it. 'But I lost it all to that', he concluded. He didn't move his head this time, just his eyes but Evelyn didn't have to turn around. She knew what was opposite and it would be the same culprit that drained her father. It had all the lights and glamour to excite every passing gambler and had been extended three times in the last few years. She knew little more than that but figured the extra capacity spoke highly of its success.

'Now I only lay down one bet a year and I've been waiting for today, saving my takings'. He studied her face for signs of disapproval but she'd settled back into character now and was giving away little. Giving up he looked to the skies instead, conscious that he was the first to break their uneasy stalemate this time around. 'And I think it's going to snow tonight, in fact, to tell you the truth I'm pretty damn sure.'

'Apparently not' she offered. I watched the news before I came out.' Aware that she'd shocked him slightly again with her choice of viewing, she gained some satisfaction from his realisation that he didn't know her quite as well as he thought.

'Then we'll have to agree to disagree young lady, but if I was you I'd be in more of a rush.'

She misunderstood his meaning, assuming in her understandably paranoid state that he was hinting that she'd have no time for him. She stood firm. She'd prove him wrong.

'There are people who need you, so as much as I've enjoyed our time together...'

It angered Evelyn to think he still assumed so much. Surely by now he'd know better? It was incredibly presumptuous to assume she had others in her life but he seemed incredibly sure.

'What else do you want my lady? The coat off my back? You know I would lend you it but I'll still be out here when it snows tonight.' He looked straight at her. 'Tick, tock, tick, tock, tick, tock'. He couldn't be clearer that their conversation was over. She attempted to engage him again but he wouldn't let her, he knew she had somewhere to be and that she didn't have long to get there. Every time she spoke or tried to interrupt he simply raised his voice until he drowned her out. She'd had about enough of not being listened to tonight and didn't give in easily.

'Tick, tock, tick, tock, tick...' he pointed across the road without stopping his insistent chant. As Evelyn conceded and turned away she saw the bus stop and assumed he was keen that she didn't miss the last ride. That would make sense; he must know the schedules for this street like the back of his grimy hand and he wouldn't want to have donated to her for nothing.

He watched her break into an uneasy canter as she crossed the street and disappeared around and behind the bus that had just pulled up. Smiling he continued his repetitive song that had now become almost tuneful as he walked, hands in his pockets back into the alleyway.

CHAPTER ELEVEN

They were leaving. He stood there on the verge of delivering his few, but essential lines and they were leaving. Across the school hall everyone else sat still and attentive. Some were genuinely enthralled by what was happening on stage whilst others looked past it or to either side; they were unable to take their eyes off of their particular child even if they were not in the spotlight or even in character. They were doing nothing more than being who they were but that was enough to be watched intently, by their family at least as if they were giving an Oscar winning performance.

Looking back, Noel realised how little he'd changed since this particular Christmas. People had never really understood his keenness to be the centre of attention one minute only for him to recoil into the shadows the next. Quite why he'd audition for a lead role on stage when he'd sink lower and lower into his seat whenever he was part of the audience and a volunteer was required didn't make sense to anyone; yet the reason was simple. The difference was preparation. If he was going to be the focus of attention he wanted to impress; it was as plain and straightforward as that. And without time to prepare or the chance to practice and perfect he'd rather not take part at all but that was the appeal of theatre… it could be rehearsed. Its other charm was that the rest of his family were not in the least artistic and so had never even attempted acting. There would be nothing to compare his performance with and therefore his sisters could not better his; not yet anyway. This might steal the limelight from his Caroline's first steps, her first words, her first… everything! It seemed like whatever she did was a momentous occasion and as at the time he was unable or unwilling to remember receiving the same undiluted attention himself, all he wanted was the spotlight on him both literally and metaphorically. He'd sat crouched behind the make shift barn door, crudely cut from cardboard and now slightly torn from the four previous nights shows but still he continued running through his lines quietly in his head. He even answered himself, knowing the replies he'd receive before continuing with his own script and working his way through the whole scene, oblivious to all around him. He was focused on nothing else except getting this right. He'd been impressive enough every night this week but instead of soaking up the praise he sought criticism. When he couldn't find it he'd altered his tactics and renamed the feedback he was looking for and labelled it 'constructive criticism'. This, it turned out was easier to come by. His friend's parents were shocked to be interrogated by a boy no more than eight years old; some even found his obsession with dissecting every aspect of himself until he found something wrong concerning but they eventually relented. Whether this was to pacify him or not would be something else for him to ponder in later life but at the time he took it all to heart. He worked on every thread of advice, real or invented until he'd mended every conceivable crack that could dim his chance to shine. After all it was the very reason he'd invited his mum and dad specifically to this last Christmas Eve performance; all they would see would be the polished and perfected recital. He'd built up to tonight and all the previous displays were little more than dress rehearsals.

But now, the one thing that could pierce the wall of concentration he'd constructed since the start of the second act invaded like a marauding army that he really should have seen coming. It rose slowly at first, like it always did getting higher and higher in pitch until those around either winced in pain or shuffled away, keen not to appear rude or uncaring but unable to take the ear splitting sound any longer.

Noel's preparatory hand gestures and facial expressions froze as he mimicked his character. It rendered him in an unnatural position as he recognised the sound, but he'd gone from being able to hear nothing except what was in his head to not even being able to listen to himself at all. All he could hear was the shrieking and wailing, not only because he knew who it was, but more due to knowing what it meant. It dominated everything including the conversation outside that had always been easy to hear through the flimsy props before. He strained to hear his cue but couldn't even make out who was speaking, let alone what was being said. The panic that grew inside him caused the few words that punctuated the screaming to blur into each other, much like his dad's records when they were played too slowly. Panicked and disorientated in the blackness behind the set he was even starting to lose his sense of balance. He stared into the dark intently, hoping that someone, anyone would have predicted the sudden difficulty he faced. Surely someone would direct him but if there was anyone there, he couldn't see them. He considered whether it was worth trying to attract somebody's attention but couldn't risk more than a whisper as he squinted in the vain hope that his eyes would adjust even a fraction more than they already had in the lonely time he'd spent there. He looked for outlines, shapes, anything that resembled a person and therefore a possible escape.

Outside the cast waited for the enthusiastic welcome they'd received with precision timing for five nights running now. And they waited some more. Again, his class mate faked an unconvincing knock on the makeshift door by stamping his foot, harder this time on the wooden stage. There was still no response. Anyone else would have assumed that there was no room at the inn and moved on but not everyone knew the script like Noel. They'd learnt their lines according to cue and any disruption or deviation at all meant proceedings would come to an embarrassing stand still for everyone. After a third attempt the door was flung open from the stage side to reveal Noel, still folded in two and totally unaware that he'd got his wish; he was centre of attention without even realising. It only became apparent when the laughing had grown louder than his sisters whining and he turned to face his public.

Even if he could remember what he was meant to do or say it

was unlikely to be noticed and was guaranteed to go unheard. He was sure that the teachers standing in as technicians didn't leave the spotlight trained on that doorway for as long as it felt like but with it pointed right at him he couldn't see the audience at all having just left the barely lit backstage crevice. But he could hear them laughing and could imagine them pointing. Keen to direct attention else where the circle of yellow light travelled the stage and his eyes adjusted with enough time to see his parents shuffle awkwardly out of the assembly hall exit, baby in tow and without looking back.

He'd been too young at the time to predict quite how much that one occasion would affect everything and he'd now never grow old enough to understand why. But during the year ahead his life changed dramatically. At the time it seemed to take forever to pass but this time around it came and went in the time it took the now familiar light to fade. It was just as well as all it held was the twelve month aftermath of his moment in the spotlight.

Until that time he'd been popular amongst a small group of friends. They were the offspring of parents as over protective as his own and they shared the same interests. But he'd gone largely unnoticed by the majority who were usually busy doing what he'd never be allowed to although that was preferable to being their target. But that spotlight had done its job and brought him to their attention and he couldn't regret it more. He'd endured endless impressions and references for months but eventually they happened less and less often until nobody could really remember why they victimised him, but nine year olds don't need a reason. The more he withdrew, the worse it became until he found himself as excited about the holidays as he had ever been but for all the wrong reasons. Whilst everyone else awaited their presents and the chance to over indulge, all it meant to Noel was fifteen consecutive days off school. As an adult he could see what a shame that was; what a waste of childhood but at the time it was all that mattered.

He'd be at home like the rest of his class and they'd be equal again. That was the theory except his misery seemed to follow him and the thought of returning plagued him everyday without exception. He held his head high for the sake of his parents but was unable to discuss it with them; he'd made that mistake before and they'd become involved. They were well intentioned but their interfering had little effect other than to amplify what was happening. He also knew their expectations; they had things in mind for him and being a victim wasn't the foundations on which they could build the man they'd planned to raise. He didn't even tell his Nan but it was for an entirely different reason... he simply didn't have to. She seemed to know somehow and that was one of the many reasons he hardly left her side for a fortnight.

CHAPTER TWELVE

She did her very best to disguise the urgency in her walk as that of an important woman in demand rather than an extremely embarrassed wife in severe pain, clinging to the respect of her subordinates.

Wishing herself literally anywhere else Ivy walked as quickly as her stunned body would allow but the deep aching in her lower spine restricted her. She wanted to wince with every movement, even cry out at times but her pride wouldn't allow it. Hers were a very exceptional set of circumstances that earned her every reaction except sympathy as she limped violently back to the relative safety and seclusion of the office.

As she made her way awkwardly past each of the bystanders scattered around the yard she found it helped to think of each of them as hurdles, each one that she passed taking her just a little closer to the finishing line represented by the edge of the printing area. Not only did that serve to divide her difficult journey into manageable sections that she could aim towards one stage at a time, it also dehumanised the workers and that made the humiliation slightly easier to bear. Her imaginative tactics were working, but then they had done for a while now and she'd promised herself she'd stop. It always helped in the short term and made life easier for a few minutes at a time but the repercussions just kept piling up. Her friends and colleagues had warned her. They didn't know the tricks she played on herself or the way she transformed people into symbols but they did know she'd changed almost as much as her colleagues' attitudes towards her had. The closest of her friends had even told her so but she simply couldn't see it. Either that or she stubbornly refused to until those same friends started to call in on her less and less. Their lives apparently became increasingly hectic and their reasons more inventive until eventually the only explanation was the truth; that they were right and she was simply impossible to be around. The admittance in itself should have been a step in the right direction but if it was, she stumbled immediately afterwards

She'd almost become addicted to the shields her imagination had grown to allow her. She'd only found it again a few years ago and barely remembered it from her childhood when it provided magical lands and weird and wonderful friends before it deserted her totally. But when she really needed it she was able to create a world in which everything was alright and she was often successful in guiding others to believe the same.

But sometimes the mask slipped and the illusion was shown for exactly what it was. And falling off the back of that lorry was one of those times. As she lay flat on the ground she could practically see her alter ego lying beside her, merely a corpse. By the time she'd got to her feet she didn't have to look at her audience directly; she could picture the scene. They'd all secretly be thinking she got what she deserved, but what made it worse was that she probably did. With more time and under less pressure she might congratulate herself that she at least realised it, even if she was equally sure she was a long way from admitting it in public but there were too many eyes bearing down on her now to think that rationally.

She imagined them struggling not to laugh. That each of them released their smirking faces the second she'd passed, ready to snap it back to a solemn look of concern should she look over her shoulder. They imagined she'd love to catch them out; to actually have an excuse to single them out and a reason to victimise them rather than just for her own amusement. But she wanted the exact opposite. The thought of actually seeing their disdain towards her was too much. She could try and ignore it or even laugh along but having nothing left but her reputation for discipline she'd have no choice but to react with hostility. But right now she just didn't have the strength to do anything but sink away, however ungracefully.

She threw the door behind her in frustration but caught it before it reached the frame. Had she allowed it to slam it would have only brought more attention her way and that was the last thing she wanted. Nobody would be able to claim they thought she was fine and would be duty bound to come and check on her not knowing that she'd give her last cigarette for a lock on the door. But even with the strongest barricade the windows would still allow the world in so she crouched silently below them. She just needed a few moments out of sight; space to breathe, but whatever she called it; she was still hiding the way she'd promised herself she mustn't.

Word of what happened had found its way across the factory floor like it always did. It was received very differently depending who heard and reaction varied from a sense of vengeance to genuine concern depending if it was from those who'd never seen past her outer shell or the select few who'd known her longer; knew her better. But being well acquainted meant that they had tried and failed to help before and had just grown tired of it. On another day they may have made a token effort, but knowing it was useless it made little sense missing the start of the office party; it'd be the only part they'd remember anyway and maybe talking to her later wouldn't be quite as painful after several glasses of Champagne. As soon as they confirmed that she'd walked back into the building unaided from the yard and could assume the injuries were minor they'd made their way upstairs. Only one left the office in the opposite direction ignoring pleas from his colleagues to join them.

CHAPTER THIRTEEN

It had always seemed strange to Noel how his mind never failed to recall emotion over sense or reason and he'd often wondered if others were the same. Looking back he remembered how he felt at these times far better than the people or places they involved. He hadn't realised when they'd been happening, but they had shaped his life and the way he'd lived it. He'd learnt a particularly hard lesson this year but he'd never shown his gratitude or acknowledged its value. To do so would be to admit just how wrong he was and so he'd buried it along with everything else he would rather not accept. Having failed to ever take a mature look at what had happened, all he associated with it was being made to feel terrible for not wanting to give up something that was rightfully his.

Sadie had recently given birth to five puppies and as much as it broke Noel's parents' hearts to split the litter up, the possibility of properly looking after six fully grown Labradors didn't bear thinking about. They'd advertised the offspring in several local papers and their timing was lucky. As it was so close to Christmas they'd had little trouble in finding new homes and had even turned down several definite sales as they were determined that they'd only let the puppies go in pairs so that each at least had a brother or sister to grow up with. They were very aware of the concerns that came with this time of year and made a point of inviting any prospective buyers to stay a while under the guise of celebratory mince pies and cream coffee whilst they underwent an intense interrogation. If they had any doubts as to their long-term intentions or their ability to provide they'd use Noel's attachment to the brood as an excuse as to why they couldn't say goodbye.

Noel had been fascinated for the first few weeks after their birth but the novelty had started to wear off and with the promise of new toys tomorrow his excitement was shifting in other directions. Add to that the promise that he could keep the money made from selling the pedigrees and they suddenly held even less appeal. His parents worried about him suddenly having more cash than he'd ever known but it only seemed fair as technically Sadie was his; he'd always looked after her better than anyone would have predicted and so it was decided they'd keep just two of her brood; partly to be humane to her but also for the sake of their son. Sadie wouldn't live forever and the loss maybe made more bearable if her legacy lived on.

They had revoked all of their advertisements and taken down the posters now they'd made all the sales that they intended to; they were left with two perfect specimens and one other for which they'd never held much hope. The last to be born, she was basically healthy but was missing her right hind leg and as such had been all but ignored by her mother and her siblings. The humans she shared the house with had made a real effort with her but it hadn't helped her fit in. They'd affectionately named her Stumpy but what amused them back then seemed brutal and inappropriate now. Stumpy seemed happy enough in her own little world and if there were no serious obstacles she could move around without too much trouble; just not as fast as the others who she insisted on trying to follow *everywhere*. Her clumsiness meant that she struggled to keep up with Noel too who, having just entered double figures still possessed the boundless energy of most boys his age; and he'd grown frustrated playing catch up rather than fetch.

Noel was still torturing his mum with 'if I guess it will you tell me' questions about tomorrow when the doorbell rang. His dad grabbed the remaining spare change and what was left of the assorted chocolates. He ensured they were the ones that nobody ever chooses and made his way to the front door. The amount of carollers this year had left his wallet thin and his generosity was wearing even thinner but answering the door just one more time with those so-called treats would mean he wouldn't be force-fed them over the next few weeks.

He opened the door, not to a choir, but to a man and he was a rather embarrassed looking one at that. He expected the stranger to initiate the conversation but strangely he didn't; on any other night he'd have guessed him to be a salesman but surely not this evening? Unable to bring himself to be rude enough to ask him directly what he wanted, he simply said 'evening' but raised his voice at the end of the word to make it sound questioning. The stranger hadn't been ignoring him; simply examining a scruffy piece of paper he held in his hand in the dim and shifting light which must have contained their home address judging by his opening question;

'This is number 5 Greenlands Street?' He employed the same phrasing Noel's dad had to turn a statement into an inquiry.

'Certainly is… can I help at all?'

'Probably not at this hour and I'm sorry to disturb you but you don't know unless you try do you?'

'Know what? He replied, his frustration showing a little more than he intended. This had better be good to disturb a family on Christmas Eve… and if he thought his delaying tactics and shivering were going to get him through the door before he'd stated his business he was very much mistaken.

'I'm sorry, I know it's not an appropriate time…' Before he could finish he noticed the eyebrows that had frowned at him rose in acknowledgement and he figured he should get straight to the point. '… it's just I was told you had some puppies for sale?'

It did nothing to quell the suspicion; the guy seemed too nervous to just be here for a last minute Christmas present.

'Who told you?' questioned Noel's father making it clear he wanted to know exactly what all this was about.

'Well my son actually… about four or five weeks ago. That's why I figure I might be too late'.

'So why leave it so long?' He could have told him straight that he was out of luck, but curiosity had gotten the better of him and he supposed it was because he wanted to leave it this late so that he could wrap a well-fed and healthy pup tomorrow morning without having had to care for it in secret. And to his mind that was exactly the type of person who shouldn't be trusted with so much responsibility. The stranger seemed to be surprised at being questioned so abruptly and that only confirmed the reservations that already existed, but an answer was given in full...

'Well he can be a little... ' he hesitated to criticise his own son... 'shall we say faddish. We've bought him whatever he wanted, whenever we could, my wife and I that is, and more often than not he's lost interest and moved on before he's even got it out of his package if you know what I mean? Do you have children Mr...?'

Noel's father could have offered his first name but it would have made the situation less formal so he took up the offer regardless of the awkwardness it caused; he answered matter of factly to imply that this in no way made them friends.

'Froste... and yes I have'.

'Then you'll know exactly what I mean?' guessed the increasingly desperate looking man with what he hoped was a knowing smile.

'No I don't'. The statement was corrected and intended to make him sound proud of Noel and the way he'd treated Sadie but he instantly realised it made him sound so unapproachable that he may never find out why he was standing in an open doorway at this hour. He mumbled a half hearted apology to try and realign the conversation and allow a response; the opportunity was taken.

'Oh, well anyway, that's what mine's often like so seeing as pets are very different to a fishing rod... or a games consol... or an easel... or a...' he was stalling for time and he knew it was obvious so he climbed straight towards the point. 'Well anyway, we said no to him this time and put our foot down for once. But the thing is, well instead of either trying to wear us down until he eventually got his way or just forgetting about it after a few days he's actually *saved* and I'm sure you know what that means?' He was at last greeted with acknowledgment.

'I think every parent knows what that means' he concurred but wasn't sure that he did; could he really remember a time when Noel had done the same? Did the boy even really understand what it meant? He doubted it but he wouldn't admit it; he considered that perhaps this late night visitor was more honest than he'd been given credit for as he continued with his explanation.

'Every week we thought he'd spend the money on something else but he never did, he just kept adding to it … his granddad even tried to call his bluff and offered to take him on holiday but the little tyke asked if he could just have the money to go towards his own as he didn't need much more. So as a father I'm sure you know why I'm here?'

With just a few well chosen words the stranger had turned the situation around completely.

Noel's father felt awkward using the same tactic that he'd dismissed but he went ahead anyway...

'It's freezing, come in Mr?'

'Stephen's fine' came the response.

'It's good to meet you Stephen. Please, come in.' He rolled his eyes as soon as he wasn't being watched; he'd always been a useless judge of character and he was obviously not improving. In refusing to stoop to his dismissive level and by offering his name willingly, Stephen had proven himself to be the better man and the other to be arrogant and conceited; it highlighted the fact that he never failed to see the worst in people.

As he hurried in from the freezing conditions outside, Stephen still insisted on detailing why he was here long after he had to; not that anyone could blame him. After the initial reception he'd received, feeling the need to overcompensate was understandable.

'Anyway, the more me and the wife discussed it, we figured we'd have to find the cash somehow as the lad deserves it...there's probably nobody needs a friend more'. Noel's father suddenly regretted his decision to invite the visitor in; he'd blown his chance again by pushing the sympathy vote at least one step too far. He was setting himself up to try and barter the price down on something the family didn't even want to sell. He expected to be asked the price any moment now and that it would then form the basis of the conversation from now on but he was wrong. All he was questioned about was whether the particular litter they'd began to raise made friends easily and whether their temperament was appropriate for children.

Noel's father again found himself unsure as to whether he should reconsider his thoughts but it would be betraying his family and make a mockery of the decision they'd already made together.

'It's not that I don't understand Stephen, because I do. But I'm afraid you're just too late; we sold the last pup a week ago...' just as he said it a hyperactive Labrador puppy charged across the hall after a ball Caroline had thrown.

Stephen looked at the man before him with a justifiably accusing and confused look on his face whilst Noel's dad back pedalled and altered his sentence. He tried his very best to make it sound as if he was always going to finish with '...that we want to sell. We were always going to keep one in fairness to its mother and as much as I hate to say it, so that she isn't missed too much when her time comes.' Stephen wasn't the only one who could play the loving father card and now he grimaced in disappointment and looked at the floor. It wasn't what he wanted to hear, but he did understand.

'Well, as I said, you don't know unless you try'.

'I can't argue with that' agreed Noel's father. At the most incriminating time a pathetic sounding yelp came from down the hall; both men heard it but only one pretended he hadn't. Noel's dad continued talking as casually as possible and may have gotten away with his charade were it not for the guilt written all over his face. Stephen wasn't sure that he hadn't imagined the noise but seeing such an embarrassed expression only served to confirm what he'd heard. As the situation sank in he changed his friendly tone.

'Listen Mr. Froste, if you don't want to sell to me, whether it's because you want to keep them, don't think I have the money, or just plain don't like the look of me that's alright, you've only got to say. But you should at least have the decency to be honest with me'.

The man of the house, the family head and the successful proprietor of a growing business now felt no older than his son. He was lost for words and didn't know what to do. He resented being made to feel like that in his own home but he knew he'd put himself in that position. His tone was forceful but apologetic; a strange combination seldom heard.

'I didn't want to get into it to be honest and wanted to save putting you in the position of rejecting a retard but if you want the truth...' Stumpy saved him the bother by half limping, half galloping but whole heartedly trying to follow her appropriately named brother Skittels after the ball. 'Well there you go,' confessed Noel's father. 'She's probably the best tempered of the bunch but not so much fun for a young lad and not what you had in mind is she?'

'Neither was my son but he's loved'

Noel's dad chose a quizzical look over the obvious questions. 'My *retard* son's in the car' continued Stephen. Sure enough, a silhouette could be seen in the passenger side. 'See I didn't think this would take more than a few minutes either way and so didn't want to wheel him to your door incase the answer was no, he doesn't know why we're here. If I come away without a puppy then I was just delivering this card'. He held up an envelope. He'd certainly thought this through. 'But if you let me buy that puppy from you then she'll spend the rest of her days with someone she *can* keep up with... although I'm sure you'll understand if we change her name from Stumpy?'

The defeated Mr. Froste had no words in direct response; who would? Let me just speak to my son he said. He showed Stephen to a seat in the kitchen and nudged the obligatory mince pies towards him but didn't imagine for a moment he'd take one as he disappeared to find Noel.

'But why?' Noel complained. 'If he wants her then surely she's worth the same?' His dad had explained the situation in full and now knelt opposite his son trying to equal their heights. He wanted to make it easier to relate to him and from that point of view it made the logic clearer. In fact the boy wasn't *entirely* wrong. For a ten year old he had a surprising grasp of economics and that would usually make a parent proud but this was a somewhat specialist case.

'Yes, but it's also about what she's worth to you. You don't play with her much now and by the time the summer rolls around you'll want to be outside and that'll suit her even less. There's a different perspective that you're not seeing.

'Dad, you said I could keep whatever money we made?'

'And you can! That's why I'm *asking* you what you want to do instead of telling you. It's your choice, just we never thought we'd sell…' he sighed as he said the word Stumpy, 'so you'll have had all the money you expected and I thought you might want to think of the lad sat out there who can't even walk? Noel just looked at him. 'It's up to you' urged his dad.

'Ok, I've got enough money Dad' Noel's hair was ruffled by a fully grown hand as he watched his dad stand up looking visibly relieved. 'I didn't want to get rid of her anyway, she's cute'.

Noel's father stopped dead just as he was about to walk away and knelt back down.

'If you like her so much, try and do what's best for her, she won't be cute forever and that boy's younger than you. He'll need her around long after she's just become something that stops you playing with your friends… do what's best for her.' Noel had learnt the subtleties of his dad's phrasing and this was nothing but a command. His dad willed him to make the right decision and not to force him into this situation.

'But you said it was up to me and now you're telling me she's going whether I like it or not!' Noel spoke nothing but the truth and his father knew it. Drowning in his own hypocrisy he forced out the words he knew formed a blatant lie.

'I said it was up to you whether you *sell* her or not!' They both sat there for a moment knowing that wasn't the case at all. Even Noel's mother who'd overheard everything was in no doubt yet nobody would say so. Noel's response came more from anger than from greed.

'Then I want paying!

In increased frustration his dad raised his voice, the words 'but there's one leg missing!' could not have been more appropriate as they charged up the hall way.

'Well then knock a quarter off the price!'

There was little could be said to that and Noel's father rejoined Stephen with Stumpy in his arms.

'Just look after her like she deserves' he demanded. 'I meant what I said, she's the most loving of the litter and so that's all I want for her.' Stephen nodded and offered his assurance along with his money. Noel's father gently pushed his hand back and repeated himself 'that's *all* I want for her'.

Not sure whether to be grateful or offended Stephen reiterated that his son was handicapped, not poor, but was met with the same response.

'Please, we never thought we'd sell her so we're not counting on the money'.

Stumpy looked back just the once as she disappeared out of the door, tail wagging as if to prove everything she did have worked just fine. Moments after he'd heard the door close and the car drive away Noel's father had come in and dropped the money; seventy-five percent of the original asking price by his sons side without a word.

Whilst this was of course a memory of sorts, he'd seen parts of the evening that before could only be pieced together or assumed. He was never there for much of what he'd just remembered but he saw a different side to the story now and a whole new aspect of his dad's personality that he'd chosen to forget.

CHAPTER FORTEEN

His total inability to leave any situation without having the last word or at least the physical equivalent had made Nick later still. The cumbersome vehicle that he drove did not lend itself to making up for lost time either and it took what always seemed like forever to gain enough momentum to gather anything more than an ambling pace. In the steadily building traffic it was frustrating having to repeatedly slow to a complete or virtual stop as he was unable to weave his way through the maze the way others occasionally managed to.

Still fuming from his confrontation with Ivy he had not been allowed to simmer down as every time he felt his anger begin to fade, another car would pull out around him, overtaking and forcing him to strain his struggling brakes and never once allowing the needle on his speedometer to exceed twenty.

He approached another turning absolutely convinced his limitations would be taken advantage of again. He had no doubt that yet another driver would assume he'd feel obliged to let them do so and would be gracious enough to accept it; but he was equally certain that he'd prove them wrong if he was given half a chance this time. They were all the same, darting out ahead of him long after the point that he could bring all twenty-three tonnes of his lorry to a graceful halt but he was determined that he'd made his last emergency stop for someone so presumptuous; the next of them would have to wait their turn.

Seeing the coupe edge forward, Nick began to lean on his horn to freeze the guilty party in their tracks but it was already too late. They'd already proceeded too far into their manoeuvre and stopping now would leave them directly in Nick's path so his actions had little effect other than to quicken the other driver's acceleration; but not to the point that Nick wouldn't have to concede and that simply wasn't going to happen. By the time the driver of the coupe had come to the same conclusion he had little choice but to fumble with the gear stick before hastily forcing it into reverse. His passengers were thrown forward in their seats then almost instantly hurled back into them with such sudden change of direction. He was shouted at by his wife for his erratic driving but was far more concerned with whether there was enough space behind his car to allow the retreat. Nick could see that there was plenty and knew they were in no danger but doubted they'd known the same; he hoped he'd caused a significant amount of panic as he thundered past to instil some much needed manners in the future.

With his mind fixed firmly on what little was left of the day, Nick didn't instantly associate the car now clearly fighting to overtake him with the incident that was now a good ten minutes ago but less than half a mile behind him. It lurched forward and sank back several times, its progress dictated by the oncoming traffic but eventually it took its chance and sped along the side of the lorry. It had barely passed before pulling in hard ahead of it, coming to a stop as abruptly as anyone would dare in the shadow of such a massive and imposing vehicle. Its driver wasted no time in leaping from his hastily opened door and it became painfully obvious to Nick exactly what was going on. He didn't need this; he could do without the delay or the likely broken nose that would no doubt accompany it but he wasn't going to wait for it to come to him either. He went to throw open his own door with all the confidence and determination he'd need to show if he was going to intimidate a younger and worryingly fitter looking man, but he got his ridiculously oversized fur trimmed cloak caught in his seat belt. In the process of untangling his awkward body he'd almost pulled himself half out of his equally generous trousers and by the time he'd redressed himself he was on the receiving end of some particularly threatening language; he'd already lost his chance to gain the first word and in his experience that put him at a distinct disadvantage.

'What were you thinking old man? You damn near killed us you...'

Nick wasn't the only one being yelled at. The driver's family were screaming at him; trying to pull in his reins and pleading with him to come back.

'I mean what the...' as angry as he was, he was still a family man and good enough at playing the role that even now he restrained himself, refusing to swear in front of his daughter, and so seamlessly exchanged his next word with what had been his first choice, '... hell is wrong with you?' Whilst purposeful and fast, his approach was controlled enough that a passerby could be forgiven for not recognising his intentions. Yet his face said everything and Nick knew it as he lurched awkwardly out of the cabin, hoisting his exaggerated belt buckle up and over his belly as he did so. The action forced his polystyrene shaping in the opposite direction, almost taking his trousers with it. He had to grab at the cheap material just to keep himself fully clothed and to save them falling to the ground completely; there was little that could have defused the escalating situation so instantly.

The determined looking man stopped in his advancing tracks having been ready to take on just about anyone else but Santa; but seeing him emerge so comically from the lorry's cabin, he was suddenly aware of his child's excited squeals of delight behind him. He searched his options as if he had some, until he surrendered to the only choice there was. He was all to aware that his three year old may never recover from witnessing her hero being beaten to a pulp and it certainly wouldn't win him any father of the year awards either. She might never forgive him and even if she did, her mother certainly wouldn't. His expression started to reverse, his face looking strained and ugly as it contorted until his features found their place again. He now smiled broadly whilst shaking his head. As if this wasn't enough to show he was standing down, he threw his hands in the air as a gesture of submission.

'I'm sorry' he said laughing at the same time, 'I know how busy you must be... I can understand the rush.' With that he turned on the heels of his designer trainers and walked away shouting 'You know she wants a bike right? And don't forget the stabilisers' more for the amusement of his little girl than for Nick to hear. He was kissed on the cheek by a wife that had never been prouder of him and they filtered into the traffic, a little more safely than before leaving a stunned and silent figure still standing purposeless by the roadside.

Nick remained speechless. The whole thing had begun, occurred and ended without him uttering a word. As the adrenaline had surged through him he'd totally forgotten his appearance, but catching his shadow the surreal moment made sense. It was the first time he'd been grateful for the ridiculous suit but he couldn't help resenting the fact it had saved him. There was no time to pity himself now though and with time a growing concern he squeezed himself back behind the steering wheel and continued on his not so merry way.

CHAPTER FIFTEEN

It was as amazing how much could change in a year as it was frustrating at just how wrong he could be. Noel hadn't given Stumpy a thought for months, his father had been right about that, but it wasn't for the reasons he predicted. It was because he missed someone else much more. Nobody mentioned the dramatic difference it made at all, despite the fact that to an outsider looking in, every Christmas Eve that went before it was identical in its structure and schedule. Looking back he wondered if it would help if they had veered away from the usual arrangements but it was the lack of acknowledgement that hurt the most. It was unnatural to ignore it completely; overcompensation was understandable and even to be expected but this was so much more. It was painfully obvious that his parents were going to extreme lengths to ensure that everything remained exactly the same as it always had; even to the extent that their festive ornaments were arranged so identically every year that you could literally see where they stood all year round.

There was a system to Christmas in this house just as there was everywhere else in their lives and it had always led to the text book family holiday, at least on the surface. Fun would be administered in an orderly fashion and more often than not it worked. Noel may have wished for more spontaneity on occasions but the festive season remained something he always looked forward to and for that reason he'd never complained. His parents were perhaps right to not meddle with a formula that had served them well; but they had attempted the impossible this year and were the only ones who couldn't see it.

They could open their presents at the same time, walk the same route during the obligatory afternoon stroll and watch the same old films as if nothing had happened but what they couldn't do was fill that empty chair in the corner. It seemed twice the size it used to and secretly, whenever they thought nobody would notice, not one single person could help looking at it.

And on the game would go. Each of them catching another staring trance like into the space that kindly old woman used to sit and pretending not to notice as that would have meant admitting that things were not as they should be. The attention to regimental timing would be greater than ever tomorrow as the day was replicated and recycled from the year before. Noel remembered that he wouldn't have been surprised if even the same conversations were played out like a script reading at some macabre rehearsal in which they'd leave gaps and silences where his Grandmother would usually answer. Worse still, perhaps they'd answer *for* her, impersonating her distinctive and ancient voice without actually realising as they had whenever they could get away with teasing her; they knew what she'd say anyway. Not only could her response be predicted, but the exact words used would be an odds on bet. The tone and even the nuances in her voice never changed like there were only so many sentences that had existed in her world and there was only one way to say each of them. As frustrating as that was for everyone around her during her life, it only seemed to exaggerate her absence now and they'd all give anything to be driven to the point of insanity by her just one more time. It made him miss her more as there was no way to forget her, even for a moment. Almost anything could trigger the memory and then he'd hear her lecturing, righting the world in the way only she could. Maybe she wouldn't be that easy to impersonate after all.

It wasn't the first time everyone had behaved like this, it had been the same throughout the year on every birthday that passed but depending on who's it was, the schedule changed slightly anyway so it had never been so obvious as it would be tomorrow. Noel couldn't help but resent them for making an awful situation worse. He'd been the closest to her in the end and was suffering the most now.

Nobody would forget and she would always be missed, yet leaving her seat spare at the table just seemed too much.

But now, with the benefit of hindsight only adults seem to be able to learn from, he couldn't believe how insensitive he'd been back then. He'd been so caught up in his own grief and how his parents' actions seemed to prolong the agony that he hadn't even considered their feelings. But if that seemingly never-ending Christmas he remembered all too well had taught him one thing it was to live life differently from the way he'd been taught. It wasn't that he thought there was any single thing wrong with what their celebrations always included; in fact, until that day he wouldn't have changed a thing. The flaw wasn't with the people themselves or the way that they chose to spend their life... it was the fact that they wouldn't last forever. The perfect day was impossible to maintain indefinitely and when a part of it inevitably went missing its absence was all the more notable, affecting everything and everyone.

Maybe next year he'd do something a little different. He didn't particularly want to and he knew the idea would not go down well at home but he didn't want this to happen again in the near or even distant future. If things were not always the same then change wouldn't hurt quite so much.

For the second time in his life Noel influenced a family decision. Whilst he dutifully refrained from raising his conclusion during that eleventh Christmas, by the time his twelfth came around with the eruption of yet more inexplicable light, he'd had several conversations with his mother about his concerns and had been listened to. He'd never know if they'd had the same, secret thoughts themselves or whether he'd genuinely set her thinking, but either way the result was the same.

It was the first year they planned to be anywhere but at home and Noel was sure that, whilst it was largely unsaid, they all hoped privately that doing so would disguise the loss this time around. Whilst he again found himself ahead of the day itself he remembered it well as it lived vividly enough in his conventional memory.

Instead of dwelling on the uneventful evening in front of him, he found himself concentrating more on the day that followed. It was unrecognisable from any he'd known before it and had changed completely, altering the routine exactly as it was supposed to with just one problem; it just didn't feel quite like Christmas if they weren't at home. He couldn't establish exactly why, but he could feel everyone else thinking the same even if they wouldn't admit it.

They were all spoilt for presents that year; people who usually avoid thought and expense suddenly became generous when they knew they be handing the gifts over face-to-face rather than through the post or other relatives. For his parents it meant no actual gain as they'd anticipated this and spent extra themselves to avoid potential embarrassment and so it was merely a trade off; but to Caroline and Noel it was pure reward. Noel had never forgotten the inexplicably strange feeling that was at odds with the usual preconception of a child's mentality but he realised that there might be more to all this than just receiving. Even before the morning had passed he knew that by the time the day was over there would be more gifts than could possibly fit in the car for the return journey. He'd had to take Caroline and literally go through everything, picking and choosing which to take home now and what could be done without until next week. It wasn't easy and the decision was guided by his mother who was desperate not to cause offence to anyone who had to see their offerings scrapped for the time being on the pile of less essential toys.

The day passed quickly as they travelled all over town and sometimes outside of it, but it was otherwise tedious. Without the extreme distractions of his more intense recollections he again found he was able to see through the image to the crowd who were still bound by a more traditional sense of time.

If things continued to follow this very distinct pattern and time was stretching to the height he had left to fall, he must be about half way down by now. At twenty-four years old he'd now relived half the Christmases he'd ever known but was unsure whether that thought came with relief or dread. He'd found plenty more reasons to condemn himself that he hadn't even considered whilst staring over that ledge; but he'd found a few to contradict his decision too. There were moments that he should have been proud of himself for if he'd only thought of them from a less critical angle. And for every occasion he felt he'd been hard on himself, there were at least a dozen that now, with all the facts laid bare before him he realised how harshly he'd judged his family. They were by no means perfect but there was nothing he'd change anymore and a couple of things he'd have liked to have said but to do so was nothing more than wishful thinking now.

To that end it really didn't matter how long he had left in this world. He'd learnt so much about those he thought he already knew too well, yet whilst he knew there was nothing he could do with any further knowledge, he craved it regardless. He looked behind him as best he could, trying to gauge whether he still had as far to fall as he had already travelled but it would have to remain one of his many theories. With the air gushing up towards him and wrapping his tie around his face it was impossible to judge exactly, but everything below him had grown considerably in size and that in itself was an indication of the speed at which he was moving.

CHAPTER SIXTEEN

Ivy stopped looking out of the office windows and instead looked down at herself. After all, that was where the problem lay. Her sodden, ripped dress forced her to close her eyes momentarily as if that meant she would forget the price tag; but she could see it there wherever she looked, dangling in front of her and representing a full weeks wages just as it had done in the shop. She didn't earn an unreasonable salary by any standards but it wasn't enough to fund the extravagance she'd shown lately and she certainly didn't earn as much her demeanour suggested. Only accounts and management knew her real title and her above average, but still unspectacular position within the company but she'd managed authority beyond her station in a way that nobody really understood. She just had a way of making life so difficult for anyone who defied her that it was easier to let her have her way than to oppose her but she was less proud of that fact now than she used to be. It was worth nothing when she got home at night and whilst she was never the one to make the coffee anymore and nobody would dare steal her biscuits, not a single person ever offered her any either. And if they did it was only in an attempt to avoid her wrath and to be in her good graces, or as close as they could get, for the rest of the day. She was still able to find the bright side though and wondered if that was such a bad thing as she continued to examine herself.

She wasn't grossly overweight, but she was at least a full size above this dress's capacity. It was obvious in this slouched position, but in the shop she'd convinced herself otherwise as she held herself in an unnaturally straight and stretched poise.

She took a ring out of her purse and slipped it over a perfectly manicured finger. It still fitted perfectly as if a day hadn't passed.

She held it up to the light as if checking it was real, but it wasn't the gold she doubted, it was the memory. Had it ever been quite like she remembered and had things really changed so much?

She prodded herself slowly but firmly in the stomach and watched intently as her painted nail started to disappear until she eventually lost sight of her knuckle as well as it was enveloped by the creases of her stomach and the silk of the red dress but she stopped short as it reached her wedding band. She was fairly convinced she hadn't actually gained weight since the last time she wore it, just that she didn't worry about it before and it had therefore never really registered.

The way she'd just reacted represented the last two years perfectly. She'd shut the door to keep everyone out and hid in the corner incase someone saw the real her, yet in complete contradiction she felt hurt that nobody came to rescue her. But why would they? There was a party to attend after all. The thought of everyone else having the time they deserved only emphasised the contrast of their situation. She wondered what they'd be saying about her, if anything at all; she wasn't even sure which was better. She tried to stop thinking about it and considered the time instead and looked up through the glass towards the same clock that she'd forced Nick to rely upon.

By now the shadows that had frequently darkened the bottom of the door crossed it less and less and the same straight white line of light that had shone beneath it had remained uninterrupted for sometime. It meant it was likely that she'd be able to travel the length of the printing press without being spotted, but that would only get her so far. But by taking the long route through the editorial department she could then leave via the fire exit. There was no reason she couldn't get out of the building that way totally undetected; but not without sacrificing her car. Even that wouldn't have stopped her and she'd have gladly made her way home without transport if that meant a lasting escape but there was a major flaw in the plan; she wouldn't be able to get through her front door when she got there. Her keys still lay next to her makeup bag in her desk drawer and that, unfortunately was in the main office upstairs. And there was no chance at all that the enormous rectangular room would be anything other than full to the brim, possibly with reporters and researchers desperately trying to finish their working day, or maybe with a more varied crowd rushing for the first serving of crudely made cocktails, but either way it would be bustling. She knew just sitting here wouldn't provide the answers but another few minutes wouldn't hurt either.

She went to change her position to bring relief to her aching back but for the first time in quite a while the light in the room shifted; only slightly but enough for her to notice. She sank back again into the same crevice then retreated further still when the door handle moved. If she tucked her legs in far enough she might not be visible from the doorway but bending her knees even a little sent pain shooting along her spine; she winced and grimaced her way through it. She felt the temptation to lean forward slightly to see who it was; to judge just how embarrassing it would be to be caught in this pitiful state. Anyone above executive level and it would be resignation worthy, but as the breeze brought the distinctive scent now filling the doorway to her she recognised it instantly and realised her situation could not be any worse. The pungent mix of expensive aftershave and cigarettes had always seemed the most pointless combination to her... and it still did.

'Just come up to the party Ivy'. The same self-assured confidence dripped from the words of characteristic certainty.

She stayed silent and even held her breath. Against the usual ferocity of the printing press she'd have been unlikely to be detected, but with the last of the huge machines having been run down just a few moments ago the round the clock chaos had descended into an eerie hollow space in which even footsteps echoed and now the slightest sound would give her away. But the suddenness of his approach hadn't allowed her to prepare and she was oxygen starved within seconds. After what must have been a minute he was still there, waiting and listening. As it was obvious he wasn't going to give up anytime soon, she slowly exhaled before panic set in any further. She deflated slowly, as if punctured, but she wondered if there was any point in being so careful. He'd know she was here the same way that she knew who stood in the door way now. He'd even know her facial expression. Why shouldn't he? She knew his; he'd be smiling a disappointed smile, concerned for her but unashamedly pleased with himself at being so right... again.

'Come on, this is madness' he continued being careful to aim his diagnosis at the situation rather than the person. He hadn't come this far without learning a few lessons but she still heard it her own way. She gritted her teeth at the very thought of her sanity being questioned. He had no idea of her situation anymore and he certainly hadn't seen what happened to her in the yard.

'Everyone's waiting for you, at least come and have a drink... or if you're hurt, let me take you to the hospital but either way, don't just sit down here by yourself?' He obviously had no doubt whatsoever that she was there and his confidence in his instincts annoyed her. She so wanted to disappear, not just so that she could avoid the confrontation but so that he'd be talking to himself; so that for once he'd feel the fool. He'd been wrong before but even then she seemed to be the only one that could see it. Everyone, even her own friends shared his point of view every single time but she still insisted it wasn't because he held the moral high ground; it was simply because his opinion was always so much more articulately put. She thought about those arguments and as usual, even her subconscious shared all the tones and characteristics of her own voice and it was always difficult to disagree with yourself.

In the background he continued to plead his case for her to join her colleagues and the montage of their voices, one a physical reality, the other inside her head brought back the home they'd built together. It didn't seem so long ago anymore.

She was there again now. The best and the worst of their time swirled around her with glimpses of the pastel walls, intricate lighting and subtle style that ran throughout the property they'd designed together. They'd agreed to create the closest thing possible to a maintenance free surrounding; it wasn't an uncommon decision but perhaps their reasoning was. They simply wanted to spend as much uninterrupted time together as possible; how could it be that back in the real world and at this present moment she'd give anything just for him to leave?

'Or we could talk right here?' he suggested. It really is about time don't you think? Silence again ensued. 'It's all we've ever needed. Just time together... to talk without anyone intervening and without you running away.'

Up until now Ivy had just wanted him to stop talking. But if that wasn't going to happen then she'd better make the most of the one thing he truly loved; his voice. Every time he spoke she used his words to cover the sound of her awkwardly shifting herself along the tiled flooring. Her dress was beyond repair so she virtually dragged herself in lunges towards the door of the next office; it heralded the entrance to a smaller and much less comfortable room but at least it had a lock on it. Ivy had avoided it before knowing it would be cold and cramped but she could suffer that if it meant putting more distance between herself and him.

As the voice became increasingly desperate, it also became louder and that suited her just fine. She was able to move further and faster that way.

'Just at least let me know that you're listening?' The door of the adjacent office slammed as if in response and was instantly followed by a key turning in the lock from the inside. She still had a way of making a point.

Now all Ivy needed was a distraction and a reason to feel strong again but she couldn't victimise anyone from here. Yet as she leant back against the nearest wall she realised that wasn't necessarily the case; she could bring one of next years tasks forward. It wasn't even being cruel and if looked at the right way it could even be seen as a kindness of sorts. She took the receiver off the nearest phone and waited only a short time for an answer; she introduced herself as if

her voice wouldn't be recognised then got straight to the point...
'I'm afraid I have some news for you and thought you'd want to know sooner rather than later....'

CHAPTER SEVENTEEN

Noel continued to try and stay focused on the ever growing world below and the calculations it suggested; not because there was any point, but because if he could concentrate hard enough on something else, it might ensure that the scene he was expecting any moment now may pass unnoticed. He should have known better.

If there was a reason for all of this, at least part of it must be to learn the lessons of your own life and that made what he was trying to avoid essential viewing. Before he could even try and resist it he found himself not at home, but still with his dad who had been incredibly determined that he wouldn't make the same mistake this year; he hadn't even taken the chance that they might sell out. Having asked for every possible opinion, he'd taken them all on board and with a budget of one month's wages he made a choice that everyone, not least the jewellery shop owner assured him was guaranteed to please. The delicate crystal fragments glistened, smooth and perfect against the extreme contrast of his rough and work weary hands that still showed how he'd started his business in the first place. Noel had always thought his father lucky to be able to afford such luxuries but moments like this reminded him that it was nothing at all to do with luck.

'So, what do you think?' he had asked Noel eagerly. He rephrased his question before it was even answered. 'Do you think she'll like it? That was what he really wanted to know so it might as well be what he asked. He looked genuinely pleased with his choice and Noel felt sure the question was rhetorical. Besides, what did he know when it came to ladies jewellery? He had about as much taste when it came to high society fashion as anyone else who'd only just reached their teenage years but he relished the inclusion.

'She'll love it Dad, especially the way it...' he searched for an answer articulate enough to warrant the grown-up way he was being treated. He'd been asked his thoughts on a necklace that cost more money than he could even imagine and he appreciated that regardless of the fact he'd been questioned *after* the purchase was made; but being considered at all was respect he wasn't used to and so consoled himself with that. Noel knew it was probably in direct response to his rant last week about not being a child anymore and so he searched for a word fitting of the adult he longed to be. He started the later part of his sentence again... 'especially the way it... sparkles'. Sparkles? Was that really the best he could come up with? He was disappointed in himself regardless of what his father thought. He reached out enthusiastically to hold the treasure he was offered, already worried about how uninterested his ignorant statement must have made him sound but his dad was already holding it up to the light and laughing.

'It certainly does... with that price tag I'd be disappointed if it didn't sparkle.' He continued to chuckle unashamedly, totally unaware of how much his son hated it.

It was only now that Noel was fully grown that he could see how ridiculous and innocent these moments he'd let haunt him had been. Back then he could tell that his dad's laughter wasn't natural and it was just as obvious now; but the way he interpreted it couldn't have been much more opposite. For years he'd held this moment against his father, honestly believing that he was trying to prove him to still be a mere child by highlighting the idiocy of his answer but now he could see he was just trying to show him that it simply didn't matter. He'd misjudged the man time and time again and it was never until it was too late, or just too difficult to talk about that it dawned on him.

Noel watched him examine the gift like a connoisseur, but was fairly certain that he didn't really know what he was looking for. But he did understand money and the fact that it was this very piece that the jewellers had chosen to feature on the front cover of their brochure this year spoke volumes. It was a cunning ploy that would probably work; it virtually guaranteed that Mum would know its considerable value already, but if she didn't her friends would be sure to ensure she did. It was sly, but it was also wise after her reaction to her previous gift.

By the time they'd got home Noel had read every page of the accompanying booklet that fitted perfectly into the delicate, emblemed box to compensate for anyway he might have appeared disinterested earlier. It didn't look large or fancy enough to contain something so expensive, but as he was repeatedly assured by his mother, simplicity often equals taste. He supposed taste could well therefore equal expense. He intently watched his dad wrap and re-wrap his new pride and joy, attempting to bring the presentation up to the same lofty standards as its contents but it just wasn't working. It wouldn't have been so frustrating had his dad relented and paid the service charge which would have ensured his present was not only wrapped, but tied in ribbons as well; yet despite the comparative insignificance of the cost he'd disagreed with the principal so strongly that he'd refused, and not without making his point well known. It didn't matter how much he regretted it now, it was too late by far and he was ruining what little wrapping paper he had.

Noel could do it. On that they would secretly agree and he'd make it look better than any shop attendant ever could but it wasn't an option. Noel knew better than to intervene but he failed to understand why. He didn't see how a man could be so proud he couldn't ask his son to help him with something so menial; it was for that reason alone that he never offered.

He kept quiet as he watched the fully grown man, usually the perfect example of efficiency and practical thinking grow increasingly frustrated that he was unable to do anything but ruin the materials he'd spent so much time choosing. He knew if he carried on like this he could hope for no better than a crumpled mess and tried one last time. When he failed in his final attempt he threw every sheet with all the power of a man his size but was insulted by the distance it travelled. A heavier object would have flown across the living room with pointless but satisfying speed. But this instead floated softly down towards the carpet and slid back toward him as if mocking him. In response he picked up the cardboard box, knowing that with the weight of the crystal inside it would fly a lot better but he came to his senses before he had even raised his arm.

He was embarrassed. Not only because of his creative inadequacy but also because he knew how easily it could be solved yet he couldn't bring himself to ask. And to have openly acted so childishly in front of his young son just two days after lecturing him on the immaturity of tantrums made him feel no better either; the boy's dignified silence only served to make it worse. He left the room without apology predicting he'd have plenty of time later; he shouldn't have dived into it when he was in a rush anyway. That was never the way to get things done right as he must have told Noel and Caroline a thousand times.

Now alone in the room, Noel figured it was time to get to work himself. He'd already failed abysmally with regard to his promise to have Christmas preparations firmly in hand weeks ago and certainly didn't want this running into tonight. His mum was out with Caroline until later this evening and having just heard the front door slam he wanted to take the opportunity to wrap their presents without the fear of anyone walking in. He was also aware of the incredible amount of mess he'd create in the process of making them look something special and that despite the effort that went into this every year, Mum would be paranoid about scissors on the carpet, Dad would term the glitter as 'excessive' and Caroline would simply tear through the lot like a freight train.

There was just one thing he had to do first. Not because of the addiction he'd convinced himself he had, but because he could not bear to miss such a rare opportunity. From a strategically ripped pouch in the inside of his jacket he pulled out a battered packet of cigarettes and slipped one from the pack. With so few chances to smoke since school broke up for the holidays they'd last him over two weeks at this rate. And with the constant transporting between the darkest corner of his wardrobe and his makeshift pockets, the corners of the packet were almost worn right the way through.

He made countless attempts to flick his lighter the way he'd seen it done so effortlessly in the movies, trying to look sophisticated in an otherwise empty room. This was usually the point at which he was laughed at, but that was exactly why now was the right time to practice. He inhaled a lungful and smirked as he bobbed his head in a self congratulatory manner, but only for a moment. It was followed, as it nearly always was by the spluttering reminiscent of his Nan's old car just before it was condemned. He coughed uncontrollably to the point that it panicked him, but as he recovered he stood up hoping it would help. He wasn't sure whether it did or if the second drag simply came as less of a shock. It shouldn't. He'd been doing this for a while now. 'Addicted for nearly a fortnight' as he would often say when seen after school.

Only now, as he careered down the side of the building could he see the ridiculousness of it all, but at the time it was a serious and realistic bid for popularity. He winced knowing there was more to come... and it was worse but at the very least it was reassuring that he was doing the right thing now and it laid most of his previous doubts to rest.

Now he had the situation and his lungs under some sort of control he walked over to the living room mirror. He finished that cigarette without taking his eyes off his own reflection, pausing only to admire, or to criticise himself from various angles, shamelessly trying to impersonate his favourite film characters at his most ambitious then desperately attempting to mimic the more popular kids at school as reality set in.

When he was finished he set about creating organised bedlam. After several return trips to the stash in his bedroom cupboard, the living room was covered with ribbons, tape, strings and every kind of wrapping paper. He received a reasonable weekly allowance and the paper round he'd inherited from Karl, the only real friend he'd made that summer had helped but it still didn't go far at this time of year. He'd only managed to obtain a fraction of the presents he'd planned, but he'd always had a way of making even the most modest offering look impressive… but it took time; time and crayons.

Following an initial flurry of activity he sat admiring the stack of gifts in all their glory, but it only represented half of his horde at best. He needed to press on, but not before another cigarette break. He waded through the carnage like a conquering hero enjoying his just reward but stopped dead at the sound of the door. It must be his dad but he'd been surprisingly quick considering the implications of the note he'd left behind.

Noel stubbed out the cigarette and was quick to start fanning the smoke still curling in the air. Visible signs were important to erase but so was the unmistakable odour and with the few minutes or less that he had he knew it would be difficult, if not impossible. Had he lived in a strictly non-smoking house he would be caught for sure. But then again he would never have taken the chance in the first place. But his mother smoked, if only occasionally but it was enough to excuse the faint smell of nicotine every now and then, but nothing this strong or recent; she'd been out all day. He opened a window but was careful not to move so far away that he could not shut it again the second the living room door handle moved. By the time it did, he dared to realistically hope that he'd been blessed with enough time.

His dad had taken longer than he'd predicted and the agonisingly slow opening of the door hinted as to why. It had all the hallmarks of someone struggling with the handle and a tray of drinks and he'd witnessed it every Sunday… suddenly it all made sense. Noel was a teenager now and the promise was being kept, it was time he tried his dad's legendary Vodka based punch. The excitement that would usually have generated paled against the significance of the extra time it bought him; it was easily enough to close the window. He checked his secret pocket as he made his way over but there was nothing there… nothing at all. He looked along the windowsill and the mantelpiece shelving but still nothing. He scanned the floor in desperation. There were very few clear areas of carpet left as he'd deliberately covered everything he could in case of a surprise invasion but now, rather than preserve his family's surprise it worked against him. Most of the lumps and bumps below the brightly coloured paper made hills and valleys that gave no clue as to what lie beneath, but then he saw it. The small rectangular bump probably only screamed 'cigarette packet' to him as he knew he had something to hide and his dad would probably regard it with no more suspicion than any of the others, but it wasn't a chance worth taking.

Noel hurdled his way across the lounge and dropped to his knees at the offending point, skidding along like a dancer reaching their show's finale. He shot a hand under the paper to retrieve what would incriminate him but his time had run out. With just a split second to make the decision he brought his other palm down flat and hard, crushing the paper and everything beneath it flat to the ground until it showed no visible signs at all. He sighed with relief knowing that even with just pennies in his pocket; he could replace that packet easier than he could his parents' trust.

'Noel! How many times?' Shut that window if you're going to have the heating on!' The reprimand had been a small price to pay, and if it hadn't been about the draft it'd have been about something else anyway; at least it ensured the mess wasn't mentioned. It was noticed, but it was acknowledged with no more than a slow shake of the head before he laid his tray down and set out the jugs and glasses with an ominous 'I thought we'd try some of this before your mother gets home'.

A little over an hour later the jug was as empty as the glasses and Noel remembered mixed emotions. He at last felt like a man to have been smoking in the morning and drinking in the afternoon and was so convinced of his rapid progression that he kept feeling his chin for the first signs of stubble. He was also full of frustration that he couldn't fully enjoy the moment for what it was. He'd been unable to escape the fear that his dad wouldn't be able to resist tidying just a little and a squashed packet of cigarettes were every bit as incriminating as they would be perfectly intact but he needn't have panicked. His dad left the room without a fuss as with so many last minute visits to make before he could relax at home for the holidays the room was Noel's again soon enough, even if it was spinning slightly.

With the threat of detection over, Noel smiled to himself. Not only at not having been caught, but that he was given a dedicated hour of his dad's time despite his heavy schedule. All this accompanied by the slightly giddy yet euphoric feeling brought on by the punch meant that this was shaping up to be a better Christmas than he'd have predicted. It wasn't fashionable to enjoy Christmas at his age but it was the one time of the year he didn't mind not fitting in. It was a shame he couldn't smoke a cigarette to celebrate; well not a straight and undamaged one anyway. He thought he'd better check their condition just in case it wasn't fatal and there seemed little point in waiting any longer to whisk them away to their hiding place as he imagined he may have used his quota of good fortune for the day.

He slumped awkwardly to his knees surprised at just how much coordination he'd lost due to the alcohol and swept back the paper still smiling but the expression didn't last long; as the wrapping fluttered back down to the ground a sickness came over him like he'd never felt before. It had nothing to do with his consumption but everything to do with what he saw. The box was hardly crumpled, but had been flattened almost perfectly so the writing on its side was still perfectly readable. But instead of the government health warning and the nicotine content, there was a gold lettered assurance from the town's most exclusive jewellers that the contents were the genuine article.

Noel felt empty, helpless and wanted to run but there'd be no escaping this. He wondered how he could tell anyone, let alone his father what he'd done and when would be the best time if ever he mustered the courage. It certainly wasn't something he could put off for long but perhaps telling him before he'd settled any outstanding business was not the best plan. If he waited until the others were home there would at least be someone else to calm the situation; it wouldn't change what had happened but it might change the immediate response.

He decided that was the best option as it also gave him perhaps an hour to think up an excuse as to how it happened but there was no way he could avoid the blame; he considered trying to convince his father that he'd carelessly left it on the floor and it had been trodden on accidentally. He'd still get yelled at for creating a mess that meant it had not been seen but it was at least an accident and they always incurred less punishment but upon thinking it through he became convinced that there was no way it would work. Had his father left the necklace behind under different circumstances he may just have doubted himself, but there was no way he'd forget the fact that he'd grabbed it in such anger. All of Noel's concentration seized on that very thought, however disgusted he was with himself, he couldn't stop thinking about how that was his only possible escape and his scheme evolved without him even wanting it to as he thought about just how much trouble he was going to be in. His arm moved involuntarily under the paper and took hold of the misshapen box. He pushed and pulled it, manipulating it back into its previous dimensions and placed it exactly where it had been.

CHAPTER EIGHTEEN

It had been a mission just to make it to the hospital and its turnstile entrance had presented a whole new set of difficulties but Nick felt considerably better just being there. He marched down the corridor towards a nurse who was headed in a typically hurried manner out of her office. He didn't know her, just vaguely recognised her as he did so many of the other staff; there were very few who remained total strangers to him. At least that meant they ignored his attire now. Several others acknowledged him as he negotiated the obstacles that littered the maze of corridors to the ward in which his wife lay. Not that he wasn't grateful; it was reassuring to know that despite the sheer quantity of human traffic that passed through, his was a face that belonged to a person and not to a crowd. It was the people that took the monotony away as the masses of trolleys, temporary beds and wheelchairs were the only thing that altered the route and prevented him from defaulting to autopilot along this labyrinth that, if asked, he could draw to scale.

'Hi Nick.' It was such a simple greeting but it caught him by surprise to be spoken to at all, let alone by name. He was obviously talked about in the coffee room more than he thought. His instant reaction was to check the young man's name badge but it offered nothing so informal as a first name. By the time he could say anything the moment had almost passed but he gave chase and then a response.

'Hi, my wife... how's she doing?'

'I'm sorry, I don't know the latest, but Dr. Rebrest will I'm sure.'

'Yeah, that's who I usually speak to; it's just that I haven't been able to find her today. I've been looking for her for maybe twenty minutes now so wondered if you could help?' he lied. He exaggerated the time massively so that he could be excused for seeking a favour.

'You really need to speak to her and I know she's in today, I saw her not so long ago'. He looked both ways along the corridor as if about to tell a secret. 'Let me just dial her department for you'. With that he disappeared back into his office, holding the door open as if inviting Nick in. The invitation seemed a little over familiar but he'd always found the majority of people here to be obliging to say the least. He watched the medic's youthful speed and precision as he dialed looking like he'd learned the pattern rather than the number.

'No!' Nick realised he sounded a little too abrupt, especially when considering the circumstances so he adjusted his tone. 'It's ok, don't waste your time, I know you're busy. I know her, I'll find her, don't worry.'

'You sure? It's really no bother.'

'Sure, honest' Nick smiled to assure him he meant it but it was also with genuine thanks; he was sure there were more important things to be worried about in a place like this than trying to save him a few minutes. The consultant replaced the receiver, nodded appreciation of Nick's understanding of the situation and his consideration before scuttling off as intended, disappearing before the door had even closed. Nick jammed his boot in before it was too late and set about mimicking what he'd just witnessed, checking both ways that he wasn't being watched before entering.

His plan was a hopeful one and it relied heavily on there being a contact list somewhere in the room but it appeared this wasn't the case. The consultant obviously had remembered the number as Nick scanned the tiny office for a chart of some sort. He wasn't hoping to be lucky enough for individual numbers, but surely there must be a departmental extension list? As he checked the desk instead of the walls and pin board he realised it didn't matter. For someone who hated the advance of technology so much he had a strong and sudden appreciation for the redial facility.

He didn't even take the time to sit down. He simply lifted the receiver and pressed the button labelled 'LAST CALL' then hung up instantly realising it related to the one above and that he'd just called reception.

'Bloody technology', he grumbled under his breath. He went to clear his throat then thought better of it. He wasn't even going to attempt an impression as such, but sounding a little unlike his usual self could only help.

Fortunately the phone ringing in Robyn's department had caller display and so was received under the obvious assumption. The efficient lady who answered was quick to offer to transfer him through appropriately and whilst that would lose him the advantage of the digital display lying on his behalf, he now had an entrusted employee to do it for him. Even if he didn't sound entirely convincing he doubted she'd question him after being forwarded by a friend and colleague. The annoying clicking of the connection was followed by a sudden, but slightly harassed...

'I'm surprised to hear from you so early?' Whilst it wasn't an overfriendly reception it was familiar, relaxed and comfortable. Nick figured he'd better adopt a similar approach in recognition.

'Well you know what it's like, earlier you start, earlier you finish?' There was a pause followed by a slightly confused...

'Well in theory. So what can I help you with?' Only I can't be too late getting away tonight... parties and... stuff' Robyn added the last few words as if inventing them as she went along.

'Yeah, yeah of course. It's the same here so I'll get straight to the point...'

'Really?' replied Robyn, seemingly no longer in such a rush. 'I'd have thought with it being your first Christmas together you'd be anywhere but partying?'

Her acute perception had suddenly put him on the defensive and he knew he'd already tried to be too clever for his own good.

'Of course. I just mean I've got a few stops and presents to drop off before I settle in for the night. You know, so we can be together without worrying about anything else for a few days.'

'Sure, alright'. She was either suspicious or just too busy to press the issue any further but she certainly wasn't gullible either. He'd have to be more careful and refrain from the niceties, especially as they were about to give him away.

'Well anyway, I was wondering about Grace Sainte on Arethusia ward. What's the situation with her as she's shown no improvement for sometime now?'

'I'm aware what ward she's on Shaun and we discussed this at the start of the week?'

'I know, I know. Just you were a little vague and I wanted to be sure what's planned before we leave for the holidays... you know what it's like, the minds never off the job and if I've got to spend from now until New Year thinking of patients I might as well be thinking about what's actually going to happen instead of what might.'

'There was nothing vague about it' she retorted in her characteristic defensive manner. 'It was just undecided. But only because we were waiting on those last tests and they show no improvement as you rightly said at the time, we've got no choice... we'll have to go ahead.'

Nick sighed silently so as not to show his frustration and closed his eyes. He doubted she was being especially guarded or she'd have questioned him more directly as she was certainly not shy when it came to confrontation. But she wasn't giving enough away either and he needed this conversation to be as short as possible; partly because Robyn would not be slow to catch on to what was happening but also because the real Shaun could return at any given moment.

'So there's absolutely nothing more we can do for her?' He took the opportunity to ask the same question he'd asked so many times before as under a different guise he might get a more honest; no, that was unfair... a more *direct* answer. In defence of Robyn and everyone else he'd spoken to, nobody was ever guilty of offering him false hope. They'd softened the blows sometimes and he suspected they were often economical with how much they told him whilst dwelling on the positives wherever they could be found. But however bleak the future appeared they'd never actually *lied* so far as he knew; in fact he wondered if Robyn was even capable of it. Sometimes it was even arguable that perhaps she should on certain occasions, but that was easy for him to think when he didn't have to live with the repercussions. He remembered bringing it up once during one of their late night five minute chats that never failed to turn into hours.

'The trouble with lying is that it's so dishonest' she'd once stated in typical factual fashion. The simplicity could not be argued with and it made him feel awful just for raising the subject in the first place. But it also filled him with confidence that he'd never have to read between the lines with her and that he'd never receive an answer as blunt as he was about too.

'You know that if there was anything... absolutely anything at all then I'd be doing it and...'

'So there's not?' Nick had chipped in with a tone so casual that it suggested he was indifferent to the answer but he still couldn't refrain from trying to hurry the truth whilst silently reprimanding himself for interrupting her.

'I was about to tell you why I've had to make the decision but if you want it straight?'

'Just you said you were busy and I'm...'

'Well the answer's no. We've tried everything and it's done little or nothing. But either way, not enough.'

'So?' Nick dragged the single syllable word out as if that could replace a sentence. The shock of being told in such definite terms had been harder to digest than he'd imagined. He knew her matter of fact response had been due to her frustration with such basic questions coming from an office that no doubt contained all this information on either of the two computers opposite rather than lack of compassion for his wife, but it angered him to hear her talked about so coldly; so methodically.

'So we've no choice but to move her on. She'll be more comfortable there' continued Robyn.

'There?' Nick was keeping to one word responses knowing his voice would crack if dared utter anymore. He could feel himself shaking; he knew exactly where 'there' was but wanted to hear her say it. He wasn't sure why. It was sadistic but he wanted the absolute clarity before she figured out what was happening.

'Shaun?'

'Yeah'

'Why are we even having this conversation and how...' before she could finish Nick saw the handle of the office door depress and was caught halfway through ducking behind the desk like some pathetic school boy who hadn't done his homework and was trying to evade the teacher.

Robyn still held her mobile to her ear but had stopped talking mid sentence. Now she just stared at a man wishing he hadn't even tried to hide. If she'd have looked angry he'd have felt less guilty but her expression was more one of disappointment. She'd began to make her way towards the office upon answering as she was never one to talk on the phone if it could be discussed face to face but a combination of the questions and the mannerisms that didn't quite suit had aroused her suspicions and she'd quickened her pace.

'I had to know' offered Nick rising to his full height; considerably taller than the child he felt like. He had been confident he could justify his questionable actions but now all he could feel was a sickening combination of embarrassment and humiliation. The best single word for it was that he felt *sorry* and for a man as proud and as obstinate as him that was rare indeed.

'Did you really think I wouldn't tell you?' After everything, did you really think I'd...' Robyn hesitated, desperate not to lose her professionalism but couldn't help consider using a word she despised yet still she controlled herself... 'mess you around at this stage? Really Nick?'

He couldn't remember having ever heard her swear but she'd just come so close she'd actually begun to pronounce the word. Having watched her struggle to snatch it back Nick realised his actions had obviously cut deep; knowing her like he did he shouldn't have been surprised. Nobody else he knew prided their honesty more highly. He wondered if that was simply because he knew so few honest people but his surmising clouded what he should have been concentrating on; a response. Something, anything to justify what he'd done but no words came.

Robyn quickly tired of waiting and continued, breaking the silence much to Nick's relief.

'Look... look at this'. She marched forward and slammed a handful of documents onto the desk so hard it made them both wince despite seeing it coming. She awkwardly shuffled her schedule to the top of the considerable pile and just pointed to the doctor's scrawl under the 19.15 entry. It read arrange meeting with 'Mr Sainte' but it was all he could make out before the scrawl descended into nothing more than scribble but she'd made her point eloquently enough.

'But I asked you this morning and you wouldn't tell me?' She raised her voice now but shut the door behind her to compensate. 'It's not that I wouldn't tell you at all. It was that I couldn't tell you *there* and I couldn't tell you *then* in front of who knows how many people and within earshot of your wife! But I would have told you, I had even planned to tell you as soon as either the facilities were available or the circumstances were right. Do you really think I'd have wanted...' she corrected herself '... do you really think that *you'd* have wanted to receive news like that with an audience? With no explanation?

Nick just looked at the floor. He was shocked to be laid into like this considering the situation but at least he understood why.

'I mean look at you! Would you really want anyone to see you like this? I know you better than that.' She changed her stance seeing she'd done enough damage and listened to her own observations; Nick looked broken. He was punishing himself anyway so she saw no reason to keep lashing out any longer however much she needed to douse the flames inside. She somehow managed to adopt a softer approach.

'I called at your house this morning' she said. 'I mean in person... not on the phone. I didn't want to have this conversation with you here. Can I see you later? I could come by after work? I should be finished up here in an hour or so?'

Any anger Nick had felt was seeping out of him at the thought of her coming by his home before her shift and then, even after what he could now see was outrageous behaviour on his part, still offering her time this evening. He began to feel as sorry for her as he did himself.

'I think the time for discretion may have passed' he suggested still looking at the floor. 'I appreciate your consideration but please, just tell me now. You don't have to hold back'. Robyn slowly walked over, careful to be quiet although she wasn't sure why; it just seemed appropriate somehow.

'I really don't mind doing this later?'

'Please, now Robyn. For my benefit if not for yours?' It was virtually begging and she couldn't stand it.

'Well we're starting this conversation from a different point to which I imagined you crafty old fool' she began, desperate to dispel the awkward atmosphere between them that she had previously believed consigned to history. She ducked her head below his, overtly looking for a smile or at least some sign that they were back in familiar territory where they both needed each other in equal measure. He wasn't displaying anything other than an understandably solemn glazed expression but her exaggerated actions were comical in themselves and he knew they'd never cease until he gave her some sign that she could speak freely. He forced a grimace which she spotted beneath his thick beard and even though she wasn't convinced he meant it, she appreciated the effort.

'So seeing as you've rendered my preparatory speech irrelevant, what do you need to know Mr. Sainte?' For all her efforts to remind him of their closeness she suddenly found herself angling for distance again to deliver this, the harshest of news and reverting to his surname may just help a little. 'Ask me openly and I'll tell you straight… if that's what you want, but you've got to be sure'.

Nick nodded his head in agreement whilst looking a little confused at the manner in which she'd started addressing him but it wasn't important enough to raise the issue. There'd be plenty of time for that.

'What happened to the last ditch attempt as we've been calling it?' His words were slow and exacting.

'The operation itself? Nick just repeated his gesture to confirm.

'It was always a long shot which offered no guarantees and we've always known that. And the chances of it working were slim and…' Nick looked up at her with an expression intended to remind her of who she was talking to as he could hear her slipping back into her official mode of speech.

'But it was at least a chance' he interrupted. 'Chance can be a wonderful word. It's my favourite in fact.' He waved his hand in apology and allowed her to continue, bracing himself as she did so. She accepted the gesture.

'Nick, the operation was, as you rightly say a last ditch attempt and therefore a chance worth taking. You know if there was any likelihood at all that it could work I'd recommend it. I'd even *insist* on it.' She fumbled clumsily with her papers, again searching for the file that contained the exact findings of Grace's case then gave up realising they really didn't matter at this stage. 'She's just too weak now. She quite simply would not survive the operation or even the anesthetic'.

'So you're…'

She interrupted him knowing exactly what he was going to ask and certain that if she didn't finish now she might not be able to at all.

'Yes, I'm sure. Everyone here's sure. I sought outside opinion and they were sure as well Nick, I'm sorry. If there was any doubt at all we'd test again, believe me. But there is no doubt and so we're moving her tomorrow. I know it's not much notice'.

'Not much notice? Tomorrow's Christmas bloody day!'

'Not here it isn't. And it won't be there either. It's a working day as far as everybody involved is concerned and they'll be as focused as they would be on any other date I assure you. We'll do our best for our patients; especially our favourites'. She believed in what she was saying and would never have a word said against the system but despite siding with the truth she could no longer look directly at him.

'A hospice is not the best you can do by her, honestly, I know her. She'll just... just...'

'They're far better equipped than us. A lot better suited and will do everything they can to make her as comfortable as possible. They're trained differently and can handle it better than anyone here.'

'But here there's hope, here there's possibility?'

Robyn gently took his face in both hands, raising it until he looked directly at her, however involuntarily. His eyes seemed to shimmer but the tough old bastard wouldn't cry. She expected nothing different. This was the hardest way to tell anyone but she knew him well enough to know that without this he'd cling to his illusion like a vice.

'Not anymore, there is no hope left Nick; only the chance to make the best of the time she's been given'. She spoke slowly and precisely as if to a child. 'I'm sorry, I truly am.'

The door opened and Shaun walked in a few steps having not looked up from his folder then stopped momentarily when he noticed he had company before turning without question and retracing the way he came. Robyn had said nothing to him; she didn't need to as he'd taken the hint and followed her eyes... out the door. The look on Nick's face had told him everything else and he'd gladly deal with almost anything rather than one of *those* situations as they were known around the wards.

Much to Nick's surprise, Robyn had followed suit by leaving him too. One of her attributes was knowing how much was enough and right now Nick needed time. She paused at the door just to whisper 'you know where I am' before disappearing and leaving Nick alone with his thoughts.

CHAPTER NINETEEN

From Noel's point of view, another year passed but not without him paying severely for what he had done. He'd managed to convince his own father that he'd crushed his precious gift when he snatched it, and blinded by the mist of his temper he couldn't be sure that it wasn't the case. He'd given Noel the benefit of the doubt and so bore the brunt of its repercussions.

For twelve whole months Noel had stayed silent whilst his parents slept in separate beds and barely spoke to each other. At the time he wondered how a present, or lack of could have such consequences no matter how much it cost but it wouldn't be until years later, when a relationship of his own had fallen apart that he'd truly understand the situation. It wasn't, and never had been the gift itself that had almost led to his parents' separation; it was the lack of thought that it represented.

Noel come to realise that had his father never bought gifts of value, emotional or otherwise, it may not have mattered so much. What hurt his wife the most was that he used to; that his feelings towards her must be regressing until she feared there would eventually be none left at all. He'd begun to forget their anniversaries more and more often and when he did remember, his offerings had become less personal. But the only thing worse than forgetting totally was lying about the reason. She had made her feelings clear regarding his temper before so the last thing he could confront her with was what he believed to be the truth and so he had created a near perfect story as to why he was empty handed on another Christmas morning. He thought it through meticulously, planned every intricate detail and even sunk so low as to involve Noel who'd felt so guilty that he fully embraced the chance to try and help keep the peace. Not only had he participated, he'd made suggestions and pointed out flaws in the scheme until between the two of them they'd come up with the perfect story.

With the benefit of such unexpected hindsight, it was tragic that their teamwork had to be under such shameful circumstances but it did at least prove it was possible for them to work together. Afterwards Noel had shared a whole new batch of punch, stronger than before, not as a bribe as it wasn't needed; but as a reward for his loyalty. Reliving it now made Noel feel every bit as sick in the pit of his stomach as it had back then but in whichever time he focused his mind, it was already too late to change what had been done.

Both he and his father should have known that no matter how well thought out, the story might serve to cover the details of the actual events but it would never actually be believed as the truth. In the end, despite all their plotting it was the mannerisms learned over eighteen years of marriage rather than holes in the plot that revealed him as the liar he'd been forced to become.

Noel had said nothing until now. He would only know the date by the calendar, as it was at total odds with the atmosphere inside the house. It was different to any year he could remember. He'd seen the best and the worst of them in this house but each and every one had brought talk of the next without exception. Only this time when they spoke it was like there would never be another. Caroline played in the middle of the floor, still a little too young to notice anything was particularly wrong, but at fourteen Noel could see the signs and where they were leading. He'd secretly hoped that time would mend the damage the way he'd heard it could but his parents had only grown more distant as the time had gone on. It was more obvious tonight than it had ever been and it couldn't be clearer what would happen if he didn't do what had to be done.

Noel looked at his sister and wondered if she'd be playing just as happily if she had to choose which one of her parents she was to live with and which to see at weekends. The joint effort that could be heard in the kitchen now as their parents prepared the turkey together was reminiscent of what he now knew to be his first memory when they'd hauled that huge video camera above his cot like the partnership they were always meant to be; only now it was done in near silence. The raucous sound of kitchen utensils was the sole clue that they were even in there as neither of them said a word to each other. Their fractured relationship wasn't healing at all; the cracks were splintering outwards and could now not be far from reaching Caroline even if she didn't know it yet. For all the jealousy he felt towards her he cared about her but it had taken this to realise it.

Looking back now he was actually relieved to recall that he'd made his decision as much with her in mind as himself and that at least meant his humanity wasn't yet lost. For the two of them he'd found the courage he needed and got up off the sofa trying to subdue the thought of just how much easier this could have been if only he'd acted before the situation had become so desperate.

Caroline was hardly distracted from her game as her brother walked past and through the archway towards the smell of cooking but when he returned half an hour later she couldn't take her eyes off of his face. She watched him edge silently around her, turning away when he noticed her watching and disappeared up the stairs. At the time, Noel could have seen nothing of her once he'd ascended more than a few steps towards his bedroom, but now his vision remained long after it was physically possible. Intrigued, he watched her drop her toys without giving them another thought and walk determinedly after him as if nothing in the world could stop her. She marched on only to be scooped up by her dad before she'd even reached the stairwell yet still she tried to claw her way after him. Her loyalty was as surprising as it was touching, especially at such a young age. It again brought back the regret that he hadn't congratulated her on the successes she'd achieve just a few years from now rather than begrudging her them just because he couldn't match a single one. He wondered if she ever knew he'd felt that way and tried to comprehend why he could suddenly think of a thousand questions to ask her when he'd spent so long not even wanting to answer hers. She'd asked about this particular night every year, yet like the coward he was he'd avoided talking about it convincing himself that she wouldn't care anyway; once again he'd been corrected and he started to grow genuinely concerned at what, if anything he'd ever gotten right.

Whilst he had now reached the upstairs landing, he could still see his sister's face but had given up trying to guess at how as he thought he knew why. She looked like she could sense his pain as one floor above her he collapsed on his bed, face first and without even attempting to break his fall. He just wanted to fall asleep like the child he used to be and in some ways still was, but it was for all the wrong reasons and it was more difficult than ever.

This time he was grateful when another of the now familiar bursts took him away and to another time; a better time in such stark contrast it was hard to believe they were only a year apart. It was a chance to prove himself after having let people down so badly but he had at least achieved something. He was sure of that when he saw his parents enter the hall hand in hand and as close as they had ever been; they'd never let him forget what he had done but his confession had been worth it just to see them the way they should be again. Now he suspected they were the schemers as he was convinced the plethora of excuses they claimed would keep them from tonight were invented; he didn't blame them as they probably feared this would be a repeat of what had been his first, and up until now last stage performance and nobody had encouraged him to try again.

In fact, having merely suggested that he was trying for a major part in the school play everyone he knew had suddenly talked to him with an urgency he hadn't known for sometime. They discouraged him with varying advice, some more honest than others but the message was always the same; 'don't do it to yourself Noel.' Worried they might have a point, he'd auditioned in complete secrecy as far as his friends and family were concerned; he didn't want to give them the chance to wallow in the satisfaction of being right if he failed abysmally.

It turned out to be a wise move as he originally hadn't been cast in a leading role at all and with an ulterior motive for wanting to be part of the production that was of no use to him at all. He'd dropped out all together rather than form part of the chorus and instead offered to understudy for all the major male parts. This was unheard of in a school that placed little importance on drama, but for the put upon teachers it was a gift not to be dismissed. They'd been let down at the last minute every year as far back as they could remember and that was one of the many reasons they dreaded the nativity play and so snatched at Noel's offer as if it was solid gold.

Learning all of the lines and each of the songs was thought to be unrealistic in the dedicated rehearsal time they'd been given, but Noel was more than prepared to supplement it with his own. He did little in the evenings anyway other than draw pictures that he'd never show to anyone, so by sacrificing a few hours a night he was sure he could do what everyone was telling him he couldn't. He was certain because he had something the rest of his class did not... motivation; and there she was... Angela Goodhall.

She was by his side and together, they were in front of an audience but Noel was again able to separate his thoughts from his vision; he remembered how he got there and the memory was as bitter-sweet as he'd come to expect.

Over a month ago he'd begun watching Angela walk, almost glide on stage every Friday when the whole class were made to watch rehearsals and to join in where possible but if being an understudy gave him an excuse to see her five days a week that was fine by him. He'd shown very little interest in the dramatics society, in fact he felt self-conscious having to shout out his name at registration time but when she was cast without audition in the leading role that all changed.

It didn't take long for him to work his way up from backstage hand to onstage actor and he won his choice of two fairly minor roles when the Farell brothers were arrested for shoplifting just two weeks prior to the first show. They were subsequently banned from the school play as it was deemed inappropriate. Their parents argued that of course but it made no difference and as such, Noel had a decision to make. He surprised everyone by taking the lesser role, all the time worried that someone would work out why; that they'd suspect he was taking the character that had the most interaction with Angela but nobody ever did. It was probably because nobody really cared or it could have been because nobody ever associated his ignoring her for two years with him being obsessed with her. Despite being in the same class he'd never quite managed to bring himself to talk to her without an inexcusable reason but this was it if ever there was one. It might be scripted, but it was conversation.

His parents had grown used to Noel hiding away in his room from to time to time so had thought little of the hours he'd spent with the door shut, rehearsing his lines and singing under his breath, waiting until Thursday evenings; the only time in the entire working week when he had the place to himself and he could sing out loud. He was caught between wanting to practice as much as possible just on the off chance he'd get the opportunity to stand in as a lead and not wanting anyone, especially his parents to know how much he wanted to. He'd stopped telling Karl things like that as he knew how it sounded; he didn't want him or anyone else to think badly of his parents. They wouldn't try and stop him to be vindictive or even to save themselves the embarrassment they suffered last time. But they would intervene nevertheless even if it was only to protect him. They knew he wouldn't have the excuse of being seven years old this time around; he was more than double that age and they remembered all too well that teenagers were no more forgiving than children.

But even if he could convince them to let him make his own mistakes they'd never see the point. Theatre was art, like his drawing and his painting and just like them it was for people who couldn't do anything that had a point to it. In short, art was for dreamers and dreamers were never something that had run in his particular family. He didn't need to ask out loud to know what their opinion would be; he had no doubt they'd advise him that his time would be far better spent on homework than playing make believe. At times he thought about confessing his other reason for wanting to take part but guessed that it would only make them try harder to stop him as it would only open him up to greater potential hurt.

So he continued in secrecy whenever he had the chance and with the help of the school's sympathetic music teacher that turned out to be enough. As he grew in confidence he started leaving his script behind, certain of his lines long before the other, more experienced actors could even look up off the page. They arguably had more natural talent and certainly had more training but they just weren't taking it seriously. To them it was just the same old school play that they had to take part in because their parents insisted trying to justify the fees of their theatre coach. This only added to Noel's jealousy whenever he had to be within the same vicinity as Mike Fenton.

Mike not only got to play the part of Angela's husband, he didn't even seem to appreciate just how lucky he was. He had a strong voice that actually suited the musical arrangements the teachers had written but Noel quietly suspected that this was no coincidence and that they'd been composed with the spoilt bastard in mind. He gritted his teeth whenever anyone commented on how the songs complimented Mike's range but slowly he'd noticed that even Mrs. Britches was losing patience with her leading man as he continued to show less dedication than he owed her. Like every other teacher in the school, she thought her particular subject to be the most important and insisted on absolute commitment to her project whilst the students were pulled in every direction by every department. It was impossible to meet the conflicting demands; the only way was to choose what was important to you and to throw yourself into that whilst ensuring that homework was at least done on time and to an acceptable standard. Mike had made his choice and devoted the majority of his time to the sports in which he excelled and Noel was ready to take advantage of their differences.

It may have even been Noel's new found ability to leave his script behind that provoked Mrs. Britches frustration with the rest of the cast and their continued dependency, but what riled her most was the fact that so many pupils couldn't even remember to *bring* them. This lost about ten minutes at the start of every hour long rehearsal whilst scripts were copied and distributed until eventually she ran out of patience. She'd been particularly confident in her threats this year, perhaps knowing that she had an understudy for the first time allowed her more flexibility, but whatever her reasons she at last issued her ultimatum; that the next time somebody forgets their papers or their props they would be excluded from the production altogether.

For days Noel glowed with expectation but her warning appeared to have worked. Everyone involved had taken her seriously this time and their memory seemed to have instantly improved. With less than a week to go the cast remained unaltered but Noel noticed Mike walking around the hall looking uncharacteristically nervous. It was obvious from over heard conversations that the star of the show didn't have his script as he scanned the periphery of the stage. Noel found excuses to stay within ear shot and learned that it hadn't been forgotten, just misplaced and that it was definitely somewhere within the vicinity.

Never one to attract any particular attention Noel was able to move freely and unquestioned, scanning the floor, the seating and even the backstage area but still couldn't take his eyes off of Angela for long and he hated that he wasn't the only one. She continued to attract admiration wherever she went and pretended not to notice as she talked to her usual group of friends. Noel couldn't help but stare until one of them noticed so he quickly returned to his search and diverted his eyes to the floorboards again. He found himself staring at a slightly worn gym bag which certainly took second place by comparison but at least it was hers; and beneath it the corner of a dusty sheet of paper jutted out. He made his way over as close as he dared and nudged Angela's bag with his own. Able to see more of the paper, he was still unable to see the printed words but he could see that they were highlighted in luminous yellow, just like Mike's always were.

The sudden lull in the chatter that had filled the hall always meant the same thing… Mrs. Britches had entered and it forced Noel to make a decision that would have otherwise lingered. He dropped his bag, obscuring any clue as to what lie below it and made his way over to the others.

Exactly one wonderful week later the slightly revised cast met again but this time to prepare for their first performance and Angela laid her bag next to Noel's. A lot had changed since she'd watched him take the stage opposite her as her new husband. She had felt outraged that such major changes had been made so close to the first show and panic had rendered her unable to think clearly enough to realise that had the threat not been made reality, Mrs. Britches would never again be able to effectively direct her class. But for lack of options, Angela had initially taken her frustrations out on Noel; not because she disliked him particularly, she didn't even have an opinion on him but she knew that without him she'd still be singing with the same person with which she'd rehearsed all these weeks. Even the teacher had shown concern at the time left to perfect the several duets that formed the core of the show but nobody should have worried at all. All of the hours Noel had put in had paid off and now neither he, nor Angela could hide their smiles, yet nobody was more stunned than Noel himself. He looked visibly surprised at his own voice. He'd only ever practiced without accompaniment, but supported by the piano it sounded sweeter, the pitching more confident and the acoustics of the music hall helped him in ways his bedroom never could. His range might not equal Mike's, but he sang with feeling *to* Angela rather than at her; that alone made it sound twice as good to anyone who heard it… but none more so than his co-star.

Over the past seven days they'd both grown in their abilities and what had started out as an uneasy pairing had evolved into the onstage chemistry Mrs. Britches could previously have only hoped for.

And by the time the first performance was due the two of them had the confidence of the whole cast, their only concerns were that an audience may effect what had been going so perfectly. And it might have done had either of them even realised they were there, but when on stage together they paid little attention to anything or anyone but each other and by the time the closing bars were played Noel hardly heard the applause despite the fact his father was standing and clapping his hands above his head. The words didn't need to be said; the pair had become a couple and their worlds didn't need anyone else anymore.

If he hadn't remembered the metamorphosis himself and was watching what he was seeing now as an outsider looking in, he'd have never believed only twelve months had passed as the colours again faded to white only to re-emerge perfectly seconds later. He felt different, acted different and even looked a little more like the man he'd imagined himself to be. The stubble he'd waited for so patiently had grown to the extent that he could attempt shaping it even if it wasn't really thick enough yet but that was only one of the reasons he was treated unrecognisably. It seemed inconceivable that a single circumstance could affect so many areas of his life; but it undoubtedly did. And by the time December the twenty-fourth was ready to be crossed out on yet another calendar it seemed that even the worst days of the year just about to end surpassed any he'd spent before it. Not a single evening had expired since those rapturous applause a year ago in which he hadn't seen Angela. So many of his new found friends had started, finished and forgotten about their own relationships in a matter of months whilst Noel's remained everything he wished it would be... more in fact. Whenever he'd pictured what life would be like with her, he'd only ever imagined that the time they actually spent together would be affected; that every other aspect of his life would remain as it had been but the reality was almost the opposite.

It hadn't been that apparent in the days following the finale of the show that had started it all, as his school had met each other for the last time that year during that final performance and whilst suddenly eager to congratulate him, they were also keen to get home for the holidays. It meant that the hall had been virtually deserted when he and Angela shared that first kiss. Whilst both teenagers secretly hoped it was the start of something far more lasting, it hadn't seemed real to them until someone else knew about it. And as they were both far too embarrassed to tell their families their romance went unnoticed; they remained who they had always been... just happier. Even when they arrived at school together on the first day of the new term there was only a faint stirring throughout the corridors as everyone struggled to catch up before class and presents, parties and arguments were discussed in great detail. But the topic of conversation degenerated as the day wore on until the inevitable rumours started to circulate. Could *he* really be with *her*? Bets were made, supposed witnesses spoke out, stories were invented and in time, exaggerated. Both Noel and Angela lapped up the attention and reaped opposite benefits. He struck at base level and gained all the kudos of dating one of the most attractive girls in year eleven, knowing it was a poor excuse for popularity but making the most of it all the same. She broke barriers with that certain group of pupils that had always assumed her to be far too arrogant to go out with anyone that didn't have shelves full of sports trophies as testament to how superior they were. This small but influential group of academics had previously been all that had stopped her reaching the lofty honour of being voted head girl, but she'd shown another side to her and now, with their support there was nothing to stop her. By the next term the title was hers.

Noel too became a representative of his class without even trying. He hadn't really done anything different to before he was one half of the school's premier couple, it was just that it had at last been noticed. His paintings no longer hid behind inferior work but were held up as examples of creativity. His sketches apparently didn't make him weird anymore, merely talented. He had a voice he never knew existed, both when speaking in class and when singing as he was now encouraged to do, not only in music lessons but in assembly too. Nobody wanted to separate a winning team so he would always perform as a duo with the partner who made him what he had become and the duets could not be competed with by any of the countless impressionists that had begun to copy everything about them.

In hindsight, perhaps the adulation he enjoyed from his peers should not have come as such a surprise. Dating someone as popular as Angela was always going to at least raise his profile and all he'd needed, all he *ever* needed was for people to look and listen. And when they did they realised there was far more to him than the quiet boy who'd never sit near the front of the class and shied away from the football pitch. As a grown man he'd come to understand the shallowness of childhood and so could forgive the sudden change in attitude to some extent, but he always thought it wrong that even his teachers changed their attitudes towards him; they should have been unaffected by his classroom status but he couldn't see that back then. He just continued taking his opportunities where he found them. Eager to accept their sudden praise he had become too arrogant to realise how false it all was until it was too late.

Even his parents treated him differently. His mum was only too pleased not to have to worry what he was up to alone in his room as he now seemed permanently attached to someone he openly called his girlfriend. And for the first time his dad could see a possible financially secure future in his son's artistic abilities now that they were pointed out instead of condemned at parents evenings. Had Noel tried to convince him that he could pursue a career that embraced his talents he'd just have received the standard response detailing the merits of practical solutions to real and actual problems. The home they lived in and the holidays they enjoyed would be presented as testament to this. Yet now his father was reading the same arguments on report cards it appeared his opinion had changed completely. Suddenly he encouraged his son's music to the point that he paid for private tuition and even enrolled him at theatre school two evenings a week to Noel's absolute horror.

It was ironic that as soon as Noel's artwork had become appreciated, he lost interest in it completely, preferring instead to do nothing in particular with Angela; but that was not nearly as tragic as finding himself committed to a theatre course he'd only indulged as an excuse to talk to his obsession. His plan worked and served its purpose but had now backfired completely. He could see that his family's motives were unselfish, but with his father's hypocritical insistence that 'talent' as he now called it should be developed, Noel was a fully fledged member of the local dramatics society with no real interest in ever performing again.

The solution and compromise didn't take too much figuring out though and with Angela switching classes it meant another two nights together. They both dismissed warnings that spending too much time in each others company would become a problem. Sometimes they laughed off the accusations, on other occasions they defended their commitment to each other fiercely; it depended more on from whom the denunciation came from more than how it was worded but they always remained resolute. For three hundred and sixty four days they shared each other and their time without an angry word or even a disagreement. It would be an impressive achievement for mature adults but for the hormone fuelled sixteen year olds at Everstead College it was unheard of.

They ensured this was public knowledge and even boasted about how they'd spent an unblemished year together but they were premature. They'd only made it so far into December as they ignored the subject that could break them until the last possible minute but now it was again the twenty-forth day of the month and now they had to face it. It was the one hurdle that it would seem few couples could clear without falling. History was littered with the graves of relationships that had withered and died under the ultimate question… whose family should they spend their first Christmas together with?

Noel brought the subject up first. He was quietly confident that she understood his love of Christmas despite his occasional cynicism that he still carried around from eleven years ago but he tried to sneak it into the conversation just in case. The chance of her agreeing that the day should be spent at home with his family rather than hers without even noticing was certainly slim but it was worth trying. He had all his arguments ready and he could not put it off any longer. His defence mainly revolved around the fact that they spent most of their time at his home, so it was hardly fair to desert his family on the calendar's most special day. He doubted he'd need to make his point, but it was best to be prepared just in case it wasn't that easy. And it wasn't.

She'd quietly amassed an arsenal of weapons with which to counter attack and she wasn't at all afraid to use them. The row ignited and flared into a fireball that could not be controlled; having never fought before they had no idea how to handle it when they did. Noel had been so sure that it must surely mean that they weren't right for each other after all and had said as much out loud before he'd had a chance to think it through. With all the shouting still ringing in his ears he did little more than watch as she left without saying goodbye to anyone and slammed the front door behind her.

CHAPTER TWENTY

As the bus pulled away Evelyn matched its pace on foot and used it to shield her casual escape as she made her way further down the street and out of sight until she was no longer visible from the alleyway. She wasn't ungrateful for the handful of coins she'd been given and that was exactly why she didn't want to cause insult, but there was simply no way she was taking public transport. It wasn't her style these days but more to the point, it'd only bring back memories of her slightly eccentric but entirely protective father who took the bus rather than drive himself whenever he could. He'd ensure that they never had to share their space with anyone by enthusiastically beckoning whoever boarded to sit next to him; it was an absolute guarantee that they wouldn't and she smiled at the thought of him using human nature to his advantage and comfort. His reverse psychology seemed to work on almost anyone except her and the very few people who understood how his complex mind worked. She learnt to avoid thinking about him for too long and it was a good excuse to look for a more comfortable form of transport and the thought of sitting amongst so many staring eyes in her state of undress didn't make it anymore appealing.

Convinced that she'd kept up for long enough, she allowed herself to slow to a mere walk and at least partially indulge her knees that had been screaming at her to stop. It also gave her a chance to think without interruption for the first time since she's been launched down those steps. She'd known precisely what she didn't want to do but hadn't had time to consider the options available, yet she had a habit of finding them where most people couldn't. She looked around, twirling on the spot to save twisting her neck again. She sighed knowing she was already a physical wreck and it wasn't even seven O'clock yet.

She certainly couldn't go on like this, at lunch time today she'd told herself that she was fine... she even believed it for an hour or so, but now it seemed like an eternity ago. But at least it had existed at some point in history; she certainly couldn't see it in the future anymore, however distant. It hadn't always been the case but what little hope there had been was repeatedly kicked out of her, sometimes quite literally. Each time she'd slipped a little further down the tunnel, but with the very last shaft of light that had been her job she'd dared to believe again.

It wasn't a career everyone would be proud of but it was one that paid; and more importantly, it was one that came with accommodation. She looked up the wall of the building to where she should have been staying tonight... it was true she'd let them down again but she never thought they'd take it this far on Christmas Eve. She'd need to hold onto that; it was someone else's fault and all the time that was the case she deserved sympathy, Champagne and sympathy. But as the clarity of soberness began descending slowly, she considered the possibility that perhaps this time she'd given them no choice. She tried to remember whether it was eight or nine 'last chances' they'd relented now and was certain that if she could remember that many, then in reality it was more likely to be twice the amount.

If she really had brought this on herself, how many other people had she falsely accused for various unenviable situations? Maybe she didn't deserve Champagne *or* sympathy, let alone both; and if that was the case, perhaps she wasn't entitled to any of the things she'd felt deprived of... she didn't like the way this thought process was going and so repressed it. It was always satisfying to do what she was good at and with so much experience she was an expert at this.

She looked down again at the change still clasped in her hand and then in the opposite direction, directly up towards the clock tower high above her, the crowning glory of the once powerful Wainsbridge Media corporation but she assumed even they'd fallen on bad times recently as they'd began to sell the uppermost offices to be converted into flats. She'd heard that since the owner lost his wife, he lost his grip on the company to some extent as well; it was strangely reassuring to know that even the rich had their weaknesses but right now it wasn't helping. Even if he had to sell off half the building, it was still vast and she couldn't even look forward to a bed that night. Everyone claims to have their problems but as far as she was concerned they should put them into perspective.

She suddenly noticed just how far the enormous minute hand had moved and just how much time she'd spent doing nothing more than thinking; wishing even and gazing at what was usually the tallest point of the city. It had been superseded now though by the neon star, taking the honour and hovering at least thirty foot above. It reigned supreme for one month a year and it would again be the case until the first week of January. At night you couldn't see the thick scaffolding pole that held it there and it appeared to hang in the sky as if by magic, but magic was illusion and for the first time she was starting to realise exactly that. It had to have something propping it up, and so did she. If just looking at it made things clearer, it wasn't so impossible that being close to it would hold all the answers. She walked towards it as if each step nearer would lead to a solution she'd never considered until now without contemplating why but her path was blocked. Yet another victim of the crawling traffic had broken down and been pushed to the side of the road. She assumed it had just overheated but it was hard to believe it could happen to even the oldest of motors in these freezing temperatures yet still the steam rose the second its owner lifted the bonnet. He noticed her looking and felt the need to offer his explanation, possibly to prove he knew what he was talking about.

'Piston broke' he shouted above the din of the road. Evelyn wasn't sure whether his diagnosis was aimed at his vehicle or her but either way she didn't doubt he was right. She just didn't know how he could tell by looking but she was indeed still nowhere near sober and the fistful of coins in her hand was all the money she had to her name… but it might just be all she needed. The vapour continued to engulf the car and had forced the queue behind to come to a complete standstill as they could barely see to overtake. The taxi that was now trapped three cars back was a familiar sight at this time of year but all she could see was the angle. She rushed forward, almost tripping over a dog which didn't seemed at all bothered despite the fuss her owner was making over her as he checked she was alright; Evelyn just rolled her eyes and ignored his cursing.

She peered through the window and pulled open the cab door. She was relieved to see a friendly face; at least by comparison to those that had stared back at her so far tonight but it wasn't without understandable shock. It said everything as she stood there dressed for the stage but it wasn't mentioned. The driver was either being compassionate or was totally apathetic. She hoped for the latter and upon further inspection became sure it wasn't the case. He certainly appeared to have all of the attributes essential to her scheme so she persevered. The lack of questions had saved her the embarrassment of answering and for that she was grateful. If he wanted to pretend to ignore the obvious, that was fine with her.

'Hey…' she paused searching the dashboard for his identification, '… Joe!' she completed her greeting with such a friendly and familiar tone he was half convinced he must know him. Plenty of people seemed to around here.

'Merry Christmas to ya!' she continued, suddenly aware she might be over doing it.

'And the same to you Miss; so where are you headed tonight' he replied. He didn't want to appear abrupt or unconcerned; the girl was quite obviously injured but the traffic would soon start to build behind him and the car in front seemed to be readying itself to pull away. Evelyn didn't even know the answer to the question and so simply ignored it.

'Whereabouts are you headed?' he semi-repeated. 'As that depends whether I can take you. I can't go too far a field as I'm due home soon.'

It wasn't a total lie; he was eager to get home but he could be a little late if it brought more money in but he was trying to find excuses. The near total gridlock was sending his equivalent per mile rate to an all time high and he'd already had two customers short change him this evening after realising they couldn't afford the fare and he doubted he'd ever receive the cheques they'd promised, but at least they paid the majority; his last fare had simply fled upon mention of the charge and disappeared into the crowd. It wasn't that he didn't care about the girl; she was in obvious need of a little charity but he just couldn't return home having worked Christmas Eve with little to show for it, not after the arguments his overtime had already caused.

'And in this traffic even short journeys are working out costly' he added. He was quietly ashamed of just how enthusiastically observant he'd been, but he assured himself that even the most faithful of men couldn't have failed to notice her lack of clothes. They left little to his imagination but he couldn't help but look for a pocket, a purse or anywhere she could keep some form of payment, but she interpreted his glances otherwise. She looked down at herself, mimicking his darting eyes and faking offence instantly gaining advantage of the situation and forcing Joe to stutter an apology, unable to bring himself to challenge her intentions.

'I'm sorry... I just, well I didn't expect...'. Having drawn him into conversation Evelyn wasted no time and was half way inside the cab before he could limp to the end of his sentence. She'd slammed the door shut behind her before she'd even landed in the passenger seat. With the difficult part behind her she smiled her most innocent looking smile. She knew it looked at odds with everything else about her so she exaggerated her shivering just incase it was not obvious enough already.

Joe just stared at her, careful to not break respectful eye contact this time. Now he'd have to level with her but with every second he saw himself reflected in those pleading eyes it become more unlikely he'd be able to throw her back out into the cold; against his better judgment he decided he might as well just take her anyway and rely on her honesty. Maybe she'd have cash at home; she wouldn't be the first not to have it on her. He reluctantly surrendered.

'So where to?' He was already a little tired of asking.

'Well can you take me uptown please?'

'Sure, which part?'

'All of me' she replied. It was her joke and even she hated it but it kept her talking and made it easier to judge the man in the driver's seat. The fact that he bothered to fake a laugh said volumes about him.

'Do you know exactly where you want to go... or where it's near at least? Just uptown's not particularly specific?'

'I've only ever been by train so I couldn't direct you via the roads, but it's near Cuddlestone Park'.

'That's miles away isn't it? That'd take best part of two hours *without* traffic? It's uptown alright but it's not even in *this* town?'

'So then you'll have a very merry Christmas with no money worries won't you?' she chirped motioning towards his meter but despite her perfect smile she shifted nervously in her seat. Joe took his eyes away from hers and stared in the rear view mirror at the traffic queue forming behind him; it was the perfect excuse to look away.

'I can't' he muttered as if he didn't want to be heard. Evelyn's face started to drop realising this may not be as easy as she'd imagined.

'I would, its just I've really got to get back... the kids will be waiting up for me' he lied. They'd be going to bed right about now and once he'd missed that critical moment, the urgency of his return dropped considerably.

'I've got twins you know... both the same age' he offered, hoping his lame joke may soften what was fast becoming an awkward atmosphere and in a attempt to reverse the sympathy vote but Evelyn didn't give in so quickly; she couldn't. She answered without extending him the courtesy he'd shown her and didn't even portray a sign of amusement.

'Then you'll need the cash' she retorted. 'And the sooner we go, the sooner you'll be back home'.

She honestly thought she'd retained her winning smile but it had become little more than a grimace and Joe hadn't so much as moved, let alone backed down.

'And I can pay if that's what you're worried about?' her tone of voice had changed and it made what had been an impossible situation a little easier on Joe. Her sudden sarcasm had dislodged her halo; he'd be able to face her again. 'Not right now obviously, but when we get there I'll pay you... and for any time you have to spend waiting for me to write the cheque' she continued. 'Unless of course you'd rather someone else earned the money?' she added, raising her hands, her father's favoured reverse psychology her new weapon of choice.

'Believe it or not, I'd rather that, tonight anyway. That's how important it is that I'm not late back' Joe sighed. 'But there're plenty of us around this evening, you shouldn't have too much trouble finding another cab.' He knew that was unlikely to be true for two reasons at least. Partly due to the overwhelming demand, but also because she was unlikely to find such a naïve taxi driver anywhere else on these streets.

Evelyn was the first to break this time and looked away, pretending to be distracted by the view from her window and buying herself time to think. She hadn't expected that response but she knew it was a lie or he'd have simply radioed his base for another car. Either he was sure they'd all be booked or he knew her game... more likely both. He'd probably seen straight through her as apparently it wasn't so hard and that would mean he knew he wouldn't be getting paid.

Joe's eyes wandered again with the new opportunity to double check what he'd thought he'd seen; it was surreal but it was true. She'd covered the wound as she got in but seemed to have forgotten about it if that were possible. He could see the blood smeared in an attempt to disguise it but the streaking had only made it more obvious.

'Whereabouts are you bleeding from?' he asked reluctantly, not sure he should be restarting a conversation.

'Never mind where I'm bleeding from, you just worry about where I want to bloody go like any other cab driver'.

Joe wasn't certain at first whether it was another awful joke but it appeared not; she'd genuinely misinterpreted his meaning and whilst he didn't deserve the reply he got, it did say a lot about the way she was obviously used to being spoken to.

Joe continued slyly, trying to look for the wound itself but the investigation could be worse. Even an average looking girl of her age would attract attention dressed like that, but with the exception of the blood still trickling down her leg she was perfect, or as close to it as he'd ever seen.

Evelyn turned sharply back only to catch his gaze before he could realign it.

'I saw you looking earlier'. Her voice had softened again, almost to a purr. 'I take it you like what you see?' She gave him little time to respond before continuing, much to Joe's relief as he had no idea how to answer that. She placed her hand on his thigh and squeezed gently, turning in her seat to strike a more inviting posture.

'I've told you I can pay' she insisted 'so I assume you don't want my money? So what exactly do you want Joe Cribley?' she asked having glanced again at his badge. That trick had always worked for her. Using their name; their full name if possible made it more personal whilst making them feel important. She had a talent for making people believe she thought of them in the same way they thought of her, however unlikely it was. She had the ability not only to change their world, one minute at a time but more importantly, to change their perceived place within it; in their own mind at least. They'd convince themselves that she was with them because she wanted to be and that they were the exception to the rule.

It would be more work for her this way, but it might just be for the best. It would save her having to run to escape the fare on injured legs as the pain wasn't easing and besides, he wasn't so bad. Significantly older and a little indecisive for her but he was far from repulsive and that was increasingly becoming a treat. She ran her hand further along his leg, not realising she was staining his trousers with the blood she'd tried to wipe away earlier; she was too busy feeling proud as her gesture alone appeared to alter his breathing.

'I'd be worth being late for. I wouldn't like to promise that you wouldn't regret it, but I'm a confident girl' she whispered incase encouragement was needed as the agitated traffic behind were about to force him to make a decision imminently, she just had to make sure it was the right one for her. She looked down.

'I see you like me then?' she teased taking advantage of how obvious men's thoughts could be.

Joe had to virtually sit on his hands but spoke slowly and determinedly forcing the words out as if he was unaffected.

'I wasn't lying that I have twins at home. But they could already be in bed so they might not be waiting for me'.

Evelyn was relieved. That was an example of twisted self justification if ever she'd heard one and she'd witnessed more than a few.

'... but their mother... my *wife* will be.'

The two looked at each other; neither of them had been in such a situation for years. In Evelyn's case it was nearly a decade since she'd failed to turn a man's most basic instincts to her advantage, but she'd been no more than a schoolgirl back then. She'd never really forgotten how a man of principal rendered her powerless but as she hadn't met one since, it was easy to try. When Mr. Coals had declined her offer it was because he'd have been risking his career, his reputation and even his liberty. All she'd wanted was the guarantee of a pass grade at biology but at the time she hadn't even been adult enough to see the obvious humour in that. She'd made it clear that she'd be generous in acknowledging any help he was willing to give but apparently that wasn't quite enough. His response was more than professional, it was even cold. She'd told him outright that she'd do anything to pass and he suggested revising before opening the classroom door for her to leave. It had dislodged her confidence for a while but now she understood just how inexperienced she was back then. The possible repercussions of accepting her proposal were so much more severe that it made it less attractive. She was less of a risk now and therefore a lot more tempting... and she knew it.

Evelyn moved forward but got no closer as Joe reclined at the same pace. She paused just for a moment before sinking back down in her seat like a student that had just been reprimanded. She didn't have a third plan in place; she'd never had to. Faced with a lack of feasible options she even considered just telling the truth and the whole sorry story but it just didn't seem believable enough. If she struggled to accept it why would a stranger? But she could at least try and explain why she had to make it to Cuddleston Street and plead with him to take her there but she didn't think about it for long. Even having just offered so much for so little, begging was still a step too far and she doubted it'd work anyway.

Struggling to control her anger and without a word she went to get out of the cab but this time he reached for her. That was more like it... she'd got to him alright and this was the delayed reaction. She turned to face him again with the first genuine smile of the week.

'I can't take you to where you asked, but I can take you to hospital. We'll be there in less than twenty minutes even in this traffic and you can get that looked at' suggested Joe nodding towards her knee. 'You might even need stitches.'

Evelyn didn't want to waste anymore of his time explaining why she wouldn't accept. There was no point. It was irrational and all she needed was someone else telling her that and Joe seemed genuinely kind enough that he'd take the time to try. She opened the door and swung out her legs but was grabbed again, this time on the shoulder. Joe reached onto the back seat before offering her the raincoat that lay there. Neither could think of the words to say so they both stopped trying. The horns continued to sound behind them and Evelyn stepped back out onto the road lost in a feeling she'd never known.

Evelyn knew she should thank him; she even wanted to but she waited until the taxi had actually pulled away to do so.

CHAPTER TWENTY-ONE

Even now, Noel still found himself blinking in the aftermath of the flash that transported him forward in time and he found himself single again as he knew he would. Angela hadn't come crawling back to him in the New Year the way he'd been promised but he'd eventually stopped waiting for her to miss him and had at last listened to his friend's advice. He still had plenty and even without being part of such a popular couple, the fact that he *had* been remained and he manipulated it for all it was worth. To listen to him anyone would think he'd simply outgrown Angela and the decision to break up was his entirely; it allowed him to maintain a grip on the image he'd gained and he'd play the part as long as anyone would watch. Tonight was a condemning example of just how far he'd go to keep what could be so easily lost.

Whilst he'd enjoyed the praise and thanks at the time it was largely due to his ability to believe what he wanted to and to manipulate others until they did the same. He'd passed his driving test earlier that year on his third attempt but so few people knew it wasn't his first that even he had started to believe it. He'd spent an unfeasible amount of money on a car that he could barely afford to insure but the fact that the bank owned everything but the steering wheel was again only known by those who absolutely had to. The type of person that could attract a girl like Angela was expected to drive nothing less than a three litre engine car and so that gave Noel no option but to live up to his own manufactured image; even if it meant working every hour he wasn't at college in a job he was too embarrassed to mention.

As he steered his defining possession around a particularly tight curb he couldn't help but think about his real friends who he'd all but driven away. They weren't as exciting or glamorous as those that he associated with now but he wouldn't have anything to prove with them either. He could have spent the evening in their company or have returned home but his parents had many of the family visiting and that would mean one thing; detailed discussion about Caroline's latest accomplishments which gave him just two options. The first was to involve himself enthusiastically; the second was to be all but ignored. Neither particularly appealed to him tonight.

Instead he bypassed the whole ordeal by taking a change of clothes to his part-time job with the intentions of heading straight to the local bar as soon as he and his overworked colleagues were dismissed. Most of them had the same idea and had accompanied him there, leaving their own cars at the office. Some only stayed a few hours before ordering a taxi home but they were replaced by others who'd gone home to change and returned ready to celebrate until closing time. And on it went, the constant replacement of co-workers and acquaintances keeping the gathering at a fairly constant number and his image alive both to himself and anyone else detached enough from the crowd to notice. He'd tell everyone who'd listen that he'd not been there that long himself and with nobody except the barman to prove him a liar he hadn't had to explain why he had nothing better to do.

At first he'd avoided alcohol, aware of the lengthy stretch that lay before him. Everyone had been allowed to finish work early despite the fears they wouldn't and whilst he could drink with the best of them, with around nine hours ahead of him before last orders he thought it best to pace himself. He'd start later knowing that once he begun he was he'd unlikely to hold back and would become a victim of his own increasingly excessive nature. He figured drinking himself into oblivion would erase the loneliness that today had only amplified whilst simultaneously avoiding another sleepless night. It might even mean he could shorten Christmas day itself and remain unconscious until at noon. His sense of worth was now indelibly linked to his popularity, however fabricated and a day without his public meant a day in reality and they could never pass quickly enough.

The afternoon passed like it was impersonating an entire day and when closing time eventually came he staggered out of the bar doors, flinging them open with twice the force he needed like a cowboy leaving a saloon; it was like he was desperate to leave until that point but then he just stood there almost motionless as they hit the wall and bounced back toward him. It was only the pistons at the hinges that slowed their return, allowing him to catch them again and save himself from being knocked backwards.

Having made his way outside using the wall to stabilise himself, the prospect of him crossing the car park without anything to prop him up amused the growing audience. Some laughed out loud, too drunk themselves to consider the repercussions whilst others watched in horror and concern as Noel awkwardly pulled his car keys from his pocket; one couple in particular studied him more carefully than the others.

Noel took a moment to steady himself then proceeded, literally holding his arms out to balance himself. His intense concentration was rewarded by allowing him one foot in front of the other in a slow but relatively straight line. He smiled arrogantly as he crossed the even ground, impressed with what he was accomplishing but then tripped on the first curb he came across. He was overtaken by revellers who left their seats some time after him but had reached their own cars, got in, started the ignition and driven away before Noel had even reached his vehicle. By the time he'd finished stumbling across the gravel many of the parking bays had emptied.

Noel had been followed but had moved so slowly it made trailing him difficult and caused his pursuers to engage in false conversation just to stall but now they kept a discreet but watchful eye on him as he spent another few minutes just separating his car keys from the others. They stayed in the shadows as he made several attempts at unlocking his car door before falling into its bucket seat.

He sat there a few moments taking deep breaths before attempting to find the ignition, aware of being approached as the engine fired. He over revved and slowly slipped the gear into first but moved it back into neutral, freeing his hand to depress the button just a few inches away. The knocking on his window ceased as soon as it began to slide down.

'What's up?' he asked, blurring both words into one to the point it was difficult to distinguish them. Past the man and woman standing directly beside him he could see the car park empty further and that he was now the subject of considerable attention. People waved to him and blew him kisses as they left the grounds and made their way home.

'Evening, is this your car?'

'Sure is, I get asked that a lot. I know I look a little young but I figure I'll grow into it eh?'

'I guess, given time. You like a drink or two?'

'Certainly do! I'm a vodka man myself. I've not got any in here though if that's what you're hoping?'

Both of the strangers ignored the slightly odd assumption that might have been humorous under less serious circumstances, but they also supposed that being approached by an unidentified couple would leave the driver little choice but to grasp at whatever seemed even slightly logical in his current state.

'Would you be able to tell us where you're headed right now?'

'That's a strange way to ask for a lift but if I'm going your way… why not? I expect cabs are hard to come by and besides, it's Chris… Chris…' he kept pronouncing the 't' in Christmas as a 'sh' and had his sentence finished for him.

'It's Christmas alright but we have no intention of getting in your car with you'.

'Why not? It's nice?'

The more human of the two strangers almost sniggered but straightened her face instantly when she realised her partner had noticed and had answered without a hint of amusement.

'It's very impressive indeed. Must have cost a fair few pennies

I'd imagine?' surmised the immaculately dressed gentleman now standing back and admiring the machine. 'But for a start it's only got one spare seat?'

'Then I'll just have to choose one of you' Noel replied looking at the woman directly and winking when he had her attention. Unimpressed on every level, her partner bent down and learned into Noel's car.

'Alright, alright man, I get it... she's with you yeah?' spat Noel trying to get the words out as quickly as he could. Without any acknowledgement he was asked to get out of his car, the fact that he was talking to plain clothes police officers apparently justification for leaving the comfort of his heated seat.

'If you insist' was his sarcastic response. There were still a few witnesses left staring from their own windscreens as he exited the car.

'Officer, I know your job goes on whether it's the holidays or not but I've got people to see' added Noel.

'Well you should have thought about that earlier, they're going to have to wait now. I can't imagine you're that eagerly awaited in this state.' His typically condescending manner was bordering on stereotypical but was unusually accurate even if his justification was not. Nobody was anticipating his arrival, eagerly or otherwise and Noel shot him with a look that betrayed his formerly glazed expression.

'Now assuming you're capable we're going to have to ask you to blow into this tube as we need to establish whether your alcohol level is over and above the legal limit.'

'There's really no need at all officer, I've not touched a drop, honest.'

Both officers were unconvinced and staggered at the blatancy yet he continued to be insistent.

'Seriously, not a drop. See?' Noel stood on one leg, unsteady but continuously for sometime whilst both officers took it in turns to recite the official lines they were required to in readiness for the easiest arrest of their careers. They'd finished long before Noel had tired of trying to prove himself sober via various balancing acts; they were entertained but undeterred.

'Look!' commanded Noel. 'No need to even dirty the tube!' He was ignored completely and handed the breathalyser without the dignity of a response. He took it guessing he'd delayed proceedings enough and exhaled fully, surprising the police woman particularly who was expecting a half hearted attempt in the vain hope that his consumption wouldn't register; she'd seen that trick more times than she cared to think about. Noel handed the breathalyser back with surprising confidence. The police woman forced her way past her partner to receive it and left him to take Noel by the arm and to read him his rights.

'Aren't we being a little hasty sir?' enquired Noel as the woman hadn't even looked at the reading yet. As a formality she indulged him. She examined the display, then looked closer as her pompous expression changed. She gave it back to Noel insisting he blew harder this time. He obeyed; but not before questioning them again.

'So how many accidents would you say are attributed to drunk drivers officer?' asked Noel frowning as he said it to indicate concern. The policewoman obliged and answered him straight.

'Nearly ten percent, now please blow into the tube.' She'd lost any signs of a personal approach that had been evident earlier, yet still Noel remained helpful; he formed his words clearly this time.

'Well are you sure you're targeting the right people as surely there are stone cold sober drivers out there causing over ninety percent of the problem!' Still they remained stone faced and insistent.

'Just blow into the tube.'

Having made his point Noel did as he was ordered and even excelled the effort that could reasonably be expected of him before dutifully returning the device. She'd watched him with unfaltering attention but he hadn't tried to cheat in any way. She again checked the display then handed it over for a second opinion. The impatient looking man who refused to let go of Noel took just one look before releasing his grip on what he had been so convinced was a drunkard's arm.

'Why look so shocked?' questioned Noel as he straightened his clothes and tucked his shirt back into his trousers. 'It's nothing I didn't tell you if you're honest, assuming you're capable' he added remembering their sarcasm towards him and no longer bothering to go to the effort of slurring his words.

'But zero? You even admitted drinking?' insisted the woman trying to sound casual as if she wasn't disappointed.

'I admitted liking a drink or two. I very much enjoyed my last Vodka just a few days ago in fact. But I told you straight that I hadn't been drinking tonight... I think hadn't touched a drop were my actual words' Noel motioned to get back in his car.

'Wait just a minute!' demanded the more visibly confused of the two officers but his partner having deduced exactly what was going on lay her hand on his forearm in a gesture designed to subtly encourage him to let it go with the least possible embarrassment.

'Wait for what exactly?' questioned Noel. 'I'm as sober as the two of you; my car's fresh from the showroom and hasn't done three thousand miles yet so I'd be surprised if it wasn't road worthy... I'm not even guilty of lying to you!' There was no response at all so he continued playing to what little audience remained knowing that word would get around, 'so if you'll excuse me officers, I'll wish you seasons greetings and be on my way'.

With that he sank back into the warmth of his leather seat and slammed the door on them both. He wondered what they were saying as he drove away and it made him smile.

Once out of sight he switched his mobile back on and the messages began to pour in with one text alert failing to finish before the next had even started. He thought he'd be able to wait until he got home to read them but didn't even make it halfway. He pulled over into a bus stop and had hardly applied the handbrake before he was speeding his phone's cursor through its commands. He instructed it before the options even appeared on screen and become impatient when it took too long to respond but he was at least quietly grateful that it was picking up signal for once

The first few messages were very similar, basically congratulating him with assurances that he was owed whatever favours he'd need in the future. It made him grin if only to himself. He couldn't take sole credit for the plan but he deserved considerable praise for its perfect execution. The high pitched bleeping of his message alerts continued so frequently that he couldn't answer them as fast as they were coming in. So instead of reading them all in order he began scanning for who they were from instead. There were a few surprises including thanks from those who had never really made an effort with him and even those he'd sometimes got the feeling didn't particularly like him but tonight it seemed he was everyone's friend. He'd never really understood those people; there were more of them than he felt comfortable with but now he could see what they saw. All it took was viewing himself from a different angle; someone else's perspective. Having had his life analysed by a virtual stranger in the short time he'd spent above the clock tower he'd had doubts about himself; now, having sped vertically past it he was certain. Almost everything that attracted people to him was fake, bought and the result of endless pretence.

With hindsight Noel knew that his performance back then had done little other than generate gratitude in those he'd allowed to drive home illegally. He'd since even thought they *should* have been arrested yet at the time he couldn't think so selflessly; he had been as pleased with himself as he could possibly be. But he had ceased to be proud of such recklessness years ago and now he was no less than disgusted with his behaviour. It was hard to watch.

For over a decade now he'd counted himself lucky if anything worked out in his favour at all so this was more than he'd hoped for; he'd made new friends *and* upstaged the authorities but they were both insignificant compared to what else he'd achieved... he'd won Angela's attention again.

Her name was amongst many others on his mobile's display screen, but it seemed to glow a little brighter than the rest. He hadn't seen her number displayed since he'd given up sending texts intending to provoke some kind of response from her, but there it was; and it was not in reply either. It was totally voluntary... unless of course she'd sent it by mistake. It annoyed him that he should jump to that conclusion but all kinds of doubts had slowly crept into him like rot recently. He hesitated to read it just in case he was right, scared that it might totally ruin what was already likely to be an unspectacular Christmas but he couldn't stop himself. It was certainly for him and judging by the language he imagined Angela would rather it stay that way. His performance and questionable morality had shown her another side of him and as far as she was concerned, it was a far more interesting side than the sensitive soul she'd believed him to be.

She'd be drunk by now. He knew that much as she was a long way from sober when he noticed her but pretended not to this afternoon. But thanks to his charade in the car park she'd been saved an expensive taxi fare as the police watched him unflinchingly and ignored the inebriated swarm as they headed towards their cars whilst the law's back was turned. To someone like Angela that would make him a hero; the man of the moment as he had been when they met two years ago and nothing else could attract her attention more. Noel knew he was being used but the pride he had left didn't seem worth saving and with a proven ability to ignore the facts, her offer didn't need thinking about.

He typed a reply as suggestive as he dared and pulled away again... fast. She was famously indecisive and he didn't want her sobering up or having too long to consider the repercussions. The more he thought about what could be, the heavier his foot pressed on the accelerator but he watched his speedometer intently knowing there was a good chance the officers he'd left behind would follow him, praying for him to break the speed limit. He imagined even the slightest deviation from a text book perfect manoeuvre would be enough for them to pull him over now. Yet knowing how careful he had to be he could still not resist carefully typing his replies to Angela's increasingly obscene messages whenever they arrived, convinced that any delay could be the excuse she needed to change her mind.

He stayed within one mile of the speed limit but maintained it around bends that would be impossible in almost any other car. His eyes rotated in a manner that almost became ritualised... phone, road, speedometer, road, rearview mirror, phone, road, speedometer, road, rearview mirror... As he predicted a patrol car emerged from the darkness behind at a distance just short of harassment. He shook his head whilst keeping a watchful eye; after all the things he'd done to try and win her back, it wasn't until he'd truly given up that she showed any interest at all. He wondered if that was coincidence or if it was the exact opposite; whether the very act of ignoring her was what he should have done all along. He was also very aware of the similarities between the response to his performance tonight and the show he'd achieved on the school stage. Both had resulted in near instant popularity that outshone her own. He tried to ignore it and drove on, he wouldn't let that thought or any other ruin the night's double victory and convinced himself that she wanted him for all the right reasons.

Having grown used to the headlights coming towards him, the light wasn't so disorientating this time. It usually faded to reveal a different scene entirely but he found himself still alone, away from home and surrounded by darkness only now there was no windscreen to keep him from the elements. Noel remembered thinking how typical it was that it snowed this year; the one time he could remember having to be patient outside in the cold for anything.

So far as he could tell, he was always thrown forward into the next Christmas Eve at whatever time of the day would teach him the most. Without a clock in sight, his only clue on this occasion was that it was already dark; *very* dark and he hadn't met her yet so that narrowed his guess to within just a few hours. Judging by the fact that his own footprints were already beginning to disappear, he knew this must be sometime into what he remembered was a frustratingly long wait. It seemed just as ridiculous now as it had done then; more so in fact as he knew he should have listened and saved himself a lot of pain. Having watched what he went through when Angela had refused to return his calls, Noel's parents had made it difficult for him to spend time with her even after they'd got back together. They weren't so naïve as to try and ban them from seeing each other but they could rule out meeting in their family home. For a while it hadn't caused much of a problem and the couple had simply met at her mother's house until the reason they had to come out in conversation and she took such offence that she enforced identical rules.

The two of them had gone through the summer meeting in secret to avoid as many lectures as possible despite both being adults. Without a place of their own it was the easiest option, or at least it had been until this weather arrived. Noel daren't even attempt to take a rear wheel drive sports car out in these conditions and so having walked for half an hour, he now waited as long again for his girlfriend to arrive. He hated the term 'girlfriend'. .. it didn't seem enough anymore. She was more than that as Noel failed to see anything but the good in her. He'd buried every other concern about her so deeply he'd literally forgotten they ever existed.

He looked at his watch again, checked the time and raised his head just in time for an exceptionally well packed snowball to hit him square in the face. It seemed anything but playful but he gritted his teeth, restraining himself from launching an equally aggressive attack on the figure peeping from behind a relatively distant wall. He awaited an apology assuming her aim was off but apparently that wasn't the case. The pain should have eased almost instantly in such extreme cold but it hadn't; he thought of all the things he wanted to say then replaced it with a sickly sweet greeting if only to ensure a similar reply but all he received was a horrified look that worsened with her every approaching step.

'What? What's the matter?' questioned Noel, looking behind him wondering what could cause such a reaction, but it soon became clear that Angela was looking right at him. When he opened his mouth to again ask her why the taste of blood was unmistakable.

Almost an hour later the two of them sat in the accident and emergency centre waiting for his broken nose to be seen to. The bleeding had nearly stopped but not before the loss had taken its effect and left him feeling slightly detached from the world around him. It had taken so long to get there and he'd bled most of the way leaving a worryingly clear trail in the snow. He watched Angela who also looked like her mind was somewhere else. She'd been uncharacteristically quiet and now sat looking at the floor. He felt sorry for her; it was an accident after all and she had been so excited about the meal they had booked with her friends, some of whom he'd never met.

'Maybe you should still go?' he suggested thinking his question to be rhetorical.

'I can hardly go when you're in this state can I?'

Again hers was anything but a question and so was answered as expected rather than with what she meant.

'You can't really help here can you? We could be here for ages and there's little point in us both going hungry is there?'

Had she been looking at him she'd have seen the disbelief on his face as she lifted herself off of her seat and began to straighten her many layers of clothes in preparation to leave.

'You'll catch me up then?' Her straight face and sincere tone indicated she was serious. Noel got up too. He'd be better off standing to unleash everything he had to say but again he held his tongue. Rising so quickly had made the world spin around him again and he had to pause to establish his balance. The few seconds it took gave him time to think and to realise this wasn't the time. There were a surprising amount of people around and that in itself would be to her advantage. He'd become embarrassed long before she would, and by the time the inevitable shouting began he'd already be trying to calm the situation not wanting to attract an audience. If he fought his case now he'd have only two options and neither were attractive; he could surrender again the second it became heated or he could stand his ground only to spend tomorrow alone. This conversation would be more appropriate in private and waiting for that opportunity would give him chance to think things through anyway. He kept telling himself there would be a better time as the confrontation would not be easy anyway bearing in mind that he had just technically *told* her to leave; and at least this way he wouldn't have to wonder if he was single or not until Boxing Day. All of these thoughts busied his clouded brain to the extent that he couldn't stop his initial reaction in time. Even having decided against using the words they rang out regardless with all the urgency he felt.

'Don't you walk away Angela!' He winced as she turned around instantly. She looked through the top of her eyes at him in the way she always had done when she was waiting for him to do something she'd make him regret.

'We haven't even exchanged presents yet?' It was an obvious but believable recovery. She walked back towards him but her expression softened with every step before she kissed him on his jaw, she couldn't reach any higher and Noel daren't lower his angle so soon after the flow had clotted, in fact he tried not to change position at all.

'We'll do it later shall we?' It was another one of those orders that could be denied should it ever be challenged. Noel's frustration grew but to be fair, she couldn't know that he had no intentions of following her to the restaurant. He knew he'd feel in no state to impress anyone, let alone her friends but if he tried to explain that now it would put him in a position he'd do just about anything to avoid. She'd say something that would make it impossible to suppress his emotions anymore and then he'd never get to give her the small but very significant present that he grasped tightly within his pocket. He'd rather wait a few days than forever so he nodded his head obediently. He wanted to say something meaningful knowing that he wouldn't see her until after midnight now but that would hint at his plans.

'See you for dessert then.' He said smiling as best he could before letting her march away.

He dropped back into his chair unable to believe just how different tonight was now going to be compared to the evening he'd hoped for. There were plenty of places he could have met her that would have been easier but he wanted the perfect surroundings and that small area of woodland covered in snow was as picturesque as any scene he'd ever witnessed. There would have been nobody to interrupt the simple lines he'd rehearsed over and over in his head, much the same as when they'd stared opposite each other and met properly for the first time. He took his hand out of his pocket as it was still wrapped around her present; a ring so thin in places it was hard to believe it had cost so much until you looked at it closely. The workmanship was obvious when studied, and whilst he hadn't drawn for years, he imagined he'd be able to sketch it from memory having spent so long admiring it. This was the forth time he'd intended offering it along with the difficult accompanying question, but each and every time something had happened to ensure it was postponed. It wasn't always as extreme as a broken nose, but then it didn't have to be; even the slightest deviation from his idyllic and meticulously thought out plans would be enough to make him wait.

He thrust it back into his pocket again and looked around the huge waiting room. It was largely occupied by those he assumed had already celebrated a little too much or had simply picked a fight with whoever was closest but then it occurred to him that people probably assumed the same about him. He tried to stop being so presumptuous but the place was entirely too busy to be populated by the victims of pure accident.

No doubt the majority of them had brought it on themselves yet not one of them waited alone. They all had a partner of some description. Few, if any would draw the same admiring glances that Angela attracted without effort; but they were at least there whilst she was in a taxi that she apparently couldn't afford when they were on their way to the hospital.

He tried to take his mind off his understandable concerns and the very real problem of staying conscious but now he'd stopped bleeding completely he at least had the knowledge that his strength would only improve. He started counting backwards from one hundred in an effort to occupy his thoughts but he instead found himself guessing how those around him had been injured. Some were obvious, others less so, but he came to his own conclusions one at a time. Every time he'd almost diagnosed the entire room, his stock was replenished and another case would enter through the main doors. This individual was helped along by two concerned looking women. The staff reacted like they had been expecting him and approached him immediately.

'Mr. Dodson?' enquired a nurse whilst busily scribbling on her note pad. The boy was clearly still inebriated from whatever party or club he had been at and looked in sever pain, but he answered definitely enough. His arms swung limp by his side and he obviously had no control over them. Noel had seen similar before on the sports field but had never witnessed two dislocated arms on the same person.

'So would you say you were dancing *very* vigorously at the time?' asked the same nurse, he could see her identification badge now. Miss Rebrest succeeded in appearing genuinely concerned and sounded surprised at her own question but still showed a steely professionalism some would surely have struggled to muster. But she controlled her reaction far better than Noel who couldn't help but imagine just how enthusiastically he must have been partying; he almost laughed out loud but tried to snatch it back knowing how inappropriate it would be. The sudden resulting pressure as he snapped his mouth shut caused him to rupture the recently clotted wound sending it into free flow once more and giving him just a few seconds to watch everyone else watching him before they dimmed along with their surroundings and he passed out.

CHAPTER TWENTY-TWO

The sound of these cheap plastic chairs being dragged across the tiled floors never failed to grate on Nick. Since he'd heard it the very first time he'd always remembered to lift them and drop them into position, but he was the only one who did. There was just a single advantage that he could think of having missed the start of visiting hours; at least he'd not had to listen to more than a dozen people shifting their position for no apparent reason other than to annoy him. They'd all settled now as he entered the ward and few paid him any heed.

It was unsurprisingly busy today. Perhaps twice the visitors had made the effort and whether it was out of genuine affection or simply to ease any guilt before tomorrow, it didn't really matter. He was glad to see that there were just two patients remaining unaccompanied, exactly as he'd predicted and he was here to see them both. All of his wife's friends had remained loyal through the worst of times but were considerate enough to leave today to him alone. They'd known that visiting hours would be stricter today and would understand just how highly he'd value those precious few hours; it only added to his frustration at being late though as on any other day she'd have had company already. He took solace in the fact that it was a rare occurrence indeed but unfortunately it had become clear that the same couldn't be said for the excuse of a man that lay opposite her. Nick felt obliged to involve him in whatever conversation he was having, but it consistently made these moments difficult; they'd never been private enough anyway, but since he'd joined the ward it was like Nick had two patients to attend to.

If he had his way, he and Grace would be cut off from the rest of the world completely with nothing to interrupt their time at all.

The very last thing he wanted was distractions or interference of any kind but he could never quite bring himself to ignore what was left of the old man completely. Nick could think of plenty of people who'd alienated themselves and wouldn't be able to rely on anyone, but in knowing them he could understand why. This was different. The sullen figure across the ward was rude, sarcastic and could sometimes come across as bitter but his terminally weak heart was in the right place and even Nick had been able to see that.

'And how you doing you old bastard?' asked Nick becoming conscious the children in the room a little too late as parents all around him frowned in his direction.

'Don't waste your time talking to me, I'm dead' came the frank yet frail response.

Nick smiled as he sat down without looking away, 'I know you won't like it Ed but I reckon you're wrong?'

'I am, I'm telling you. I'm dead. I must be; I woke up this morning and nothing hurts!'

Nick smirked faintly. It was typical of Ed's humour. Even his witticisms contained complaints but then who could really blame him?

'And less of the old bastard, you can't be far behind me or at least you don't look it' continued Ed. 'You seem to be catching me up in fact, look at the state of you.'

Nick shook his head as the same parents scowled again at the repeated term of affection, but Ed wouldn't notice this time anymore than he had the last; it wasn't the type of thing he worried about anymore. But that didn't mean he wasn't right. Everybody here had grown used to seeing Nick in costume now and barely took any notice but it also meant that they now looked past it and as such, it had obviously failed to disguise the amount he'd aged recently.

'It's all in the mind as well you know. I'll decide when I'm old' Nick laughed.

'I used to say ridiculous things like that but I'm afraid it doesn't quite work that way' growled Ed before launching into yet another coughing fit.

'Then enlighten me with your great wisdom. Just when do you know you're past it?'

'Well for me it was on my birthday when I realised the candles had cost more than the cake'.

Nick laughed out loud but more out of support than anything else. Ed had clearly been setting that one liner up since Nick had sat down and had been looking forward to the punch line; a lesser reaction would have just disappointed him. It was clearly appreciated.

Ed quit while he was ahead and changed the subject, presenting his gratitude by showing his concern.

'So seriously, how are you doing? Didn't you have an appointment yourself?'

'I did. And it was a relief.'

'You got the all clear then?'

'No, not at all. But they blamed the booze and the cigarettes which was a relief… I thought they were going to say it was my fault.'

Across the ward a far younger woman laughed, sniggering whilst knowing she shouldn't. It made it obvious that she'd been concentrating on their conversation instead of the patient she was tending to. She couldn't condone Nick's seemingly blasé attitude to his health but she was just glad he was talking at all; and to hear him making bad jokes was even better. It meant he was still himself. Robyn straightened her face realising that her unprofessionalism had been noticed and turned away again before Nick saw her too.

'So can they do anything for you?' It wasn't like Ed to be so openly concerned and that was worrying in itself.

'Sort of. Apparently I've done plenty of damage but they've given me a bottle of pills that should sort me out. I've been told to take one a day for the rest of my life.'

'Well I guess that's good news of a kind?'

'Not really, there're only two dozen in there.'

Robyn couldn't help herself this time and winced at the comment; considering the situation it was in spectacularly bad taste but Nick wouldn't change for anyone so why should he change for any situation?

'You've got a lot longer than that in you lad and if you want an old man's advice I think you should make more of it. I know why you're here and I respect it as much as anyone else but maybe one day it won't be through choice. You'll lie here rotting and all you'll be able to think about will be the things you should have done, beating yourself up that you didn't whilst you could.'

'This is my chance to learn from the knowledge of a lifetime is it?' said Nick dismissively. Not because he doubted it was true, but because it was easier than trying to explain his side of the argument. It had been dark for hours now and time was passing faster than he'd like.

'Nobody could possibly have the knowledge of a lifetime and still be around able to tell anyone about it.'

'Now that is something I'll concede to, I can't argue that... smart arse.'

It was the perfect excuse to end the conversation there, or at least pause it for a while. Nick didn't move his chair but instead altered his angle so that he faced the bed again. It meant that he could rest the intricately wrapped gift he'd brought on the arm rest.

Robyn took her chance having noticed Nick's distraction. It was going to be hard to face him after their confrontation earlier but she wasn't going to avoid him totally. She just wanted him to be the last person she spoke to before she left the room, unsure of how their next meeting would go. If it turned sour she wanted to be able to leave the room completely for both their sakes, and to be in the position to do that she needed to make sure she'd attended to everyone else first.

She quietly approached Ed and sat gently on his bedside; she was the only one who ever did, the other staff preferring to stand or pull up a chair if they were feeling particularly familiar.

'So you figured out what's wrong with me yet?' It was a question asked without expectation. He wasn't hoping for anything more than excuses but he'd never been one to let anybody off easily.

'Not anymore than we did when you came in I'm afraid.' She knew they'd not found anything because there was nothing to find. There wasn't always anymore reason than the hour glass had at last run dry; he was simply worn out. She had no doubt he'd be following Grace within days but the only difference was that there were a few tests left to try in his case and, as always, she'd remain outwardly optimistic until then.

'So more experiments then?'

'They're tests... not experiments Edward'. Robyn was genuinely sympathetic and ignored his sarcasm; she understood it made it easier for him and let it go as always. The procedures they'd put him through would be gruelling for anyone but at his age they were a genuine strain.

'And yes, I'm afraid there are more of them. Until we know for sure what's wrong with you.' Robyn continued.

'People have wondered that for years my love. Nobody's ever really known. The last hospital put a suggestion box at the end of my bed.'

Robyn smiled and assured him that they did things differently on this ward, only ninety percent sure that he was joking.

'So did you manage to get much sleep last night Ed? I'm told you're having real trouble with getting proper rest?'

'Is that even what you'd want? Poor ol' Fred over there managed to drop off around half ten last night and the matron woke him up to take his sleeping pill at eleven.'

On the off chance that he wasn't exaggerating she didn't try and defend her colleague.

'Well we could give you the same and you can take yours whenever you think best so long as we don't need you conscious for your tests if sleeping has become a problem?'

'It'd only be a problem if I didn't want to be awake; if the clock was ticking for you like it is for me would you want to sleep?'

She looked away but answered immediately not wanting to think about his question too much.

'Don't start talking like that now, you've got to stay with us for quite a while yet, even if it's only to finish that book of yours...,' Robyn motioned towards the enormous hardback that sat next to his glass of water, 'I haven't even seen you reading it yet?'

'And you won't. Between you and me I've no intentions of ever reading it... look at the size of it! It's all far too complicated for me.'

'A present you didn't want?' suggested Robyn thinking the situation a little strange.

'No, no. Not at all. I bought it myself and just put the book mark in near the end. I'll just make sure I open it at that page when my time comes; I want the final image of me to have been reading a really impressive book; one that I'd have been proud to understand.'

Robyn looked at him intently trying to figure out how serious he was; he couldn't be... but it was a saddening thought all the same and she had to lift him out of that mode of thinking. She adopted a more authoritative tone.

'I don't believe you made it to such a grand age with an attitude like that.'

Robyn wasn't just being polite. She really didn't want to hear him talk like that but he continued regardless, leaning forward as if about to let her in on a closely guarded secret.

'It's not an attitude that keeps you kicking around and outstaying your welcome you know?

Robyn played along, humouring him only to a point as he continued to whisper.

'It's having something to live for'.

'And what are you living for?' She didn't mean it to come out like it did. She was merely asking what was most dear to him but in light of the empty chairs around him it sounded like a crueller question. 'I'm sorry', she added, ashamed at her rare insensitivity. He didn't even acknowledge her apology; he knew what she meant and it was a fair question in either sense.

'Nothing. You're quite right in your observations. I've got

absolutely nothing and that's exactly why I can't bow out yet. I'm waiting. It's boring and it's painful but I'm waiting'

The next question was so obvious Robyn didn't think she'd have to raise it, but in the interest of making this a conversation rather than a confession she did so without hesitation.

'What for?' She was whispering too now although she hadn't intended to. She could see Ed trying his best to lean closer still but the effort was visible so she moved further forward to save him struggling but he'd told her all he intended to. What kept him waiting was his secret to keep and all he had left.

CHAPTER TWENTY-THREE

He heard the door slam and felt the suspension dip before he even knew who'd climbed on board. Joe turned around to look over his shoulder, eager to see just who hadn't even felt the need to check he was available before helping themselves. Joe had a mental image of exactly what he could expect to see. After all these years he'd learned these streets and their little known side roads so well he'd bet he could draw the city's map just from memory but the intricate details he could picture paled in comparison to what he'd learned about people themselves. All those psychiatrists with their university degrees would have nothing on his understanding of so-called typical human behaviour. He was sure he was wasted sitting here behind this steering wheel but without a piece of paper to prove his knowledge, that's exactly where he'd stay.

But maybe he should accept he didn't quite know it all yet and that just maybe there was still more to learn as the pair in the back seat of his car were decades younger than he'd imagined. He could've accepted being inaccurate in his estimations but he was about half a century out; in his experience, the older the couple, the more likely they were to leave their manners on the street. It was an unpopular preconception but he believed it to the extent that he found this a complete surprise. It was so unexpected in fact that he lost his pre-rehearsed line and in the few seconds it took him to compose himself again and find the words he'd decided to stop looking. Joe had intended to use his new found ability to stand his ground again in case he lost it forever. Whilst he'd felt sorry for the girl he'd refused earlier, he also felt something he hadn't for sometime; he was reasonably sure it was pride and for the price of a taxi fare it would seem cheap at twice the price. However much he knew he needed the money, he needed this feeling that he'd missed so much even more. He'd struck a blow for marriage and its commitments already this evening and now he was going to make a stand for manners but he'd already lost his intentions.

The faces in the back made their excuses without a word and didn't even know it. It was remarkable how much he could tell just from their expression. He couldn't be sure of the actual events of their day, but he knew exactly what kind of day it had been. He recognised that look from the mirror at home and his wife would see it tonight when he crept back in, except she wouldn't cut him the slack that he was about to offer his passengers.

All the words he'd planned and even looked forward to delivering became less and less likely to escape until only a disappointingly meek 'So, where to?' was uttered.

'Just the other end of town please' came the sombre reply. 'It's not the weather for walking'.

'But it might well be quicker' advised Joe, ever honest to the point he'd suffer for it, but at least they wouldn't be able to argue the fare if they did decide to stay. Neither of them responded, not directly to him anyway and instead just spoke to each other. Joe took that as a decision and pulled away from the curb.

'We should probably both be saving our money?' suggested one. He waited for a response from his friend but all he seemed interested in was the condensation that had formed on the window next to him. The droplets that had been their breath slipped down the glass whenever their combined weight become too much. He wasn't quite sure whether his colleague possessed a secret interest in nature or was simply spellbound by the glaring symbolism of the day but he thought it wise not to ask, just in case it hadn't been noticed.

Joe hit the brakes again having taken the statement as an indication that the decision maybe reversed but even he grew tired of waiting and accelerated, as much as he was allowed just as the sole, frustrated voice in the back urged him to do just that. Eventually someone let them join the traffic that had been creeping past but there was every chance it was warmer outside the car; Joe was sure the atmosphere would be at least. An awkward silence ensued, so difficult to break that he started to wish he'd just gone ahead with his original response and refused to drive; even a minute of this was hard to bear, but how long it would actually take to wind their way to the journeys end was anyone's guess. Joe abandoned any thoughts of joining their conversation and just listened to it instead.

'We've just got to keep trying, and that's all there is to it'. The passenger immediately behind the driver's seat had changed his previously gentle tone and it had become rather more aggressive, no doubt in an effort to command attention. It was abrasive, but under the circumstances it was still to everyone's relief. It clearly wasn't the first time he'd issued similar advice that day and he was obviously getting tired of making the same point. Another few seconds passed in which nothing but the muffled, indistinguishable noise of the world outside could be heard before Joe turned the radio on. It was rude and was not the action of the defender of manners but he was finding it increasingly hard to care. Maybe everyone was right after all and he would be much happier if he surrendered his morals and just did what he wanted; everyone else seemed to just look after themselves.

'Declan please, its bad timing and it didn't need to be put like that but it's really nothing we didn't know is it?' He cleverly kept tailoring every statement to beg a response, but each and every question was posed in vain.

From the drivers seat it was already obvious that this Declan's friend was a good one, despite the aggression in his voice. The confidence and the directness with which he was demanding answers suggested they'd known each other for years so he didn't worry about another scuffle in the back of his taxi. He just kept his eyes fixed on the car ahead and his thoughts aimed towards the morning, yet a part of him never could help taking in the conversation and tonight was no exception.

The voice continued, 'And it's nothing we wouldn't do...' the hesitation was short lived, 'is it?'

'Yes it is it David,' Dec used his friends full name and mimicked the way he'd been addressed, 'it's very much the opposite to what I'd do and hope it's nothing like what you'd do either! I know what this place is like the same as she does and I also know that's why nobody ever watches the channel...', he paused for breath having already said far more than he'd anticipated and twice as loud. '... or reads the so-called stories but it's hardly our fault is it?'

'It never is, it *never* is. Nothing's ever got anything to do with you has it? Well whose fault is it? Hers? This city's? We made her a promise and we haven't kept it and that's all she's saying.'

David knew there was very little point in trying to get him to agree, not just yet anyway, but at the same time he couldn't watch him avoid taking any responsibility whatsoever. If anyone was the innocent party here it was surely himself but he wouldn't go so far as making that point. Not right now. Playing the martyr would weaken his point that this wasn't as personal as it seemed and it wasn't even about people; it was about business, profit and loss and nothing more.

'She's just taking it out on us. Whether we're paying for her stubbornness, her charade of a marriage or if that dress just isn't allowing the blood to her head doesn't matter... we're still the victims here. Why are you defending her corner anyway?

Joe was sure he recognised at least one of his passengers but couldn't quite place him. He kept a weary and watchful eye in his rear-view mirror as Dave pinned his colleague back into his seat to stop his evermore excessive gestures damaging the sensitive recording equipment which sat between them; combined, it had cost Dec his entire savings and he wouldn't want it ruined through temper.

'I'm not defending her and believe me, I'm nowhere near her corner. Ivy's a bitch. We both know that. So does everyone else. And yes, she only did what she did today because of what happened and to show us, and more to the point, to show everyone else exactly who's in charge. But my point is that it was going to happen anyway. We'd have just found out in the New Year... *after* we'd blown our wages and our bonus. She's done us a favour without even meaning to.'

He looked his friend straight in the eye hoping to see reason reflected back but there was only ignorance. The old adage was always proved true without exception; nobody was perfect and stubbornness was Dec's defining defect. He had a complete and utter inability to think about the bigger picture and to put himself in another's place. David awaited the next defence, unsure of what exactly it would be, but altogether certain that it would arrive regardless; he didn't have to wait long.

'Favour? You've got as much money in the bank as I have? We can't afford to lose this and she shouldn't be taking it away.'

'Do you really think it's that simple? Why shouldn't she? Why shouldn't she sack a pair of inexperienced hopefuls who oversold themselves in the first place and haven't produced anything she couldn't already get since? We took a gamble and we lost. That's all there is to it. You even suggested the terms yourself and now it hasn't worked out you're acting like she owes us a living? It was always a risk and she actually pointed it out to us. I think surplus to requirements were the actual words she used but still we insisted...'

'But it's not our fault?' Dec's voice was calming now; the tone more forlorn than accusing. 'Just nothing ever happens in this city...'

'Exactly. Just like she said it didn't, but still we insisted we'd find the stories and we haven't'.

'But it's not our fault' repeated Dec, even quieter this time. If that was all he had in his usually fully stocked armoury, even he knew it was true.

'No. It's not, but it's not hers either'.

'And to do it over the phone, that's just not right.'

'Well there's something we can agree on, there really was no need for that.'

Dec searched the damp streets outside his window for a reply other than that which he'd been pointlessly repeating but when he found none he just inhaled deeply and sat back. Surely this couldn't be happening. He'd given up so much and now he'd end up right back where he'd started; a waiter in an unexceptional restaurant with nothing but an ambition to make his name in journalism. And having spent who knows how many years worth of tips on a college media course and a camera to capture his stories, he'd resigned from the diner in which he'd dreamt the future for so long. With all the confidence and self-assurance of an experienced hack, he'd walked into that Wainsbridge office knowing he was just one final interview away from changing his life. He'd promised the woman front page stories that would increase her papers circulation and images worthy of the national press but now, a short three months later, despite his very best efforts he'd been able to offer her little more than local petty crime and school fetes that were already amply covered by her existing staff.

David was right, she had warned him that there was little else of real interest ever happened in the local area and if it did, the chances of those involved talking to anyone other than a respected and established reporter were next to none. But presumably quietly impressed by his enthusiasm and courage she gave him twelve weeks to prove himself and his partner to be everything that they claimed; and that was the worst part; dragging David into the same pretence and unpredictable gamble by assuring him that everything would be worth it and that he could escape the dreariness of his monotonous but well paid accountancy job. At the time it all seemed to make sense, in his own head at least but now he wondered just how convincing his speech could have been, but it was passionate and as always, it pushed all the right buttons to ensure he didn't have to take the journey alone. He never had to. After eleven years of living in each others pockets he could hardly remember being alone. He didn't even like the thought of it anymore but his selfishness had now obliterated a promising career.

Dec knew that jobs waiting tables were relatively easy to come by but high profile office jobs were not so easily found yet still the two of them reacted in opposites. He knew it wasn't David's choice in the first place and that he'd lost the most for the sake of someone else's ambition; it was why he'd backed down and it was why he remained silent now.

CHAPTER TWENTY-FOUR

Noel was glad not be driving as from the passenger seat he could enjoy the illuminations streaking by as Angela thundered her car towards the one place they'd avoided all their lives. He wished she'd take her time and try to make the most of what they were doing but both she and Karl, who sat dutifully in the back were here under duress so he didn't complain. The two of them had tolerated each other since Noel had decided he didn't want to compromise to the same extent anymore; he was tired of choosing between the two worlds in which he existed and keeping the people who inhabited them separate. He needed Karl to remember who he really was; he remained the only true friend Noel had ever known and he'd relied on him to varying degrees for years now. But he'd rather nobody knew as it took Angela and people like her to give him the persona he allowed the world to see. It was clear that both of them were determined to get this over and done with as soon as possible for totally different reasons but at least they'd come along as they'd promised.

The evening wasn't working out exactly like he'd planned, but it was without any major problems and the project as a whole had gone better than he'd ever imagined. He leaned over and looked in the rear view mirror at Karl, wedged firmly in the back seat between two massive stuffed toys and smaller, wrapped gifts occupying every available space, making it impossible for him to move. He was the only one in the car not wearing a seatbelt yet he was probably the safest; it was hard to imagine him going anywhere in the event of a crash. Noel smiled at him hoping he was just as happy but the stony look on his face, at total odds with the giant rabbit to his right indicated it wasn't likely. As soon as he realised Noel was looking he adopted what he imagined was the appropriate expression but his mind was with his fiancé, a quiet and timid girl who he had yet to even mention to Noel.

'We'll be done in just few hours; it might not even take us that long?' Noel assured them and couldn't have felt better when that later turned out to be true. They were nearly finished and as was always the case, each others company had beaten the cold and the frustration of navigating these alien streets. Even Angela, by far the most vocal protester admitted to having enjoyed at least parts of their mission. Karl was busy talking about how it had at least been worthwhile just to see the look on the children's faces and had even ignored the persistent calls from home for once. Noel was relieved but doubted they felt quite like he did; he'd managed to provide almost all of what they were now delivering and so imagined he'd gained the most satisfaction. He was also immensely proud of the fact that it was his idea; he'd seen it through almost unaided and now, because of him, Christmas would exist in places it would otherwise have not. He'd been told as usual that he wouldn't manage it and that to motivate anyone to contribute these days was an uphill battle but whilst they weren't wrong, he'd climbed anyway and from up here he liked the view much better.

After passing out due to blood loss last year he'd been brought back to consciousness by the last woman he'd seen before he fainted. Whilst that should have been Angela, it wasn't. It was Ms. Rebrest and she looked as sincerely concerned for his wellbeing as she had seemed for the patient who'd enjoyed dancing a little too much. At that moment he remembered thinking that her Christmases must feel considerably more fulfilled than his own and in that instant he'd decided to do something about it. She was making a difference in the world and he was sure he could too. After she was satisfied that he'd been patched up as well as he could be, she'd left him to recover quietly. Having been deserted he'd been left with too much time to think. Noel had questioned what a modern Christmas had become and promised himself that whilst he wouldn't deny himself all that he enjoyed about it, he'd achieve something worthwhile next year whether that made him old fashioned or not and he began to think about quite what he could do and how. The obvious was to pledge money to an appropriate charity, but rightly or wrongly he'd been brought up with a distrust of such organisations and besides, that was a little too easy.

The year ahead passed and he'd done little towards that hastily made promise other than to make time for the friend who had always had time for him and that was why Karl was here tonight, much to Angela's disgust; it wasn't good for either of their images.

But as winter fell again, the season provoked all the usual discussions and it struck him just how many homes are full of unwanted gifts and toys that'll never be used and that it couldn't be that difficult to ensure that they were. It was painfully obvious to him that whilst they might only be collecting dust, to someone they were the perfect gift. Whilst so many of his colleagues and particularly his family were desperate to find space for new luxuries, others were more worried about where even the most basic of essentials would come from. By encouraging his friends and colleagues to donate what they no longer needed, they could ensure that Santa visits where he's needed most Christmas and that seemed something well worth working toward. At first it had seemed not only thankless, but futile too. Yet gradually his efforts were rewarded and as more people jumped on board, the more it made others stop and think.

As the momentum gathered, he'd needed to pursue people's halfhearted promises less and less and the donations became more frequent until the ever growing pile of gifts served to silently advertise the appeal without him even trying. Most who'd contributed were keen to promote their own generosity and made sure it came up in conversation which in turn effectively spread the word even further.

As it turned out though, that was the relatively easy part as having made the necessary calls he was not short of organisations willing to take them off his hands but he was determined that the gifts should not merely be sent on blindly in the hope that they'd find their way to where they'd be appreciated; as far as he was concerned they needed to be matched against actual Christmas lists to ensure they reached someone who was actually wishing for that very donation. And the only way to achieve that was to be personally involved. He'd anticipated handling the whole project himself but gradually dragged those closest to him along and now, with the gifts carefully wrapped and being hand delivered they were making a real and actual difference where it mattered... just like the nurse who'd inspired him had done, and probably still did.

'Who says Santa doesn't exist?' he asked excitedly. His enthusiasm was his best and his worst asset and sometimes grated on even the very best of his friends, but tonight they shared it, albeit not to the same frustrating extent. He was obviously pleased with himself but he had every right to be.

'Too right Noel, and it's been an eye opener that's for sure!' observed Karl.

To varying degrees they were all lucky and they realised that now more than ever before. Each had their own problems and fears but they'd rarely gone without and had certainly never known the lives they'd witnessed tonight; it was humbling. It had also proved most of their preconceptions wrong and that dignity didn't cost a penny. When handing over the gifts they were often greeted with faked surprise as if there had been some kind of mistake. After several drops offs and much discussion they decided they'd probably react the same way and so played along accordingly, insistent that the gifts should be accepted, even if they were mis-delivered. Others were openly grateful, the recipients offering grubby embraces and sugary tea from cups that shouldn't even be touched, much less used to drink from even if they could spare the time. Fortunately they couldn't and so needed no excuse.

There'd really only been one annoyance that night and even that had been little more than inconvenient. Most of their deliveries had been in one area which on paper at least was ideal; except that having got there it became obvious that the area resembled all the characteristics of a rabbit warren. Instead of the long, relatively straight and brightly lit roads they were used to, these seemed to cross and intersperse each other which would have still been manageable had the street signs not been overgrown with foliage or customized with spray cans. That would ordinarily be intimidating, but looking around it seemed more likely to have been caused by nuisance kids rather than anything more sinister. Even so, they'd rather not go blindly into the many dark alleys and passage ways that led from one street to the other more times than was necessary. It would take an extreme set of circumstances to make them resort to asking children for directions, but in their increasing frustration the trio admitted an early defeat.

Pulling over to a pavement that outlined a small patch of untended lawn Angela wound down the window and called over to the group of children loitering around it. Noel guessed they must be no more than ten years old, maybe eleven at the most and remembered how different he'd been at that age. Whilst he didn't expect them to be particularly helpful it was worth asking so he didn't try and stop his girlfriend from enquiring. Karl was busy making the most of having space to move, but still leaned away from the car window in case of confrontation. Perhaps surprisingly, it was one of the younger looking boys that came over.

'Nice car Miss.' was the unexpected greeting.

Completely thrown by the compliment Angela thanked the boy, instantly more hopeful of help and always glad to receive a compliment whether it be for her or her possessions.

'We're looking for Cuddleston Road, I know we must be close to it but would you know exactly where that is?'

Karl and Noel looked at each other and raised their eyebrows in unison. To listen to Angela talk you'd think she was conversing with someone of at least her own age. She'd had little experience of children and it had never been more evident. The boy also looked confused having never been approached in such a manner. His clothes suggested he was well into in his teens but his voice enforced Noel's original estimation as he responded with a particularly high pitch.

'I certainly do. But it's a few streets away. Go down to the end of this road... turn left, then right and go on for about a mile'. He replied, mocking her accent and the characteristics of her voice. His own hadn't broken yet and that meant his impression was strangely accurate and feminine. Quite predictably, the only one not to notice the over pronunciation and almost butler like tone was Angela herself. The others would keep it that way for the sake of the peace and smirked as they wondered if they would have ever spoken to an adult with such sarcasm when they were so young. Angela thanked him in an equally official and well spoken manner and then pulled away. The ordeal had been considerably easier than any of them would have expected.

Over half an hour and several miles had passed before they gave up and returned to that same patch of grass to find the little bastard that had sent them round and round in circles. With such an age gap they were not entirely sure what they'd do when they found him but he was unsurprisingly nowhere to be seen anyway. It was getting later now and they guessed that even liars have bed times.

Sitting there feeling more than a little humiliated they simply sighed and shook their heads when they saw the sign that had it not been for the gathering standing in front of it would have been perfectly visible. It read 'CUDDLESTON ROAD' in big, black letters directly ahead of them and was only partially obscured by graffiti. They could only imagine the amusement they'd caused and just how loudly they'd been laughed at as they drove away.

'Well, we're here now so shall we?' suggested Noel sensing the atmosphere changing back to that with which they'd started, if not worse. Knowing they were in the right road now, the house number had been easy to find and they readjusted their expressions as they rang the door bell. A large and harassed looking woman answered the door trying to hold a baby under one arm whilst gripping the handle with the other.

'I'm sorry' she said, apologising for the obvious chaos that was inside. 'Do you want to come in?' she asked before she even knew who they were. She noticed they looked taken aback at the invite so justified it with a concerned sounding 'I'm told it's bitter out there tonight'.

Noel thought she must be one of the last of an incredibly rare breed. Whilst most people were asking people for identification these days before they were allowed across the threshold, at number twenty-four Cuddleston Road you didn't even have to state your business. It was both refreshing and worrying in equal measure.

'Thank you, thank you very much' Noel was grateful to have his mood and his faith in people turned around so instantly, 'I've got something for you, but I've just got to go back to the car for it... we just wanted to check someone was in before we unpacked it that's all' he added the explanation thinking his statement sounded a little strange without it.

By the time they returned he could see that the gifts and two large hampers they were about to deliver would be much needed here. The kindly woman was now surrounded by four more marauding children and that didn't include the one still in her arms. The woman was not old by any means but looked years past being able to have given birth recently; the struggle must have taken its toll.

She was the most open in her acceptance; perhaps kindness left no room for humility as there was no pretence at all this time as she gushed 'Oh, I'd started to give up. I was expecting you earlier', she looked embarrassed, more by her apparent ingratitude than the charity itself, 'but bless you for coming at all' she added quickly.

By now she was encircled by three bouncing, shrieking young boys and a girl who must be the eldest; she was quieter but beamed with unadulterated joy. Noel soaked it up, knowing that this was the moment he'd want to remember from tonight in case it never happened again; the minute or two that made all the hours he'd invested worth it. He examined each of their excited faces, the third of which was barely recognisable in its delight but it was familiar all the same. The boy looked no more than ten years old, maybe eleven, but despite his fashionable and presumably fake designer clothes he looked so much younger than before as he now proceeded to jump up and down on the spot, no longer as concerned with impressing his friends as he had been a short while ago.

Noel's first instinct was to explain exactly why it was they were late. It would have dissuaded his guilt over causing so much anguish whilst ensuring punishment was later dished out to the boy in a way he never could. But at that moment the little liar who now looked a picture of innocence caught himself being looked at and did nothing but stare straight back. There was at least a decade between the two of them, they lived very different lives and to some extent spoke a different language but everything was said without a single word.

The realisation in the young boy's face was exaggerated and obvious, displayed in a way only a child can, clearly both sorry and terrified of the scolding he was sure he was about to receive. The family pushed and pulled between themselves exchanging pledges and promises that would be kept if only they could open their presents now, but they were quickly laid to rest by their mother. Karl had obviously been observant too and was about to speak out but received a forceful elbow to the ribs to discourage him. Noel was confident that saying nothing would teach the lesson better than bed without dinner and for the first time he considered that maybe he would make a good father some day. He kept the same, uneasy mutual gaze until ready to walk away and heard a familiar high-pitched 'thank you!' as he did so. Whether it was for the presents he'd delivered or for his discretion he wasn't sure, but either way it was good enough.

CHAPTER TWENTY-FIVE

Robyn had provided a distraction and given him the chance he needed. Nick looked at his wife's face, down her body and along the leads that stretched the length of the bed and back again. Until recently she'd looked her age and showed evidence of the luxury cruises and all-inclusive holidays they'd enjoyed whenever they could. They never left long enough between trips that she'd lose her tan completely and he'd always be thankful for that. They could easily have waited, saving their opportunities until Nick eventually kept his promise and retired without ever seeing this coming. He wondered if he'd be able to forgive himself for that but at least this way he didn't have to.

He carried on studying her despite having done the same yesterday, and the day before that, and the day before that but he never lost interest on the little things that remained as reminders of the life they'd led. It was perhaps impossible to have enjoyed themselves the way they did, or rather the way they *had*, without gaining a few pounds but she'd kept it under control and with such a busy schedule it had never presented too much of a problem for her whilst Nick had to breath in whenever he weighed himself just to read the scales; but at least he made the effort back then. He'd stopped caring since and rather than utilising a fruit and vegetable diet to lose a few pounds a week, he'd often employed a pure alcohol diet where it was possible to lose a few days. And when he did eat, he ate out finding that kept his kitchen spotless more effectively than any cleaning product he'd ever used. He didn't think about himself enough as Robyn constantly told him and it was no different now as he turned his attention back to Grace.

After she lost the ability to do the things she'd always taken for granted she'd literally changed shape in everyone's eyes except Nick's; he hadn't even noticed. Without the regular use of her muscles, they now seemed to hang loosely off her bones; she was now emaciated by comparison with the woman constantly smiling in the photographs he still kept on display at home. Nick was asked to move momentarily and couldn't quite understand why it only took one orderly instead of two these days to adjust her position and save the bed sores she'd never even feel. The slightly built youngster moved her with ease, but Nick just assumed it was due to technique rather than strength.

To him, she was Grace. Nothing more and nothing less than and that was fine by him; it was all he ever wanted her to be. She'd remained beautiful throughout the years just like the countless country singers he listened to promised she would, but the real point of the matter was that he truly wouldn't have cared if she hadn't. Looking back now he found it hard to believe that physical attraction had ever mattered to him, even when they first met. But since then, not the dated dress sense, the thinning hair or her sinking form had made any difference to him at all. To him, she was as evergreen as that tree he should be delivering that now symbolised everything it shouldn't. But the fact that she was still being manoeuvred without a hint of exertion was evidence that his eyes had deceived him all these years and he'd learnt to be grateful for certain lies they told. If they'd been so convincing throughout her lifetime he hoped they would do him the same honour for the rest of his as he barely recognised himself anymore; not just physically, but in the decisions he made as well.

Since the disease that had now all but consumed her had begun to take hold, he'd found himself capable of thoughts he'd never known. He fantasised that it was a person, an actual someone that he could blame; at least that way he could have his revenge. The kind and gentle man that he used to be, the pillar of the community that he could scarcely remember now would take it by the neck and squeeze with a grip that closed with a deliberately controlled pace. Too fast and it would be over before he could absorb the justice, too slow and it might doubt his intentions. He'd keep this pressure up until it was on the very brink and then he'd do it again and again until he'd give in to his every instinct; to tear it to pieces like it had done him.

'Nick?' There was no response at all. Not even acknowledgment.

'Nick!' It was louder this time and authoritive enough to pull him out of his trance.

'Sorry Robyn, you ok?' Nick's voice was still distant but at least he was back in the room with her.

'I am. I'm a little more concerned about you?'

'Well then you should stop it. You spend too much time worrying about me and you've got your own life to lead and your own problems to deal with.'

'Not as significant as yours.'

'Maybe, maybe not, but you've got enough of them.'

'Uncalled for.' Robyn recoiled as she said it.

'I didn't mean it like that but it's true. I just mean you should spend a little more time on your own life and that daughter of yours'.

He looked at her waiting for agreement but realised it would be a long wait. They both knew it wasn't the place, and it definitely wasn't the time.

Robyn managed to change the conversation without saying a word. She simply looked at the intricately wrapped package that Nick had now laid on Graces bedside. At some point he must have laid his wife's hand over it, accepting the exchange on her behalf.

'So can you tell me or is it a secret?' asked Robyn keeping up the pretence that Nick had always maintained, acting as if Grace could hear them.

'It's no secret at all. It's very much the opposite in fact. She's known she had it for years.'

'So how can it be a present now? If she already owns it?'

'Because she's never worn it… she was always waiting for a better time; the perfect occasion. He managed to laugh a little as he said it. He couldn't think of anything sadder but he could see the irony too and he wanted to show Robyn he was alright as it'd make the whole conversation slightly easier and he had yet more advice to give.

'It's only a ring', he continued, 'and she's got plenty of them. It's not even especially valuable, she just really liked it. Strange isn't it? There was no particular reason but you should have seen her face when she knew I'd bought it for her.

'I doubt she was that surprised. I get the impression she never wanted for much?' Robyn had formed a question but she knew the answer. She said it more as a compliment than anything else. Nick just smiled and accepted it quietly and humbly. He knew he'd always done the best he could for her.

'She could always have whatever I could afford... sometimes even things I couldn't, but this wasn't quite that simple. We saw it on a day trip; just moments before we had to leave on the last ferry so she thought she'd missed her chance. Well I managed to convince the firm I worked for at the time that their next quarterly meeting would be ideally situated on that little island and as a favour they pretended to agree. The very next month I was back there and I managed to track the jeweller down. As I said, you should have seen her face. It made it more than worth the trip.'

'If only I'd have found you first Nick, poor Grace wouldn't have stood a chance'. Nick laughed out loud.

'And neither would my poor old heart, I've seen the skirts you wear out of work.'

Robyn blushed; liking the fact her figure had made an impression even if it was on a man almost twice her age. She looked like she was pushing her thirties but in reality she was clinging to them for dear life; her unenviable financial difficulties wouldn't seem quite so inescapable if she was younger but now, with a daughter to support it was getting increasingly difficult to see a way out.

Their banter was attracting disapproving glances but it wasn't unusual; to an outsider looking in it would sound like shameless flirting. Whether the age gap was acceptable was a matter of opinion, but the fact that the words were exchanged quite literally over his wife's body should make it spectacularly inappropriate but it was exactly that which made it acceptable to both sides. Nick found Robyn attractive, not just physically but he admired her unfeasibly strong morals too. And Robyn genuinely wished she could meet someone a little more like Nick; neither of them made a secret of this but both kept it in perspective. It wasn't even something they tried to disguise anymore. They were comfortable with it even if those around them weren't. The only concern that Robyn ever had was that her professionalism could be called into question if she ever forgot to be mindful of who was listening.

Her thoughts were interrupted by Nick's sudden action. Without warning he began tearing the paper, slowly but deliberately and without taking it out from under Grace's hand which rose and fell in time with her husbands. It was no accident and he played it out like some twisted puppet master doing whatever he could to see the life within her again. Robyn wasn't sure if it was sickening or quite simply the sweetest thing she'd ever seen, but either way it broke her heart. She watched him rip the last of the paper away and open the tiny box as he spoke.

'Just make sure you learn from others mistakes, if you want to make me happier… just promise me that. I've not got much to give you for all you've done for me, but I can at least offer you one piece of simple advice.'

'That's not true Nick, and you know it but I am listening' she assured him, throwing a glance over her shoulder to check that she was the only one who was.

'Treat every single minute you have with the respect it deserves'. His voice was trembling only a little less than his hands as he fumbled with the ring, trying to free it from its mount and slip it over Graces finger. He'd taken today's news even harder than she'd predicted. 'Every day's a special occasion so don't ever wait for one to come along... look what happened when Grace did.'

Robyn nodded but failed to convince the old man that she was taking his words as literally as he intended. He wasn't surprised;

she's young and therefore felt as invincible as he did at her age but he hadn't been surrounded by death on a daily basis. It appeared it was age more than surroundings that dictated your awareness of your own mortality. Whilst still considering that thought he continued.

'I know you're just humouring me but it's the single best piece of guidance an old fool can give someone with so much ahead of them... but I wouldn't have listened to me at your age either. And yes, I can remember that far back before you say anything.'

Robyn just smiled broadly and continued looking at the floor letting her friend continue the flow he'd fought so hard to gain.

'And I don't blame you, I know it's only natural; it's just that I don't want you to have regrets. I've very few but those I have are all due to what I've waited to do; things I *haven't* done rather than things I have. Every single one of them, but I was just like you. Tell me, I bet in your twenties you couldn't have cared less what people thought of you? Am I right?'

Robyn looked at him directly while she answered.

'Looking back I'd say you're right although I didn't realise it at the time'.

'Of course you didn't. But it was only when you were in your thirties and spent every minute guessing at others opinions that you realised just how free you used to be would you agree?'

Robyn laughed out loud as she was shocked at his accuracy.

'Something like that' she admitted.

'Then you should believe that sooner than you think, you'll be in your forties and the good news is you'll at last be a little wiser but the bad news is that it comes with the unfortunate knowledge that most people never gave a shit about you. Although if you're lucky, a few people will, but they're the ones that were always going to anyway and you wasted all that time worrying about it when you could have been concentrating on making yourself happy. And that's exactly what you should do Robyn; look after yourself and make yourself happy... and your daughter. At least until there's someone that can help do it for you.

'Which is looking increasingly unlikely. All the good men seem to be spoken for', she smiled as she said it encouraging Nick to take it as the compliment it was intended to be but he wasn't going to let her change the subject so easily.

'How would you even know? Really? When was the last time you actually gave yourself time to look?'

'That's the problem. Doing so much overtime here leaves no time at all to meet anyone.'

'It's only overtime if you're getting paid Robyn.'

'I know' she sighed.

'If you're not, it's just voluntary work'

'I know, I know, I do listen Nick, even if it sometimes seems like I don't'.

'It's no good listening if you're not hearing a word I'm saying though. You've got so much to offer and it's appreciated here, but it's been long enough now… you can and should be able to start seeing someone without feeling guilty.' Nick was surprisingly focused on her considering what he was having to deal with today, but maybe that was helping him through.

'So my aunts and uncles keep reminding me… they're encouraging and they're only trying to help but I just wish they'd leave me to do things in my own way.'

'I'm not trying to lecture you, I just…'

Robyn interrupted him before he apologised as there was no need.

'No it's fine; it's different when it's you as you know me. They're just saying what they think I want to hear whenever they think I want to hear it. They're at their worst at weddings, every time they assure me that it won't be long until it's my turn and I just don't want to hear it you know?'

'I do,' Nick assured her, smirking at sneaking a marriage vow into his reply. 'I was in the same situation for years but I just kept saying the same to them at funerals… that kept them quiet.'

Robyn laughed out loud again. Nick really was awful but he could raise her spirits, if only for a few minutes at a time and that made him priceless. Nick was always pleased to amuse her whenever and however he could but he also knew they were again deviating from his point.

'Seriously though, I'm not saying you should give any less of yourself to what you do, it's wonderful. I'm just saying don't do it for so long. Stop spending all your time here rather than at home. I know the patients need you but there's other staff too. And if you keep working outside hours for free you'll never resolve that debt of yours, try not to let it rule your life.'

'I understand what you mean but it's a lot easier said than done.'

'I know it is, honestly I do. I'm not saying don't deal with it; I'm saying don't let it rule you. And before you say it, there is a difference.'

'I'm just trying to be a grown up'.

'Well don't rush it, age is a high price to pay for maturity'. Just spend a little longer doing what you enjoy. Spend more time with your little girl rather than everyone else's here. Arrange your own dates once in a while instead of your friends. Don't have dresses that you save for special evenings, wear it in the garden if that's what you feel like doing.

'And you live by this advice do you?' Laughed Robyn trying to lighten the mood by picturing him mowing the lawn in his best frock.

'Well not exactly, but I've drunk all the whisky I'd let age for years and what's more, I drank it from crystal that previously only saw the light of day once a year.

Robyn suddenly felt guilty trying to make light of such sincere guidance. 'So I guess you're saying life should be experienced rather than just survived.'

Nick at last sank back in his chair, satisfied he'd been understood.

'As always Robyn, you've put it so much better than me; but yes, that's basically what I mean.'

'Well I thought you were very eloquent' she assured him in a half mocking tone that would make the flattery easier to accept. 'I shall wipe the words 'someday' and 'one day' from my vocabulary. If it's worth seeing, listening or doing, I'll see, listen or do it because it feels right and not because it makes sense.'

'No you won't. We both know that, but do your best at least?'

'You've got a deal Mr. Sainte. And with that I'd better be off before I promise anything else. Come find me before you go yeah?'

Nick didn't answer. He just smiled and turned back to Grace as the young consultant left the ward. 'She won't change a bit will she my love?' Grace answered in her own, silent and motionless way and for the next hour Nick had a similar conversation to that which they'd held every day for the past few months. He never once looked at the power cables and wires which led to the various machines that keep her constant company but he never forgot they were there either.

Throughout the one-way discussion Nick never mentioned where she was being transferred to just in case she really could hear him; he didn't want her to even have to think about it. He didn't doubt the ability of the people who'd take care of her from tomorrow onwards and in fact he admired them already. He couldn't understand how people could do that for a living but was thankful that they could; the world needed their kind and it would be an infinitely worse place without them. But he could actually feel his heart break every time he looked at his wife and imagined her in their care, but they'd have to do it all day; every day until her time came, whenever that may be.

He tried to shut the picture out, knowing that she'd hate it even more than him. He couldn't help but feel he was not staying true to his vows and that he wasn't showing the dedication and loyalty she deserved.

CHAPTER TWENTY-SIX

They had agreed to do the same again the next year following an incredibly twisted justification fuelled by Noel's desperation to feel the sense of purpose he could easily become addicted to. It had taken him nineteen years to achieve something he was truly proud of and now he found himself in his twentieth, he wanted nothing more than to do it again. He'd argued with the others that the boy had only been mischievous, and far from being ungrateful, he would have actually learnt a valuable lesson from last year's outcome. Angela in particular was unconvinced but she also knew that giving in to Noel just once could easily be turned into at least a dozen victories of her own later so she joined him without protest.

Despite the obvious problem of having predominantly the same people to call upon for donations and knowing that this time they would only have a year's worth of clutter to clear they again managed a car load; the success of the previous effort encouraged people who now had no reason to doubt it would work and so gave generously. Only this time there was no squashed Karl, in fact there was no Karl at all. In the course of the last twelve months he'd not only announced that he had met someone, but he'd fathered their child so Noel hadn't even asked him to come along tonight. If he was honest with himself, Noel knew that he probably would have done but he found him hard to be around these days. Karl was supposed to be jealous of him, yet Noel had found it was increasingly the other way around. He missed him being there but insisted to Angela that he preferred it this way and without his less than perfect map reading skills they completed most of the night's deliveries much more efficiently than before. Having more idea of where they were going helped, but they'd also developed an approach and a system that streamlined the whole process.

Again, there had basically been the two groups of families; the openly grateful and the coyly embarrassed and having discussed it they now had appropriate banter for each. Their list of homes was basically the same as before with only a few alterations and it had been nice to be recognised. It also erased those awkward first few moments of confusion and now, with one more stop to make they tried to recall the reaction they could expect at this particular address as they searched for a place to park. Looking around it was amazing to see how excessively decorated and brightly coloured the narrow street was despite its obvious deprivation. Enthusiasm must cost the same as pride and as they'd already discovered, that was somewhere between a little and nothing. Either that or there had been a major superstore clear out sale that he didn't know about.

The cars were stacked as fridges and freezers inexplicably took up valuable parking space. He and Angela circled the block several times before agreeing that he should do the honours whilst she stayed behind the wheel, repeating her route and keeping her eyes open for when Noel had made his delivery.

He approached the front door, again looking forward to the now familiar feeling of making someone's day, but could hear the shouting coming from within. Muffled through the brick walls, it wasn't entirely clear what the screamed 'conversation' was about and it was partly obscured by dogs barking who were quite possibly on the receiving end of the abuse. He set the two bags of presents and the huge hamper on the ground, but out of view. It was another worthwhile part of their revised tactics; most times the children would be at the door before their parents, but sometimes they weren't. And without the gifts to attract their frenzied interest it was possible to have them smuggled inside, therefore keeping them a genuine surprise for the morning. That way, as far as the children were concerned the credit was due to either their parents or Santa rather than some stranger at the door and that was ideal as far as Noel was concerned.

He hesitated before ringing the doorbell, trying to make sense of the racket as this was starting to sound like a particularly inconvenient time but he couldn't make sense of the riot of competing sounds. He listened intently before coming to his senses. At nearly nine o'clock on Christmas Eve, he wasn't in the position to call back later. He couldn't even put this address at the back of the list and return later as it was the very last one.

He pressed the door bell firmly before he could agonise over the decision any longer, knowing that the simple action took away his options altogether. He decided too many things that way; some of them important and for that reason it was then frustrating to have to resort to knocking with the letter box just to be heard. He hated it when people did that to him; it always sounds so impatient.

The additional noise only seemed to rile the dogs further but the human voices ceased instantly and through the misted glass of the entrance he could see a shadowy figure approach. It pulled the door open forcefully and stood without any hint of shame in nothing but its underpants demanding to know what Noel wanted with a less than articulate, but admittedly to the point, 'What?'

Had Noel not remembered the youngsters that lived here he may well have just picked up their gifts and left but for their sake he persevered, unable to blame them for the ignorance with which he was met. He asked for their mother suspecting that she'd remember him; he didn't relish the thought of trying to explain himself to the caveman in the doorway and why should he?

'Is Rosalin there at all please?

'Rosalin?'

Yes, Rosalin...' Noel sighed, hoping it wasn't noticed before taking an educated guess. Perhaps three syllables in quick succession had been too much so he tried shortening the name. 'Rosie, is Rosie there?

'Depends who's asking?'

Noel was losing his patience. It shouldn't matter who's asking so he totally ignored the question.

'Can you just tell her I've got something for her, something she wants? Thanks.'

With that he was punched square in the face. Not amazingly hard, but it was enough to knock him backwards and over as it was the last response he expected from the Neanderthal man who was still surging towards him. Rosalin was now half way down the stairs and running to get between them before her partner could do any more damage.

Embarrassed to have been knocked down so easily Noel sat quietly in the car on the way home. Twice already he'd considered defending himself to Angela who returned only to find him on the ground. He'd thought about explaining how unprepared he was; that he hadn't been flattened as such and had half tripped over the hamper but he knew that would just make things worse. Before Angela had even seen him the whole misunderstanding had been unravelled and he'd been apologised to but it wasn't nearly enough under the circumstances. Apparently the shouting and screaming that he'd heard had been the later stages of a raging argument between Rosalin and her charming new fiancé who'd heard rumours that he wasn't the only one. Despite her denials he was convinced there was someone else and when Noel had appeared at the door insisting on seeing her, primitive assumptions were made. Noel guessed that jumping to conclusions was the only exercise he got judging by the look of him but he certainly knew how to use his considerable weight to his advantage.

The car was steered around another corner and its lights caught the side of an end of terrace house and more importantly, the street sign that was bolted high upon it. Angela stopped the car abruptly spotlighting it perfectly.

'I don't believe it.' She mumbled.

'Must be so nobody can vandalise it' suggested Noel, grateful for the silence to be broken at last.

'What? I don't mean I can't believe it's up there... read the bloody thing!' A few seconds passed as Noel squinted to read the words and then digest their relevance. He didn't say anything, he just sighed so heavily his whole body seemed to deflate with it; it seemed to sum up the situation perfectly.

'Quite'. Agreed Angela.

'So what do we do?' asked Noel who was speaking to himself more than his girlfriend. He knew what her answer would be and also that he wouldn't agree. There was no response so he continued for the sake of something to say. 'No wonder she looked surprised'.

'No wonder' replied Angela, unable to disagree. Both of them sat there just staring forwards, the car still resting on its handbrake, neither of them willing to think too hard about what they'd done. The metal plaque ahead of them was difficult to see but had been screwed as firmly as possible to a badly deteriorating wall; it signified the end of one road and the start of another. The first didn't lead into the next as they'd assumed earlier tonight and put simply it meant that the old woman at number five Salisbury Avenue had the presents intended for number five Richmond Road and that, unfortunately explained a lot.

When they'd rung that particular door bell a little over an hour ago they waited longer than usual for it to be answered. Anything over a few seconds was abnormal as expectant children ran for the door or parents rushed to beat them to it in an often useless vain attempt to keep the arrangement a secret. But they'd almost given up on this address and were on the verge of walking away when the door sneaked open, snapping the security chain behind it taunt. The face peeping out from the gap looked a little confused to see two strangers standing in her porch. Even when they announced who they were and why they were there they saw no recognition in her expression. They played their role as usual, at first looking perturbed and then even a little anguished to have been sent out so late at night to the wrong address. Had they been questioned as they often were with regard to which house they were looking for it would have invited them to confirm the address but that conversation never happened. They'd been in a similar situation before and expected the gifts to eventually be graciously accepted as if to do the young couple a favour, but looking back nobody had ever acted quite as well the lady who still looked genuinely confused. They'd had to literally *insist* that the presents were for her and had even left a little frustrated at her stubbornness; Noel considered that she should be nominated for an Oscar.

Noel was the first to start laughing.

'That was the very last reaction I expected from you' said Angela without even taking her eyes off the view ahead. 'I really didn't think you'd see the funny side?'

'I don't, I just really don't know what else to do. I mean...' Noel hesitated, he was about to admit that his dad had been right but doing so would bring up another debate that he really didn't want to deal with, especially not now. To avoid the situation he made his father's point but raised it as his own.

'You try and do something worthwhile and... well it doesn't really work does it?' As he said it he considered his still swelling face and the money this mistake was about to cost him.

'Don't start. You've made someone happy which is what you wanted... just not who you thought.'

'Angela? The woman's got a box full of toys and books for five year olds. How happy is she going to be with that?'

Angela rolled her eyes and looked out the opposite window, 'Then let's go and ask for them back then? Come on.' She motioned her hand towards the door handle as if to get out although she knew she'd be stopped.

'We can't. It wasn't just toys... there was food and ornaments in there as well; and they're wrapped up. I wouldn't know which ones to take back. She'll have started cooking the turkey by now' he said, exaggerating just slightly. 'How are we going to knock on her door?' Noel was getting increasingly agitated thinking about tomorrow morning at five Richmond Road but he couldn't dwell on it for too long. 'I'm sorry Mrs. but you know those gifts we've just *insisted* are yours? Well give them back, they're not!' He said the line in a strange voice which in itself was odd considering it was an impression of himself.

'Noel, stop it. We've got two options and we've got to pick one and then get on with our own Christmas'. He was becoming melodramatic and she couldn't stand him when he got like this.

'And maybe this should be the last of your little projects'.

'Maybe.' Or maybe not he thought to himself.

'Let's just take them back or go home, it's getting late.' He couldn't believe how heartless she was being about this; she hadn't even considered the family who were relying on them but would now have nothing.

When they arrived back in familiar territory having spoken little during the journey, Noel got out of the car before it had even stopped and walked straight over to get in his own. He'd started the engine before she'd been able to catch him but she was now banging on his roof.

'What about dinner? What are you doing?'

Noel started to reverse.

'You get out of there or we're through!' She ensured she sounded like she meant it and Noel knew she did; he doubted anyone had ever ignored her quite so completely. He even wondered if it would do her good but whether she'd realise that or not was an entirely different matter. She was still standing on the drive way as he drove to whichever shop remained open to replace everything that needed to be in Richmond road by the morning.

CHAPTER TWENTY-SEVEN

Nick collapsed into the driver's seat that was as beaten, worn and as full of holes as he felt. He didn't even pull the cab door closed behind him, but instead just let it fall lazily onto its catch in its own time as he just sat in a trancelike state, looking very intensely at nothing at all.

How long would it take? Was she already gone? He was no doctor and he wouldn't even come close to understanding the endless technical explanations he'd have to endure at the inevitable trial, but what he did know was that by disconnecting the wire that never failed to distract him, he'd severed her ability to breathe. He'd effectively strangled his childhood sweetheart; the last remaining love of his life. He might as well have placed his hands around her throat and squeezed the life from her so from the second he broke the circuit, she must have had as long as she could have held her breath for. Whilst he didn't know exactly how long that was, he knew that he couldn't have even held his own all the way back along the corridors, through a reception and across the entire car park... and he was comparatively healthy.

She was gone. And probably before he'd even walked clear of the last narrow hall; but he hoped that she hadn't even lasted that long. He'd like to think that she passed on before he'd even left the room; that he was at least close to her at the time even if he couldn't actually be by her side as he should have been. She shouldn't have been alone. She deserved better.

He wished now, and would probably always wish that he could have stayed those last couple of vital minutes, perhaps even the few seconds it would have taken her weakened body to fail her for the final time. But he'd already pushed visiting hours past their official close as he always did but tonight he wasn't alone. Rather than leave him to see his own way out in the trusted manner they had done for years, the staff seemed to hang over him like circling vultures. They must have been unaware of how appropriate that was. In his paranoid state they seemed suspicious, but they were no doubt just determined to claw back every possible minute, eager to return to their nest where their arrival was awaited with more excitement tonight than any other. But if he could have just been forgiven those last ticks of that dreaded clock he wouldn't have to wonder whether she inhaled or exhaled her very last breath.

But still the dignity, perfect manners and polite control that defined him were alive and well and accompanied him in the cabin now, as they always had. Whilst he was surprised at his restraint, he was also strangely proud but more importantly, he knew she'd be even prouder... it was what she would have wanted; no tears and no self-pity. Just the strength she'd always admired in life. He'd promised never to let her down and even now at the very moment he'd never stopped fearing since the day he met her, he would keep his promise.

To his surprise he found himself checking the mobile he might as well not have had for the last year. It was really only used for emergencies now as his social life had all but disappeared but he flicked the cursor back and forth awkwardly. He used it so rarely that he had to follow the onscreen prompts just to reach its sorry excuse for an address book. Most of its listings consisted of hospital departments and the people who worked within them, but he was searching for an entry that hadn't been highlighted for so long he couldn't recall what he'd saved it under.

The selection arrow scuttled along, overshooting its possible targets and reversing repeatedly like someone who's lost but very, very late for a meeting. He scrolled past 'D' where it was unlikely but at least possible he'd filed the number under 'DAUGHTER' before trying to find it under 'M'. When he was still left without the result he so desperately needed he tried yet another approach having noticed that he'd listed others by their surname, but scrolling threw the 'S' section proved that theory wrong too. Had he erased it in anger after his last desperate attempt to reach her had been rebuked yet again? If there was any mercy left in this sorry world that wouldn't be the case. He used to know the number by heart but he could no longer remember a single digit. He dragged through the entire alphabet, his eyes darting to keep up as the list looped and started again until there it was... saved under her childhood nickname. It shouldn't surprise him; even as he struggled to come to terms with her actions he'd never stopped thinking of her on such an affectionate level.

The cursor was still now except for its expectant flashing. It knew the next natural command but Nick seemed unprepared to give the order, like a soldier who'd searched for the enemy only to find he couldn't pull the trigger. He inhaled deeply as his thumb still hovered over the dialing key but he just couldn't bring it down.

He'd had to read between the lines, but over time he'd come to understand why she never visited, so why spoil her illusion now? She wouldn't be able to hide from it forever and eventually the news would find her wherever she was but she must be due to give birth to the grandchild he doubted he'd ever know any day now; if she couldn't handle reality before, today would not be the time to force her. Yet still he lingered in uncharacteristic indecision... memories and thoughts wrestled within his mind but the fight was over before the referee had even entered the ring.

As he lowered his phone he noticed policemen; two of them. They were walking with the brisk pace that always suggested purpose and were headed towards him. He'd been one of the many to criticise the force for so many reasons including appalling response times but even he'd have to admit this was impressive; typical. They'd not be interested in his reasons or his motives; he wondered if they'd even be overly interested in whether he was guilty if it would get their arrest figures up for the month. He was sure they wouldn't take anything he had to say into account at all and for that reason he sometimes regretted not joining the force himself; after a career in the service industry he longed for a job in which the customer is always wrong.

Nick was sunk so low in his seat that it was entirely possible that from ground level neither officer would not have seen him yet. He inched lower still on the off chance they were working from a description of *him* rather than his vehicle as even they couldn't fail to fit him to the vaguest of descriptions considering his outfit.

He wriggled awkwardly, trying to manoeuvre himself down as far as possible but succeeded in little other than riding his oversize velvet trousers uncomfortably between his legs making any further decent too painful by far. Aware his hat must still rise above the windscreen he snatched it off before holding himself silent and motionless; an impressive achievement considering his compromising position.

He could hear them approaching, the grating static of their radios overriding their clichéd and over emphasised footsteps that punctuated what was still no more than a muffled discussion. He'd held his breath more out of anticipation than any genuine risk of being heard. As they neared he began to pick out individual words until entire sentences became clear; they must be almost level with his door now.

'I didn't catch that Sarge please repeat?' The voice lacked urgency but retained a certain respect; like that of a man who should have already clocked off hours ago but knew the repercussions of not responding. Another burst of static and then a heavy sigh followed.

'Sarge, neither of us caught your last transmission, could you repeat?' Nothing; until he began to ask again in a clearly frustrated tone only to speak over the orders being re-issued which this time came through perfectly clearly but both men stopped to allow the other to speak. Neither uttered a word; desperate to receive the elusive message this time, each patiently waiting in a stale-mate of silence. Both parties waited an embarrassingly long time until they doubted the response was coming at all, they surrendered in unison and began exactly the same sentence again in faultless synchronization, only louder and increasingly aggravated. Neither could be more eager to know their commands than Nick, who remained perfectly still but close to cramping up, jumping involuntarily as the side of the cabin shuddered.

He could only guess that one of the officers had kicked it in annoyance at their complete inability to be able to coordinate a two way transmission but that must surely mean they didn't already know he was in there? He allowed himself a much needed breath.

Having repeated the same routine perfectly, again cancelling each other out, the side panel was thumped inwards again. Just two inches away an officer had landed his forehead heavily against the door where he stood, one hand over his face having given up completely and handed his radio to his partner hoping he'd have more luck.

The two officers must have separated as the weight was still clearly pressed against his cabin but the pleas for a clear reply now sounded distant again. The receiver had probably been walked away so that the near constant swearing coming from just the other side of the door could not be heard over the air.

'Right, she wants us in the town centre as there's an APB out on a dark blue estate, registration A80... something or other attempting a getaway. Three suspects, allegedly dangerous... description to follow apparently and...'

Nick could make out nothing further than that but he didn't have to. Sitting up straight was relief in itself and without the imminent threat of arrest he was ready to take his opportunity, but without the distraction he was hit by the enormity of what he'd done.

He was caught by the wave; it's the only way he could describe it, like an oceanic surge that he just couldn't stand up against no matter how he'd readied himself and however much he knew it was coming, he just couldn't stand against it.

In a sudden outburst of aggression the phone split in two then exploded as it hit the windscreen; the toughened glass withstood the blow, much to Nick's anger as he desperately needed a destructive release. The abrupt force had caused the already damaged jaws of the glove compartment to fall open; Grace's various medicines and pain killers from those more merciful days when the disease could be controlled spilled out, falling into the brown paper bag he'd been so thoughtfully presented with earlier as it dropped towards the cabin floor. Nick snatched and in one motion launched it so hard he succeeded in splitting the screen down its centre, but still it refused to shatter; at least one of them could withstand the abuse. The bottle remained in one piece as it rebounded against the dashboard, rolled along and fell awkwardly onto his hand; it was like a message so clear that it could have been written in neon.

The wave crashed around him but washed way, allowing him a few moments to breath and consider his options in the screaming silence before the next rolled in, more powerful this time. He fought the rising tide just to stay afloat, his breathing quickened and deepened but he found himself wishing it away and for the first time in his restrained, text book life he felt truly out of control. There was something stronger than his will after all and it was taking hold of him.

His legs kicked against the dash sending the remnants of his mobile jumping into the air only to be sent flying again upon their brief landing. His fists, clenched as if to defend against the onslaught, or even ready to take on death itself if only it were possible, hammered against the steering wheel like it was directly to blame.

He was parked near the exit, and as it opened onto the only public road in or out of the hospital his surroundings remained busy with people having also just said goodbye, although in their case, it was less likely to be for the very last time. They took a wide berth around the lorry, the commotion inside its cabin so furious that the entire vehicle rocked on its suspension just as Nick's old estate car had done the night his daughter was conceived. The emergency department continued to churn out the injured and the inebriated in equal measure and as concerned strangers they made double takes, surprised that the lucky bastard inside couldn't have had the consideration to have driven to a more secluded area before having his way, but they smiled wryly all the same, totally unaware of the colossal pain it contained.

It rolled away again, as waves and swells do but just as predictable was the fact that there'd be another chasing behind, and the thought made him pray it would be the one that drowns him but he reached for the bag just in case it wasn't.

With shaking hands he scanned each bottle of pills. He'd learnt a little about the ingredients they comprised of over the years, never once thinking he'd ever use the knowledge for anything other than Grace's comfort. He made his selection hurriedly; eager to take advantage of the sudden lull he'd been so generously afforded but his trembling fingers struggled repeatedly with the childproof cap. In a different space and time he'd have laughed at the irony, but right now it was nothing more than exasperating. With strength he hadn't possessed for over twenty years he forced the cap through its safety catch rather than under it, snapped its so-called safeguard and threw back most of its contents trying to beat the next attack. He shook the container viciously, trying to dislodge the few tablets that hid stubbornly under the ridge. He tossed it aside and cracked open another; he managed it with comparative ease and sank its fill too like a drunk trying to race closing time at the bar.

He swallowed what he could before pulling his Christmas bonus from the bag and ridding himself of the pills metallic taste as he washed them down, wincing at the strength of the whisky but soldiering on regardless.

CHAPTER TWENTY-EIGHT

The ground was nearing now and it reinforced his belief that he'd meet it the moment he was literally able to see himself climb the fire escape of the very building alongside which he was falling. He was convinced that time and distance had made a pact and were working together; that would mean that the vision of his twenty-fourth Christmas would be his last and that made the fact that he was now reliving his twenty-first all the more daunting.

He braced himself in expectation but again managed to focus his thoughts on the scene before him. It was amazingly clear considering the detail it included that would not be too dissimilar to reality had it not been for the smoke that choked it; there were people everywhere. It wasn't only remarkable due to the sheer size of the crowd; their proximity to each other was just as memorable. They all clutched their glasses against themselves, unable to hold them any other way as they shuffled and competed for position. There wasn't even the faintest shaft of light between the bodies whilst strangers were herded together as close as the lovers but as Noel came down those stairs he could pick one individual out above all others. He'd spent the three years since unsure whether he should be grateful for the timing or whether he'd have rather lived with the illusion but nothing wouldn't change what had actually happened. Noel could see him; he stood there as if he had nothing to hide, smiling as broadly as those surrounding him and enjoying the atmosphere. He was dressed for the occasion and paying the bartender for what must have been a dozen double whiskeys.

Noel again lip read 'keep the change' as he had back then and it was a relief. Until now he'd always wondered if he'd merely remembered it that way; if bitterness had somehow altered his memory. His whole world seemed to focus on those seemingly generous words as everything else may as well have fallen silent. He was out of earshot but could see that the sentence had been thrown away with a casualness that pierced him, opening a wound that he never realised had failed to heal until now.

With hindsight, it was amazing that he had recognised him at all as dressed so immaculately he looked every inch the city gent. Having since tried to convince himself that he'd made a mistake, Noel had justified it with the fact that it would be forgivable after a few celebratory drinks as plenty of guys in suits look similar. But now, given a second uninterrupted view that he never imagined possible he was absolutely sure. There were certain features that distinguished him whatever he wore and all the anger and embarrassment stabbed again in midair just like it had that night. But he wasn't ashamed, even now; anyone would feel it.

Almost a week before Noel had walked the length of that High Street, no doubt with a smug expression on his face knowing he'd bought all his presents whilst others were in a state of emergency. This was the first year he'd felt happy with the gifts he'd bought. He'd sold out on his ambitions and resigned his talents to hobbies in which he'd never found time to indulge but his new job was at least well paid. Before his desk job he'd had to resort to offerings everyone would swear they loved and he'd done his very best to believe them, but now, with his second pay rise in six short months he'd finally been able to buy what he could enjoy giving. He genuinely looked forward to presenting them more than anything else and the organisation and thought that had gone into ensuring he'd avoid any disappointments was impressive by anyone's standards. He was ahead of almost everybody he knew so far as planning was concerned with the intention of enjoying the season for all it was worth rather than being vaguely aware that it had happened as it passed in a streaking blur. He walked slower than those surrounding him, taking in the decorations that lined the street partly because he wanted to, but mainly because he could. They were less sophisticated back then, but what they lacked in technology they gained in simple charm. With so much to look up at he'd never been sure why he happened to look down; but he did and it was a very different picture.

There, sitting beneath a massive wreath so elaborate its cost could have no doubt fed those below it for a week sat a beggar. Their kind were usually easy to ignore but his tattered coat moved independently from his body. Noel couldn't help but look again and was caught staring. The beggar moved his jacket slightly to satisfy Noel's obvious curiosity. The dog that made its appearance was small even for its breed and Noel would know; the puppy looked just like a miniature Sadie and with Labradors coats more suited to a domestic environment it shivered with such intensity that the animal appeared to have no permanent or definite outline. Noel kept walking alone but was accompanied by the thought that last years events had put him off his own charity appeal. He felt guilty having not replaced it and the feeling kept up no matter how much he quickened his pace. He'd thought he could live without that annual feeling of worth but he missed it more than he'd predicted.

It would have been easy to simply stop and rifle through his pockets for the loose change that he'd no doubt lose or waste anyway; but where was the redemption in that? It was too easy and not even helpful; he'd witnessed plenty of tramps claiming to be hungry yet reeking of booze. Money wouldn't help him and it certainly wouldn't help the canine ice cube still sheltering in his coat. So instead he continued on his way with a better idea that developed with every footstep.

He returned half an hour later with two carrier bags but stopped out of sight to contemplate the actual handover; he hadn't thought that far ahead until now. In his somewhat limited experience, these people survive in one of two ways; by having donations thrown at them or by rummaging through bins for whatever they could find. It wasn't that he was in anyway nervous or apprehensive about talking to him but he was concerned about the manner in which he should approach him. It was easy to work through the scenario in his head but every line he rehearsed sounded condescending somehow so he stopped thinking about it and strode up to the pair hoping for inspiration.

Noel considered bending down which in itself might seem belittling; like he was engaging a child, but he figured the alternative was to wait for the beggar to stand which was hardly any better. If he rose to meet him that would only serve to give Noel an air of self-importance and that was the last thing he wanted... or worse still, he'd stay seated in which case humiliation was all he could expect. Given the options Noel knelt. Looking directly at him, he tried his best to ignore confused onlookers who'd only ever seen coins donated, not time or respect. A city suit talking... actually *talking* voluntarily to the homeless? What was the world coming to? Surely he could just put money in a tin like everyone else? Or even set up a direct debit to a charity if he was determined to be such a saint. Noel remembered being oddly amused by the undisguised and almost accusing stares; almost like he was some kind of traitor. He guessed that nobody imagined that the two men could possibly have anything in common but they did and Noel at last knew what to say.

'I used to have a dog very similar to yours.' It came from nowhere but he was instantly convinced it was the right choice. It immediately put them on a level of sorts. 'And mine didn't like the cold either' he continued whilst digging around in the noisy plastic until he found the blanket he'd just bought. 'I had to get the soppy thing one of these for whenever we took her out in the winter but after a while she wouldn't leave home without it'. He winced at his use of the word 'home' but hoped he was again being overly paranoid.

The beggar, clearly thrown by this extremely personal and unorthodox approach expressed his gratitude through his companion.

'Now what do you say?' he asked the ball of fur so small it could be held in one hand. It merely continued to whimper but both men possessed the uncanny ability to hear what they wanted to. 'Lucky says thanks' assured the tramp in a voice unlike anything that Noel had expected. It was funny how you could have expectations of total strangers.

'They're a very polite breed' joked Noel.

'Aye' was the uninviting response but it was delivered with a smile and his eyes fixed firmly on the bags that now lay on the ground.

'She used to like these as well...', Noel nudged the offerings forward along the pavement. The tramp looked at him as if for permission to examine the contents before taking the hint. The bags were virtually pulled apart in the search but it yielded nothing of interest to anyone except Lucky.

Noel felt a sudden surge of guilt. He had no doubt he'd done the right thing in buying food instead of giving money and was just as sure that this was the best way to ensure Lucky justified his name for once but maybe the distribution could have been a little more equal.

To Noel's surprise the beggar showed no obvious disappointment and, picking one of the larger tins held it aloft in front of Lucky like he expected him to read how delicious his next meal would be but the dog looked indifferent.

'Still learning is he?' enquired Noel hoping it would be taken in the spirit it was meant rather than sarcasm.

'Give him chance man, he's not three months old yet!'

The response sounded sincere and was delivered without even looking leaving Noel to wonder if it was ok to laugh. He chose not to.

'So what's his master's name?' They continued to use the illiterate puppy as an excuse for conversation but the tramp looked surprised to be asked and hesitated before answering.

'Bill... Fenley. Old Bill Fenley lad'.

Noel was surprised he referred to himself in that way, mainly because he didn't seem that old at all and he guessed that nights spent on these streets would age anyone prematurely. Old Bill rotated the can in his hand looking for a way to open it.

'Other bag Bill'. Suggested Noel and stayed crouched in his difficult position, watching him dive into it and find a tin opener near the top.

'You think of everything lad and I'm grateful to you for thinking of us at all'. Lucky's interest changed dramatically as the lid was peeled back, his nose twitched and he launched himself out of his new blanket like a furry cannon ball. Had the tin not been full it would have consumed him all except his hind legs kicking out the top. Both men envisioned the same and smiled at the thought.

Bill continued to search the bag as if looking for something else and it was only then that the deflated expression Noel had expected earlier appeared. He'd obviously figured on one bag each.

'Looks like it's all for you Lucky' he muttered, although his last word sounded more like an observation than a name in that context.

'Not at all', Noel was quick to take the bait. 'I can only carry so much'. I'll be back before the can's empty' he promised nodding towards the tiny gorging eating machine next to him.

He made his way up the street again without feeling like he'd been backed into a corner. Instead he felt better than he had in a long time, a year in fact, and at the cost of another shopping trip it was a bargain. Once inside the supermarket he filled a basket but stopped and examined it for a while. It was crammed with a socialite's wish list but he was feeding the hungry, not providing canapés for a dinner party. He retraced his steps, replacing most of the contents with a less appetising but massively more wholesome selection.

Later that night, alone in the apartment he could now afford and long after he'd handed over his carefully chosen selection, the feeling he'd enjoyed earlier had begun to wear off. He knew that what he'd done was better than nothing; a lot better. Yet it solved nothing either. Tomorrow, or maybe the day after they'd both be hungry again and they'd both be cold and it would be as if he'd never met them.

The next day he got to work early so that he could extend his lunch break but when his boss was late in Noel used the time to make a few calls. By midday he was back in that same stretch of the road and again wondering what to say. He adopted a similar approach figuring familiar territory might be wise.

'He even looks fatter'. This time Noel spoke before he'd even reached his new friends. On his approach he noticed just how much change was mounting up in Old Bill's dish. It was a lot more than yesterday so either he was having a good day or he was cunning enough to clear it regularly. For a moment he felt angry at the thought of him giving a false impression but when you stripped it down it was basic marketing. With so little, what was wrong with trying to do the best he can? Everyone was guilty of the same and Noel knew that included him; he did it for a living.

It was obvious he was recognised but his approach was greeted with more enthusiasm from Lucky than from Bill who looked like he felt awkward.

'Hey, where's his blanket Bill?' It was obvious who he was talking to but he made a point of saying his name so he knew he remembered.

'Woke up and it was gone. I'm sorry'.

'Bastards'.

'It's amazing what you get used to young man'. Lucky had been pressed against his owner like he was trying to enter his rib cage but edged towards Noel the first chance he got. As he surged he tumbled down the grubby coat in which he lay but landed upside down but in Noel's hand rather than the pavement.

Noel was shocked; not only due to the feel of the puppy's bones, all too obvious against his hand but more by the fact that *he* was a *she*. His first instinct was to ask the obvious question but he caught his words before they escaped. Under the circumstances it wasn't the most pressing issue. Knowing it was clear he was about to speak, he merely changed his words and got straight to the point.

'Now tell me to mind my own business if you want... I don't know anything about you and maybe I've overstepped the mark so as I said, tell me if that's the case won't you?' He waited in vain for a response. 'I took the liberty of making a few calls this morning and to cut a long story short, it doesn't have to be this way'. Still he didn't provoke a response and even considered retreat but pressed on. There were basically two options open to Bill and he was living one of them. If Noel presented him with the other, at least he'd have done what he could and might sleep a little easier tonight; since he'd moved out he'd found himself with too much time to worry about problems that weren't even his own. 'I've made a few calls, well quite a few actually and basically you could be housed by Christmas.' There was a short but awkward silence before it was broken, and this time not by Noel.

'How?' Noel explained in full but wasn't entirely convinced Bill was quite as ignorant as he seemed but figured he must be playing dumb out of gratitude. It made sense. Just a single 'I knew that' would play down Noel's efforts and the polite thing to do was to keep nodding appreciatively; and that was exactly what he did. Once he was confident he understood what was admittedly a basic procedure Noel handed him a piece of paper. 'Now that's the number to call' advised Noel.

'And this one?' questioned Bill referring to the writing below it.

'That's my number, and my name's Noel' he explained, unsure as to whether he'd mentioned that before. 'I'd be grateful if you'd call me... when you know what's going on or if you're not getting anywhere. Either way I'd like to know'. With that he dropped a pile of change into his collection rags.

Bill smiled, 'Sure I will... Noel. And thanks, thanks very much'. Noel just gestured acknowledgement as the elder man kept shifting his position having looked decidedly uneasy throughout their conversation. With everything said it seemed like the ideal time to leave until he held out his open palm expectantly. It surprised Noel but why couldn't a homeless man be a gentlemen. He took Bill's hand and shook it firmly. His job had taught him the importance of a firm and confident handshake and he engaged enthusiastically, pleased to have been accepted over the social fence that divided them. He examined his grip when it wasn't met with equal force but the tattoo that was now visible on the opposing wrist only served to emphasise the likely differences in their upbringing so he thought little of it. It was only when he looked up that embarrassment sucked his pride away as his friend's posture and expression made it clear he'd merely extended his hand to take his puppy back. Now it was definitely time to leave.

Days passed and Noel had heard nothing. Everyone had told him to expect exactly that but the idealist in him believed he'd receive a call to the extent that he was actually shocked and concerned when he didn't. After nearly a week he returned again to see Bill but he was nowhere to be seen. In the closing minutes of the hour he spent patrolling the street he stood in the spot where the beggar had sat and looked out from his perspective at the shops and organisations across the street. They were full to the brim with pedestrians who'd all claim to be rushed but had somehow found the time to browse the window of Fenley's, which thanks to his humble confession had long since become his mother's jeweller of choice. Fenleys… and right next to it was the police complaints depot or 'the old bill' as so many around here called it. His heart sank at the thought of his efforts to help someone who was so desperate to avoid it that he didn't even give his real name.

Every emotion he felt in that moment was present and correct again as he stared at the bar and the dozen double whiskies; he imagined how 'Bill' must have cursed him for bringing him dog food and vitamin bars instead of just throwing the cash that obviously kept him in tailored clothes and swanky wine bars but Noel was able to take a little pleasure in it. He also drew some consolation from having driven him out of his regular haunt with repeated helpful visits but it couldn't compare to the rage he felt… the wasted time, the needless concern and worst of all, the complete lack of trust he was worried would never leave him.

There was so much he wanted to say and even more he wanted to do. He could even picture himself evening the score but it was just a fantasy... a dozen whiskies meant twelve men, eleven of which were not likely to watch Noel attempt any sort of primitive retribution. But Noel couldn't share the building with him either, and he'd have to leave now before he did something he knew he'd regret.

As he dragged himself back across the car park at an embarrassingly early hour and without explanation to the friends he'd arrived with, he suddenly suspected that he had the opportunity to leave with another. The sound was unmistakable and as before, it was a reaction to both hunger and the cold and it was coming from around the corner.

He didn't hesitate for a moment; he followed the whining and untied Lucky from the wrought iron railing and carried her to his car. He'd take care of her until she was healthy but then his apartment, however trendy, wouldn't suit her. But he just happened to know a couple who knew how to look after Labradors and missed having them around.

CHAPTER TWENTY-NINE

Just another example of peer pressure; if you dropped the excuses and all the pretence, that's exactly what it was. Robyn wasn't sure if it was funny or pathetic that she'd spent the better part of yesterday convincing a fourteen year old girl that she shouldn't feel cornered into losing her virginity just because it was the fashionable talk of the classroom; or that she'd spent her so-called lunch break lecturing another that just because her friend's abuse alcohol, it doesn't make it a good idea. Yet here she was, walking a little short of three miles home on a freezing winter's night, simply because she couldn't decline a second sherry.

She could have politely and inoffensively drank a toast to Christmas with the other surgeons, nurses and consultants and would still have been able to drive home legally, but instead she sank one after the other in the name of reputation. She shook her head and raised a disappointed, almost sarcastic smile as she pictured herself behind the podium at the local secondary school earlier that week giving a speech on sensible drinking.

She felt a fraud. Not because of the amount she had drunk; it hadn't been that excessive and she'd hardly have felt its effect if she hadn't skipped another meal today; it was simply the senselessness and the childishness of her reasons.

In that regard she was really no better than the wayward delinquents she advised. Whilst her teens and even her twenties were becoming an increasingly distant memory, she remained single and amongst the younger of her peers. Some of them were relatively new to the hospital, but the reputation she'd gained at University, only some of which was deserved, had preceded her introduction.

Back then she'd been found at the very centre of every party and event the campus could throw at her with little regard for the unforgiving hangovers that always accompanied them. She ignored them as a necessary side effect until she found herself pregnant with no recollection of the conception at all. It had been a wake up call unlike any other and for a while she couldn't have regretted it more. She still wished the manner in which it happened was very different but she'd not change the result for the world. She'd not exchange any amount of freedom for the miracle that was Abbie, but giving birth to her at that particular stage in her life had meant that she'd never gained the financial stability she'd planned for so long. Every stage of Abbie's life brought new expenses and Robyn had spent her career struggling to provide and paying debts that had already mounted.

The sudden responsibility had changed Robyn as a person and altered the way she lived to the point that those closest to her thought she'd actually over compensated. She'd become the epitome of clean living whenever she had only herself to please but she still often felt torn between being the women her committed life demanded and the girl she used to be. In truth, the moments of indecision were few and far between as she rarely had time to be anything other than a mother and a saviour; and if the opportunity arose to be anything else she chose not to take it, knowing those precious hours would be better spent catching up on well-earned sleep rather than crawling in at three o'clock in the morning. Her best friends knew how much she'd changed which meant Nick was well aware and that's why he'd spoken the way he had earlier that day. But she did nothing to dispel her socialite image with those who didn't know better. She didn't encourage it as such, but by never answering any questions directly she let others fill in the blanks; and the conclusions they often jumped to never failed to amuse her. She couldn't help but feel that this other life made her more… interesting, even if it didn't actually exist anymore. It allowed her a much needed alter ego, totally at odds with her whiter-than-white work persona that she'd employed since those days working towards her degree, but it was this new, reliable as clockwork reputation that had helped her climb so far, so quickly within the hospital ranks. She was sometimes criticised for being too inflexible and for following procedure to the letter, so she'd happily wear her party-girl hat until someone eventually noticed it no longer fitted. It hadn't done since the last of her friends married but tonight she'd been surrounded by expectations and for the sake of a few drinks she'd oblige rather than disappoint.

She'd let them watch her sink two of their watered down drinks to each of theirs before slinking off to whatever party they imagined awaited her; most were not even aware that Abbie existed as whilst she took her work home with her, she was never so unprofessional as to bring her home to work. Acting the part of the available woman would mean she could avoid the truth and the inquisitions that would never stop accompanying it. Besides, it would only damage the little chance she had of any future relationship with the new consultant in the cardiology department; exceeding the limit might even result in a shared taxi ride home if she played her cards right. But the opportunity to suggest it came and went and still nothing had been mentioned as he'd disappeared back to the beckoning of his profession the second after the toast had been made. She supposed his dedication was admirable enough even if right now it felt like rejection. And maybe he'd find the fact that she already knew in which direction he lived a little proactive anyway? She'd tried littering their few attempts at conversation with hints at car sharing but there'd been no reaction to speak of. Perhaps he'd rather not and there was no more to it than that but it was also entirely possible that she wasn't as obvious as she'd thought; the demands of her position had taught her the value of subtlety but sometimes she employed it too much.

It had been an exceptionally long day and she'd have liked to have stayed where she was just for a while longer even if only to talk about nothing in particular to who ever was willing to listen but she *had* to get home. Her little girl was well looked after at her Grandparents' house and would be happy there until Robyn joined her later this evening but she still had to get to her flat, pack her case and call Nick despite his insistence that she didn't have to; the impossible schedule made it all the more frustrating that she was having to make her way on foot.

She sighed again, thinking back to what Nick had said earlier; did she really still worry about what others thought to such an extent? And now, having tried several times to call a taxi and eventually given up, she also wondered how it was possible that she was qualified to advise on life and death situations yet she didn't possess the mental capacity to calculate the likelihood of being able to book a cab so late on Christmas Eve. She was certainly paying the consequences now.

Bracing herself against the deteriorating weather she couldn't help but think of the comparatively warm embrace of the driver's seat she could so easily have been in right now then realised that wasn't quite true... had she driven home she'd be there already. She scolded herself and tried to stop thinking of her car, still parked, perfectly of course, back at the hospital.

Those Sherries were not her only recent regret. She couldn't deny, even to herself that she'd change the last half hour if she could; she'd have retraced her steps back through the corridors to the cloakroom if she'd have known it'd be quite this cold outside. But at the time, having been asked her holiday plans for what honestly felt like the hundredth occasion today she didn't have the time or the energy to answer anymore; particularly when those enquiring didn't really have the time to ask. But it was impolite not to, so all day, that's exactly what they'd done... all trying to appear genuinely interested in each others mostly fabricated replies and now everybody was running late; so for all their sakes, she'd made her way home without returning to the cloakroom for her winter coat. She'd hardly broken the journey though and the chill was already eating into her; with hindsight those few minutes would definitely have been worth losing now but she'd hoped saving them would mean she'd be with Abbie just that little bit sooner. All day she'd scurried around and stole glances towards her wrist watch in a hurry for no better reason than she felt she should be on Christmas Eve. There was no chance at all that she'd finish her shift early, it was more likely she'd be late but she'd joined in with the others as clock watching was as traditional as putting up a tree on Christmas Eve.

Robyn hadn't had the time to prepare for her stay at her parents but as they were taking Abbie out for the day she wasn't due there until later tonight. She knew that Nick was right and that she should be with them already but it wasn't that easy. She did her best to concentrate on what she could see rather than what she knew; she'd driven along this stretch twice a day or more but really hadn't paid any attention to the transformation that had taken place. It may be for the wrong reasons but it really was impressive. She tried to take in the grand spectacle but found herself noticing the smaller, more natural details too. Icicles had started to form, providing evidence that the temperature really must be as low as it felt but she grinned silently as the optimism for which she was known refused to freeze; at least it had at last stopped raining. This afternoon's brief spell still lay in the roads and had started to crystallize; perhaps it wasn't so bad that she hadn't driven; she'd rather get home slowly than dangerously. She was grateful that she'd left between showers as without her coat, a drenching when she was already shivering would do her no good at all; she didn't have to be a doctor to know that.

Robyn stopped in her hurried tracks as the first drop landed. She'd been so lost in thought that it startled her as it splashed, wet against her cheek. Surely not? She wasn't even half way home yet. It felt like punishment for her stupidity but it still didn't seem fair. There was no point in attempting to predict the clouds and whether they were moving in her direction; the sky was far too dark to tell and it wasn't worth guessing. Instead she tried to judge just how much shelter the shop canopies would provide and so looked down the street rather than skywards.

Had she done so, she'd have seen a woman, awkwardly leaning from her apartment window trying to get some much needed fresh air into her lungs now that her friend had left without managing to finish her pizza. That was ok though as what her neighbour left behind would make an unconventional yet much anticipated breakfast in the morning. But that was *hours* away and right now she didn't feel quite right. The sudden cold and natural breeze often helped her whenever the feelings of sickness became too much; the habit saved her actually leaving the flat but it had become increasingly challenging over the past few months. Since her pregnancy began she'd gauged just how much she'd grown simply by how difficult this seemingly simple position had become. Her shape now meant that without stooping into an unnatural and painful angle she was held away from the wall below the open window by her own bloated body; the resulting poise was more uncomfortable than the dizziness she was trying to ease.

As she'd evolved, so had the problem but it was easily overcome; she simply filled a suitcase with all the clothes that she could no longer squeeze into and had Donna lay it flat on the floor where it served as a makeshift step. By standing on it she elevated her protruding stomach above the windowsill and found that she fitted perfectly into the open space. It allowed her to tilt herself so that her shoulders and everything above them were outside and overhung the wall of the building; it gave her sense of the wider world without the interaction she'd rather avoid. Sometimes watching those below her brought a sense of optimism but not tonight; she couldn't see a single person who was actually alone and so they had nothing in common with her. All she could begin to compare herself with was the abandoned roadwork's that looked even lonelier when surrounded by the crowds who ignored them totally; like her, it had barriers to keep them out. Another tear welled in Mary's eye but there was no point in wiping it away; nobody was watching and she needed both hands to hold herself steady anyway.

She was surprised at having become so upset quite that quickly and blamed what she could on her hormones and the rest on the view; that at least could be easily dealt with and she closed her eyes tightly. As she did so, she forced the tear out; it wasn't the first and followed the existing trail, crawling slowly down her face. For a moment it clung to her chin as if it was afraid of heights before letting go, just like the last had done and followed it down towards the street where Robyn remained halted by indecision.

The young consultant was determined that she wasn't going to turn back at the first spit of rain but she took the hint as her face was splashed yet again. It was hardly a downpour but it was how they all started; those shop entrances would soon be packed as everyone joined her in trying to stay dry and that would mean the pavements would be as gridlocked as the road itself. The thought was enough to turn her around; even she, the highly respected Robyn T. Rebrest MRCP could admit she'd made a mistake.

It was a far longer walk home than it was back the way she'd came. She estimated about half a mile versus two. She'd stride back to the hospital, face the barrage of niceties, recycle the pretence that she's inundated with plans that would make anyone jealous and be out again, *with* her coat and her sanity, god willing, more or less intact.

CHAPTER THIRTY

The over enthusiastic embrace confirmed all of his worst fears and the subsequent kiss on both cheeks cemented them. If he could possibly escape he would and Noel searched his mind for possible excuses, but as the door slammed shut behind him he knew it was too late. They said it was to keep the heat in, but it felt like it was to prevent him from bolting; to be fair, he was guilty of having done so before. To try and reassure his hosts he forced excitement across his face; he really ought to be more grateful to them. As a besotted married couple there would no doubt be plenty they'd rather be doing.

Karl's girlfriend was now his wife and had gained confidence with the title. She was still not overbearing in the least but now she didn't get nervous in public places and could hold a conversation without stuttering... she'd come a long way since she'd found Karl.

Noel liked her; despite the fact that she monopolised his friend's time, he found her caring almost to the point of being annoying but he'd grown enough to appreciate that. She rushed forward and planted two enormous lipstick kisses on him, one on each cheek and smacked her lips as she did so he could hear them as well as feel them... she was overcompensating to the point of insult. The thought that it could be out of genuine affection didn't cross his mind and now, just a few years older but infinitely wiser he could see what a pity that was. And at some point tonight she'd be asking him about his love life in that genuinely caring but unintentionally condescending way that married people do, especially whenever they're giving charity to the poor singletons of this world. He knew that no amount of assuring her that he was perfectly happy living his life for himself would convince her that he needed anything else other than the love of a good woman; all she'd ever needed was someone else so she couldn't imagine that it wasn't the cure for anything and everything. But at last she'd disappeared into the steam and heat that emanated from the kitchen now which should have offered some relief but she'd simply switched shifts with Karl, who despite handing over a beer straight from the can like in the good old days seemed to have changed completely in almost every other sense. Complete with checked trousers and a sensible jumper he launched into all that would usually come from his other half.

Noel at least appeared to be paying attention and listened closely enough to be able to nod and smile in all the right places but he couldn't help but wonder just how having deliberately left late he'd managed to be the first one here and in despair he realised that his initial assumption might have been an accurate one after all. He gradually and subtly adjusted his position trying to see into what was looking increasingly likely to be an achingly traditional dining room to see the table layout; there were four chairs just as he'd feared. This wouldn't be the first time a happy couple had tried to make him part of the same; it wouldn't even be the second but they didn't seem to be able to help themselves. It never failed to put him in an awkward position yet they always believed that they could get it right next time but if Noel hadn't managed to find anyone that held his interest like Angela did then what chance did anyone else have? He'd asked them politely enough to stop and had wanted to shout and scream when they wouldn't but it wasn't that easy when all they were trying to do was what they honestly thought was best for him.

He wondered exactly when they were planning to spring their most recent, pre-arranged date on him and whether they'd learnt anything at all from the last time they tried. If they had they'd at least warn him before introducing him but with each passing moment it was looking increasingly unlikely? But they'd give it yet another last try and would attempt to match him with one of their lonely, not to mention desperate friends.

Sometimes it went better than others but the more recent occasion had been embarrassing for everyone involved so it was no wonder they'd kept their intentions quiet until they actually had him through the door; they'd got him this far and now he could only guess as to their tactics as it was bolted shut behind him. Would they come clean, admit their plan and be considerate enough to prepare him or would the first he knew of his next supposedly perfect partner be when they sat down next to each other to eat? The thought angered him and it hadn't even happened yet.

He was still being talked at and walked up and down the hall, being shown the latest additions to the house and told in pointless, intricate detail exactly which factors played a part in the various decorating decisions but still, all he could think about was finding an escape route that wouldn't offend. As much as he hated the fact that nobody listened and everyone, even his friends presumed they knew him better than he did, Noel knew that there was no denying that whilst they may be doing the wrong thing; they were at least doing it for the right reasons.

He was jolted from his trance and led through the archway to his place at the table. Karl and his wife had obviously gone to considerable effort; the table was immaculately decorated and brightly coloured crackers were displayed neatly and uniformly, two per place. Were they really in Karl's humble semi-detached? Noel remembered the boy that didn't see the point of a tidy room but this was kept like a show home; either he'd changed beyond comprehension or was now ruled with an iron fist.

'It'll be a squeeze when the others get here' observed Noel, wanting to remind his hosts that he was here under the assumption that it was a dinner party. He disguised his sarcasm only slightly. He didn't want to upset anyone but needed them to accept what they were doing for what it was... blatant lying. Karl looked suddenly awkward under his accusing stare as would be expected but Marie was giving him a similar look. Noel could only assume that she was either unaware that he was invited under false pretenses in the first place or that she'd been assured he'd already been made aware that the situation had changed.

'I thought you'd told him, why haven't you told him?' she demanded looking expectantly at her husband. She had certainly changed. Noel's question hadn't been answered directly but it had triggered a bid for the truth so at least he didn't feel ignored completely. It was actually convenient as he was able to step out of the conversation and that suited him just fine. Karl made a timid attempt at a reply.

'Well, you know how it is Christmas Eve, people say they can make it then their family interferes or something else comes up... you know?'

Karl was pleading for help and Noel gave it to him. His understanding gesture of agreement was met with visible relief; both men knew it was the only way to get him there. There was no pleasure to be had from watching his most trusted friend squirm and stretch for further explanation and there was nothing to gain as he'd already interpreted the situation; perhaps this time at least one of them had learnt their lesson and the other had just never found a good time to admit he hadn't. It looked like Marie was coming to the same conclusion and seemed like she was willing to lay the subject to rest; for now at least. The reason for the deception had been assumed but it still didn't explain where their latest victim was and why Noel had not yet been told just how much there was to love about her.

Now that everyone felt slightly uncomfortable he might as well bring up the issue of the empty place himself as it was laid as lavishly as their own and the soup had already been served; if their other guest was running late at least he'd have the chance to plead with them not to try too hard on his behalf once she arrived. He considered how best to tackle it as his pride wouldn't allow him to pretend he hadn't noticed the situation but before he could say anything their son bolted through the door and took his position at the table; Noel hadn't even known he was home and just hoped that his surprise didn't show.

Noel couldn't remember the last time he'd been so grateful to anyone under three feet tall; he'd been saved from embarrassing himself completely by the toddler's impeccable timing. Had he entered the room just a second later Noel would have launched with brimming confidence into an inquisition regarding the whereabouts of his prospective suitor. The resulting silence would have turned him back into the speechlessly shy youngster that only Karl remembered and he wanted to leave that past where it was.

The feeling of relief began to mix with the jubilation that tonight would be pressure free and that he'd at last made his point adequately; he'd been listened to. It would seem like a small victory to anyone else but Noel had a way of building the little things into issues so tall he could spend weeks, even months in their shadow. Turning down a proposal should only add to his ego but instead he would agonise over the effect it would have; it was a rare combination of caring in the extreme matched only by the arrogance of the assumption they were damaged by his rejection. He felt a little guilty having suspected, charged and convicted his hosts before the evidence had even arrived but they had put themselves in the line up over the past few months; he wouldn't let it ruin the night or his sudden feeling of freedom.

Nothing was expected of him. He'd have to make an effort with their son but by comparison that would be easy; had the chair been taken by a woman he'd crumble under the pressure. But everyone knew he was inexperienced when it came to conversing with children so he could make as many mistakes as he wanted without worrying the person underneath would be revealed; this wasn't an ideal situation but he was going to make a real attempt at enjoying the occasion for what is was. It was the very least he could do.

Trying to tread a careful line and judge the level of conversation that can be had with an infant eating machine Noel struggled to choose an appropriate manner. He adapted quickly enough though as between slurps the boy was surprisingly articulate. Noel's subjects of choice could have been more appropriate, but at least it created plenty for everyone to laugh at which lightened the atmosphere instantly. The doting parents just appreciated the effort being made and Noel was perfectly happy to be the subject of mockery so long as nobody was around to see it. By the time they'd finished their starters he was surprised to find that he was actually enjoying the evening but promised himself he'd never tell another soul as long as he lived.

Marie excused herself to make final preparations for the main course, but it was only when she and her questions left that Noel had the chance to consider the other side of what had really happened. If there was a negative to be found anywhere, he could always find it, even if it sometimes took him a while. He was aware now of the delusion he'd been under; Karl was ecstatically happy with his new life and his wife seemed even happier. They believed totally in what they were doing and the more he thought about it, the more convinced he was they thought it the answer to every problem. They hadn't listened... they'd simply given up on him. The result was the same but somehow the cause seemed more important now. He'd taken a strange enjoyment from trying to convince others that he was better off alone, but now they were starting to agree he almost felt panic.

Suddenly feeling so different, it became difficult to humour his new friend and to pretend they shared an interest in spelling and basic arithmetic; whilst Noel had enjoyed his company, it was a welcome relief when he scuttled away from the table to squeeze in just one more game of hide and seek with his imaginary friend. Noel had the feeling that it was behaviour that wasn't usually tolerated but tonight it permitted two old friends to snatch moments when and where they could.

It was amazing the difference a few laughs had made and both men clicked into place again the same way they had done since secondary school. Gradually the conversation moved beyond that which was usually spoken at the family dinner table and Marie guessed as much from the next room as the hushed voices faded until they could not be made out at all. She smiled and didn't hurry herself; she could accept that they had things to talk about that she may not appreciate.

Karl threw the occasional glance over his shoulder to check who was listening more and more often the further back in time they travelled, only now realising just how much he had changed and understanding for the first time why Noel might have kept his distance recently. The subject was switched momentarily and in perfect time with the opening and closing of the dining room door and then ceased altogether with the arrival of the main course. Karl adopted a different manner, sat up straight and began talking about gardening in a cover up so obvious it wouldn't have fooled the toddler, let alone his mother who just smiled, not even pretending she didn't know the score.

She looked and sounded proud as she laid down the feast before them. It was impressive yet nobody would have thought so judging by her son's reaction as he dashed back in response to her call.

'What's wrong' she asked him. 'Its turkey, very similar to chicken and you like that?'

'I know, we've had it before. Just I thought we were having something different that's all?' His response was met unfairly with a guarded defence by Karl, not because he had realised the misunderstanding, but because he took it as a complaint. He was unnecessarily to the point.

'Mum's been in there most of the day' he snapped both embarrassed in front of his guest and defensive over his wife's effort but backed down instantly; the boy hadn't been rude or even unappreciative, he just looked confused but knew he was in trouble and used his facial expression to great effect .

'Just didn't think we were having this again' he explained. His dad looked reluctant to respond but his mother was keen to find out what had caused such disappointment.

'Of course we are darling, it's Christmas… its tradition'.

The youngster was old enough to know when he'd been lied to and turned towards his dad, 'but you said we were going to have a great big loser for dinner? I thought it might be one of Mum's French dishes?'

The clattering of cutlery ceased as everyone, not knowing who to face just looked at their plates. It was like someone had dragged the needle across the family record and now there was near perfect silence until it was broken by the one who had caused it.

'What?' It was all he could think to say. He started to wonder if he'd repeated one of *those* words he wasn't allowed to but was sure he hadn't. He tried to justify what he was convinced he had said.

'It's not that I don't like roast dinners, just I was expecting something else that's all' he whimpered, on the verge of tears. 'Sorry?' he offered as a last line of defence.

Noel was the first to react and did the only thing he could. He didn't want to say anything at all but forced himself knowing that someone should.

'You don't need to be sorry' was his uncomplicated but honest assurance. He got up from the table and declined to add anything else. He didn't need to; the situation couldn't be clearer. He paused where he stood for just a second, wondering if there was any other way to take what had just been said as he had a habit of misinterpretation but this time he was certain so he turned and left the room with a simple 'thank you'.

It served to acknowledge the thoughtfulness and the thoughtlessness that was behind the evening and for now he didn't care which way it was taken. He half expected to be called back or even physically stopped before he reached the front door but he wasn't. Perhaps he shouldn't be so surprised; the married couple were probably grateful to not have to deal with such an awkward and embarrassing situation as they wouldn't know how. Noel showed himself out and as he closed the porch behind him he couldn't help but wonder if and when he'd hear from them again and at which point Karl had stopped looking up to him and begun pitying him instead. At that moment and for the next few years he remained clueless but now, having seen his life replayed it couldn't be clearer, it would have been when he began pretending to be someone he wasn't.

CHAPTER THIRTY-ONE

Whilst some of the strangers had lost interest and continued on their way, a few were still staring, shifting their position and angling for a better view. Nick was obviously not alone in stretching visiting hours to their very limit and that meant that he was still surrounded. They were no doubt well intentioned and their unflinching attention was more likely born of genuine concern rather than childish prying but that's what it felt like to Nick; they should mind their own business and worry themselves with someone who actually *wanted* to be saved.

Through gritted teeth he fought back against what couldn't quite be defined. It was too hopeless to be outrage yet so much more violent than despair and it continued to control each of his limbs, manipulating him like some cruel and destructive puppeteer. It forced him to resume his frenzied and relentless assault on the dashboard until that swelling mass within him could no longer be contained. It had expanded beyond his chest and stuck momentarily in his throat before finding its way out of his body as an indescribable bawl, not part of any language on earth but understood throughout the world.

Its release hideously contorted Nick's face in physical pain; it even *sounded* like it hurt and caught everyone by surprise; including himself as its tone found its way through glass and steel to the ignorant bystanders around him that now appeared still, shocked and confused... and focused very directly on him. He couldn't bring himself to make direct eye contact with anyone through his now damaged windscreen but instead caught darting glimpses of them, watching for any signs that he'd drawn more attention than he could afford.

He didn't need a clearer view or to be a professor of body language to interpret the reaction he'd provoked as it was undoubtedly one of apprehension for his welfare. It would have been too much of a coincidence for none of the numbers being frantically dialed into mobile phones to be for an emergency dispatch to save Father Christmas before he died from the heart attack, stroke or whatever other seizure he must appear to be in the grip of.

Nick at last managed to restrain himself and did his very best to at least appear composed, but what was left of his brain was telling him that it was already too late to call off the response. An ambulance, most likely accompanied by a police escort would already be en route; he'd better leave now if he didn't want to be here when they arrived.

It wouldn't take anyone long to figure out what he'd done and an ambulance crew would probably know just by looking. They'd graciously save him as they'd been trained to do, therefore immediately condemning him to his living nightmare of life without Grace, and eventually life without freedom. He couldn't face the indignity of trial and the resulting sentence... not without her. He couldn't face *anything* without her; or at least without someone.

He had no idea how many pills he'd swallowed or when they'd take effect, but surely they'd allow him time to attempt to lose himself in the city traffic, but not enough that he'd care if and when the authorities caught up with him? He didn't need to buy himself much time at all.

Without even having to look down to insert the keys into the ignition, he started the engine keeping his eyes fixed expectantly on the hospital doors. As real life replaced his vision they burst open as predicted before he could even pull away. It could have been to receive any other emergency for all he knew but as paranoia set in he was certain they were coming for him.

He accelerated as fast as the lorry's considerable weight would allow but quickly reprimanded himself for drawing yet more attention his way. There was now more staff at the entrance but they looked confused, as if looking for something. It must be because they'd found Grace. He didn't expect them to take much time to solve the equation but this was unprecedented. He breathed deeply trying to rationalise and calm himself; he'd never visited in a company vehicle before so they wouldn't necessarily know what to look for. All he had to do was drive like it was any other day and blend in. Even a thirty foot lorry could be inconspicuous so long as he didn't panic, but panic was an understatement as a middle aged woman slammed herself against his cabin door, imprinting her face against the frosted glass and startling Nick to the extent that it took his seatbelt to hold him down. It was the same lady he suspected had reported his worrying behaviour and she was now screaming something through the window at him, pressing against it as though that might help force her words through, but over the pain in his head and the revving engine he might as well have been deaf.

Nick moved the lorry forward in reflex but instead of backing off and retreating, the women reached up, snatching at the door handle like it was her own life at stake. He snapped the lock down a split second before she could invade the relative tranquility of his cabin. Her grasp was so fierce that she was dragged a short distance before she either lost her grip or gave up the struggle. With nothing to personally gain, her persistence was nothing short of saintly but Nick would have kicked her off if he could. He just wanted to be left alone, but watched his wing mirror with amazement and even anger as the stubborn bitch got up, waving her arms frantically and beckoning the hospital staff that now careered towards them. Everyone involved was trying to help but right now he'd swap them all for the heartless majority of the cities inhabitants who'd gladly ignore him.

He shifted gear and thundered himself out of the car park, watching with relief whilst one of life's few good people shrank as the distance between them grew, all the time continuing to choke on his exhaust fumes. After the next turn he'd at least be out of view and could only hope that once off hospital grounds he'd cease to be their responsibility and might seem a little less worth chasing.

He started to reflect on just how long an overweight, overdosed old man dressed as Santa could evade the authorities on Christmas Eve in a vehicle that could barely shave its way through the crowded city streets on what must surely be the busiest day of the year. He questioned his judgment but found himself unable to focus on more than one thing at a time with any clarity and there was a bend in the road ahead; he'd better make that his priority. As he negotiated and crept his way around it he had to brake suddenly to narrowly avoid collision with a motorcycle, its agitated rider clearly in a rush and desperate to deliver the pizzas that only just remained on board. The lorry had only delayed him by seconds but he seemed infuriated; Nick could only assume he was already having a less than perfect day and he now seemed no less frustrated to be stuck behind an animal trailer. With live cargo onboard, its driver had to drive carefully and he certainly wasn't going to compromise that for an impatient teenager who was repeatedly leaning on his pathetic excuse for a horn. It was typical of the date, but everyone seemed in a hurry on the one day that time couldn't matter more to Nick. Countless vehicles of every shape and size battled to make their way in the traffic so it was difficult to believe that anyone was in a rush to join it, yet three men with enviable freedom sprinted to reach a car parked outside Fenleys as if they'd already spent far too long inside. They didn't know how lucky they were, if Nick still had the strength and the coordination to make his way on foot that's exactly what he'd do.

As he stopped at the next set of traffic lights he again considered whether he could manage walking as it would be a lot easier to disappear as a pedestrian than as a driver but he was already starting to feel weaker; and besides, leaving his lorry on it's handbrake at the crossing would ensure him attention that he could really do without. It wasn't an option and he needed to concentrate on what was viable. If he'd have realised he'd feel this fragile so quickly he may have done things differently but he had no choice but to deal with reality.

He was heading for nowhere in particular and if there was a quiet side road within the vicinity he'd have taken it but there wasn't; not today. He had to keep moving on his way to somewhere and it might as well be his next drop off; if he made it at least they'd have their tree. He could then take a little pleasure in knowing the last thing he did was selfless and neglected to think of the psychological damage that could be inflicted on who ever eventually found him slumped in the drivers seat. He again checked his rear view mirror for flashing lights but could see none; that didn't mean that they weren't around the corner though so he'd have to keep competing for every available inch of road.

CHAPTER THIRTY-TWO

Noel desperately wanted to close his streaming eyes now; more so than at any point during his fall but not for any of the reasons he had expected. It wasn't even due to the reflexes he had been so sure would turn out to be his master. He felt sure that he was in control now but it was a sensation he barely remembered. He was glad to feel it just one more time and would do everything he could to ensure he savoured it for the rest of his life; both seconds of it. He concentrated on that thought rather than the panic that rose within whenever he allowed himself to consider the advancing pavement. It looked so much more threatening now that he was just a few storeys above it and it appeared a lot less perfect too.

He'd previously imagined the moment would be over in an instant but now he could see the imperfections of the ground below, the reality again sneaked its way past his defences. It insisted on a premonition that saw part of him hitting the concrete slabs before the rest of his body caught up; it might be his chest but not necessarily as his body was beginning to twist. Either way, for a split second there would be pain like he'd never known as his ribs caved in but he'd accepted that as punishment for what he'd done. But now that sentence could be so much harsher than he'd ever imagined; now he knew how long these tiny fragments of time could last in whatever dimension he'd found himself and fear crept in like rot. Virus like, it spread until he found himself unable to block out the thoughts that his barriers had up until now kept at bay; he pictured actually seeing peoples horrified expressions as he entered their sphere of vision and it didn't bear thinking about; he wondered if for that last split second he'd literally be able to follow their gaze as they trailed his descent until at last it ended.

That was how far he'd fallen now, he could see individual people and he dreaded recognising a face in the crowd; but worse still was the thought of someone recognising him. He hoped with all that was left of his soul that nobody would look up and that his landing would be somehow shielded from view. For the first time he thought about what he'd done not from his own point of view or from that of his family or friends; but from the perspective of the innocents that, through no fault of their own could be about to witness a horrific sight but mercifully everyone seemed to be distracted by a near collision across the street. It had begun to cause such chaos that it was distracting. He arced his head to try and see it in more detail but before he could he was again rescued and transported to a different kind of hurt, and for what must be the final time he saw what wasn't physically there.

The rain ran off the same car as it had when Noel sat silently outside his parents' home three hundred and sixty-five days ago. It was one of two places to which he'd been drawn when he'd left Karl's house trying to come to terms not only with what had just happened, but with what must have begun some time ago. He'd have despised being thought of like that by anyone but the fact that it was someone he felt sorry for just multiplied the insult. He'd left Karl's house defiantly thinking there was any number of people he could call on... but as he drove away it dawned on him that there really wasn't; on any other evening there might be, but not tonight. It wasn't a time to be with anyone but those you're closest to and that left him on the outside looking in.

He'd driven for some time before giving in and then parked opposite his dad's truck for just as long, staring through the kitchen windows. His family were eating dinner, sat in the places they always had and pulling crackers before desert the way they always would. When he saw they still kept what had been his chair vacant he'd even gone as far as opening the car door but slammed it again when he imagined having to explain himself. It would be easier to drive on... even seeing *her* again would be easier than invading a house that used to be his home, however much he'd wanted to.

But when he arrived outside Angela's driveway he again found himself frozen by the fear of rejection. He might have sat there all night had she not made the approach; as her friends grew older and wiser they'd seen through her in a way that Noel never could and had all but deserted her. She and Noel were both alone for all the same reasons and she'd been busy staring out her bedroom window at nothing in particular until Noel pulled up; she'd recognised the car instantly. For the third time they used each other, not just for the night, but throughout the entire year ahead.

That was now twelve months ago and he found himself with her as a twenty-three year old woman struggling to believe he'd met her as a fifteen year old girl. They were no better suited now than they were back then yet still they continued their particularly vicious circle. Nothing had changed, he waited for her now as he always had, all the time promising himself that he'd leave, just to teach her a lesson but knew he never would.

Noel looked at the phone beside him as it flashed its message alert, but as it faded, so did its apparent urgency. She had already taken far longer than he expected but that wasn't exactly out of character. It was too early to worry and genuine concern really would be the only excuse to give in to temptation. Especially as he'd argued so strongly earlier that temptation really wasn't an excuse for anything.

He looked at the illuminated clock which was once again the only source of light in the car and switched on the radio to occupy his suspicious mind; it constantly reminded him of the time of year as if anyone wouldn't be well aware. He found himself absent mindedly flicking through the conversational stations and popular music frequencies, unsure of what he wanted to listen to until he eventually made a decision. He surprised himself by turning the dial back and retuning into what sounded like a live broadcast. It was clear and the quality was impressive but it had that raw, hollow sound that technicians would never allow in a pre-recorded transmission. Noel imagined the obviously large choir were singing from a church and being a local station it must be nearby.

He smiled to himself. He wasn't sure how many times he'd promised himself and others that's exactly where he'd be next Christmas Eve. It somehow seemed like the best place to be and he'd always meant what he said at the time. Yet he never managed to convince himself it was the *right* place to be. To arrive for midnight mass having ignored the building and its people all year round seemed as hypocritical and convenient as his annual charity events. He turned the volume up a little, the glorious resonance emanating from his surround sound speakers. By shutting his eyes he was there in the church until that same electronic jingle broke the moment and he was reminded of his tiny passenger; the mobile started him thinking again. He'd been jealous of that phone for years. It was never far away from Angela's side and forever held her attention; he hated the greedy little bastard and so couldn't help wonder what had suddenly been so important that she'd leave it behind... what... or who.

He despised the fact that he thought like that now. He knew he shouldn't but he just couldn't stop himself. Rightly or wrongly he'd never had his doubts before, but the rumours he was sure he should ignore had damaged his confidence in her. He knew having never been with anyone else didn't mean she couldn't or wouldn't, it had just never entered his head before. Her insistence that she hadn't been unfaithful even whilst they were separated had been the main reason he'd taken her back; he needed a companion with that kind of loyalty now more than ever. He drowned out any suspicions he had with whatever worked at the time; and right now it was an exceptional choir.

He'd had opportunities to at least try and put his mind at rest through mutual friends who might know more than him. There was even the chance to listen in on telephone calls on more than one occasion but he didn't want to give in to that kind of behaviour. He liked to think that it was due to trust rather than fear that he'd remained resolute. An attempt to investigate was to accuse her, and once that started there was no telling where it would end. But a little part of him that he didn't like to visit too often wondered if that was the sole reason; as much as he'd never admit it to anyone else and could barely confess it to himself, he simply didn't want to know the truth just in case ignorance was preferable. He remembered all too well how it felt when he left her before and more importantly, how he didn't feel anything at all for so long afterwards. It had made him numb. But lately he'd wondered if the constant anguish and the inability to concentrate on anything other than what she was doing was worse than the risk he'd be taking. But the one thing he did know was that giving into his impulse to pick up that phone was as wrong as it would be to look at her diary.

His arm shot out as if it had made up its own mind and wanted to make sure he couldn't re-engage his brain in time to stop it happening. His eyes were still shut so his grip was awkward but he snatched it from the passenger seat with amazing accuracy. He brought his thumb down, confirming that he wanted to read the message even though he wasn't sure and with a deep breath he opened his eyes. He'd braced himself a little too early as he struggled to interpret the abbreviations until he realised he was looking at it upside down. It gave him another chance to do the right thing; to trust Angela and give her the benefit of the doubt but he didn't take it. He twisted it, reading as he turned with every word wrenching his insides just a little more than the last. The thought of her scheming and planning to see them both in one night seemed somehow worse than the fact that she'd been cheating on him.

He considered retaliation only a moment or two then realised there was no dilemma at all. He sent a simple message back; he hoped the words 'she's all yours' would seem final enough to tell them both how he felt.

He pulled away blindly. He wasn't going to waste any tears on her but his eyes had welled and his vision was blurred to the point of distortion. He had to escape but was forced to shunt his car back and forth as he edged his way out of the car park, now full to capacity.

Checking her advance, he twisted in his seat and felt the engagement ring he'd bought five years ago pressing through his trouser pocket, but the day he'd waited so long for had never been further away; at the time he had no idea what to do with it but if he'd have known then what he knew now he'd have sold it the first chance he got and put the money to better use; it might be impossible but that's exactly what he'd do if there was any way he could.

By the time he'd successfully steered himself to freedom Angela was practically at his door. But there was no way he was going to allow her to open it; he mustn't let the poison in. If he did it would seep into him again... the lies would be toxic, but so cunningly administered that he'd welcome them. They would be convincing enough that doubt, his most hated of enemies would burrow itself in until it was him making apologies. The only remedy that had ever worked was distance so he kept driving.

Checking the phone again as his screaming tyres found the main road he checked the message was still on the screen. It was and it hurt just as much reading it the second time. He scrolled down to illuminate the parting shot and twisted in his seat whilst simultaneously bringing his window down far enough to allow him to throw her phone towards her but he couldn't help himself; he threw it *at* her.

Wiping his eyes allowed him to see that he was already too far away to be able to read the look on her face when he looked back but her body language conveyed perfect confusion; she'd obviously never managed to find whoever she was looking for in the heaving crowd and had therefore never seen the message Noel had sent in reply. As such, she'd have no idea why he was leaving without her... he could sort that out.

Until now he'd never known if he achieved hitting his target but from his new and multi angled view he could see that he'd missed, but only because she saw the missile coming. His aim was surprisingly accurate and had forced her to dodge but before all he'd been able to see was the enduring vision of shattered glass that had flown before his eyes. The darkness of the world outside had twisted and turned around him, swirling in a mass of confusion in which nothing was clear.

From that terrifying moment, right up until this very night everything about his life had been lived to cover the guilt he dare not feel about his recklessness. His was the only vehicle able to drive away from the accident and, however much it disgusted him now; that was precisely what he'd done. He'd blamed it on his frame of mind, he blamed it on Angela and he'd blamed it on the weather; he'd repeatedly reassured himself every single day that if it had happened before or after that night he'd have stayed; that he'd have done the right thing. But the fact was he didn't. He'd put as many miles between himself and the scene as he could with the petrol he had left in his tank yet he couldn't help but look behind him as he accelerated away. The carnage was spread across the road and it was hard to imagine that everyone lived to regret it; the next day he found out that was true.

Even with all the excuses in the world he still held himself ultimately responsible and right the way through January he'd frozen at every phone call, convinced that whilst his registration couldn't have been taken, Angela would know what happened and would have reported him as some kind of twisted revenge. His freedom was testament that she hadn't, yet he was sure it was due to her own feelings of guilt and knowing the part she played rather than through protecting him. There seemed a little justice knowing that she was there to see it and he questioned whether it haunted her like it had done him. Within a month he had his answer; she'd moved away without telling anyone where. In Noel's experience it was evidence of a guilty conscience as he'd considered doing exactly the same but something kept him where he was; perhaps he just knew that disappearing without a trace would attract attention that he'd so far escaped.

For the next month he avoided any form of news and hoped it would return the favour. The local papers were recycled without being read and every regional report exchanged for another channel until he felt sure the headlines concerned people and places that he'd never seen. It had worked and until she unlocked it tonight on the building's edge he'd kept it all in that same dark place he reserved for all the things he wished he'd never said or done and the apologies he should have made but now never could.

But tonight it had found him on that ledge and in the most unlikely of situations and he'd learned exactly what he'd driven away from and the consequences of his selfishness. An innocent man had died and his daughter was left mourning the loss to the extent that she was actually jealous of his passing. Noel wondered how he'd lived with it for so long. He looked through his twenty-fourth Christmas onto the unforgiving pavement that eagerly awaited him; but why should it have mercy? This was nothing he didn't deserve; he couldn't bring her father back however much he'd want to and this was the only redemption he could offer. Just talking to her had made him doubt his role in the world and quite what he was meant to bring to it. He'd been given so much whilst she'd had everything taken away yet in just being herself she had more than he could hope for.

Based on that alone he'd started to wander down that lonely road that always leads to pondering the point of existence, but for a while he thought he may have found it in her. Perhaps. Yet the moment he thought himself to be the reason for her pain that indecision was over. He'd accused, tried, sentenced and all but executed himself believing that if there was a jury, they'd be undivided in their condemnation but as he watched the evidence play out he found reason to appeal. He watched intensely, seeing more than he had done before as he was no longer blinded by panic.

The same shards flew horizontally through the air as they had done a year ago but it happened *before* he'd made any sort of impact whatsoever. What he saw was an exact replica; almost. Everything looked and sounded just like he'd remembered it. It proved his memory accurate in every sense except that the loudest of those thunderous, colliding sounds actually preceded the moment he was shunted across the road, the force whipping his head back and ensuring he missed seeing the few vital seconds that followed.

He'd driven into an existing accident rather than causing it and had careered head on into a motor cycle that no longer carried it's owner; it may be due to luck alone but he was starting to realise a lot of things were. It didn't make what he'd done any less irresponsible but it did mean he'd done no more damage than writing off a bike that was already crumpled beyond recognition. His comparative innocence could not bring anyone back from the grave but it did wipe the blood off his hands.

The weight that had hung on his shoulders lifted to the extent he couldn't be far away from floating back up the way he came as his exoneration tipped that fragile balance back again but the decision he'd made could not be reversed. Even having witnessed the impossible he doubted gravity would change its rules just because he'd changed his mind and that made his immediate future inevitable.

He wasn't merely a day's worth wiser than yesterday; he'd gained the knowledge of a lifetime, even if it was unnaturally short he'd all but ignored it the first time around. That's what it had taken for him to quite literally see the light. He'd done and said so much that he wasn't proud of but at least he regretted it, he'd made plenty of mistakes but most were either for the right reasons or out of simple naiveté but he'd done his best to put them right... eventually. If he was honest with himself it hadn't taken this long to realise it but he'd convinced himself it was irrelevant as he was repaying a life with a life and however differently he may view his family and friends now, his debt alone kept him from regretting his decision.

But now regret was *all* he felt. Regret that he couldn't spend more time with those that were owed it and regret that he couldn't become the person he'd be if he had the chance again. The irony was that he wouldn't have to change who he was at all; he merely had to stop pretending to be someone else. He'd been his own worst enemy all his life and had spent it trying to please all the wrong people whilst those that really cared about him paid for his misjudgments. He'd give anything to let them know that he'd at last learnt what mattered but once he left that ledge behind, hitting the ground with a clearer conscience was the most he could hope for and if nothing else, he'd been granted that.

CHAPTER THIRTY-THREE

Robyn didn't even have to look where she was going. She knew these corridors better than the streets in which she grew up and that allowed her to keep her head down, staring intently at an old scuffed and folded letter. It was only a reply to a query regarding last quarter's gas bill, but it had been already paid now and the debate resolved, so it was no longer of any use other than to serve as an excellent excuse to avoid eye contact and the resulting rehashed conversations she'd rather not have.

She furrowed her brow in an effort to look so lost in thought that others would forgive her passing them by without acknowledgment. Had she seen her own reflection she'd have realised she was overacting and that her expression was so exaggerated that had anyone noticed, that would have actually created their talking point. But nobody did... at this time of night they were now as wrapped up in their own plans for the next few days as she was in her winter coat as she purposefully headed back along the obstacle course that was the B Ward, gradually thawing as she went.

The few remaining staff who weren't too busy for small talk could see by her impressive pace that even if they had time, she didn't. She thundered onwards, blinkered towards the exit but as she'd learned over these last few months, you can try and change the way you live but there's no changing the person you are and she began to take an interest in those around her.

The hospital was on skeleton shift and rightly so after all the extra working hours its staff had endured lately. Overtime was as certain as inflated prices over this joyous time of year but whilst the accident and emergency department would be barely able to cope as revellers revelled a little too much, the wards housing the long term patients remained unaffected and had settled for the night. It made a lonely place; like a ghost town when compared to its usual breakneck pace and it suited Robyn for the first time ever. But without her even realising it, her escape had progressively slowed until she'd been surprised to find herself standing on tiptoes and peering in through the thick glass set in each of the ward doors; from the other side she imagined they must seem like those of a prison in this eerie half-light. It was so much quieter than usual which was to be expected with around half the usual staff on duty, but it never failed to surprise her. She felt for those working the year's most dreaded shift but knew it must be even harder for those that couldn't leave; those whose condition was just not stable enough for them to go home, even if just for the holidays.

She creaked the heavy door open gradually, one squeak at a time, until the resulting gap allowed her to ease her head through, even if it meant squashing her 'party' curls. She'd created them for no better reason than to convince her colleagues she had a life outside of work so it didn't matter. They'd served their purpose; everyone had assumed they signalled she had places to go tonight and she hadn't corrected them. She sometimes wondered if she was any healthier than the patients she surveyed as she scanned the room. Her anguish for their condition was eased as she was greeted by a surprisingly peaceful sight; it was a silent night indeed.

'Merry Christmas' she whispered, carefully gauging her volume and ensuring she was loud enough to be heard across the sizable room, but not to the extent that she'd wake anyone who was already sleeping. There was no reply. Without an immediate response there seemed little point in staring into the semi-darkness and she considered what a thoughtless thing it was to say. How could they even hope for a merry anything?

She paused just a moment longer, just in case before beginning to shut the door again gradually. She'd delayed for as long as possible; hoping for a reply that would prove her thoughtless words had not caused offence. When no such reassurance came, as unlikely as it was, she wished it to be because they were all asleep and dreaming dreams... even if they were increasingly unlikely to come true. The shaft of light that she'd allowed into the room narrowed until it was all but gone as she guided the door through its worn and rusted hinge yet the words made it through just before it fell shut.

'Merry Christmas my love... and bless you!' She didn't even know which of the poor souls had whispered back but it didn't matter. Even on the days when she wondered why she came to work there'd be moments like that to remind her. It took less than two minutes but now at least twice as many people were happier than they were before and that made it time well spent. The time it'd take to check the three remaining wards suddenly didn't seem quite so long if that's all it took to make her feel a little better about herself, and if it spread a little Christmas cheer to others as well, all the better. Besides, having started to warm up a little now she was in no hurry to expose herself to the elements again even if it was with the benefit of her jacket.

The next door was opened in the same careful, considered manner and the beam it allowed in was sharp and hard-edged, effectively highlighting each patient. It crept across the room, passing over them as if scanning them individually. It was harsher than the subtle light that had softly swept the previous ward before as the long florescent tube directly behind her had no consideration at all for rest or slumber. She wondered if she should skip this ward. The brightness had already caused a few patients to stir and she supposed she may well be doing more harm than good. Undecided she held the door steady before returning it to the frame but in doing so she held the spotlight on Grace; everything looked exactly the same as when she saw her last... and it shouldn't. By moving the door just a little further she could illuminate the left side of her bed and the equipment that surrounded it. Now able to see it clearly, Robyn was certain that her tiredness was not fuelling her imagination; the drip fluid had hardly dropped.

She edged herself through the doorway and into the darkened room, the shadows moving around her like ghosts as it creaked shut behind her. Robyn was respected enough and all the right people were predicting a bright future for her but she was a long, long way from being the most qualified consultant in the hospital. Nor did she have the highest IQ or the technical skill of some of her colleagues but right now she understood what most of them wouldn't. Even the most intelligent among them would be scratching their head; it may encase a brilliant mind but still they'd be trying to figure out how something like this could happen. But Robyn understood all too well; and wished she didn't.

She was impressively knowledgeable when it came to medicine and had learned more than most about procedure and protocol, even outside of her own remit, but what she knew without study or revision was what made her so good at her chosen profession; she knew people. It was the reason she always had to break the saddest news and it was why she didn't have to question what she was looking at now.

The lead powering the units as essential to Grace as air itself lay two inches below where it could have served her. It was incredibly unlikely that something so essential could be dislodged accidentally and even more unlikely that it could happen without being noticed and instantly corrected, but it wasn't entirely impossible. However, the cable didn't just lie abandoned as if caught in an oversight that didn't bear consideration, but was tucked back under the unit and hidden away in a manner that suggested the unthinkable.

Robyn suddenly felt a coldness that couldn't be dressed against as it swelled up from within her. She sank to the ground, unsure whether it was to investigate further or that she felt so physically sick she was no longer able to stand. Either way it brought her eye level with the plug powering the failsafe warning system installed just incase such a disaster should ever happen. It was pulled far enough out to disconnect, but not so far as to fall from the wall. To her at least, this laid the final piece of the puzzle and the picture was much clearer than she'd wish it to be.

CHAPTER THIRTY-FOUR

So this was it. The light that would introduce his final day on earth was bleaching the colour out of his vision again. Noel knew its passing would bring memories so recent he'd barely had time for them to fade in the slightest but with a revived interest in life he'd be grateful to see anything other than the infinite nothingness that awaited him.

In reality he was only yards away from where his fall was about to take him but in his mind the situation couldn't have been more opposite. He was staring skyward towards the building having made it half way up the fire escape that scaled its full height. He moved one hand over the other, now literally dragging himself onward, unconvinced that it was even the direction in which he wanted to travel. He wondered how many before him, if any at all had made the same ascent. It was a fire escape after all; far more renowned for providing an emergency route *down* rather than up and he was certain nobody would put themselves through this by choice.

The burning pain he'd felt in his legs had found it's way to his arms as he'd begun to rely on them to keep him going but at least it served to take his mind off of just how far he had already climbed. Heights had never been his strong point and he was fairly sure he'd shy away from even standing too close to a balcony edge at this level; if someone had told him yesterday he'd be marching relentlessly up these rickety and seldom used steps with just a single metal banister separating him from the increasingly considerable drop he'd have found it hard to believe; if they'd have told him it'd be his decision to do so he'd have found it impossible.

He'd done his very best not to look down, particularly through the worryingly large open spaces between the steps, but every so often he couldn't help himself and each time the world below looked a little more like a child's play set. He wondered how small the cars would look next time he dared glance and considered whether it was even worth knowing as he became increasingly convinced that he was merely chasing shadows and that all he'd achieve from this was confirmation that he did indeed have an overactive imagination... and most probably legs that would ache for days.

It didn't seem to matter how irrational he knew his phobia was, he couldn't quite control it. There was no arguing that a fall from even three or four storeys would most likely be your last so another few would put him in no greater danger. But whilst he knew this to be true, it hadn't helped him much up to now. And even if it had, the sheer exertion was proving a problem in itself. Under any other circumstances he'd have paused every few flights to catch his breath and to stop the acid in his legs building quite so steadily but whilst he began to doubt those few stolen moments would make any difference at all, they just might. And in case they did matter, he'd been careful not to attract attention to himself, treading carefully on the metal steps that threatened to send a metallic alarm ringing and vibrating along the hollow steel construction every time his awkward stealth failed him. Being so careful not to announce his approach to whoever may or may not be up there had made the journey painfully slow. But now, sobering from the effort he was making and the focus it demanded he fully expected to be returning down the same escape, none the wiser as to what he saw; or at least *thought* he saw.

The structure was sturdier than he'd anticipated and as his confidence in it grew, he started to swing himself around the railing corners as he repeatedly followed their crisscross pattern, one flight at a time, leaving the familiar security of solid ground further and further behind. He'd grown increasingly dependent on them and wondered if that was now all that was holding him up as exhaustion and vertigo conspired against him but he daren't let go to find out. He hurled himself around another railing, fully expecting to be faced with an identical flight of steps just as foreboding as the last but instead looked up the stairwell and onto the open, featureless sky.

He could now see the summit and counted the last remaining steps as he took them one gasp at a time realising that this may not turn out to be a waste of time after all; if nothing else it highlighted that maybe he should take advantage of that corporate gym membership instead of creating excuses not to?

He was as relieved as he had expected to be but he was so surprised at his sense of achievement upon reaching the rooftop that he almost forgot why he was there. His legs were buckling and his throat so tight he couldn't swallow but he might as well have just conquered Everest. As he leaned back against the brick wall that no doubt housed the generator, it felt as though just one more step would have been one more than he was capable of taking but he wondered if he'd have felt the same had he climbed half as high or twice as far. The mind has a way of doing that; excelling the body beyond itself, however impossible it might have seemed afterwards, or even before.

His previously immaculate suit now clung to him, wringing wet but unable to dampen his smile as he looked out onto a view he'd never seen before despite having grown up in this very city; he was even born in the hospital at the end of this street. The height alone brought new realisations; whilst the throbbing and conflicting mass of decoration competed for attention on the street, there were far subtler and personal displays in the windows of flats above it. They were understated by comparison and whilst he didn't know if they were restricted by taste or budget it really didn't matter; they seemed more sincere and all the more pleasant for it. It seemed a shame it had taken him this long to notice them but with the distractions on the ground he couldn't imagine the last time he'd looked above them which only served to make the fact that he took the time to tonight even stranger.

The festive trees he could see through the windows opposite said more about the people living there than could ever be deduced from the car they drive or the clothes they wear. The obvious attention to detail was a stark contrast to the boldness of those below and with this angle the High Street's shameless excess was even clearer. He was able to take in more of the scene below from this perspective than he ever could when he was a part of it and the glow it emitted was immense. From the ground its centerpiece looked simple enough; a sleigh that was all but ignored by day but did admittedly look spectacular by night as it hovered above the traffic as if by magic. The complex and jet black cabling that powered its ample lights and held it in place were invisible when viewed against the night sky but from up here looking down they were clearly defined against the increasingly frosted pavement below. Behind it he could even see a giant inflatable snowman, imaginatively named Frosty according to the plastic scarf hung around his neck. Yet despite his excessive size, from street level he was hidden to the extent that he'd never even been noticed behind the stall erected, larger still on the sidewalk in front.

Noel shook his head back and forth, tilted it back and closed his eyes, trying to compose himself. There was no point in revelling in glory, real or imagined and there was certainly no sense in him soldiering all the way up here only to lose potentially critical time at this point.

Still breathing like he might not get another chance he leant out from behind the wall that had shielded him, scanning the expanse of concrete that sprawled before him. It was divided only by a few power cables that led his gaze right the way to the opposite edge of the building. He traced them nervously to where the silhouette he'd so hoped would either not exist or turn out to be nothing more than an extension of the old furniture that was bizarrely scattered across the rooftop, presumably discarded to make way for its excessive decorations that had replaced them. His first wish was in vain. It was still there... like the shadows he remembered but it was so reassuringly shapeless that it could still be anything. It did nothing at all to prove it to be what he'd feared, but that was in no way evidence that it wasn't either.

He narrowed his eyes in an effort to concentrate his focus, studying the motionless outline for any clue it was willing to give, but subtle hints may go unnoticed from this distance. Reluctantly surrendering his shelter and support he crept lightly forward no more than a few elongated paces before stopping dead in his tracks; the outline moved, only slightly but it was in a different direction to the breeze that he'd only just noticed and he knew what that meant. It meant, unfortunately, that he'd been right.

He debated whether to announce himself, intently aware that any sudden moves could provoke a reaction that would live with him forever; he could even be blamed. To let himself be known was to take responsibility for the outcome and considering the situation, that did not bear thinking about. He knew exactly what to do and it was to do nothing except make that call. Now that he'd at least established the facts he could call the police and be on his way having done what he could.

He pulled his cell phone from his pocket and had even started dialing before he'd noticed that all too familiar flashing screen. His model was indeed, as the advertising promised, the most compact and sleekest looking mobile on the market, but an ability to pick up a reliable signal obviously wasn't so high on the designers' priority list. Up until now he hadn't even minded it lacking its primary function. Its failing to fulfill its one real purpose in life had saved him from making many a call he'd regret the following morning. In those difficult late night hours when licensing laws snatched away his much loved distraction he'd not only been tempted to disturb people better left alone, he'd gone so far as to actually try only to be saved by its stylish inadequacy every time... and he'd been grateful. But now, more than ever he desperately needed the criminally expensive device to be more than a fashion statement... and it wouldn't.

He looked at the various cabling, wires and transmitters surrounding him and sighed. With that kind of interference, adjusting his position for signal was futile. He looked behind him towards the stairwell and back again. If he crept away now, whatever happened would have nothing to do with him. He'd have influenced nothing and that just might save him anymore guilt than he already felt. He carried enough around with him as it was.

He must be about half a dozen paces behind what he could now see was a person, oddly dressed for her age… and gender, and she was perched precariously on the ledge as if it was a park bench. Predicting the likely outcome of provoking a sudden reaction he started to move backwards as carefully as he could in a perfect slow-motion rewind of the last thirty seconds then suddenly paused, his realisation rooting him firmly to the spot.

Would he really be less to blame if he sank away now? He wondered how many people, and more to the point, how many security cameras would place him at the scene? He might not get away with it this time and if he was recorded retreating after so obviously understanding the situation surely he could be accused of… murder, manslaughter, aiding suicide? It didn't matter which, he didn't want any of them associated with his name.

The only thing worse than doing something was to do nothing and he turned his attention to what, if anything, he should say. Or would that cause her to decide on what she was obviously already considering? Maybe he just needed to snatch her away and not take that chance? These options and their seemingly endless combinations and variations raced each other for preference but he was caught short before they'd even neared the finish line by the girl's voice, as decided and focused as he'd ever heard.

CHAPTER THIRTY-FIVE

Robyn just stared with mixed emotions, amazed at how surprised she wasn't. In a desensitised world that could now accept so much this was surely one of the last true taboos. After years of struggling and arguing on either side she'd worked out where she stood on the death penalty and had eventually formed an opinion she honestly believed in. She'd stood firm with regard to her position on abortion but this... this remained unresolved, for her at least; but obviously not everyone had failed to decide. Right now though, looking at Grace it was hard to think Nick was wrong however much she wanted to; however much she was duty bound to. As a consultant sworn to save and prolong life she knew she should be outraged; but she couldn't bring herself to be. Her eyes welled but she wiped them dry as if there was anyone to notice, but everyone around seemed to be sleeping peacefully; some more so than others.

She tightened her jaw as if that would somehow lock the tears out and keep her thoughts in as she tried to consider more than the one obvious option. She knew she wouldn't want to be the judge or the jury when this made its way to court. Without knowing the people and their history it was an impossible task and one that wasn't to be envied. But the fact was that she did know them; she knew Nick anyway, probably better than she knew many of her more conventional friends. She saw the very closest of them twice a week and her own mother maybe once a fortnight yet she shared her life, and more recently, her car with Nick two days on, one day off; more if she worked overtime. She remembered the first time she'd met him. She'd been the messenger when Grace was diagnosed and at that point it had been the worst day of Nick's life. She'd delivered so much unthinkable news to so many undeserving people since that she felt almost ashamed that she'd recently lost the ability to even remember them all. They'd become cases rather than individuals and she'd sworn she'd never let that happen. How could she still be human when she could orchestrate moments they'd never forget whilst failing to recall them with any real feeling herself?

But with Nick it was different… at the time she'd never been put in that awful position before and she remembered every excruciating moment; it almost caused her to abandon the profession she'd worked so hard to join. She'd been present at some of the most horrific accidents and scenes of carnage imaginable and had famously even planned lunch whilst casually observing a heart transplant but seeing a heart actually break was something entirely different and she wondered if she'd ever recover from it. She'd even gone as far as writing her resignation letter and the fact that it was Nick that talked her out of it was just part of what she had to thank him for. She'd not only learnt to deal with those situations but she'd actually become accomplished at doing so; she was often congratulated on the fact but she secretly wondered if it was really anything to be proud of. Were such controlled emotions an asset or a weakness in the real world? It had been the subject of many discussions and Nick had even taught her to joke about it and to see herself like everyone else did; she often wondered if he truly realised he'd saved her from so much more than just throwing away her career. After so many failed relationships and having witnessed first hand what people can do to each other she'd almost lost faith in humanity but seeing Nick by Grace's side might not have given her trust, but it did give her hope and to her that was as essential to life as water and oxygen.

Always the realist, she didn't even imagine that anyone would ever look at her the way Nick looked at his wife but she didn't need them to. To see just half the want in their eyes would be more than good enough for her as she was certain she'd already missed her chance by being born a generation too late. Nick had grown up in a different world and she wondered whether, with the last of the true romantics nearing extinction, we'd soon need old black and white movies to even witness such commitment, let alone feel it. There'd always been the dictionary to remind us that loyalty shouldn't be confused with convenience and necessity, that love wasn't a monthly contract and that 'I do' doesn't mean 'I might'. But she didn't have to live in that world already. Nick and people like him weren't just a memory yet, but they were an endangered species and she was here to protect them as best she could for as long as possible.

She'd spent years in education and lost entire months in books to be able to advise patients and their families correctly and honestly yet she'd learnt more at Grace's bedside than could be taught at any seminar or learnt in any library.

She bent down, slowly at first and pulled the lead from under the unit. The plug was smaller than her clenched fist and cost less than the taxi she should have taken home but ultimately, it was the difference between life and death.

As panic swelled inside her, every option paired with an emotion then squared against the enemy. Guilt stated its claim screaming that she'd forced the situation by issuing the transfer before reason stepped into the fight, arguing its case just as convincingly. They then had to join forces against both loss and sadness tearing away at her but she knew the battle being fought must be nothing at all in comparison to that raging within Nick. He was a complicated man who'd tried hard to give the impression he'd cope better than he ever would. Her first instinct was to call him but to do so would be admission that she knew and that would later turn into incrimination. She wanted to be there for him like he had been for her but she felt angry to be put in this position where protocol dictated that she raise the alarm; it was the only thing for a consultant to do and as always, duty called.

CHAPTER THIRTY-SIX

'I might not have heard you coming if you'd have taken the lift'.

Noel stood dead in his tracks as she looked back over her shoulder. He hoped she was joking but either way her sarcasm at least gave away that it was lack of fitness rather than a lack of stealth that had given him away. She must have heard his breathing hailing his approach before he even knew she was real. It was slowing now but was obviously still heavy enough to be heard above the traffic below; it was embarrassing. He really would have to look into that gym membership.

She'd known that someone was behind her, but had been understandably convinced it must be company security or perhaps even the police earning their wages. And on double time for working Christmas Eve, it was the very least they could do. She got ready to despise whichever form of authority it turned out to be as she didn't need to be acquainted with them to know their kind; anyone who made a living lording it over whoever they could wasn't her type of person.

As her eyes adjusted from the kaleidoscope of colour below to the contrast in which Noel stood, her vague surprise at the lack of uniform turned to disbelief as she managed to focus. She recognised him instantly but remained expressionless. To let him know that he stood out from the urban circus in which she first saw him was a compliment she wasn't prepared to give, she doubted he'd need it and she was sure he didn't deserve it after the way he'd left her in a crumpled heap. She remembered him dodging her as she fell to the ground in case she creased his suit all too well. She'd played it over in her head to the extent she now felt like she knew him and that just exaggerated her surprise to see him here of all places. It was the exact opposite to what she'd expected but she'd seen simple curiosity take control of people before; nobody knew how to mind their own business these days. It was ironic that she had to go to these lengths to be noticed but it was too late to make a difference now. He'd played his own small part in convincing her there was only one answer to all the questions that plagued her and so he deserved to see this. She could only assume his being here was some form of repentant heroics but if that was true he was wasting his time; she'd needed rescuing for months but had now grown tired of wanting to be saved... but that didn't mean she wasn't intrigued. Another few minutes would make no real difference and she delayed her intentions.

She started to lift herself backwards but couldn't move quickly without the danger of falling. She was all too aware that this type of behaviour was typical of the thousands of attention seekers who cried out for help with similar displays of desperation. Anyone watching would probably doubt her conviction the second she retreated but they'd be wrong, she knew her own mind; she just wasn't in a hurry.

Noel decided to ignore the statement regarding the lift as he was still unsure whether he should take it seriously. Rather than risk looking foolish he started the conversation again.

'You look like you could use some company?'

'That's presumptuous.'

Noel drew a deep breath. This wasn't going to be easy.

'Well am I right?'

'The last time I was interested in a man's company it was because he owned it.'

Noel wanted to answer with the disdain her attitude deserved and under any other circumstances he might have done so but the situation was too delicate and he approached it from a different angle. Maybe she was right, maybe he had assumed too much so he sought permission to intrude.

'Do you mind me talking?'

'Not if you don't mind me not listening.'

Noel was losing his patience. There were a thousand places he'd rather be and he'd certainly appreciate a little gratitude for having conquered those steps whether it was needless or not.

'Look, if you're not interested in anything I've...' Noel was cut short and was again left unsure of how to react.

'No, no, it's ok. I always yawn when I'm interested.' If she hadn't smiled faintly as she said it Noel would have walked away but he was prepared to accept it as a sarcastic sense of humour... for now at least.

'So what are you doing up here?' He realised it was a ridiculous question but he was struggling. He still didn't know what to do and he was increasingly unsure of what to say.

'I think we both know why I'm here, but you... why you're here is a lot more interesting don't you think?'

Noel had to admit to himself that it was a fair question. If he wasn't quite sure what he was trying to achieve then she didn't have much chance of understanding at all. But it was the first invitation to converse that he'd received and he didn't want to waste it. He used it as an excuse to walk a little further forward. Evelyn was grateful as it saved her from straining her aching neck any longer and she returned to a slightly more natural angle.

'It might be more interesting' confessed Noel, 'but it's hardly as important is it? I'm not the one sitting on the ledge.'

'A fair point, and well made too.'

Noel's relief was obvious and having been offered the slightest hint of respect he dropped his guard a little but the awkwardness was still there.

'You're not going to tell me why are you?' Noel knew the answer but it felt like less of a defeat if he suggested it.

'And why would I do that? Telling you won't change anything will it?'

'I don't know... won't it?' If she could answer questions with questions, so could he. I might be able to help put things in perspective if nothing else? I know a lot of people... whatever's made you feel like this, however bad you think things have become, I bet I can tell you about someone I know who's worse off.' It was a clever remark as far as Noel was concerned; he really did have more contacts than most and there were plenty of depressives among them. If her problems were genuinely more serious than theirs, he could simply invent deeper issues; he'd tell a story so tragic that he was sure she'd be counting her blessings in no time but he'd underestimated her worryingly rational point of view.

'I'm sure you could...' she replied. 'Everyone could fall further and harder; but I'm tired of it. I've got my health and my freedom and I know I should be grateful for that but it's just not enough. I'm not naive... I know things could always be darker but I've reached my limit; the decisions mine to make and I've made it whether we talk or not. It shouldn't have to come to this before someone will listen anyway"

Noel was thrown off course and only just managed to stay on the same subject as he responded defensively.

'You're right, it shouldn't. But I've never met you before so I've never had the chance.'

Evelyn delayed her response just a few seconds wondering if it was worth letting him continue thinking that was true. It was the first admission that he didn't recognise her at all but ignoring it was certainly the easiest option. Explaining otherwise wouldn't help her now... although it might just help him. She opted for a compromise. She reached behind her and lifted the back of the jacket that until now had covered her completely. It allowed a freezing rush of air against her skin but it wasn't in vain; she could actually see the recollection on Noel's face. It felt satisfying, albeit in a cruel way but right now she'd take her pleasures where she could.

'I'm sure you can see my point of view?' She tried to coax him into feeling as guilty as he should but she really didn't need to. If he'd answered her question honestly regarding what had beckoned him here, it was predominantly selfishness; but not anymore. Instead of pitying himself as an innocent bystander dragged into a situation in which he might be implicated, he now knew he could well have contributed to the events that caused it and that gave him an entirely different perspective. He'd been convinced he was here because of her and the thought that it could well be the other way around gave him a responsibility to resolve this. Explaining himself seemed the most natural place to start.

'Listen', he paused where he'd usually make a conscious effort to use her name but realised he didn't know it. 'About before, I thought I'd seen someone I know… well, someone I used to know and… well by the time I saw you I reacted without thinking. That's all it was, a reflex. An involuntary reflex.'

Evelyn prolonged his agony by not acknowledging what was obviously meant to be an apology but was delivered like an excuse. She just looked directly ahead into the emptiness of the beckoning void. In truth it was just more physically comfortable to return to that position but she wouldn't let him know that. She wanted it to turn the screw a little further and a lot more painfully.

Noel looked at her, glanced back at the steps and then to the sky above. He took a deep breath and with it inhaled the possible consequences of what he was about to do and stepped forward decisively. If actions always speak louder than words then this should be deafeningly clear.

If Evelyn had been shocked to see him arrive at the top of the stairwell she was nothing less than stunned to see him settling, albeit extremely nervously beside her. If she hadn't felt him brush against her she would have doubted it was actually happening. He cautiously lowered himself into a space so small Evelyn had to shift to her left to accommodate him. Noel had to literally force each carefully thought out manoeuvre, it took all of his effort to override his every instinct that craved safer ground. Evelyn wanted to say something although she wasn't sure what so just kept quiet and very, very still, not wanting to distract the concentration that couldn't be more evident.

As he settled himself he tried not to think about how much more difficult it was going to be for whoever got back on their feet first but at least that meant he was thinking positively. With nothing in front of them to balance themselves it would be a delicate act indeed but he consoled himself with the thought that to be concerned about it, he must at least believe it was likely to happen.

'Just promise me that whatever you do, you'll at least warn me first? I'm not keen on heights and I like falling from them even less.' Noel hadn't intended it to sound like a genuine request but his voice betrayed him in coming over as anxious as it was serious. Evelyn's expression was equally solemn and her reply did nothing to settle his nerves.

'I never promise anything… to anyone.' It was the second time tonight she'd had to make that clear so she ensured she was understood. 'And more importantly, I never ask anyone to make promises to me. That way nobody can break them.'

Noel emptied his lungs hoping that the fresh intake of air would somehow help him come up with a response but he didn't have to yet; she was taking the opportunity to make her intentions clear in a subtle acknowledgment of what Noel had asked of her.

'The only promise I've made is to myself; and it's to keep my eyes open all the way down… it's supposed to be virtually impossible but I like a challenge.'

As if to prove she wasn't bluffing and that his presence hadn't changed a thing Evelyn let go of the wall next to her and fumbled with Joe's jacket, covering herself wherever she was exposed; she knew it was strange considering what had been her job until tonight but she wouldn't have to live with her strange traits and contradictions for much longer. Having released her grip she was pleasantly surprised at how easy it was and so she braved a search of the coat until she found what she was looking for. She pulled a lighter from the inside pocket and reached back in to produce a battered and squashed packet. It gave Noel a glimpse of her suspenders and he looked away out of decency. Evelyn wasn't used to that reaction and was unsure what she thought of it; it wasn't the first time he'd surprised her tonight. She fixed him with a fascinated stare and started smoking.

'Those things will kill you' warned Noel, grateful to be given an excuse to change the subject. It'd be a hollow cliché under any other circumstances, but right here, nineteen floors up and taking their lives in their hands it was enough to make her laugh with him and not at him for the very first time. Noel coughed but didn't ruin the improving atmosphere by complaining about the smoke but it wasn't as easy to ignore as it should be. He needed to focus now like never before but found it increasingly difficult as he struggled to name the feeling that was starting to overcome him. He'd suspect that it may be vertigo if he'd dared to look down but he'd made great efforts not to and so ruled it out as a possibility.

He blinked as if that would clear his head. He'd had a few drinks earlier that night but not enough to make him feel like this. The sensation was different somehow and besides, it was a little late for alcohol to start taking effect. He knew as well as anyone how it worked and it was unlikely to take him by surprise. He was virtually sober now and there was no way this was some kind of relapse. He looked at the cigarette Evelyn was smoking. She still paid it more attention than him but he'd only just realised why.

'And I don't think that's going to help you think straight.' As he said it Noel swiped at her hand to stop it returning to her mouth but without a tight grip the 'cigarette' was ejected from her fingers. It fell, still lit to the ground below but Noel was prevented from worrying about any potential hazards it could cause as it tumbled towards to canopy below. He was far more concerned with the girl's overreaction as she had raised her arm dramatically in self-defence. Noel felt instantly guilty. It never even occurred to him that she'd think he was about to do anything other than protest against her habits but it only highlighted how different their lives had been.

'It wasn't mine anyway'. Evelyn reacted childishly. She spat the words like an infant, but it also happened to be the truth; she'd been surprised to find cigarettes of any description in the coat pocket but had been astounded to find they were laced with something other than nicotine and tobacco. She'd have thought someone as principled as Joe who'd shown annoyingly impressive will power would have shunned that kind of weakness, but it only served to emphasise what she'd thought earlier; everyone has their problems however much they may vary. And it appeared even such a dedicated a family man wasn't exempt; he obviously had issues that he needed to escape from, if only for a few minutes at a time.

She doubted Noel would believe she was telling the truth but there was no sense in trying to convince him and she didn't care what he thought enough to even try. But she did know that by flinching at his sudden action, she'd hinted at her past and she'd rather not give that away… it was one of the few things she had left. However much she hadn't wanted to, she knew that she'd given away a secret but she didn't try to snatch it back; she just watched the smoldering embers as they continued to fall until they were lost in the distance. It certainly gave perspective to just how high up they were but it was surprisingly easy to get used to it.

Noel had obviously adjusted already and she'd been sitting there much longer than him. She looked at him shocked and with an exaggerated form that made her feelings clear. The sudden action would have startled her anyway but it was another risky move on his behalf. He wasn't only on the ledge; he wasn't even holding himself steady any longer; it had taken her longer to take such risks and she was the one that wasn't supposed to care. As she looked away she couldn't help but smile. She'd never worked out if she brought out the best or the worst in people; she'd done both already tonight but she always seemed to affect them in one way or another.

'I think you needed that a lot more than I did? Would it be fair to say you're a little highly strung?'

Tired of being told this by everyone who thought they knew him Noel answered defensively.

'Not at all, I don't have to be highly strung to know dragging on those things isn't going help you'.

'And how exactly would you know that unless you'd done the same yourself?'

'It's called an education', snapped Noel. He realised it might be unfair but he couldn't stop himself. She'd been personal so why shouldn't he? He needn't have worried. His comment seemed to have no effect at all. Either she didn't take offence because she wasn't lacking schooling at all or she really couldn't care less about his opinion but whichever was true, she looked a long way from being offended; she was actually smirking. She was getting to him already and it obviously amused her.

'So you've never tried it?'

'I figured if I try it and don't like it; what was the point? If I try it and do like it; well then I've got an addiction I'd be better off without'.

Evelyn looked at him blankly. To her mind a simple question deserved a simple answer and there was no need to dress it up or justify it. She replicated the pace and tone of her words exactly and tried again.

'So you've never tried it?'

Noel looked away, embarrassed to be condescended to but not quite sure how to retort.

'No I haven't.' He mumbled his reply like a schoolchild answering his teacher.

'There you go!' Evelyn had adopted a mocking tone. 'You can just say no after all.'

'And obviously you can't?' It was a better response and one of which he was quietly proud until he realised she might think he was questioning her sexual attitude rather than that which he thought they were discussing. True to form, he clarified what he meant. 'Your addictions I mean... you can't say no to your addictions.'

'I knew what you meant and that's not at all true. I can say 'no' to nicotine, alcohol and drugs; just they never listen.'

Noel joined her with a lopsided smile because it was only half funny. It was witty enough but it was pathetic too.

'So you've got no addictions then?'

Noel sat up proudly as if he'd just been asked by his parents or anyone else that would be impressed with his answer.

'None.' He kept his answer deliberately blunt this time to prove he could. He watched Evelyn shake her head. 'You don't believe me?' he questioned.

'Of course not. Addictions are only dependencies and everyone's dependent on something.'

'Not everyone' insisted Noel, lying as only he could.

Now sat beside her he could see the physical damage he'd already caused even if the psychological remained a mystery. 'I really am sorry about earlier'. It was unexpected and seemed to come from nowhere.

Again she refused to accept his apology but eased his guilt slightly by assuring him that the wound looked worse than it felt. It still hurt and was actually starting to sting a little more but the long coat had dragged the bleeding all over her legs and now they looked a real mess. Noel continued to try and make peace.

'My mind was somewhere else.'

'With *someone* else don't you mean?'

Noel looked at her not looking at him; she sounded... jealous? But how likely was that? Even with her makeup smeared across her face, being this close meant he could see just how striking she was. Under any other circumstance he doubted he'd be able to bring himself to talk to her at all. He snapped himself back out of his senseless fantasizing. She was just feeling vulnerable and must be craving attention from anyone; not him in particular so he saw no harm in continuing.

'That girl, I don't know if you saw her...'

'I saw her.'

'Well she's nearly put me where you are now several times.'

Evelyn whipped around to face him once more.

'Don't patronise me!'

Noel angered initially at being spoken to like that again, but she was right. Angela had given him plenty of sleepless nights but she'd never tested his will to live. It was insensitive to suggest that she had. He was terrible at this.

'Maybe you should be talking to someone else? I'm not trying to get away, really I'm not. But I'm really not helping either am I?'

Evelyn didn't answer but the fact remained that he was helping a little. Not with what he was saying, but with the fact that he was there of his own accord. If she was honest with herself she didn't want him to leave but there was no way she could say as much. Without knowing it, Noel took the pressure off by speaking again.

'The signal on my phone is unreliable at best, but why don't we try it? There must be plenty of people you'd rather talk to than me'.

'Is being presumptuous your only forte?'

Noel didn't give up so easily. He believed in what he was doing but it would have fortunate side effects for him too. This would become someone else's problem and he could be home within the hour; he'd tried to resolve this himself but as far as he was concerned he was only succeeding in making matters worse. He'd understandably gone off the idea of meeting up with anyone and his bed seemed more inviting tonight than it ever had before. He pulled his phone from his pocket. As he had hoped, being on the edge of the building had helped; they were at the farthest point from the transmitters and the network signal had returned to an acceptable level.

'Come on, who do you want to speak to.' Noel had learnt not to expect an answer by now so such an instant response came as a surprise.

'My Dad.'

Noel handed her the cell phone. She looked at it, seemingly impressed with its minimalist style.

'But I'll need a stronger signal than that; he was killed a year ago.'

It wasn't the response Noel was hoping for but at least she was talking now instead of just speaking. He was surely getting to the roots of the problem and that meant that his being here was serving some purpose. He wasn't sure whether to probe any further on such a sensitive subject but if she hadn't wanted him to she wouldn't have been so specific. She'd have said her father had passed on, perhaps, but he took her admitting he'd actually been killed as a subtle sign of trust. It limited where he could take the conversation from here though; she'd told him when it happened, to ask where seemed irrelevant at this stage.

'How?' His voice was quiet, understanding and Evelyn was surprised to find herself replying.

'Car accident.' She said the latter word like it couldn't be more inappropriate.

'You don't sound like you believe that was the case?'

'If it was the bastard would have stopped wouldn't he? Not just disappeared off the face of the earth?'

'Maybe he just panicked?'

Evelyn looked at him like the insensitive cretin he could sometimes be and he moved on quickly. 'But that's no excuse, so the police...'

'Never found him... or her. Even if they had, what would happen? Maybe a few years behind bars but more likely a fine and a suspended sentence.'

'And that's not enough is it?' It was Noel's honest opinion but he also knew that's what she'd want to hear.

'No, that's nowhere near enough. If it was an accident then I don't know how much easier it would be to accept. But I've been over and over everything and it was either down to driving over the limit or with extreme recklessness and it should only be paid for with what was taken.'

Noel nodded slowly again in agreement. Take the accidental element away and it basically became murder in relative terms, if not legally. Her opinion would be thought barbaric by much of the population, but possibly as many would argue she was absolutely right. The way in which she said it left him in no doubt that this wasn't the first time she'd justified her feelings.

'So did the investigation lead anywhere? Did the police ever explore all the avenues and...'

She finished his sentence. Now she was finally talking about this she couldn't race through the details quickly enough.

'No. But I did for months afterwards and it never got me anywhere. By the time I started to accept I was never going to get to the truth I'd lost everything. My job, the house... even my friends.'

'Some friends they must have been?'

'They did what they could. They put up with a lot but in the end I just put them through too much.'

Noel sat listening to every detail of what brought her here. He said little and just listened as she opened up to him unlike any stranger had done before; possibly unlike anybody he'd ever known.

CHAPTER THIRTY-SEVEN

'Deep breaths, deep breaths'. It was all Ivy kept saying to herself as she approached the main office door. Her approach had been slow as she listened for any clues that would help her timing.

She could see the clock and she knew the party schedule off by heart; after all, she'd decided it and had the design of the memo changed three times or more. Now she wondered why; the first draft was perfectly fine. Was it just because she could? It probably was and that meant another two people to add to her growing list of people she really should apologise to, or at least make peace with but she'd have to consider that later. Trying to compensate for everything she'd done could take all of January so she planned to make an early start when she returned to work in the New Year... if that was even possible. The humiliation might be too extreme to bear and that very much depended on the outcome of the next few minutes. If she handled this badly her resignation may well seem like the only viable option. She'd lost whatever awkward brand of authority she'd created and she was sure her departure wouldn't even be noticed, let alone missed. But then a worse thought struck her; her leaving *would* be noticed, it would even be celebrated... maybe more than any departure in the history of the company. Entire departments would be able to breath easy again. If only she'd have been able to see herself so clearly before maybe she could have done something about it. But it had taken being thrown off a trailer and two hours in a darkened room with absolute zero distractions to come to that conclusion and she wondered under what other circumstances that could possibly happen. Maybe if this had been last year she could recompense but it was surely too late now with her colleagues, her directors and worst of all with Richard.

She conceded that her husband may have had a point; she hated the thought of him being right yet again but perhaps he was. Maybe all they really needed was to be alone for long enough to set the record straight but if she couldn't stop herself from running before, why would she ever be able to? There would always be somewhere to flee and that would save listening to the truth she was so scared of hearing although that's exactly what it would take for her to live again, with or without him. It would fill in all the blanks but maybe some part of her craved the everyday torture of ignorance as that kept possibility alive.

She was thinking with honesty she'd avoided for too long and that could only be healthy. But it wasn't anything she hadn't been repeatedly told; it was just that she found her friends easier to ignore than her own conscience which obviously had no intention of giving up on her so easily. Unlike them, it wouldn't go away when she asked it to. All the advice in the world could be kept out but now it came from within things were not quite so simple.

The constant and raucous noise from the other side of the internal wall kept a sense of urgency that she could do without though and she'd have to save any further deliberations until she was on her way home. She felt too fragile to be anywhere else. The sounds on which she was focused hadn't begun to fade as she predicted they might, but they had changed… and from having attended countless similar events she knew exactly what it meant; it represented her one chance to do what she had to without being noticed. She sneaked a glance of confirmation through the glass panelling in the door, twisting for the best possible view whilst remaining unseen. It was as she thought. It was that time of the evening when they presented the year's awards. Mostly they were not worth winning and the majority were always for comedy value rather than genuine acknowledgement but there were often a few worthy honours. But as far as Ivy was concerned it all amounted to just one thing; the audience's eyes were firmly fixed on the speaker and to her mutual relief and dismay they'd chosen Richard for a third year running. She couldn't really disagree as he was popular enough not to be ignored and possessed the charisma needed to deliver the always cliché ridden script in a manner that few could get away with.

She could accept the reasoning behind it but that didn't mean the result wasn't just as cutting. There seemed no greater way to emphasise the massive chasm that divided the way in which they'd each coped with their separation than this; him up there commanding the attention of the entire room whilst she attempted to slip out the fire escape unnoticed. If she was going to start accepting reality though, this seemed like an appropriate place to start.

She entered the room whilst he was midway through a presentation that actually interested the crowd and not a single head turned. Knowing the noise her heels would make on the polished floorboards she took them off and made her way quietly across the room. She did so with a confident pace and was careful not to creep knowing it would just look conspicuous.

Relieved to have made it to her desk, she slid the drawers in and out whenever a new nomination was made or the applause rose beyond a lazy murmur. It would have been considerably easier without the lights dimmed but they'd been virtually switched off to give the amateur looking spotlight its maximum effect. She was forced to feel her way through the clutter, grasping at anything that even remotely resembled the shape of her keys. With increasing desperation she became less careful with her timing as she took to the cupboards but in their mostly drunken state, still nobody noticed. Any other time she'd have hated the fact but for now she was grateful to be totally ignored.

Usually she'd be glued to the announcements, busily committing them to memory for use at a later date but right now she wasn't even listening. She was lost in her hunt until the words leapt out at her so loudly they startled her; 'Ivy Wainsbridge'. How could he? He knew more than anyone that she wouldn't want the attention yet he called her name like he was presenting an Oscar. She had been certain that whilst he was admittedly facing in her direction, from such a distance and with the stage lights pointing towards him he'd never be able to see her but she'd obviously misjudged the situation.

She ran for the office door without even thinking. Tripping over a chair leg in her frantic rush caused her to fall against the relative stability of a nearby desk but her weight shifted it across the floor, its rubber mounts squealing her location as they were pushed violently across the boarding; now everyone knew where to look. She scrambled back to her feet and allowed herself time to shoot Richard just one hurt and accusing glance before she escaped.

Had she stayed she'd have seen him lost for words at last. For a few seconds he just stood by the microphone staring into the now illuminated rear of the office as the spotlight had searched for the disruption. He looked torn, indecisive and for a moment he was. He didn't like it. He sided with duty and made an attempt to resume his speech but it was barely comprehensible. He resorted to his notes, something he'd never do unless he absolutely had to and again tried to pick up the thread but it was useless. He just handed the notes and envelopes to the closest colleague and left the stage without a word, breaking into a full run through the parting silence as he did. He didn't give a thought to the stunned apologies about to be made on his behalf but there was little explanation needed.

As he careered out of the doors he stood for a moment in the corridor trying to decide which would be the most likely direction in which she would have fled. He started to turn left as that was the quickest route out of the building and therefore her most likely course but as he moved he stepped onto her abandoned stilettos and thought again. Continuing would lead him down the stairs to the fire exit. The corrugated metal steps would be painful without shoes and the trek over to the car park even more so and she'd know that. He spun on the spot considering the other option; it would be easier for her but it was definitely further and she'd be every bit as aware of the extra time it would take to get to the reception. One way was as likely as the other and he squinted into the half lit gloom of the corridor, the annoyingly difficult to read electronic displays above the elevators were moving even if it was impossible to tell which way from here. Even so, the fact that they were flashing at all meant that someone was undoubtedly on the move. He made up his mind and took off towards them. Now close enough to read the indicator and knowing the elevator was heading down, the likelihood that it carried Ivy increased. Richard didn't even slow down as he reached the end of the corridor gaining every second he could and crash landing into the button like the optimist he was; they just might re-open the doors to reveal what was technically still his wife. The lift had already left the floor, but only just. He could hear the ancient and lethargic contraption begrudgingly amble towards the floor below. He tore off and descended the stairs, missing so many steps before each heavy landing he was lucky to hit them square but the gamble paid off and he'd made it down to the next level in seconds. From the stairwell he could see he had just missed her on that floor too. By the time he'd raced down a second flight he'd almost made up the time difference between them but not quite. The level indicator by the lift shaft again faded just as he got to glimpse it. He was keeping up at this rate but he had to beat it... and soon. Already heaving for breath he'd start to lose his pace after another flight and he'd already been lucky not to break an ankle. Every time he skimmed the top of another return he braced himself to hit it at an inhuman angle. Time, luck and oxygen were all running out.

He daren't risk trying to travel any faster than he was already and figured the only time he could gain was that in which he kept pausing to check for the lift's position. For the next two flights he ignored its progress and instead channelled every second into overtaking it in his descent. He took a final leap clearing a full four steps and lunged instantly sideways out of the stairwell. For the first time since he started this insane chase the little orange light flicked onto his level rather than away from it. Now all he had to do was press that button before it passed. He reached out and slammed it back, leaving it in no doubt as to the importance of responding. He waited trying to interpret the whirring and metallic creaking of cables and pulley systems that previously meant nothing to him other than a maintenance bill. But now they meant everything and all he wanted was to hear them stop. With a worryingly abrupt crunch that echoed through the walls the mechanics ceased to rattle. Exhausted he propped himself up against the wall as they took their time opening.

When they eventually parted, neither man nor woman were prepared for the site that greeted them. From his position on the stage he hadn't seen quite how dishevelled she looked. But it wasn't the state of her clothes or the smearing of her makeup that startled him the most. It was the look on her face. She'd dropped her recent character and through the running mascara and smudged lipstick was the woman he'd fallen for. She was equally surprised as his appearance at the door seemed physically impossible but she backed away all the same.

CHAPTER THIRTY-EIGHT

The fairy lights continued to flash insistently as if their batteries would never lose power but Nick's were, and the sudden drain began without any obvious warning. His head bobbed again, only momentarily but it was enough to make him realise that he had to give in; he had to pull over the very next chance he got. He could hear the sirens getting closer all the time but there was no point at all in trying out run them as the traffic parted whenever possible to let them through. With the exception of a single estate car that risked its metallic paint work to force itself onward, vehicles edged towards the curb to allow an unfair advantage in a chase that was almost over.

Exasperated drivers found patience they never knew they possessed but for Evelyn it felt like the traffic lights had never taken so long to change as she repeatedly urged them to under her breath without really knowing exactly why she was in such a rush. Not a single aspect of her life was actually any different now to when she'd been thrown out like the trash down the steps that now faced her once again but it felt like a different world; so much so that it might as well be. One in which she could carve a place for herself and in which she had already made a difference; even if she'd needed guidance to see it. Her impatience made no difference to the lights though and they went about their duty full of their own self-importance, letting the traffic creep past and ignoring Evelyn completely. She thought again about her eagerness to tackle her problems that still lay ahead. However different they appeared when viewed from another perspective, in this case from the top of a tower block, they only *seemed* different. None of them had disappeared or even eased and it certainly wasn't that she now had all the answers;

she wasn't even sure that she ever would. But now she felt that they were worth tackling and that in itself was amazing considering how she'd planned to deal with them. Noel had been absolutely right and everything was indeed relative. The outlook remained as potentially bleak as before but it didn't have to be and she was reminded of the words which she now found hard to believe were hers… 'things can always be darker'. A simple statement but surely it signified a new beginning as far as her attitude was concerned. Despite being well disguised it was an optimistic statement at its heart.

'Come on… come on' she whined under her breath like the spoilt child she always wished she could have been but then smiled, realising that despite her recent resolutions she'd lost none of her impatience...

'One thing at time' she mumbled, if only to herself. 'And it starts right here'.

Finally the lights reached green and it had never meant 'go' to quite such an extent, yet rather than step out presumptuously, she waited for the traffic to stop completely. In the light of her elation even this seemed symbolic but she imagined that from now on, or for a while a least, having had that conversation would be a little like reading your stars or having visited a fortune teller and that she'd see everything as some kind of prolific sign. Part of her remained skeptical, still suspecting that believers made those predictions true by interpreting everyday events as they wanted to and she feared she was doing exactly the same. Real or imagined, it was working for her and if she could now see changing traffic lights as evidence that life was going her way, then she was glad to join the faithful.

For the first time in a while she looked both ways before crossing… just in case. She stepped out but was hurried by the estate, still frantically swerving until it had mounted the pavement in an aggressive attempt to overtake the car ahead. It was steered back onto the road and over the pedestrian crossing scattering the migrating crowd. They panicked at its committed approach and scowled as it left them behind but quickly resumed their path to the other side of the road realising that they were now the ones causing the hold up.

Gears shifted and clutches dipped in readiness, the drivers obviously as frustrated and eager to continue their journey as Evelyn had been. They were pulling away before she'd even stepped up onto the opposing curb but now she'd reached the exact same spot that had been the focus of her elevated but glazed attention. She turned where she stood to look back across the way she'd came through the clearing of the crossing before the gap closed completely from both sides as vehicles charged in opposing directions, intermittently blocking her view and allowing just glimpses of the building she faced.

She wanted to see it again; to watch it tower over her like it had done so ominously earlier, but through what felt like brand new eyes; she wanted to see if that too seemed so very different now. Looking above the steady flow of traffic, it remained as dark and characterless as before but as she expected, its representation had changed completely. No longer an impenetrable fortress, it was the very home of her salvation. She started to face skywards again, deliberately slowly, as she had done before in anticipation of seeing that same electronic star; only now it wouldn't be the star she may never become, but her star. Her *lucky* star.

The crowds bustled around her and even barged into her, some by accident and some out of irritation. The street had developed an unspoken rule of its own and now worked in a very similar fashion to the road it bordered. There were effectively two lanes that developed as if of their own accord whenever it was this busy allowing movement in either direction, but Evelyn, true to form stood firmly between the two. She'd choose which direction to take just like everybody else. But not just yet... right now she was star gazing.

She stumbled a little as the weight of the human pile up she was causing pushed her aside before surging past like a burst dam, but the relentless opposing torrent swept her back repeatedly. She'd better give thanks or say her prayer or whatever it was she felt she had to do now and be on her way before she was trampled. She again arced her head towards that same pitch black sky that just may not seem quite so dark anymore. If Noel could have seen her from this distance then there was no reason that she wouldn't now be able to see him clearly enough. The very least she could do was blow a kiss as she was sure he'd still be watching over her... at least she hoped so as it would certainly look more than a little strange to anyone else and she didn't want to look like a fool for nothing.

She saw him; or at least his shadow, enlarged, distorted and projected against the building, changing shape as it fell over the contours of its walls. She didn't even need to try and focus on its source, small by comparison and so much more fragile. Her heart hit the paving below as everything Noel had said as she left him behind slotted into place like a hideous puzzle she didn't want to see completed. She would have expected to scream hysterically or maybe even call for help but instead she whispered just one word that captured the disbelief she felt; then she ran.

For years afterwards people would ask why she reacted that way when there was no way on earth she could have reached him in time and absolutely nothing she could have done if she did. But still she ran; sprinted even with no plan or purpose towards him, tearing away at anyone and anything between the two of them with a ferocity she'd never known until she was back in the road, unable to take her eyes off of that awful shadow.

Battles were still being fought for every available inch and even the heavier vehicles that should be able to rely on their grip moved nervously and unpredictably in the freezing conditions. The driver of one of the many taxi's making the most of their increased fares was becoming increasingly aware of his passengers unease as the meter crept ever higher turning a relatively short journey into an expensive affair but he still hadn't capped his rates as the delaying traffic was no more his fault than it was anyone else's. He felt certain they'd bring it up any minute and having been in similar positions before he knew he'd relent and so would rather offer than get pressured into negotiations despite his pre-emptive measures earlier. He'd started the night determined to pay for the extortion they'd named Christmas in one mind numbing shift and then just maybe he could spend tomorrow worrying about the mess his twins were making rather than next months mortgage but now he just wanted this journey to end. He'd be heading home the moment it did; someone had to eat the mince pies that would already have been left on the bedroom shelving and he was so hungry he'd struggle to leave the three large crumbs that his wife would insist on. He smirked remembering her explanation.

'Father Christmas is in too much of a rush to lick the plate clean' she instructed. 'You just make sure it looks like they were polished off in a hurry.'

Her obsession with the girls believing in Father Christmas as she still called him was becoming unhealthy. He doubted that they were still convinced of his existence and thought it more likely they pretended for their mum's sake which he found both sad and funny but couldn't help the smirk appearing on his face. His passengers just looked at him without breaking the awkward silence that had now been re-established so long it had virtually become a stand off. It was doing nothing to take his mind off the claustrophobia he'd always struggled with. A taxi driver that felt confined in enclosed spaces… there was another reason to either laugh or cry. The sunroof he'd insisted on helped a little but not as much as analysing his wife's quirkiness. There was a solid days worth of distraction there. To her, the children believing, or more to the point, *not* believing was another rite of passage like tying their own shoe laces or their first day at school and she'd taken those moments hard. But they were still just children if they believed in Santa and she went to extraordinary lengths to ensure that it remained the case, providing evidence whenever she could. By tomorrow morning she'd have even spread a little soot around the fireplace and carefully dislodged a few lumps of coal. That in itself could be seen as thoughtful rather than fanatical but this was the *only* reason they had an old fashioned fireplace. She'd even disguised her hand writing to fake a convincing reply from the North Pole to letters the girls had been forced to write.

It was that very afternoon, after she'd reprimanded them and lectured on the merits of always telling the truth that he'd approached her about levelling with the girls. Partly because he could see the massive hypocrisy of the situation and could imagine the repercussions in years to come; but not least because he didn't want to contribute to them struggling in the classroom. He remembered primary school and what an unforgiving place it could be. He knew that even a hint that they still fell for their parents' lies could enter their names right at the top of the playground hit list. As sad as it was, he'd far rather that they were the first to know the truth than the last; if they didn't already. Every parent thinks of their children as bright, but both girls were genuinely intelligent to the point that he wondered quite where the genetics had come from. He wouldn't be surprised if they'd worked everything out for themselves and even had the foresight to hide it now out of compassion and an understanding of their mother. It would make them wise beyond their years but it certainly wasn't above them. They were probably working just as hard to play ignorant as their mother was to continue the pretence in an endless circle of deception intended to keep each other happy. He just shook his head at the thought and returned to the here and now.

He sat up straight in his seat in an attempt to show his concern at the duration and cost of the journey, suddenly aware of the aspiring journalists still slouched in the back seat. With that nagging curiosity returning, he glanced back once more and was glad he did; the face was still familiar and with his head held at a slightly different angle he at last knew where from. A week or more ago he'd seen it staring up at him from the kitchen table and any doubts he had were laid to rest as he remembered the conversation he'd overheard. It all made perfect sense; it had to be him. It was Dec that he recognised and it was due to the picture that always accompanied his newspaper column in which he tried to make local concerns sound as much like news as possible. Joe usually paid it no attention but this particular story had caught his interest for all the wrong reasons. He'd always had a soft spot for animals and an understandable grudge against corporate extravagance so the combination of the two had been enough to put him off his breakfast. He'd read that the Grandure Hotel planned to hold a party that would outshine their last and that this year it would include genuine elves which can't have been strictly the truth, as well as real live reindeers... that was the part that stayed in his memory. The fact that they'd be expected to perform for the drunken masses was bad enough, but tonight was apparently the last of their bookings as licensing continued to escalate and the manner in which they were being retired immediately afterwards was a little too permanent. He considered asking how the campaign to save them went but he was afraid he already knew; if it had been successful the story would have been printed in headlines so big it couldn't be missed so he avoided the subject entirely.

'Plenty have left it late again this year' he offered hopefully but without turning his head. No reply. He wasn't one to force his customers into the traditional banter of weather, holiday destinations and what time he started his shift, but he wouldn't accept being totally ignored either. However he hadn't asked a question as such and so hadn't demanded an answer so he rephrased, turning this time to make his delivery more personal.

'They never learn do they?' suddenly realising that 'they' could be the very people sitting behind him but the equipment that still rested between them suggested otherwise; shopping was the least of their worries. He again wondered where his daughters got their intellect when he'd managed to build them stables for the horses they so desperately wanted but he couldn't afford. It was typical of his determination to provide for them without the means to do so yet but the savings were adding up; just not quickly enough to grant them this year's wish. At least thinking about that had passed the time he'd spent waiting for a response and he turned towards his passengers in anticipation. It made no difference though and he reversed his attention back to the road just in time. He braked hard, *too* hard whilst simultaneously leaning heavily on his horn as a girl, oddly dressed dashed blindly in front of his already unsteady path as if she didn't know he was there.

Joe couldn't control the inevitable and he continued to surge forward over freezing tarmac. His wheels had stopped rotating but twisted without effect on the ice as he steered one way and then the other trying to weigh his limited options in the short time he had.

By colliding with the larger and sturdier estate car to his left he would take the chance of injuring those inside both vehicles, but by steering right he should be able to use the raised curb to bring him to a halt. That decision would only cost him his hubcaps but if he misjudged the manoeuvre he'd be risking ploughing into the crowds that were now even deeper thanks to the escalating commotion. There never had been be anything quite like an accident to draw an audience and this one was moments from happening; its arrival hailed by horns and locking tyres. He had a tough choice to make and just a split second in which to make it; his urge for self-preservation tempted him one way whilst logic dragged him the other.

His eyes darted in every direction trying to take in as much information as possible. He spun the steering wheel back again deciding that the muscular car beside him offered award winning protection to its passengers and even if the manufacturers claims were exaggerated, its occupants were certainly less exposed than the shoppers on the sidewalk. Both vehicles were at least travelling in the same direction and neither had managed to gather much speed yet so there was little difference between the two; at worst they'd effectively collide at just a few miles per hour. With a little luck the damage would just be cosmetic so he held his breath, taking what little control was to be had and swung right.

The priorities in the opposing car were very different as panic set in deeper with every wail of the police siren. The traffic was effectively bumper to bumper but its driver took every possible opportunity to stay ahead of the flashing blue lights edging ever closer and growing in the rear view mirror. He spotted a sudden vacancy ahead and surged forward, urged on by his brother who knew what it was like to do time and didn't want to see either of them in that situation again; not just for robbing a High Street jewellers. Desperation forced them to snatch at every possible chance to advance knowing that every single penny they'd stolen couldn't buy them the time or distance they needed. It was getting to the point that they'd have to make a decision of their own and it was increasingly becoming a question of when to abandon the car rather than if. If the police made much more gain on them they'd have to make their escape on foot but they wanted to delay such desperate tactics until the last possible minute. There was still a chance that they weren't being followed at all and that the patrol cars were responding to something else entirely in which case running would attract them to a crime they might not even be aware of yet. But if the distance between them continued to close they'd have no choice but to attempt to lose themselves in the maze of people lining the street... at least there was no shortage of potential hostages should they be forced to take such drastic action. It was a tactic that had worked for them before and they'd use it again if they had to.

Their urgency pushed them forward, much to Joe's relief as the sudden rush opened up a space right next to his taxi but he knew it would close again soon enough. It was too much of an opportunity to miss; he accelerated towards it and swung wildly towards his one chance to come out of this unscathed. He'd almost successfully guided himself awkwardly into the gap when the estate, having lurched forward with such sudden excitement had to brake just as abruptly to compensate. The taxi careered into the back with enough force and at such an awkward angle that it sent the larger car spinning on the spot in the increasingly icy conditions.

The sound of the impact caused Evelyn to hesitate and she stopped in the adjoining lane, guiltily looking back at the accident she caused rather than in the direction of the oncoming traffic. Onlookers stared in horror as the massive headlights of Nicks lorry bore down on her, its driver seemingly oblivious behind its badly cracked windscreen. They saw no signs of the hulking metal mass slowing down until the awful sound of its ancient brakes being applied and the grinding of metal pierced their ears. It was obvious to everyone watching that the lorry would never manage to stop its forward slide before it reached the girl now standing in the centre of its blinding beams, wide-eyed but rooted to the spot as if trapped between them.

Inside the lorry's cabin Nick opened his window. He had hoped that the breeze would clear his mind and having finally managed to gain a reasonable speed he'd created a flow of air that had helped for a while. But now he summoned all of his effort against the overdose and the massive effect it was having only for his concentration to ebb further away. He'd mounted the pavement, only slightly but enough that he was receiving screamed abuse that served to focus his attention again. Whatever the consequences, this was perhaps the most selfish thing he'd ever done and he needed to get off the road before he hurt or killed someone. Carol singers, more concerned with keeping their harmony than being mindful of the traffic had edged nearer to the roadside and having sung so sweetly about the holy day they now blasphemed whilst trying to alert others potentially in Nick's path. He managed to avoid them but the relief led to a lapse he couldn't afford. His head dipped again and his eyelids began to close. When they lifted it was to the scene of a young girl, frozen in his realigned headlights.

With what strength he had left he braked and leaned on the horn for whatever good it could do. It wasn't like it would alert her anymore as she couldn't look more alarmed; she could see him coming... she was staring straight at him. The massive wheels locked, but despite their tread and the weight above them they skidded on the crystallized road until it was so close Evelyn could see her own reflection in the polished grill that was advancing without mercy. Nick couldn't look into those widened eyes a moment longer and with his own life now worth less than nothing he turned the steering wheel violently, desperate to collide with anything other than her. Evelyn watched the front wheels turn forcing the entire cabin round so sharply that it continued to surge towards her sideways and against the direction in which it was now pointing. Locked in a losing battle with the momentum still pushing the entire vehicle along the icy street its huge tyres span with increasing speed and determination before at last finding their grip and powering themselves away from her. They crashed into the raised pavement towards its furthest edge until the trailer they carried began dragging the various cabling that suspended and powered the aerial illuminations weaving back and forth high above the street. Some offered more resistance than others but inevitably even the thickest stretched to capacity, snapping back wildly and narrowly missing the crowds who were already clearing the area below. The unfolding events had already attracted the attention of everyone in the vicinity and so they were quick to react, scrambling to escape the monster as it roared towards them.

The manner in which they retreated separated the entire crowd, regardless of their creed or class into a pair of simple categories; those that pushed and pulled to save themselves and those that dragged others to safety. The last of them escaped as they leapt clear of the charge but in that moment, the main beam had shone a spotlight on who they truly were. They would all have to live with the pride or the disgrace it evoked; none of them realising at the time that marriage proposals and divorces would later be based on that very moment.

The cabin's front smashed into the reception of the very building to which Evelyn had been running and on which she'd made and retracted that potentially fatal decision. The immaculate entrance was devastated but it wasn't enough to bring the beast to a standstill as it continued undeterred through the welcoming desk and towards the elevator doors coming to an abrupt and destructive halt when it reached them; it threw everything onboard forwards, closing the gap between the engine and its trailer like a concertina. It had a bullet like effect and shot the cabin ahead of itself again, impressing it into the lifts metal doors for a second time sending another tremor up the shaft strong enough to shut it down. The trailer was snatched and catapulted further through the exterior wall and strained the foundations under the deserted marble floor.

The eerie lull and stunned silence of the crowd gave way to the delayed sound of shattering glass, heavily punctuated by debris falling from the edge of the gaping hole punched into the building's entrance. Slowly, those that had dived for cover emerged and again the divide was obvious as some fled the ongoing disaster and others rushed towards it, cautiously avoiding the brick and plaster still landing like deafening meteors on and around the cabin in which Nick was slumped.

CHAPTER THIRTY-NINE

'May I?' enquired Richard but typically didn't wait for an answer in case it wasn't the one he wanted. As he entered the impossibly confined elevator he'd forced Ivy to retreat to its rear and ensured she couldn't rush for the exit. It was an inappropriate approach considering her obviously frail state of mind but he also knew this was likely to be his only chance and that it wouldn't last long. He had just the time it would take them to descend to ground level; all he had to do was to get her to listen but the minute or so that he had was unlikely to be enough. He didn't expect it to be easy and her opening line confirmed as much...

'Not now, not after what you've done' she wailed as she tried to squeeze herself between him and the sheet metal wall but the sliding doors had already began to shut. Their closing came as some relief to Richard who'd seen his wife's escape route shut off at last. It gave them extreme privacy that he could previously only have wished for.

'I've explained the best I can, as much as you'll let me and if you can't believe me maybe we should just forget the past completely?' he suggested. It was a bold statement but there was no time to introduce it subtly.

'Not that' she said shaking her head in disbelief at his insensitivity. 'That's a different story completely... I'm talking about what you did, what you *just* did'.

Richard stared at her blankly. He'd been prepared for various responses but not that. He genuinely had no idea what she was talking about.

'If you mean coming to check on you then I've explained that too, I didn't even know for sure that you weren't seriously hurt'. He looked at her awkward stance and the bruising that was starting to form. 'I still don't! I'm still your husband Ivy, you can't expect me to hear that you've been thrown off a truck and do nothing?'

She continued shaking her head, but violently as if she was trying to dispel everything she was hearing.

'I'm not talking about you checking on me? I'm talking about you turning the whole crowd towards me when you knew full well I just wanted to escape... I just wanted my home'.

'Our home' suggested Richard, 'and I don't...' he was about to conclude that he didn't know what she was referring to but he was suddenly afraid that he did.

'Ivy, I had no idea you was there' he muttered, disappointed that she could think so coldly of him.

'How could you? You know me better than that... did you really think that would help?'

Richard knew how rude it was to watch the screen behind her instead of her face but the red dots kept changing and shifting shape and had now formed a perfect ' 7 '. He didn't have time for manners.

'Enough!' he hadn't quite shouted but he was only a decibel short. The abruptness and authority in his voice silenced her momentarily but encouraged her anger as it steadily built towards rage. How dare he humiliate her and then have the audacity to speak to her in such a manner; she launched into a barrage of her own telling him exactly how she felt. Had he listened he'd have known that amongst the insults and the abuse there were words he'd want to hear but they were hard to find and he couldn't take the time to wade through the verbal litter that surrounded them. All he heard was her opening line accusing him of announcing her degraded presence. Like a rival superpower too late to launch a preemptive strike he had to mount a counter attack and make himself heard in the precious few seconds that remained before she would do what she'd done on every other occasion; bolt for the nearest open door.

The last thing he wanted to do was to raise his voice again, but all reasonable attempts to calm her failed abysmally.

'That wasn't what I was doing at all, did you not hear a thing that was said?' he demanded and continued to explain in vain. 'I'd just finished speaking about how well organised this year's marketing strategy had been and explained just how much you'd put into making sure tonight ran as smoothly as it did. I don't think the people you work with realise... I thought you deserved the credit and...' they continued to try and over shout each other, totally unaware that the war would be over if they'd only listen to what the other now had to say. Disguised amongst it were the words they'd both needed so much, but thinking they'd heard it all before it took a force more powerful than either of their will for silence to reign. The lift stopped so suddenly they were pushed to its floor; crumpling under the unexpected pressure and unbalanced by the shock but it was the sound that was petrifying.

A near deafening, metallic roar erupted from below them and shuddered upwards shaking the very floor on which they now lay like it was hunting the pair of them as they huddled together, their reflex to protect each other as natural as fear of the unknown. Once the tremor had found its prey it seemed to linger around them, vibrating the walls for what felt like an impossibly long time before seemingly becoming bored and racing up towards the ceiling looking for new victims to terrorise.

Neither of them had realised how tightly their eyes were squeezed shut until they opened them and just looked at each other in the now flickering light that looked like it was about to give out at any given moment. It made each and every action appear in slow motion and therefore added to the significance of every little gesture as Richard rose to his feet and offered his hand.

Several floors below them the front of the lorry remained held fast and embedded in the elevator doors having hit them hard enough to shut the whole system down. But whilst covered in concrete dusk, the trailer to the rear had lost none of the momentum created by the sudden change in direction and had been pivoted round threateningly under its own considerable weight. The ice did nothing to slow its destructive procession as it jackknifed; sweeping through a perfect arc but if nothing else, it made its direction clear and allowed those most obviously in its path to flee. It pushed the partly abandoned traffic and market stalls effortlessly aside and, unable to gain enough traction on the slippery surface it continued to wreak indiscriminate havoc.

It was like a colossal game of chess; every single move and each individual action altered the options of the next. Cars slid and people ran for cover only to find the vehicle they were escaping had collided with a post that had just that second been knocked flat creating a much needed haven, but that same post would steer danger in another direction towards those who were not so ready or able to seek cover.

All around people were reacting as best they could, but it was those that were able to judge and predict the constantly changing shape of the threat who were the most likely to see another day. And of these, as before, those level headed enough to retain the ability to pre-empt the advance used it in one of two ways; many who foresaw their own paths to freedom about to open readied themselves and fled... but not all.

The dog that had almost tripped Evelyn earlier tugged at her leash in whatever direction she could, instinct leading her to safety. Her owner was keen to follow except that it was painfully obvious that the couple ahead of him, watching in awe like they were not part of the scene at all were not quite as safe as they must have thought. They were at least three or four car lengths back from the perimeter of the chaos but failed to notice that less than a minute ago they were four to eight lengths away.

The bedlam was spreading like cancer yet with all the suddenness of a heart attack; and it was as potentially deadly as both combined. Cars and vans were being shunted backward and into each other until they were concertinaed lines of crumpled metal, cutting off escape routes with each collision. The able bodied of those that were trapped had to flee *over* the traffic rather than between it but not everyone was capable.

He watched it all and was torn as to what he should do. His dog was not suffering a crisis of conscience though as her leash was repeatedly yanked and stretched to capacity. He struggled to keep his grip whilst simultaneously beckoning the awe struck youngsters his way with exaggerated arm movements. He knew they were unlikely to hear him but they didn't even look. Transfixed by the scene unfolding in such familiar surroundings they were totally unaware of the domino effect coming their way. He fought an entire battle with his conscience in a split second before lumbering in the direction of the imminent collision.

He advanced as fast as he could but was caught short, still being pulled in the opposite direction; seeing no sense in risking the life of his usually loyal friend as well as his own he let go. This didn't end his struggle however as he clambered on and around the debris that separated him from those he was trying to warn. He was sure his shouting would be heard as he approached but it was no match for the crunching onslaught of battered metal. He reached out grabbing the closest of the pair trusting that the other would follow. Heaving backwards, he tried to transfer his own weight to his advantage but almost toppled over his indecisive but faithful pet who'd followed him after all, leash or no leash; she'd obviously decided she was part of a couple too.

But if tactics weren't changed the repercussions were obvious so he charged forward instead, half tackling his oblivious targets in an effort to push them clear. They noticed him a split second before he careered into them but their attention was turned back again as the car in front smashed into that against which they leant. It was so close now that they even *felt* it as the bumper collided with the bags of shopping they still held in front of them before they were thrown clear of the diminishing gap. To them the stranger had appeared from nowhere and he'd collided with them awkwardly. Whilst his weight was modest, it was launched with enough energy to send them reeling but the impact had halted his own passage leaving him caught between the car still being pushed his way and the stationary van behind; he hardly had time to scream as he saw what was about to happen. He slammed his hands against the boot as if his slight frame could stop the enormous force that rammed into him, jettisoned him backward and pinning him between the two vehicles.

Those he had saved looked back in horror as the man that should have separated the two vehicles failed to do so. He was virtually ignored as both bumpers met beneath him regardless of his standing there. Metal touched metal with no room for anything in between. Witnesses stood in shock, unable to bring themselves to look below his waist at where his legs used to be, convinced that they must now be no more than a paper-thin bloody pulp at best and trying not to entertain the thought that they could be severed completely. Most turned away, some even heaving as they tried not to vomit at the thought but his dog remained desperate to get to him, unable to clamber over the boot she was forced to crawl under the van, determined that nothing would separate them for long.

CHAPTER FORTY

Evelyn had talked for what Noel guessed must be the better part of two hours now but he daren't check. He was very aware what impression looking at his watch would give and it was best avoided. Not only because he didn't want the girl to think he was counting the minutes, but because he really wasn't; in fact he'd been anything but restless. The detail and passion with which she had spoken was more fitting of a Broadway actress than an alcoholic dancer but it had all been said with twice the sincerity anyone merely trying to portray a role could ever manage. He knew a little about that and would have seen straight through it... it would have been like looking in the mirror but this was very different.

It had been sad, contradictory and tragic to the point that he'd felt as much like crying as she did, but she never quite cracked. He admired that and it was a rare trait in a world in which a bad hair day was reason enough to break down. Resilience was certainly something missing from any girl he'd ever dated. But it was that same asset that had ultimately led her here. She forced everything inward rather than outward, all her problems creeping up on her totally unnoticed until it took one last humiliation to push her this far. But she still retained the ability to laugh and to Noel that translated as a sure sign that he'd already done what he came here to do; he must be making some kind of progress. At times her story had been nothing short of hilarious, if tragically so and together they found the funny side somehow. He'd successfully managed to find more than a few blessings she should be grateful for and he wasn't even lying; he was genuinely jealous when she spoke about her early teenage years but whatever he said he couldn't bring back what she missed the most. And whichever tone or direction her story took, it always came back to *him*... her father. She spoke of him again now and the smile faded from her face.

'Do you think it strange that I visit the place he died more often than I visit his grave?' she asked.

Noel knew what he thought as he imagined that in a similar situation he might well do the same, but he pretended to ponder the question for a little while to make his answer appear more considered.

'No, I can see why you might do that.'

'A lot of people don't. They just think it's morbid. But at least it's only a short walk to get the drink I always need afterwards.' She smiled but Noel just shuddered.

'You ok?' she asked. She had to ask twice.

'I'm fine, I'm fine.'

Evelyn wasn't sure if he was simply mocking her repetition or if he was trying to convince himself. She found him hard to judge.

Noel composed himself knowing that giving away his concerns could destroy everything he'd achieved on this ledge. But it was hard not to show just how apprehensive he was feeling. He'd never needed to act as convincing as he would have to now as the anniversary of Evelyn's father's passing suddenly had the potential to mean more to him than a reason to sympathise.

'So how long has it been?' he asked as casually as possible.'

'I told you, a year.'

'I know, but a little bit more... a little bit less? Surely you know the date?'

She was taken back by his impatience and was surprised that it mattered to him but for whatever reason it obviously did.

'A little more' she answered. As she said it she could see Noel visibly relax. 'By an hour or so' she continued.

The mist that formed in front of Noel's face every time he breathed ceased as if he'd stopped exhaling. Either that or his insides had turned just as cold as the air around him.

She looked as confused as she felt but Noel just kept pushing with unbecoming insensitivity.

'We could go there... now?' It was desperate, but he wanted just two things; to get her down from this building as quickly as possible and to know exactly where her father met his fate. If she accepted his simple offer he could achieve both within minutes.

'I'm not here for attention you know, if you hadn't shown up I wouldn't be here at all.' Her voice was determined. He'd obviously not had the effect he'd hoped for; he tried to make the situation seem trivial by ignoring her statement but it only achieved the reverse effect. If there was one thing she hated, it was people not taking her seriously.

'Come on, we can carry on talking, but in a comfortable chair and with a drink in our hand.' The sudden change in his personality left her emotionally disorientated.

'Even if such a cheap trick worked, we're a two or three hour walk away; we'd just about make it for closing time. We've both been sitting here long enough to know how hard it is down there to hail a taxi, we've got a better view than anyone' she said remembering the poor indecisive woman who obviously hadn't known whether to proceed on foot or not.

Even if his over ambitious ploy wasn't going to work, this was still the best chance he'd had of finding out what he needed to know without having to ask directly and arousing even the slightest hint of suspicion although it did risk causing offence.

'Two or three hours? I could walk anywhere in this city quicker than that!' he claimed, goading her on.

'As you might be able to, but you couldn't make it to Eccles Corner much quicker.'

With that statement Noel got the truth he craved but not the one he had hoped for. The time, the circumstances and now the place had combined making the evidence just too convincing and left no room for doubt; there was only one possible conclusion even if it was almost beyond comprehension. But what were the chances of him finding out like this when he could so easily have just walked on without ever looking up? It was hard to accept as simple coincidence but that didn't mean that he failed to recognise what he'd learned as facts. He'd already felt responsible for contributing to her situation but only now did he begin to conceive to quite what extent. He owed her much more than he could ever give but getting her to safety would go some way to repaying the unthinkable debt. Simply grabbing her was still an option but it was one that he wanted to save as a last resort.

For some reason the fear of falling wasn't as great now; he wondered if it was because he suspected it was nothing less than what he deserved but if he surrendered to such self pity there was the chance he'd take her with him. She was talking again but it hardly interrupted his thinking; could he really be considering this when he'd been enjoying himself at the centre of a party just hours ago? Evelyn spoke up, never one to be ignored.

'So that's it is it? We've done a little soul searching so let's all go have a drink?'

Noel thought about what she'd said. We've done a little soul searching... she was right. In the course of listening to her hopes and fears he'd been forced to talk about his own. He couldn't help compare his life to hers and despite his comparative wealth and comfortable lifestyle he'd gladly exchange it all for an ounce of her honesty. He'd lied and deceived everyone around him into thinking he's something he wasn't whilst Evelyn had remained true to herself, even if being her wasn't something most people would envy. Despite what she said, that was why she was still here and hadn't yet dived towards the pavement; Noel doubted she was quite as sure of her intentions as she claimed to be. Something had delayed her and that meant it wouldn't take much more to pull her back from the brink.

He'd held up a mirror to the life she'd led and he hoped he'd made her realise that despite her losses, it could have been worse; it could have been his. He wondered how many of his plastic, so-called friends would be around if he'd needed them like she'd needed hers. By her own admission she'd pushed them away and he wouldn't mind betting that if she'd let them, they'd be here now. She'd been right... they'd both been soul searching but it was only her that found one. He'd been so deep in thought that he hadn't realised he'd continued to totally ignore her.

'Well it's been nice talking to you but it seems like you've decided our conversation's over so I hope things get better for you, I really do.' She clamped her hands down beside her and used them to push herself forward. She did so with such certainty that there was little of her still in contact with the ledge by the time Noel reacted, but when he did it was with a conviction neither of them had expected. He let go of the railing with both hands and gripped her, stopping her forward slide instantly. He held her firm for a moment whilst the force he'd exerted equalled hers before he unleashed another burst of energy, half dragging her and half pulling her back and onto the roof's edge. The twisting motion that he adopted had the opposite effect on him and they virtually exchanged positions. He swung out instinctively and grasped at the metal barrier and, hoping it was as strong as it looked he steadied himself with it, resisting the temptation to yank himself back to safety as he wasn't confident it could take the sudden strain. He eased himself backwards slowly and carefully, not even breathing until the majority of his body was laid flat against the ground.

He looked at Evelyn without even trying to hide his anger. How could she do that to him? Even if she didn't believe he'd risk his own life for hers, she was still going to let him watch her fall after getting to know her. Why put him through that? Why humour him for so long only to carry on regardless?

Evelyn returned his constant stare while her opinion changed entirely. She could barely believe what had just happened; she didn't even know his name but after knowing her just a few hours he'd risked everything for her and it gave her a sense of worth that she could barely remember. With no idea what to do or say she just scrambled to her feet and motioned towards him instinctively, unsure of how she'd show her feelings but in no doubt that she had to try. But Noel interpreted her advance in his own way; all he saw was her walking back to the building's edge and he was outraged at her ingratitude.

'Don't, don't even think about it. You come a step closer and I'll drag you back down.'

The man before her was virtually unrecognisable from the timid stranger that had come so close to being the first person to ever urge her to reverse a decision. When she first met him he'd seemed nervous just looking at the drop but now he almost seemed comfortable next to it. She simply didn't understand; there seemed no sense to be made of it. The adrenaline must be consuming him and his heart must still be pounding from the situation she'd put him in. That would explain the sudden change to some extent but his behaviour had become erratic before any of that happened. It shocked her that she was more concerned about him than she was herself; the role reversal was so unprecedented not only because of its severity but also its suddenness. It had all happened so fast. She again moved towards him, this time with her arms outstretched, almost welcomingly which she hoped would change his perception of the gesture entirely.

'Don't!' He was shouting now but his aggression didn't seem directed at her. She couldn't quite explain it but it seemed directed inward.

'I'm not going too, don't worry.'

'Not going to what?' Noel questioned. 'Not going to jump or not going to leave?'

'Neither. '

Noel sighed and hoped it wasn't visible. At least he didn't have to worry about her now. Whether somewhere along the line he'd said the right thing or the potentially self sacrificing action was enough in itself he didn't know; but then it didn't really matter. Now all he needed to be concerned about was finding the space he so desperately needed. Part of him really didn't want her to go, she'd brought out an honesty in him that he'd missed but the rest of him needed her to stay away. He couldn't even look at her and right now he'd say or do whatever he needed to as long as it meant he'd be left alone.

'There's no point in hanging around now, so just go. I'm sorry about your dad, really I am, but go. If he's not around it just means your mother needs your more.'

She barely reacted, but she didn't have to. In just a few hours he'd gotten to know her well enough to understand what that look meant. It meant he'd done it again. She was certainly right about him assuming so much. She hadn't mentioned her mother at all and now he was sure he knew why. Her next few words didn't surprise him at all.

'She died giving birth to me.' She didn't delay or soften the blow; just told it like it was and again Noel admired it.

Noel ached with sympathy for her. Her life had been tougher than his ever had to be and at least she was the victim of circumstance; he'd just created all his own problems. He wanted to talk to her like she deserved, to treat her like she needed to be treated but even a hint of compassion now would keep her rooted to the spot or worse still… it might bring her closer to him.

'Think about what you're saying... just for a moment, actually think about it!' This was more than shouting, it was virtually screaming and she physically backed off as he worked through his tirade. He'd seen a chance to send her to safety and he was going to take it even if it meant she'd hate him for it.

'Your mother died giving birth to you; do you know anything about it?' He didn't wait for an answer and continued as she looked too shaken to reply. 'How old are you? You're certainly not old enough that the hospital would have lacked the technology to have predicted exactly what would happen. They'd have known and they'd have told your mother straight; they would have given her the choice. She would have had a decision to make.' He started to walk slowly towards her now but she backed off equally for every advance he made as he ranted. It confirmed to him that his plan was working and so he kept the intensity up.

'She'd have had a decision to make' he repeated just in case the words had been thought and not spoken last time. 'It's you or your baby they'd have told her, that'd have been her simple, but agonising choice. And she chose you... she chose *you*.' Noel believed passionately in what he was saying but not how he was delivering it. It hurt him to hurt her and her eyes alone left him in no doubt as to the effect it was having but he didn't back down in the slightest. He had her moving in the right direction now, and it was the goal, not the method of achieving it that mattered now.

'Now I don't know whether that's right or wrong, it's not for me to say but she decided that she should die and that you should live... and for what?'

He couldn't believe what he was doing, how ruthless he was being, but without realising it Evelyn had retreated almost as far as the stairwell now and from there the route was obvious.

'But what I do know is that she didn't do it so that you could throw yourself off a building because things haven't gone your way lately? Or so that you could drink yourself even stupider.'

Evelyn had never felt such mixed emotions but was still elated at what Noel had done for her. She'd endured a decade of men telling her what they'd sacrifice for her but in a few fateful seconds Noel had proven himself more sincere than any of them. She felt she knew him well enough to be certain that what she saw now wasn't the real him, but not well enough to know why. The equation just didn't add up but whatever the answer, it seemed he needed help more than she did... and he'd certainly earned it. But now wasn't the time and that couldn't be clearer. Either she'd touched a particularly sensitive nerve and he was genuinely as frustrated as he seemed or this was his tactics to ensure her safety; either way she considered giving him what he wanted... for now.

From across the street she'd be able to see him exit the building or descend the fire escape again and that would give her time to decide whether she could say everything she wanted to; whether it was worth the chance. She was sure it would sound too contrived;

like it would appear no more than a knee jerk reaction to such a life changing moment... and maybe it was. The possibility remained that she was letting her new found emotions rule her but at least she was worldly enough to realise. Perhaps distance would serve her well too, if only to give her time to gain some sort of perspective and to establish whether she was simply confusing his sense of duty with something else? They were from different worlds after all... he'd been honest enough to acknowledge that but still she stopped walking away; it wasn't so impossible. Worlds collide all the time. For all the points they'd disagreed on there were plenty that they hadn't. But then she remembered his face when he heard what she did for a living and she snapped back to reality.

She should give up what was no more than wishful thinking. They might share a mutual interest in painting but surely neither of them would be able to gloss over her most recent career. He was too opinionated and she had a frustratingly accurate memory. Besides, anyone who wore a suit like that and lived in that part of town didn't get where they were by not taking their opportunities and he'd had plenty of time to call her back if that's what he wanted to do... and he hadn't. Without turning around she closed her eyes and waited; it was only for a few seconds but it was long enough to become humiliating when it turned out to be for nothing. She wanted to be sure he needed something more than time but the silence made his decision obvious. She pulled Joe's coat tighter around her and walked away.

Noel was relieved and disappointed at the same time. For a moment he thought she was coming back; had she done he wouldn't have been able to go through with his promise of pushing her away. After such a long and unnecessary delay, in his pathetic mind he'd honestly thought to himself it was because she didn't want to leave. Until that moment he'd wanted nothing else other than for her to disappear but now she had it didn't feel quite right. Just a few hours ago he'd have ran after beauty like that and clung to the awkward connection he thought he'd felt but he knew he would never be able to look her in the eye.

He turned back and stared at the street below hoping the noise of the traffic would drown out the sound of her descending the steps toward it... maybe she was teasing him about the elevator after all. But for all of her strange and weird opinions that he might never understand she'd been right about one thing at least; the view from here really was stunning. Displays he'd walked past every working day took on a different shape from up here but he could also see things he thought were no longer there. Behind the seasonally erected market stalls were the various efforts of the permanent shops and cafes to entice the valuable end of year trade, eclipsed by the part-time opportunists. They even overshadowed Frosty, the unimaginatively named snowman that Noel hadn't seen for weeks, but he remembered him now. He'd watched the ever jolly inflatable rise slowly every morning on his way to work and he'd sometimes seen him gradually crumple to the ground when dusk arrived on the few occasions he left work that early. He also remembered the shopkeepers' frustration when their top hat wearing mascot, among the first and the largest of the outdoor displays to go up this year, had been lost behind the barrage of advertising that grew larger with every advancing December day. The shop keepers and store mangers had grown increasingly hostile towards each other as the competition increased and their tactical operations magnified to compensate. Sometimes it was hard to watch as they tried to jeopardise each others businesses, but occasionally they were cunning to the extent that he laughed out loud. He'd known Frosty's owners since he was a boy and still talked to them now. He remembered their frustration when the shop owner next door set up his advertising on the pavement just slightly to the right of his store with a massive banner claiming 'THE BEST DEALS AROUND'. It wasn't directly in front but it obscured the view of shoppers walking down the street but at least they only accounted for a little less than half his custom. But when his other neighbour invaded his potential to sell by erecting a 'BARGAINS RIGHT HERE' sign to his left he fought back; not with sheer scale as they had done, but with shrewdness they obviously lacked. He constructed his own sign, but it didn't boast the way theirs did; it simply read 'MAIN ENTRANCE' and he placed it perfectly between the two... and it had worked.

With so many obstructions in the street, Old Frosty had nearly been retired to save the electricity it took to keep him inflated and illuminated but for one reason or another it had never happened. Perhaps he was kept in employment for tradition's sake alone, but either way, Noel hoped his shopkeeper friend regained the trade he deserved and smiled again thinking about it now. Like so many of his thoughts, it was pointless but it was simply his mind trying to keep him off the subject that had triggered his total transformation.

If he looked down even more directly than he had been, it wasn't the glow of the street that was visible, but the cold dark concrete of the ledge and his shoes almost reached its edge; he didn't even remember returning to it yet he'd been drawn back somehow. It was unthinkable. He'd taken the chance he'd needed to when he'd pulled the girl back from the brink but he didn't need to be here anymore and he couldn't possibly *want* to be? He dedicated all his concentration to the question; this was closer to the perimeter than anyone who valued their life would go so surely that must be the answer? The thought of doing anything other than returning down that old fire escape to the crowds below didn't bear thinking about; but then neither did living the rest of his life knowing what he had done.

He edged forward until the roof beneath him ran out completely, wondering if his careful, shuffling steps were evidence that when the moment come he'd lose his nerve and would retrace his steps every bit as carefully. He wondered if this whole episode; this epic battle that had been declared, fought and almost lost in his aching head would just become another secret. Whether it would then just ricochet around his body until it eventually shot out of his mouth, always at the wrong time and always in the wrong direction.

He eased himself onward a little more as if daring fate to make his decision for him. Standing with his right foot over hanging the building by what he estimated to be about half its length, he closed his eyes momentarily, breathed the deepest lungful of frosty air he could and was taken aback as he did so. Not just by the sudden cold but because it felt like it was one more than he was owed; one more than he should even be allowed. He aligned his left shoe with his right until he was at pivoting point and even the slightest breeze could encourage his decision or reverse it. Either way it would save him having to make what was becoming an increasingly agonising decision.

He stood there waiting for the inevitable but it didn't come. The gust that he'd decided to rely upon never arrived. He literally couldn't feel the air shifting around him at all but was sure it wasn't through numbness; there was no sign of the slightest draft anywhere. Even the weather had reacted now that the secret was out and it wasn't going to help him either; he didn't deserve it. Still he waited knowing that this was impossible but it gave him too much time to think; too much time for everything he'd repressed to stay beaten down any longer.

But at least now he was alone it didn't matter anymore. With that comforting thought he fell to pieces. Maybe he did have the makings of a poker player after all as he'd managed to not reveal his hand to Evelyn as the dreadful truth caught up with him. But the ability to deceive was nothing to be proud of. What kind of man can discover he's a murderer and continue with a conversation like that? He'd spent his life accusing others and claiming to want justice but when he could deliver it himself he'd shied away like the coward he could now see he had always been. He knew Evelyn wasn't perfect, she was a long way from it but if life was a game of cards she'd been given an unfortunate hand yet still played the best she could. The one good fortune she could have had was to know the cause of her loss and that the sentence would fit the crime. But instead the cause had sat there, shaking his head in disbelief at how someone could be so careless and agreed with her when she'd suggested exactly what the punishment should be. But it wasn't too late; he could give her what she deserved. As unbelievable as it was that he was even considering it, he really could make her wish a reality. He backed away from the edge and searched his suit pockets for a pen and chose the plainest of the business cards he carried. He knew that for what he was about to do to mean anything, she'd have to know why it happened and he shakily scrawled his confession. Whoever scraped him up would see that it reached who it was meant to; of that he was sure. He might not know her name but the truth would find her; it had tracked him down after all and he had done his very best to hide from it. He read his note back and, satisfied that it contained everything it needed to he pocketed the card again with shaking hands.

Afraid to look down he stared skywards for longer than he intended to. The enormity of the situation engulfed him and the pitch black sky offered little distraction. He blinked, unsure whether his eyes were even open

CHAPTER FORTY-ONE

The trailer's approach could be seen from within the whirling estate as it appeared, vanished and then reappeared again with every revolution. Each time it loomed significantly closer than before as the car, still reeling from its earlier collision continued to spin relentlessly making its occupants sick with dizziness. They couldn't be sure whether they'd escape the lorry's reach as it swung ominously towards them but they'd rather not take the chance. They clawed at the door handles, desperate to evacuate but their disorientation made co-ordination impossible. The wheels below them gradually began to find the road and the car started to recover, each full circle slightly slower than the last but with each turn the trailer appeared to increase in size and they knew what that meant. Everyone inside and outside the car could see what was going to happen but none could intervene. The two vehicles smashed together and the smaller of them was again sent twisting like a toy with yet more force and faster still, but this time in the opposite direction.

Even loaded with passengers and a substantial amount of cash, the estate had done little or nothing to interrupt the trailer's relentless slide and with nothing larger or heavier ahead it continued to close the angle at the point it was held secure like a colossal hinge. The connecting pin was strained under the enormous pressure, being pulled in opposing directions and forcing the entire trailer back across the street as if it was actually chasing Evelyn. Despite Nick's efforts she was effectively back in the same situation and looked frantically to either side; her path was blocked to the left as the lorry was now bent back on itself and the other end was so far away she'd never make it in time even if she could force her legs to move. Realising that attempting either route was futile she could think of nothing else other than that this must be what they called karma; she'd wished her life away and now it was being taken. The trailer had become the Reaper and it was coming for her, its company logo had been difficult to read at first but it became clearer and clearer with every passing moment. It filled her entire sphere of vision for a spilt second until it blurred, altogether too close for her to focus on. Now it was all she could see and an awful scraping sound competed with the screams, sirens and alarms that surrounded her.

Although encircled by people she felt so alone in a world that suddenly defied belief. She couldn't help but wonder if the reason she found herself so unable to move was because she knew, subconsciously at least that she wasn't meant to. The papers and even the local news might later report it as a tragedy and discuss how unlucky she'd been... to be there, at that time but it didn't feel like misfortune at all. It felt as though all twenty-three tonnes of metal and grease had been launched at her; for her... like it was actually chasing her down. The way it continued to move despite the unimaginable wreckage was too bizarre; under ordinary weather conditions it would have ground to a natural halt sometime ago but it was exceptionally cold tonight. The damp had frozen *so* fast that it was as if the temperature had dropped solely to provide the ice on which helpless vehicles now slid. They were even moving at a pace that allowed everyone else except Evelyn to narrowly avoid the twisting mass as the heavy traffic had prevented most of them from ever approaching the already over cautious speed limit; had similar happened in fast moving traffic, the results wouldn't bear thinking about.

Onlookers stared open mouthed and screamed conflicting instructions from a safe distance and the relative safety of shops, some already turning away not wanting to witness the moment she disappeared under the trailer; others were simply unable to take their eyes off her. She was now half hidden in shadow as the sliding tonnage loomed over her, still clearing whatever lie in its path and creating a semicircle barrier difficult for the authorities to breach, trapping them one side of the carnage and its victims on the other. She closed her eyes so tightly it was as though she wanted to see less than nothing, unable to accept dying minutes after deciding she truly wanted to live. Now the end was here she didn't want to see it coming. This may be justice but the timing was cruel; just an hour ago she wouldn't have been so scared.

CHAPTER FORTY-TWO

The cables torn down and ripped from the sides of the buildings by the wayward trailer had fallen to the ground; once proudly holding an impressive spectacle so welcomingly above the main stretch of road, they now hung limp and useless except for the main supporting wire. With enough voltage running through it to supply the electronic mass of bulbs and fairy lights it thrashed around violently spitting raw and deadly power at anyone that dared approach it. It kicked around the driver's side of Nick's cabin as if defending it from help before twisting and jerking across the street. Unchallenged, it snaked its way along until it was caught and wedged under the wheel of the estate which snatched and pinned it to the ground as it continued to spin.

The cable caught firm on the wheel arch and slapped hard against the body work before coiling around its bumper, working its way up and around the car. Still the vehicle spun, picking up the cables convulsing slack like a winch from across the street and lifting it off the ground. It whipped into the back of Evelyn's calves as it snapped taunt, taking her legs out from under her and sending her crashing to the ground. She'd have screamed in agony but the shock stole the sound away and the impact as she landed hard on her back knocked the breath from within her. The world blurred as her head lashed back, cracking against the ice but still she watched the thick, armored cabling hoisted higher and higher above her into the air until it was pulled tight and perfectly straight. With no more slack to give, it tugged persistently at the steel pins that had secured it so successfully to the cities walls for almost two months. But now, it was being dragged away from across the street and the plaster and brick embedding the lowest of the hooks was beginning to crumble yet nobody noticed and no one really cared; by comparison to the horrific and seemingly more threatening events unfolding it seemed the very least of their worries. It continued being gradually dragged from the weaker fixings in one slow, smooth movement until it paused for a moment, a particularly well embedded hook making one last stand before being violently jettisoned under the enormous building pressure.

The next fastening suddenly found itself under such sudden strain that it too was sent flying across the street. The force was transferred unmercifully to the next again and again, each offering just a split seconds resistance before it either snapped or was simply pulled clean out of the wall until the entire row had burst away in staggered jolts all the way up to its final and most secure fixing. It held fast and determined but only for so long before it exploded sending plaster spraying and leaving nothing to stop the cable being stripped from the supporting frame to the centre of the street where the sleigh hung precariously above the escalating scene. Unleashed, it corkscrewed around the pole over which it had been wrapped. It wasn't until it yanked at the beam wiring the power lead to the mass of tangled lighting and the beautifully detailed wooden sleigh enjoying its first year of display that its reluctant audience began to foresee the possible repercussions.

They again started to look around for a haven but with the wreckage piling up around them, safety was becoming increasingly hard to find and a luxury that no amount of money could buy. The plastic restraints now struggling to hold the spectacle in place had been designed and tested to withstand minor projectiles and even severe gales but the council who commissioned it had understandably failed to foresee this.

The cablings resilience was impressive and even managed to bring the twirling estate car to its final revolution but that last, diminished turn was just one too many dragging the decorations in its direction and sending the full weight of the loaded sleigh plummeting towards the trapped gathering below. A few on the outer circle found shelter in the contorted maze that had been their cars but that left most staring in frozen fear as they saw the massive ornament break loose; others just screamed and covered their faces in pointless defence whilst the lucky ones, oblivious to where the panic was stemming from didn't see it coming until it was virtually on top of them.

The terror died with the screams as the sleigh's descent stopped suddenly, mid-fall and just short of a dozen petrified faces; the strings of fairy lights were thin enough to snap by hand individually but together in strands and stretched to their limit they were strong enough to swing danger away from the cowering crowd like a pendulum. The wooden construction was swept so closely over their heads that it knocked the hat off of a boy who'd been sat on his dad's shoulders, ironically to keep him safe from harm. It was like a pilot had woken up at the last possible second and regained control; gliding it away and onwards with its journey.

Until a few minutes ago there would have been few scenes less deserving of media attention and the best footage programmers could have hoped for would have been low grade video feed, delayed until it was over and captured on a tourists substandard camcorder. But Dec was already screaming into his mobile phone before he'd even slammed Joe's rear door shut behind him. He was in a position to get something for Wainsbridge Media that they couldn't need more. With such scenes on their doorstep the company would never find a suitable excuse to have missed gaining coverage; and with all of their employed reporters too drunk to handle a camera even if they could hear the commotion over the party inside, his promise to David suddenly had the potential to come true. He'd continually assured him that they'd eventually be in the right place at the right time and now it was looking very much like they were. The two of them could still hear Joe, shouting after them from his taxi as they sped away; it was another fare that wouldn't be paid tonight but he'd never catch either of them at the pace they were running.

David's footage would be shaky at best but he was capturing everything whilst Declan tried to double task; he guided his cameraman through the obstacles whilst simultaneously trying to get someone inside the building to beam the pictures live to their news channel. To his surprised relief his call was answered with sobriety and he accepted their promise to try, wishing with everything he had that it would be done in time; he knew that the story-book scene of Santa's full-size sleigh skimming the top of the High Street crowds on Christmas Eve then soar towards the night sky was priceless... and career saving. Executives from national stations would have paid untold amounts for the stunt but it was impossible to stage and all they'd be able to do tonight would be to watch their televisions sets, jealous and stunned that an unknown reporter got to shoot what could well turn out to be the footage of the year.

The combined strength of so many wires was strained but adequate and continued to swing the considerable weight out and away from the crowd. It rose into the air but slowed as gravity gradually took effect whilst it neared the edge of its upward curve as if posing for the cameras that flashed all around as opportunists failed to realise that what goes up never fails to come down. But the relieved crowd looked on in wonder at the fitting image which seemed so familiar from children's movies and greetings cards. They actually smiled as the sleigh reached the full height of its journey and paused momentarily, hanging in the air so perfectly and kept from continuing its flight by its entwined leash. Even under this enormous pressure the wires never snapped but the staples attaching it and clinging to the sleigh's intricate outline were not so sturdy and bent under this new and unprecedented force.

It was watched not just by those there that night, but by the thousands sat in their own living rooms as the images interrupted the broadcast being beamed live and unedited into homes for miles around. Yet in the hysteria, nobody noticed that once the initial double pinning had worked lose, the others started to follow; each stretch of released wiring lengthening the lead on which the sleigh had begun to swoop again, clearing its public by even less this time in a breathtaking display that defied belief.

It continued to turn heads as it dipped and passed the trapped gathering again, some flinching at last suspecting that their sense of security may have been misplaced and nervously watching it rise against its second backdrop. It reached its peak, but instead of hesitating peacefully as before it kicked and twisted in midair as another sudden succession of staples were ripped away from one side to the other, unable to bear the full brunt any longer. The return flight was far less graceful as it swung noticeably lower and the now terrified crowd braced themselves again for what was now inevitable. Their smiles traded back to looks of horror as Santa flew towards them on a suicide mission with his sights firmly set; his jolly expression seeming almost that of a maniac now.

Not far behind them the traffic turning into the High Street was only just realising the catastrophe into which they were headed. It took time for even the quickest thinking of the approaching drivers to comprehend the carnage that confronted them and their reactions were equally delayed as they had to look twice at the nightmare scene to believe it. Car after car shunted the one in front like dominos, but most had been moving too slow to cause any major damage if they could just stop short of what was starting to look like a war zone. Bikers were the only ones who'd been able to negotiate the congestion and had been able to maintain their speed, weaving in and out of the maze of bumpers but now, as the gaps closed to nothing in the pile up they were routed down the street. Some bounced between the cars as they were channelled onwards, out of control and struggling to stop so suddenly on just two wheels in such conditions.

The squealing of brakes again filled the frosty air as all but one managed to bring their bikes to a halt one way or the other at a relatively safe distance. But Rick was desperate not to forfeit another pizza and had been the only one to actually exceed the speed limit in a last ditch attempt to make up for his delay; he'd be able to disguise his failure to deliver on time earlier by subsidising his takings with his own money but he didn't have enough cash on him to do it again. He'd known full well that it was asking for trouble to reach such speeds on a night like tonight but he also wanted to keep his job. As he'd pointlessly explained to Mary earlier, he hated it but it was usually easy; without some life changing event to drag him out of the rut in which he'd found himself he'd probably prove the woman right and never paint again. The more he thought about her, the angrier he'd become and with the sudden heightened awareness he'd been amongst the first to slam on his brakes, but thanks to three year old tyres he was still the last to slow down. He daren't look anywhere but straight ahead. He was aware that he'd left the traffic either side way behind and was now exposed, still being propelled forward into the bedlam. If he'd had time to think of anything else except how he was going to avoid careering further into danger he'd have been quietly impressed with the fact he'd managed to remain in his saddle. It had kept sliding from under him, trying to throw him off but he'd repeatedly counterbalanced, occasionally and painfully using the cars that flanked him to keep himself upright until they'd run out. Now, with a complete lack of options and his runway almost at an end, he'd let go completely.

 Rick gritted his teeth, ready to land hard and glad to do just that it if that meant avoiding being launched headlong into the oncoming trailer still making its way steadily up the road... sideways. He had no idea what on earth had happened here but he didn't have time to wonder. He caught glimpses of his faithful bike crashing to its side, sparks flying the moment it landed as its metal components began to scrape against the harsh surface of the road. It vanished momentarily, replaced by the darkest black of asphalt before appearing again, becoming a revolving view as he too hit the ground and tumbled, half turning and half-skidding on the ice below. His world continued to twist and turn until he saw the blazing trail of his motor cycle swallowed by the shadow of the all consuming trailer.

 With little material left on the elbows and knees of his standard issue, one size supposedly fits all uniform, he'd hardly slowed as he tumbled through the freshly constructed stall that Evelyn had obliterated earlier that evening; he demolished its remains completely and again sent hot chestnuts sprawling down the street. Covered in tinsel and with streamers trailing behind him, he emerged out the other side, already closing his eyes in anticipation of slamming into bone breaking brickwork of the precinct wall. From his perspective it was all he could see awaiting him beyond the stalls to which he sped, looming ever nearer with each blurring glimpse. Opening his eyes would have done nothing to prepare him as he'd been practically gift wrapped in the process of exiting the stand and now curled into a ball to protect his essentials he resembled the results of a child's first effort to wrap a present unaided. His new position only served to send him head-over-heels, he winced through the ribbons and bows hoping he'd fracture rather than break.

But he could feel he'd stopped. He was virtually upside down and still unable to see, but he could tell he wasn't moving. Scared of the answers he'd find he concentrated on each part of his body, convinced he was yet to feel the damage but besides the grazing and bruises he'd expect from launching himself off a moving vehicle he felt surprisingly intact. Having given up trying to free himself completely, he clawed at where his face should be and tore holes in the paper, misshapen, but sufficient to see through. His eyes peered through the tunnel vision at another's staring right back. They formed part of an expression so cheery it was inappropriate to their life threatening surroundings but then its wearer knew no other look. Unsurprisingly, his eyes were as black as coal but then that's exactly the way they were made; without them, a carrot for a nose may look strange. Frosty's fixed smile remained in place even when doubled over by the force of a pizza boy careering headfirst into his air filled belly, forcing it through his seams faster than his generator could replace it. The impact had knocked him backwards, effectively flinging his arms open and forwards as if to catch Rick and now, with his plump, partially deflated body engulfing him, he looked down on the boy kindly as if pleased to have at last been of use this year.

CHAPTER FORTY-THREE

Lying flat on her back and still dazed from the fall Evelyn caught a familiar glimpse of the night sky before it was totally eclipsed by the underside of the trailer as it moved over her. It cleared even the highest point of her body by a surprisingly comfortable distance and with a new burst of hope she tried to refocus her mind. Directly above her was what she thought must be one of the axles but under a vehicle with so many wheels this alone did little to help her establish her bearings. She raised her head as far as the blackened belly of the under carriage would allow and foresaw the massive wheels no sooner than she felt them. They were already upon her and she reacted faster than she would have thought possible, snatching her head away from its path. She squealed with pain and shock as it was tugged back, the unrelenting grip of the closest tyre was pinning her hair to the tarmac like a vice; unable to roll aside to safety, she was forced to listen to its considerable weight as it cracked the ice beneath so close to her ears that it sounded like the road itself was about to collapse.

The pain grew with the awful sound, so loud now that she couldn't even hear her own screams as the tyres trod her locks further into the ground, tugging them so fiercely that her entire body was dragged towards them. Her defiant cry escaped her immediate surroundings and those that heard it shuddered, fearing the worst and afraid to look. Her head had been yanked so far back that she had to arch her body to avoid her skull being crushed against the road, but it was already pressing its grit and gravel into her scalp so hard that she feared it was not only the ice she could hear cracking; that would at least explain why it was *so* loud. Yet she wouldn't give in to it, not all the time she knew it could be her imagination.

The merciless grasp tightened until her neck and spine were bent to their limit and she was forced into such a contorted position that she could actually see the back of the wheel behind her, clamping her to the road. She was close enough to see strands of her own wet hair already ripped loose, and clinging to the tyre tread, rising up and over as it rolled but there was hope; she'd either grown used to the pain or she was gradually being released. She was reluctant to believe the latter although she was able to allow herself to ease into a slightly more human position but she wasn't free yet and her sense of relief didn't last long. Her body lay at an angle and remained directly in the same wheels path, forcing her to awkwardly and painfully shunt and drag her body around. With no time for elegance, her movement was almost epileptic, the violence of her jolting actions adding to her existing wounds but it didn't enter her thoughts; there was no room for anything but survival as she jerked, twisted and thrashed until she'd manoeuvred herself clear.

For the first time her new position allowed her to see past the wheels that still held her captive. Until now they'd been shielding her from the incoming missile that was hurtling straight towards her; the sparks that continued to spray from the bike's cheap metal frame announced its course all too clearly and she'd be grateful for the warning if she was able to react. In the corner of her eye she could see the overturned motorcycle's colossal speed, but she concentrated her efforts fully on breaking away from the unrelenting grip that still held her firmly in its path.

Growling with one final effort, she tugged so aggressively that when the sudden release sent her reeling, she was unsure whether it she'd been granted the freedom she so desperately needed or if she'd literally torn herself away but the sudden release sent her rolling along the ground. She was facing away when the extreme darkness that had surrounded her was lit up by the sparking metal screaming past so close she actually felt what she couldn't see. The sparks landed hot on her skin but died in moments as the battered motorcycle shot by at such a speed that her oversize men's jacket billowed in the gust it created.

She watched as the same wheel that had almost claimed her life rolled over one of the chestnuts still cascading down the street, leaving just the crushed remnants behind; the perfect metaphor seemed well placed to make her realise how lucky she'd been but she didn't need reminding. Turning to watch the last of the blazing trail fade as it left her letterbox view, she exhaled for what seemed like the first time since she'd landed on the ground. From her perspective the crowds were cut off at the knees and they charged in every direction as if they were in more danger than her. She hoped at least some of them were running towards Noel as she had been but doubted they were trying to save anything but themselves. She again found her thoughts return to his words, terrified that she should have seized on a clue as to why someone like him would do something so extreme and that she could have intervened. But her thoughts were shattered by a sudden and deafening crash as the trailer finally collided with something nearing its own size and immense weight.

The massive impact shuddered through the vehicle and Evelyn clasped her hands over her ears to shield against the awful sound, amplified by her proximity to the iron framework that still reverberated above her. She turned her head, aware of the movement beside her and watched with horror as another of its massive wheels weighed down on the exact spot where her arm would still remain had she not defended against the noise. She'd have wondered about the odds had the grotesque image of an entire limb, so much more than merely broken filled her head. All the wonders of science wouldn't have been able to mend the bloody pulp that it so nearly became. She pictured it so mangled and heavily trodden into the pattern of the tarmac that it'd show through the paper thin limb and for that moment she was unable to see anything else. She was so uncontrollably sick that she didn't even notice the incessant rumble having now almost passed over her completely. Her vomit resembled the liquid consistency of what everyone around would be expecting to be left of her remains but she was still more or less intact... the improbability made her heave again. She closed her eyes momentarily to stop the cycle, unable to fully take in what had just happened. Overcome with emotion and sobbing uncontrollably, she grappled with the meaning, not sure what it was but absolutely convinced of its existence. It wasn't her time... not yet.

Evelyn rolled over, never more glad to see the same old city but she was still shaking and was very aware that she was encircled by other peoples panic. In the short time she'd been hidden so much had changed; it all seemed so surreal that she'd lost any concept of time and even her certainty of what she'd ran so recklessly towards. She hoped the commotion that continued was in reaction to anything other than what she thought she'd seen and that it had been no more than her exhausted mind playing cruel tricks on her again. Forcing her head around, she tried to wipe the tears away but only succeeded in streaking blood across her face as if to camouflage herself and become part of the nightmare.

It was now obvious what caused the ear splitting collision as emergency crew leapt from the wrecked rear end of their fire truck. They'd only been called to extinguish a small alleyway blaze; its flickering glow was evident from here and with horror Evelyn realised it was incredibly unlikely not to have been started by the 'cigarette' when Noel had knocked it from her hand. She'd never felt so significant; could she really have been the catalyst that had triggered all this? If so, her presence brought a responsibility that made no sense.

The firefighters were dealing with an emergency they hadn't expected and that was clear from their apparent lack of organisation as they seemed unsure of which situation to attend first. But it was obvious from Evelyn's distance that they had to regain control of their own vehicle before they could try and quell the devastation around them. The impact from which they were recovering hadn't had the effect she'd hoped for though and was not as final as it had sounded when reverberating spitefully in her head. Barely even interrupted, the trailer continued to sweep through its destructive path but the force of the collision was felt throughout the fire engine as various equipment spilled out of its side. Hoses unravelled and extinguishers were crushed by the massive force of the blow and now spewed foam high into the air. Its revolving ladder had been dislodged, still held fast at the highest point but had extended out the back of the vehicle and fallen dangerously to the ground. It narrowly missed a group sheltering there, believing it to be the most sensible place until an ambulance arrived. One of the trucks many compartments seemed to withstand the first of an almighty force that was coming from within before the second burst it open. Pressurised canisters, presumably gas tanks of some sort had been ruptured and were now being jettisoned across the street like primitive rockets. Evelyn could see them scatter the crowd in yet more directions as everyone tried to evade being caught in the crossfire as the containers shot overhead but then rebounded dangerously off the walls, cars and buildings on the opposite side of the road. There were only two exceptions; both of them reacted differently to everyone else and ran towards the battleground instead of away from it like a pair of war journalists, one more reluctant than the other. They stayed low whilst struggling to carry their enormous baggage. One dragged the other who never once took his eye away from the lens of his camera as he captured all that he could on film. They charged across the short expanse in time to immortalise the spectacular but destructive sight of the canisters smashing through windows and into the offices that would be occupied if it wasn't for the party still raging in ignorance several floors above.

Despite the scene she was witnessing, Evelyn's attention was drawn away as screams fuelled by absolute terror found their way along through the carnage, rising above the now indistinguishable noise of an entire street in total chaos. She watched with everyone else as the sleigh, which to her had appeared from nowhere began its flight back towards a crowd already herded and trapped by wreckage; its path painfully predetermined. Clasping her hands across her face she peered through her open fingers, unable to even imagine how so much had happened in so little time. She'd never heard so many people draw breath in perfect synchronization before as everyone, transfixed in their disbelief but helpless to do anything prayed to who, or whatever they believed in as the bike, still wildly out of control hit the base of the fallen ladder. The sharp, metallic clang of the initial impact as it jolted off the ground caused the crowd to flinch in faultless time and they recoiled from the deafening smash as it was flipped and catapulted along the ladder's steep angle, tumbling all the time but guided skywards. The clattering of metal against metal ceased suddenly as it was launched, somersaulting over the fire truck and into the night.

It continued to turn and twist over and over at unnatural angles, high into the air and above the captive crowd; some watching it intently, others staring in the opposite direction and tracing the speeding sleigh instead until their gaze met where the two collided violently above them, showering them with little more than splintered debris.

Virtually undeterred and hardly damaged the bike spasmed in increasingly awkward flight as far as the deserted road works. It clipped the barrier which accelerated its continued final twist and powered it into the earth sending one last cascade of sparks into the air. In the seconds silence that followed, the cowering crowd dropped their defence just as its tank ignited; the modest 150cc engine had been driven so dry of petrol due to Rick's desperate throttling that the resulting explosion did little more than make them flinch, the resulting fireball failing to even reach the area's outer cordon.

Without exception nobody moved, standing in respectful silence of whatever greater force was at work. The white foam still jetting into the air had gone largely unnoticed but now formed a spectacle all of its own. Rising skywards in a powerful and steady stream above them, it separated at its full height and fell all around them in flakes. It drifted down and onto the flames, extinguishing the fire from the very moment it begun and prevented its spread. Nobody would say it out loud but everyone was thinking the same; it looked so much like snow as the breeze returned and blew it down the street in flurries that they only knew it wasn't the real thing because they could see its source as it continued to erupt from the fire truck.

The speechless mass of awestruck faces turned as one to see the trailer had now arced almost full circle into the already evacuated clearance and was now about to catch up with its cabin. At such an angle, the two halves of the hinge connected in a way they were never intended to and were unable to move separately anymore; one now had to force the other to follow suit. With the far greater mass, the trailer took the front with it, yanking it back out over the marble floor, across the devastated reception and pulling it away from elevator shaft completely. The force was enough to pull it out through the way it had come but not without causing further damage. Its returning angle was vastly different to that at which it had entered and so it took yet more of the building with it and onto the street, increasing the width of the already gaping hole.

Two of its front tyres burst as they were dragged over the rubble backwards which helped to slow the momentum as its position was reversed. The entire vehicle faced the opposite way and at last was beginning to grind to a halt now that there was little left to destroy except the single queue of traffic that had so far escaped unscathed. In an effort to keep it that way, every vehicle from the front of the queue right to the animal transporter at the very back had inched forwards as much as possible to the extent that the row had become so compact, some were literally touching. For most of them it had worked and it became obvious that the lorry's procession would miss most of them... perhaps even all of them but that still gave the last driver in the queue plenty to be anxious about. He sat up in his seat, nervously switching between evaluating the situation ahead and checking his rearview mirrors as the lumbering mass advanced, seemingly uncertain as to whether it should stop.

The scene reflected in the one sliver of glass that wasn't now covered in foam resembled something from a far-fetched movie. It was hard to tear his eyes away but it was becoming more and more obvious that he needed to look ahead rather than backwards if he was going to escape this. He edged the transporter further forward to try and avoid it being another, perhaps even the last casualty in the ongoing list of victims as he certainly had no desire to add to the fatalities... even if the lives he was trying to protect weren't human. He estimated that the few inches he'd gained may just be enough, but with such fragile cargo onboard he couldn't take any chances and not just to avoid the wrath of his insurance company. He had taken all the space between him and the car in front without it making much difference but from what he could see, the car ahead of that had space worth stealing. Impulsively he floored his accelerator in an attempt to ram the stationary car into, and if possible, beyond the cavern ahead.

With their bumpers already in contact there was no collision to be felt, just the steady four wheel drive pressure and the howling of the powerful engine driving them and churning the foam beneath. The transporter initially struggled to find its grip but outmatched its competitor in seconds; its occupants leaned out of their window in astonishment before hurling abuse as they were rammed forwards, but as their focus extended far enough to see what was looming, they too fled without another word. With any other cargo, he'd be right behind them, maybe even overtaking them but mucking out his trailer would take on a whole new meaning if he gave in now. He surged forward again, claiming another abyss two cars ahead this time but there was no way he could feasibly shift a third. The deck of the stable box behind him was being trampled hard by agitated hooves as if to remind him they were there but they needn't; he was very aware but was equally sure he could do nothing more for them. Tonight might have been their last performance and all he could hope to achieve was to extend their short lives until New Year but he couldn't see them ended so inhumanely... but he also didn't want to be there if it happened.

He flung the door open and leapt out to join the family whose car he'd shunted. They were still running for cover and he was catching up but those hooves still hammered their box like they knew what was coming. He turned on the spot, already regretting that his pointless sentimentality would now no doubt see him in hospital without any gain whatsoever but there was one last way they could be dragged to safety as there was still a gaping divide between their box and the front compartment. The spring coiled connection was pulled almost flat but could compact to half the length; and it might just make the difference. He wedged his overweight body between the two sections and tried desperately to pull them closer together knowing that any result at all may just be enough. Neither side moved at all. He changed his position and braced himself, he grasped each side and pulled his arms together in an enormous effort to secure a clear conscience should he survive this. He was less successful than he needed to be but twice as effective as he could have realistically hoped. It was all he could do and now he ran as fast as his inadequate body would allow him.

Nick's lorry finally collided with something it couldn't sweep aside but the rock solid bollards struck along the length of its body so low that it their sudden influence caused the entire vehicle to tilt. The cabin suffered most as its height worked against it but every set of wheels, including the trailers left the ground and rose slowly away from the road. As it twisted it revealed the traffic behind and a reminder of the night's most horrific casualty; having saved the couple, he remained pinned between the partially demolished vehicles, his dog still scrambling to get to him. Horrified onlookers saw him push down hard on the bonnet in front of him, forcing his body to slide up against the vans rear doors. The vision of what must surely be a dying man trying to lift his own torso from the wreckage would have been too awful to bear but those whose morbid fascination would not allow them to look away saw plastic shards trail from his trouser legs and he fell awkwardly to the ground. He clawed his way halfway under the van with no obvious signs of pain and with the urgency diminished the still rising lorry captured their full attention once again. The wheels that remained on the ground started to slip from under it, turning it further still but the weight of the cabin's upper half ensured it kept the greater angle. With its connecting pin now locked again it had begun to twist its trailer but not as before, this time it was forced *over* rather than around. Both sections were now on the verge of capsizing and moved so slowly they seemed suspended at this impossible angle.

The cabin still led the way, if only by a little and within it Nick was barely conscious. The drugs had been shutting his senses down before he was pummelled into the dashboard as he sent himself through a solid external wall. He'd even hit the already damaged windscreen and now looked through his own blood, spattered and smeared across it onto his beloved winged hood ornament. Along with everything else, it had been given the same crimson tinge when viewed through the glass but it remained in place, still standing tall and preparing for flight from the irreparably damaged bonnet on which the cupid like figure still perched and rose without ever leaving her mount.

Even with its path blocked, the lorry found a way of reaching the transporter that had so nearly escaped its clutches. Leaning over at the final point before collapse the statuette's raised metal arm edged closer and closer until it made gentle contact and flipped the latch on the transporters rear door. It opened and shut a couple of times as if being tested but was blocked by the cabin's bumper, now almost stationary as the lorry's front reached near-perfect balance. With the catch undone it was repeatedly tested before being held open, pressed hard against its barrier in frustration. Darkness was all that was visible through the tiny gap until a snout appeared, wrinkled and sniffing, testing the air and smelling what must be freedom.

The lorry's cabin was no longer able to maintain its uneasy poise and started to falter, picking up speed as it fell. The twisting force again locked the pin and hinge against each other, but this time the front tried to take the back with it as if in direct response to the humiliation of having been torn from its resting place just moments before. The pressure at this angle was far too great to be withstood and the solid iron pin snapped violently, instantly ending their influence over each other. The cabin unceremoniously crashed to the ground having tipped back over completely and again filled the street with the sound of shattering glass.

With nothing now to stop it, the unlocked gate swung open, a dozen reindeer pouring out and onto the street in a frenzied escape attempt. They galloped between the obstacles of this new and alien world as if they knew the fate that awaited them should they fail. Each of them excitedly explored the labyrinth caused by the wreckage resulting in a scene that in any other place or time may have looked more than a little surreal.

The trailer had yet to make up its mind and having broken its leash still hung in the air, precariously indecisive. Evelyn had not yet found the strength to stand and still lay shaking in the road staring in awe at the familiar underbelly of the freight carrier; a sight that had so nearly been her last. It had paused at the point of toppling, the deer running back and forth in its awesome shadow. They seemed oblivious to what could happen as they galloped into the circular clearing searching for an opening in the crushed and twisted metal fortress that surrounded them, yet nobody panicked. Everyone fully realised the potential horror of the trailer's collapse and what could happen, but after what they'd witnessed tonight in this strange and somehow enchanted street nobody actually believed it would. Together they watched the trailer reach its highest point and hang there, suspended in time as if their combined wishes alone were enough to stop it dead. Nobody moved; nobody spoke… they just wished… wished and stared in silent awe at a sight they'd never be able to fully describe. Even with the ground breaking camera work being captured by David they would never quite be able to convince anyone that wasn't there of the overwhelming feeling that something far greater than them was establishing its influence that night; something that would change their lives and make believers out of even the most cynical among them. The images beamed around and beyond the city would later reach a wider audience on specialist shows but the screen would never do the atmosphere justice.

The pure white foam was blood stained in places but it had started to cover everything around them making their surroundings appear as other worldly as they felt. They'd survived near impossible odds and as far as they knew, so had those that surrounded them.

The trailer was successfully willed back down to earth but it landed so hard that it now tipped in the opposite direction, the sudden impact and steep angle catapulting its cargo despite it being strapped down. Its symbolic load hit the ground evenly, sent rolling by the force with which it was thrown and helped along by the sloping road.

CHAPTER FORTY-FOUR

Neither David nor Declan moved; they were hardly able to. Rather than give up the shot, they'd stood their ground and did their very best to narrate for the benefit of viewers now glued to the news. The pair of them tried to explain what was happening despite having to guess themselves but their shaky commentary had come to an abrupt halt. They'd taken the risk that the immense tree rolling towards them would stop short but they'd misjudged its advance; whilst it had slowed to an almost harmless speed it had reached them all the same and trapped them both but still they kept filming. Those who watched the images beamed live into their living rooms had backed away from their television sets as if the tree that Ivy had wanted so badly had been charging towards them and not the reporters now surrounded by its branches.

They'd been engulfed completely, much to the disappointment of their audience that was growing every second as word of the amazing scene spread from neighbour to neighbour to the very outskirts of the city. For miles around people tuned in, those at the outer edge of broadcast capacity repeatedly adjusted their sets trying to clear the picture to see if it was really true but for them it was already too late. The evergreen foliage had totally blocked their view and now David could only supply an image of near perfect darkness. The constant rustling and scratching of fir tree needles provided the only evidence that their television sets even remained on until Declan, shaken but not defeated began his annotations again. Families hushed each other, listening to any hint of what may be going on ensuring that they were all the more startled when the thunderous and final crash of the trailer landing for the very last time was recorded without a view.

Feeling their audience's frustration as well as their own both journalists clawed at the trees twigs and branches, trying to climb free but managed the next best thing; they found their way onto its trunk which offered the only solid footing available providing the hope of a view. David needed to be higher still but every other branch seemed unable to take his weight and he was forced to accept they were stuck for the time being at least. He reached up, his camera emerging through the thousands of pins like a periscope and just in time to capture the trailer still bouncing on its punished suspension, more by luck than judgment. He used sound alone as a guide and held his camera steady in the hope that the image was indeed being broadcast and that the public watching at home were able to see what he could only hear. But for all the extra senses the viewers were allowed, they were just as shocked as he was when the shot was obscured without warning; whatever if was fell far too fast and too close for the camera to pick out a single detail. It happened so quickly it was easy to doubt that it happened at all but there was definitely something there and it had landed just below shot.

Screaming, Evelyn ran on legs even more damaged than before, oblivious to their tattered state and racing as fast as her mind. She reached such a pace that she increased her lead over the paramedic crew that had now arrived at the scene on foot, the ambulances struggling to follow them. She tore through bewildered bystanders sending them sprawling like skittles until she'd made her way to Noel. He'd gathered such velocity during his descent that the force had powered him down and embedded him into the once impressive branches of the tree, twisting him as he had landed. Evelyn scaled its side inflicting further wounds but didn't feel a thing; all that mattered was reaching the top. Once there she reached down into the needles until they pressed hard into her face as she desperately tried to lift Noel to the surface, but every time she pulled, she sank deeper herself.

She spread her frame over the branches, dispersing her weight as evenly as she could and through the evergreen could just about see him. Broken and bloodied, his limbs lay at unnatural angles to his obscured body but he returned her gaze, staring straight up at her.

'Thank you!' she squealed not sure to whom or what she should be grateful. 'I can't believe that you... why would anybody... if this hadn't have broken your fall...' she thrust her arms down together then parted them sharply to clear a path between the two of them. She continued starting questions but failed to complete any of them. There were so many to be answered that her body could not keep up. However much she adjusted her position she could still only see part of him due to the bristly sprigs that kept snapping back into position but after everything she would not be deterred. They were snapped and wrenched from the tangled mess, showering Noel with countless needles until a clearing had been made. He was covered to such an extent that Evelyn's limited view was altered rather than improved, but at least she was closer and she could see his face. That was what she wanted; it was what she needed. She beamed down on him but hope, always as fragile as glass began to crack, slowly at first then splintered in every direction.

There was no recognition in his eyes at all, no hint of torture, relief or anything other than the wide eyed stare of terror and regret. Her insides dissolved and she realised what she was witnessing. Although the moment had passed, his eyes were apparently still fixed firmly on the ground that had been speeding towards him; Evelyn felt sure that if she looked hard enough she'd be able to see it reflected as if that last scene had somehow been imprinted there. She held tight to the knowledge that he'd be proud of himself in a twisted way; he must have done what she'd suggested was impossible. Despite her certainty that he was basically all talk he'd kept his eyes open until the end having taken her challenge on as his own.

She lowered herself further still, reached out and grabbed his jacket and furiously renewed her effort to pull him towards her like closeness to life could regenerate another. If it could, she was willing to share. With one final effort she yanked with all that was left of her energy but rather than lift him towards her it had the opposite effect.

The branches were unable to withstand the sudden and considerable pressure and gave way as she fell through the trees' already gapping crater towards him. She closed her own eyes in protection against the attacking foliage taking its revenge but by the time she opened them again she was quite literally face to face with Noel.

She was far too close to focus properly but she'd swear he actually blinked. She hadn't actually seen it but was sure she'd felt his eye lashes flicker against her cheek. She didn't move, hoping that the jolt of her landing had reawakened him somehow and that she may feel the same sensation again but she couldn't. She knew she must be wishing for too much and that what she'd felt was far more likely to be needles still falling from the branches but she pulled back to analyse his face from her awkward position.

It was clear to her now that they'd been far more alike than she'd assumed. The thought of his being here as some kind of terrible accident was not one she considered for long; it was no accident. He was too far away from the building's edge when she left him to have simply slipped. She'd known he wasn't quite as happy and content as she'd initially thought but it couldn't be more evident what an understatement that was now. Surely their conversation alone couldn't have changed his philosophy so dramatically? He must have been repressing some serious issues before tonight and that would at least explain why he was up there? Perhaps he hadn't spotted her at all but had always intended climbing those steps for his own ends; despite the tragedy, the thought that she'd not been the cause of this brought her some minor relief. But if that was the case, how could he speak so passionately about life to the extent he'd made her want to live hers? She just couldn't believe it was all just an act; she'd been lied to enough times and would have seen straight through it. As much as she didn't want to believe it, she somehow knew he'd meant every single word of what he'd said and that left just one conclusion... that he'd questioned his own life in response to learning about hers. But how could the answers he found lead to this? The thought seemed to exist in her stomach rather than her head and it wrenched so hard it physically hurt.

She tortured herself with further thoughts... did he blame her in those last few minutes? Did he see the final throws of the chaos and wonder if the tree would be enough to break his fall? Tears welled and she buried her head in his blood soaked jacket rather than be seen crying on camera. She'd noticed the lense and the whining of its mechanics but had chosen to ignore it completely; it wasn't important to her. But it didn't need her attention or permission to capture emotion as raw as anyone viewing had ever seen. Not only was it intense, it was unexpected on a local news channel more adept at reporting on lost pets and trivial awards. It had stunned everyone who saw it into silence as young and old willed Noel to react to Evelyn's pain. Her exhaustion caught up with her and she fell hard against his chest, as she did so he exhaled a burst of air. She heard it and opened her eyes but daren't pull back to look at his again. She didn't let herself be fooled; it was just the bodies mechanism reacting to her weight pressing down on his ribs; but then it came... he inhaled; the sound of the passing air the single best thing she'd ever heard.

Noel was disorientated and unable to move his neck. His eyes darted around in the gloom before everything cascaded back to him as Evelyn pulled away from his shoulder and reared into view. For just a moment he wondered if he'd got lucky... exceptionally lucky judging from the perfection of the face staring down at him but as his eyes adjusted and he could focus more clearly, the blood; *his* blood glistened against her cheek so thick that it ran off her chin. As it dripped onto his face he entered the real world again and knew exactly where he was. This was no Saturday night conquest and what he lay on was certainly no bed.

Trying to move even a little caused so much pain to shoot through his body that any remnants of the notion that his time had eventually come vanished completely. The air rushing against him, the ground speeding towards him, the tree rolling into view... it all kicked around his skull unable to escape; none of it was easy to believe but he didn't doubt it had happened either. The agony was wonderful; to be feeling anything at all was a miracle and he couldn't be more grateful. But as the darkness beyond Evelyn was streaked white with what looked like snow floating down towards him, he started to wonder if he'd landed back in reality at all.

He stared further past her for confirmation that he was not imagining all this and half expected a contradictory view; it was what he wished for and everything was as it should be... the building rose skywards above him as his perspective was reversed entirely; even the lamppost towered above him now but the glow that shone down like the spotlight he no longer craved seemed weak and insignificant compared to near blinding bursts he'd almost become used to. Those inconceivably intense flashes already seemed a little less plausible but that was the past, however recent it might be and he didn't want to think about that anymore tonight. He was grateful for any possible future he might have but all he wanted to concentrate on was the here and now and he was becoming increasingly sure it was actually happening. He was surrounded by the evidence and he'd begun to accept it as the truth.

'No way?' was all he could utter before his nerves reawakened fully and he screamed out in pain. Evelyn's sheer joy and relief turned to panic as she realised she lay with her full weight supported by a man who'd just survived a nineteen storey fall against all odds and she clambered about him trying to ease herself off to no avail. Every time she shifted she increased the pressure in one place or another and quickly decided to take the advice that was now coming from above.

'Miss, just lay still, please just calm down and don't move... at all.' The commanding voice came from a paramedic, the first of many now on the scene.

'Any movement at all could cause further damage so please, stay as still as possible.'

She wasn't sure if she actually acknowledged the order verbally but she responded by complying. Her thoughts lay more firmly fixed on what she should say to Noel; what *could* she say? The two of them lay in bizarre silence as the thousands watching asked themselves exactly the same question. Viewers of all ages were transfixed; they could only piece together what might have happened and certainly didn't know how, but they'd rarely seen so much said with so little.

For such a grotesque scene it was strangely beautiful as whilst Noel's body was distorted into a shape nature never intended and it was becoming increasingly difficult to tell whose blood was whose, romantics around the city were willing each of those on screen to just say *something*... the silence had everyone leaning toward their televisions, all with their own idea of the perfect line but in later years they'd all agree that Noel broke the silence perfectly; he laughed. It seemed little more than a cough at first but it grew steadily. Evelyn seemed prepared for anything other than that and could only react by slowly joining in. As before, this in itself fuelled the other until it spread. The viewing public were unprepared but concluded if those who were injured could laugh in the grip of disaster there was no excuse for them not to join in when enjoying the safety of their homes. It somehow seemed the least they could do although it seemed massively inappropriate too; but then they heard the cameraman who'd fallen silent until now. Being closer to the scene made it easier for him to judge the moment and he could be heard off camera, his stunted attempts to withhold his emotions only served to make it funnier; it was all the permission the audience needed. The paramedics had never seen anything quite like it and continued to cut their way towards the injured with a beaming smile across their faces that contradicted the seriousness of the situation completely.

CHAPTER FORTY-FIVE

She woke suddenly as the calming sound of conversation was shattered by sirens and alarms as the panic set in and stabbed her all over. Disorientated, Mary blinked repeatedly but it all came back to her within seconds; all she'd done was fallen asleep with the television on again. If either of her parents were here she'd be lectured on the dreadful waste of resources, not to mention the cost implications, then, like the petulant child she still was beneath the façade she'd find excuses and arguments whilst knowing they were absolutely right. She didn't stand much chance of being honest with them; she couldn't even be honest with herself. Still she tried and failed to convince her own conscience that this was part of the joy of living alone; part of the freedom she'd always dreamed of yet she tuned into talk shows all day and left them on all night partly because she could... there were no reprimands and no punishments here. Yet in truth it was also for the company. Even a newsreader reporting the latest disaster or an agony aunt listening to how two sisters slept with each others cross dressing husbands on some tasteless American chat show eased the loneliness that prowled the flat like a hunter.

Now fully awake, Mary sighed in disappointment. The dream in which she'd been immersed just moments ago faded until she could remember nothing of it except that she'd rather be there than here. Rotating her head slowly to stretch her stiffened neck she checked the clock.

'Happy Christmas sweetheart' she whispered patting her bloated stomach gently but rolled her eyes as the images of another cruelly timed disaster flickered on her screen, each broadcast clip changing the ambience of her darkened room; the warm glow of the dying flames on her set illuminated her lounge and her way to the narrow hallway. As she reached down to pick up Holly, the flickering illumination vanished, replaced by red and blue, flashing intermittently as an ambulance crew began preparing to wrench a lorry door open.

'And a Merry Christmas to you as well' she insisted, lifting her cat to eye level, its tolerance of her dependency wearing thin. It looked blankly back at her, wondering how her species ruled the planet when even after seven years of trying to communicate she still expected a response. This alone was frustrating enough but any minute now the aggravated animal fully expected to be hugged awkwardly again by the confused human and pulled in all directions in the name of affection and would even be expected to look like it was being enjoyed if feeding time was to be sooner rather than later. Purring in mock contentment seemed like the most beneficial thing to do and it had always worked before but the torment was over mercifully quickly as a distraction was delivered just in time.

Through the window Mary could see that every other along the row of flats pulsed in time with hers, tinged with hints of the same colours. She looked back at her television wondering just what must be happening that would attract the attention of so many people who had countless satellite channels to choose from. She watched as paramedics crisscrossed the screen, most of them towards that same over turned lorry. It was difficult viewing made harder by its timing.

'A Merry Christmas indeed' she sighed before disappearing into the kitchen. Holly looked hopeful as Mary returned with more than she could comfortably carry but she dropped everything before she'd cleared the door's threshold. Open tins crashed to the floor, their contents spilling over it only to be leapt upon by Holly who was paid little heed to anything else as Mary's arms fell limp and useless to her sides and shock set in but her cat couldn't care less; she wouldn't have recognised anyone on the screen anyway.

But Mary did, and it was all she could do to keep from collapsing.

She lip-synced words of disbelief as she tried to cobble her thoughts and emotions together. She squinted at the screen, waiting for a close up to confirm or deny whether this was really him or some cruel trick born of missing someone so much. That beard had been the source of much embarrassment recently; twice she'd gone running like an infant to any white haired stranger on the street who didn't shave as from a distance that alone was enough to suggest the man behind it was her father. Yet that same sinking feeling would always consume her as she approached and realised that unruly facial hair wasn't an entirely unique feature. Now was not the time to make that mistake but it was the first occasion she actually wanted to be wrong.

Suddenly finding her strength again she ran to the set and dropped to her knees holding onto the sides of its casing to keep her upright. The figure on screen was slumped forward, leaning at an unnatural angle in the overturned cabin as if held precariously by something out of sight yet did nothing to help itself. Like a rag doll it retained the strange and limp position it had been manipulated into by the confines of the wreckage but still the camera crew zoomed in through the cracked glass until every blemish, crease and crevice that made his face his own was clearly visible.

She couldn't believe what she was seeing. She'd imagined every possible scenario under which she might see him again and what she might say if she did but she'd never contemplated something like this and she couldn't begin to find the words. She collapsed forwards as far as her stomach would allow burying her face against the screen. Her initial stunned silence broke into a fragile whimper. The thought of it already being too late for her to say everything that needed saying was unbearable but it came out anyway whether Nick could hear it or not...

'I'm sorry' emanated as less than a whisper. Incomplete and fractured in places where the simple words were not quite made whole as pain snatched parts away and back down within her. She tried again. It came out louder this time but cracked towards the end. As she repeated it she again heard her father's gentle voice and the simple advice it carried. The words remained the same every time he recited them; normally at the moments he deemed the most pivotal in her life, yet despite the amount of times she'd heard them she could never remember them exactly until now. She'd often faked her attention, nodding in agreement at all the right intervals but secretly thinking almost anything else; she'd been able to disregard whatever he'd said with the knowledge that he knew nothing of today's world.

He'd advised her long before he ever had Robyn to listen to the same speech and had never failed to deliver it in a voice so serious it had scared Mary as a child and so she'd ignored what should have reassured her ever since, but for the very first time it all made sense. He'd told her not to wait too long for anything or regret was all she'd know; she didn't just remember his words, she believed in them now too.

That's why her dad could cope with her mum's disease so much better than she could... it wasn't that he didn't care as much, that he was stronger or more detached; he simply had no regrets. No guilt; he'd done everything he could for her whilst he could do it.

She cried not just in mourning, but for how different it could have been; had she been where she should be tonight, her dad would be anywhere but lifeless on the television for all to see. She looked up... *lifeless on the television?* That can't happen can it? Whether it's immoral or not remained a source of debate but to the best of her knowledge it was still illegal. And even if the network had somehow slipped up and caught him in frame they certainly wouldn't *fill* it with him, zooming in for close ups? They must know something she didn't. With that in mind she studied the screen intently and as her father's eyes opened slightly she could see the same bright blue life in them as she could in hers; the family trait had never been so obvious as when her own image, reflected in the screen overlapped his. She'd never really noticed it before.

Stiffness came back to her limbs as she listened for a location but knew there was little chance of them repeating it until the end of the bulletin and so focused on what little background there was. The only thing that was clear was the partly demolished logo but there was so little left it offered no clue until the camera panned a little, revealing the onlookers that would only be found in a sizable shopping area at this time of night. Scared that she might miss a hint as to exactly where this was taking place she reached behind her with sudden realisation and without averting her gaze, blindly groping for the remote control. She found it surprisingly quickly and punched in the channel that she was sure she was already watching; the station didn't change. She was right; she was watching the local news and that only covered two major shopping centres. Only one was wide enough for a lorry of that size to pass through as she was sure the other had height restrictions. She ran to the window and looked directly down at the street below; the view mirrored that on her television screen.

Still muttering her desperate and delayed apology that had now almost descended into a chant she busied herself trying to locate her clothes but gave up in seconds, hastily pulling on her slippers instead and throwing her dressing gown around her. She stumbled over Holly and threw the front door open so hard she assumed it would bounce back and close behind her.

CHAPTER FORTY-SIX

Nick had been falling in and out of consciousness, maybe only for a few seconds but when he opened his eyes this time, it was to the site of Mary running towards him as best she could, flanked by ambulance crews who struggled to match her pace. They'd been reluctant to approach with anymore staff before the area around the lorry had been secured but now Mary had breached the cordon they had little choice but to follow whilst trying to warn her of the danger and the lorry's instability. As they neared, they vanished from Nick's perspective but Mary reached him first, appearing over the crumpled door like a sunrise despite having to climb for two. He wasted no time, all too aware that he may not have much left.

'Mary I'm sorry that…'

Nick pulled her towards him with what felt like all of his strength yet it amounted to no more than a feeble encouragement to move closer. It was all Mary needed though; she knew her father. Whilst she hadn't seen that look in his eyes for years, she was all too aware of what it meant and despite the paramedics advising against it she leant in so tightly that she felt his weak breath on her cheek as he whispered.

'You know I never stopped missing you don't you? You know I'm not angry?'

Mary pulled away a little so that she could look at him directly and leave him in no doubt as to how serious she was. Her voice was stern, ironically like a parent scolding their child, but it was for all the right reasons.

'Don't you even start talking like that. I've seen you laugh off deeper wounds than this.' She gently wiped his bloodied brow with the softness of her dressing gown. Its rich cotton soaked the moisture up to such an extent that when she pulled it away it revealed the cuts to be deeper than she thought but she never let her expression show it. 'I need you around, I've always needed you around so let's just get you fixed so you're presentable when my daughter meets her grandparents you hear me? I'm due Boxing Day.' It wasn't the way she'd wanted to make the announcement but right now she'd say whatever was most likely to give him a reason to hold on.

She was pulled aside as Nick was tended to and, unable to reach him she checked behind her to see if the ambulance crew had managed to edge themselves and their heavier equipment any closer, but with so much to carry they were still struggling through the barrier of battered vehicles. All around her the damage ranged from scratched paint work through to much, much worse with one single exception; as if protected by the same force field that seemed to follow him wherever he went, the father of her unborn child sat wide-eyed in the leather sports seat of his equally luxurious car. It was the same vintage convertible he'd chosen over her though so at least he knew how to stand by some*thing* if not some*one*. She shook her head in disbelief. Having been promised so many times by so many people that he'd pay for his selfishness she'd never really believed it and, true to form, he'd been the only person for as far as she could see that had escaped the anarchy unscathed. She sighed and looked away, but not before he caught her looking. Understandably surprised to see his pregnant ex-girlfriend balanced on top of an overturned lorry, clad in the nightwear he bought her and a sweater he was glad he'd never seen, he called to her out of reflex. It was only then that he realised she was the focus of an increasing media frenzy as rival reporters began to arrive on the scene. She just ignored him hoping he'd do what he did best and leave as she turned her attention back towards a far more important man. He'd probably only noticed her through jealousy that the cameras weren't pointed in his direction anyway.

Those tending to her father foolishly left a gap between them wide enough for Mary to squeeze through again and she took her chance before it vanished. They'd have pulled her away as she was in no condition to be there but they had even more important matters to attend to with her father and her presence gave him something to concentrate on; it kept him buoyant and he spoke again.

'I can't be there for you now Mary. And neither can your mother. However much we'd want to be… it's too late.'

'She's gone?' Mary mouthed the words as her voice failed her. By not denying it her father answered her fully. She was lost for a few seconds before her concentration returned to events she could alter and she regained her composure. There would be time to grieve later and she amazed herself with her impressive ability to focus. 'Then I need you all the more so don't you dare leave me, don't you even think about leaving me!' Her voice was back and could be heard over the sirens that still filled the air.

Unable to look at her anymore Nick looked past her towards the flashing blue lights still struggling to force their way towards them but Mary saw panic in his eyes rather than relief. Everything began to fall into place; the glazed expression, his certainty that she'd be alone, his inability to answer her directly.

'You didn't? Did you? Again the lack of response was admission in itself. She leaned in closer, suddenly realising there was a secret to be kept and managed to conduct herself with discretion; it was easier than she would have imagined. She'd never expected him to do this but now she was certain he had, she was astounded not to be surprised. 'You did what she'd have wanted, they'll know that. Everyone will know and they'll all understand. There's no way you'll go to prison for it Dad, no way at all.' She was devastated but she understood and for that reason there was nothing to forgive. But it was the very last reaction her father would have predicted; if he could have frowned he would have.

'You know that's not true darling. The law won't see it like you do.'

'They'll take you to court but they won't take you away, it'd make no sense.'

'Maybe they will, maybe they won't but either way, I can't stand in the dock being questioned as to whether I loved your mother. I couldn't go through that without her, not alone. And I won't have to... I won't have to do anything without her.' Nick wouldn't have confessed to sealing his own fate so selfishly but had seen the suspicion narrow her face; he knew that she'd already begun to figure it for herself. He'd seen her notice the empty bottles lodged against the windscreen and she'd never been naive in that sense; only a few seconds had passed and now he could see her pain as the realisation hit her hard.'

'But you're not alone, you have me!'

'I didn't. I hadn't... not when I made my decision. I didn't know that I'd ever see you again.' He paused only to cough pathetically. 'I'd not heard from you in nearly a year and had no reason to believe I would.' He regretted saying that instantly knowing that she'd have to live with that long after he was gone but it was getting harder to think clearly; harder to concoct lies and that meant the truth rose to the surface whether he wanted it to or not.

'But I want you there at the birth Dad, I need you there!'

'If I could be, I would. I promise you that.'

'You can be! You hear that? That's the sound of you being cut free.' Below him work was under way as she spoke; the emergency crew had secured the cabin and were now inside the wreckage with the hardware they needed. 'You can be in the hospital within minutes and they can fix you.'

'Not if they don't know what I've done. By the time they realise I'll be where I need to be. Just don't tell them what was in those bottles.'

'No, no, you can't ask me to do that' pleaded Mary. Her father's wandering eyes focused if only for a moment but long enough to convince her it was still him talking and not the drugs.

'I shouldn't have to' he insisted. 'Your mother didn't have to ask me. Don't tell them. Don't tell them what I've done. Promise me Mary.'

'I can't, how can you even suggest it?'

'Because it's what I want and I...' Before he could finish his sentence his mobile rang. He'd ignore it but he had a feeling he knew who it was and he had an apology to make even if it took the last of his energy. Just pulling it from his pocket took an enormous effort.

The voice was professional, clinical even and Nick didn't recognise it. 'Mr Sainte?'

'Yes?' confirmed Nick albeit it in an increasingly agonised voice whilst Mary remained in quiet, tortured indecision.

'I'm calling from your wife's ward. Mr. Sainte, I'm afraid I have news for you... news regarding your wife. I'm very sorry, she's passed away...'

'I know. I couldn't, I just couldn't sit there whilst...' he interrupted with the opening line of his confession. He had no doubt that they'd draw the obvious conclusion before he was pronounced dead and that the paperwork would be filed away and forgotten about before his funeral but even a moments time wasted on investigation was a moment to long. He didn't want the faintest shadow of doubt to loom over Robyn or any of the other staff. Pleading guilty would tie up the very last loose end and he could leave this world with a conscience as clear as possible considering what he'd done.

'We believe it was a painless passing but our only concern is that...' the voice continued regardless, insistent, impersonal and determined to complete the offering of their sympathies but Nick was equally resolute and failed to listen. He just wanted to say what he had to say and get back to his little girl who was falling apart beside him.

'I just couldn't bear the thought of her going to, to that place... and she...'

He was cut short again and this time was left in no doubt that he should pay attention. The words were short, concise and demanded that they be digested.

'We'll of course be happy to discuss any concerns you may have and we can provide you with contact numbers that will help you to make arrangements and to cope with your loss.'

Nick could hear her continue but the words competed with those inside his head as he dared to think the impossible. By now Grace would no doubt be surrounded by a team of experts. He'd witnessed them solve even the most complicated of situations time and time again so how just one of them, let alone all of them could possibly fail to notice the obvious was beyond comprehension? He'd be surprised if they didn't trip over the lead as they pulled the unit away from the wall to check it.

He decided they knew. They couldn't *not* know. They might not be sure it was him just yet but they must be aware of what had happened and how. They were either building up to telling him or they were going to send someone for him... that was more likely to be the case. Accusing him now could cause him to run or to hide as they would have no idea of the situation he was already in. And even if they were not attributing the blame to him yet, they could hardly tell him over the phone that his wife of forty seven years died under suspicious circumstances.

'I wish we could tell you why, after all this time she suddenly let go, but there are no obvious signs. We'll investigate further but I assure you we've checked everything we can...'

Nick tried to raise his voice above hers 'Please, she's gone, just listen to me for a moment please.'

Clearly agitated the woman cleared her throat for the last time in order to be heard as clearly as possible and continued in spite of him.

'There are no obvious signs Mr. Sainte, I understand that this must be incredibly difficult for you, but there are no obvious signs. No one can... ', her voice softened slightly, 'and no one *will* figure out what happened.

Those last few words were not typical of a hospital official and as the icy persona was almost dropped, the voice became recognisable again, even to his fading mind. He was sure he knew who he was speaking to despite the fact she should have left the hospital some time ago. His advice had obviously been disregarded and embraced in equal measure. There had been no sign of her trademarks or the familiarity he'd grown used to but he did recognise the tone if only in her closing sentence. There were so many things to say to her but they'd have to wait. He just smiled, allowing her charade to go on knowing that at this stage she was speaking for the sake of those around her rather than his. She'd finally broken the rules but he was absolutely certain that she'd ensure nobody ever found out.

'Thank you for letting me know doctor.' He turned to Mary looking like an entirely different man. 'Your Mum wanted to leave' he whispered. He pulled her closer, 'but your ol' Dad doesn't. So if you want him around you do what you have to.'

She stared at him just for a moment with so many questions but decided they could all be put on hold. Having placed his trust and his destiny in his daughter he felt strangely peaceful as he let consciousness go, not knowing if the site of her disappearing over the edge of his cabin would be the last he'd ever see.

Robyn smiled so subtly as she cut the phone's connection that she couldn't believe anyone would notice, but Ed was wide awake, as always and he'd noticed everything. The two looked at each other unflinchingly despite the hectic scene that was just coming to a close. Grace's passing had caused a commotion but it hadn't lasted long and most of the staff it had attracted were about to leave the room. Robyn would follow but she needed this moment with the old man; she needed to know his intentions. With nothing more than an expression of understanding they made a pact; a vow of silence that they somehow knew would be kept. When she was sure nobody was looking she mouthed two simple words to him.

'Thank you' was all that was needed and she left the ward with her colleagues to appear as accepting of the situation as they were.

But Ed felt that he should be thanking her as he reached across to make the first phone call since he'd been admitted to the hospital whilst knowing it would be his last. It had been a long wait but at least it hadn't been in vain. He opened his impressive looking book at the last chapter, laid it on his lap and picked up the telephone receiver. He began to dial a number from memory hoping his solicitor wouldn't mind him calling so late at night. As he waited for it to be answered it made him truly happy to know that if Robyn ever came back to work at this hospital or any other, it would be through choice and not necessity. She'd never known just how wealthy he was. In fact she probably assumed he was the opposite judging by his few worn out possessions but that was exactly why it should be her. She'd given him what he'd been waiting for... someone to leave his fortune to... someone deserving.

Having given his instructions he laid back, at last able to relax completely and it was better than he remembered. He allowed his tired eyes to close but only endured darkness for a moment before a burst of light appeared only to him. It beckoned and he was only too pleased to follow.

CHAPTER FORTY-SEVEN

Noel was still laughing uncontrollably, if he could stop it, he would; he was in enough pain without the extra exertion. But through a mixture of adrenaline and sheer joy he found the strength to scream 'thank you!' over and over to whoever he should be grateful. To have survived was a miracle in itself regardless of the condition he was in and he now saw every breath he took as the wonder it was.

Evelyn ignored all the advice she was given and the concerns it should have raised; overcome and assured by his reaction. She flung her arms around him causing his expressions of appreciation to turn into screams of agony but he didn't care and neither did the viewing public yelling at their television screen for her to take it one step further.

She didn't leave Noel's side as he was eventually lifted onto a stretcher and carried towards a waiting ambulance. Those that escorted him allowed Evelyn to follow assuming the pair were very much together. As painful as it was for him to do so, Noel repeatedly struggled to lift his head to see if she really was still there but his body failed him. Unable to crane his neck he tried to look down his broken body using his eyes alone but it was no good, his vision just shuddered and dulled when it was that strained. He only knew he'd reached the ambulance when its ceiling came into view as he was gently guided inside. Forced to look nowhere but straight up he'd been virtually unaware of the devastation around him but he had begun to think of that which he'd sustained. If his condition was just half as critical the initial assessment he'd overheard discussed so openly, as if he wasn't even there it would be a while until he saw this old street that he was about to leave; but at least he'd see it again and that was what counted.

He lay motionless wondering if he had a choice but he had no intentions of finding out for himself. He'd been told to stay still and that was exactly what he planned to do; he'd listen a little more from now on. As he was unable to see through the windows, his only view was through the open doors of the ambulance that tunnelled his vision into a simple box, like a screen that people wandered in and out of and the characters that filled it ranged greatly.

Emergency services ran across it and back again trying to decide which situation to deal with first. When he saw the same faces return minutes later they all looked mystified that there really wasn't much to grapple with at all. The damage was mainly structural and that wasn't something they could help with; on the ride in they must have braced themselves for casualties on a catastrophic scale but all they'd found were minor cuts and bruises. Even those who'd suffered the most needed little more than maybe a plaster or a bandage. Many were completely unaffected and wandered trancelike, trying to take in what they'd just seen knowing they'd be asked to recount the experience for the rest of their days.

Noel's hauntingly peaceful scene was interrupted by the officers having to physically drag their cuffed prisoners into custody who were not making it easy. The cable that had been wrapped around their estate had done the Police's work for them and held their suspect's captive before the law had caught up with them. Noel could only hear odd words but could make out they were being read their rights as he filled in the gaps through memories of television shows and movies. He couldn't hear the statements in full for the protests of two of the three prisoners who screamed a combination of innocence and abuse that contradicted each other perfectly. The quieter of those arrested, presumably still in shock and stunned from the incomprehensible turn of events was violently marched into view and it was him who Noel focused upon the most. The face had changed very little, but then it had been only a few years since Noel had last seen him and the wispy beard he'd shaped so thinly wasn't enough to disguise him. Noel was as sure as he needed to be but further evidence was provided in full anyway; with his arms held fast behind him, his sleeves had risen allowing the hint of a tattoo that looked all too familiar.

Justice couldn't mend Noel's broken bones but it could do an incredible amount to heal his pride. Knowing he couldn't expect to see a better sight tonight he stopped testing his tired eyes and at last relaxed. He'd never felt so sure that everything would be alright so long as he could just let it be. And he could do that now; things seemed to work out better when he didn't try too hard to force them his way and at the moment he didn't even feel like talking; he knew that the grin he could feel spreading across his face would provoke questions but he just didn't have the energy to answer.

'Merry Christmas' he thought to himself but he breathed it without meaning to. It was so quiet Evelyn only just heard him despite remaining by his side, but it wasn't meant solely for her anyway. He didn't have the strength to wish it more than once so it would have to be shared by the crew around him, the crowds outside, the family he should have been with and not least, those now being ducked into the patrol car; the thought kept the reluctant smile in place.

Evelyn turned her attention back to Noel repeating his simple phrase but in a voice softer than he'd heard from her before. She knelt by his side and winced as her grazed knees went down.

'What's so funny now?' she said mirroring his expression in anticipation.

'Can I tell you another time? Trust me, it's a long story.'

She nodded knowing what the asking of the question meant, however well disguised it might have been. A medic squeezed past her to shut the doors from the inside as they so desperately needed to be on their way but his colleagues were rushing towards him from the street asking if they had room for one more.

'If you hurry!' was the abrupt answer.

Another stretcher was hurried into view and at first glance the injuries it carried appeared horrific. The casualty was covered with a sheet and his outline dropped to nothing shortly after his waist yet he appeared to be in no pain at all; in fact he seemed more concerned about his dog which he called for relentlessly. Noel pictured the injuries beneath the cloth but couldn't bring himself to do so for long. The shouting continued from Noel's side of the ambulance doors.

'I thought you meant walking wounded... there's no real room for another stretcher in...' the crew were understandably concerned and it came as some relief to Noel who'd had to deal with enough horror for one day but all pleas were ignored under such desperate circumstances. He'd have looked away if he could, but instead had to shut his eyes; it wasn't like he needed an excuse as he'd been told to rest repeatedly. He didn't have a major problem with the sight of blood and tonight it was just as well but he had a feeling he would not want to see what was coming his way.

In his self induced darkness he found himself listening for clues that would help him solve what he didn't want to know; he hadn't changed entirely. The conversation just didn't make sense as nobody panicked for anyone but him; they must already know something he didn't and Noel dared to look again at the man ignoring anyone who wouldn't help him track down his pet... and that was everybody. When he realised just how different his priorities were to those around him he reached out to the closest person in a bid to gain their undivided attention and spoke with all the control and poise only enjoyed by those in perfect health.

'I really don't need to go' he assured anyone who'd listen. We were just on our way to my parents. I'm not even hurt and if I need you I can call. And if I can't my mother will?' The response was almost automatic and certainly to the point.

'I'm sorry sir, but you've just been involved in an accident, if you're as well as you say your parents can pick you up in a few hours.

'Honestly, I'm fine... except I'm late!'

The crewman lost his professionalism and laughed out loud.

'You're lucky to be alive. If that had of been anyone else things would be very different.'

'I know. It's the first time I've felt fortunate in a while' he said tapping the area just below his waist. It met with a hollow, plastic sound as he drummed out a short tune, most likely in a last ditch attempt to convince anyone he could that he was indeed able to be taken directly home. It didn't work.

Noel stopped looking directly at him, not wanting to be caught in case his fascination was misinterpreted. He was working out the maths and thought he knew the answer but wasn't quite ready to go out on a limb just yet; he made a mental note not to use that phrase anytime in the immediate future.

The various injections that had been pumped into him were beginning to take effect and whilst they numbed the pain as promised, it was slowing his mind too; it was a race against time until it failed him completely but the conversation didn't quicken to compensate.

'Come on?' the so called casualty added, 'I wouldn't be the first to go out Christmas Eve and come back legless would I?'

'Sir, please? The medic was determined not to encourage the cavalier attitude. 'I'm not a decision maker around here and I want to get home as much as you do, but I've got my orders and it's not like I can say you ran away is it?' everyone in the ambulance smirked unsure whether they should find that funny or not. They looked towards its target; it was obvious he'd taken it as it was intended and that he'd also given up his fight.

The medic continued, 'and the quicker we finish procedure, the quicker we'll be there. We've got someone looking for your dog so I tell you what... you make this easy for me and I promise you we won't keep you a minute longer than we have to... deal?'

'Do I have a choice?'

'None'.

'Deal'.

'Good. So I'm going to need your name and details and then we can call your folks if you want?'

'Peter, Peter Reynolds'.

Even a full name wasn't the final piece of the puzzle jostling for space inside Noel's head and his suspicions failed to slot into place as questions were asked about the technical aspects of prosthetic limbs. Peter seemed to know all the answers but was less sure of the cost implications involved; he kept returning to the subject however much each member of the crew assured him they didn't know. Noel would have to ask now or accept that he could well pass out before he lost the chance for good but his unexpected attempt to be heard was muffled by the blood he still coughed up whenever his voice was raised. It served as a stark reminder to everyone where their priorities should lie and that they really needed to hurry this along; even Peter fell silent and ceased to be an obstacle any longer. The strange atmosphere of peace and optimism betrayed the seriousness of the situation but Evelyn didn't need a new perspective. She rushed back to Noel's side and gently wiped away the blood and stroked his forehead.

'That's enough out of you Mr...' she ordered suddenly realising what didn't seem possible; she still didn't even know his name. Noel tried to clear his throat again and renewed his efforts to speak. He wasn't certain that the man lying next to him was who he thought he might be, but he was no longer scared to be wrong.

'Peter, don't worry about the medical costs. Just have whatever you need done; I can cover that until your insurance pays out'. Peter stopped midway through a sentence he'd already begun and looked at the total stranger.

'I don't mean to be rude, and it's not that I'm ungrateful but why on earth would you do that? You don't need to feel sorry for the invalid you know? I work. I've got money... without charity'.

'It's not like that', Noel was struggling but continued to explain. 'It's just I think we've got a mutual friend and if you are who I think you are then it's not charity, I owe you.' It was the first time in years he'd offered his word without doubt but consciousness was slipping from his grasp. His simple offer had to be enough as he needed to speak to Evelyn and it had to be now; he reached for her and she crouched down beside him again, taking the hint but quieting him before his lips had even parted.

'You really need to just rest. Whatever you've got to say, you can tell me later.' Noel looked at her questioningly wondering how much he should read into what she'd said. She could almost see him thinking so she put his aching mind at ease.

'I'll be here when you wake up' she whispered. 'I promise.'

It was that final word that meant everything. Evelyn promised nobody anything but Noel was sure he didn't imagine what he'd heard. He could breathe easier knowing that this wasn't the last he'd see of her and finally accepted it could all wait until another time. She continued to mop the blood from his face but there was nothing she could do to wipe away the smile.

Peter's face was contorted in confusion. Having witnessed their obvious closeness he found it more than strange that she'd found it so difficult to convince him of her loyalty. He wasn't rude enough to ask for an explanation as such, yet couldn't help but enquire as to what Noel had meant about being indebted to him. Evelyn just shrugged her shoulders. She had no idea but was a little embarrassed that it was the case; she could only guess at the conclusions that could be drawn but she didn't let it worry her like it would have done yesterday.

She was more concerned about the fact that the engine wasn't even running yet. What were they waiting for? It was still pandemonium outside but if the ambulance had made its way in, surely it could find its way out? She didn't know how alarmed she should be that Noel was no longer lucid; it would hardly be surprising due to the pain alone, but when considering the blood loss it seemed inevitable. She felt herself weakening but anyone would wish for her condition over his; she'd sustained scratches by comparison. Despite the considerable attention he was receiving, nobody had managed to stem the flow from his wounds and the suit she'd previously admired was now soaked through and heavy in places but congealing and sticking to him in others. The blood had even seeped into the stretcher's fabric and as it dripped and spattered onto the floor it was becoming increasingly impossible for Evelyn to continue blocking reality out.

She wasn't the only one who'd noticed and the mood had changed accordingly.

'What are we still doing here?' she screamed no longer needing to keep her concerns private for Noel's sake. Their moment of intimacy together had slowed her world and she'd have brought it to an absolute pause if only she could but now it hadn't just returned to real time; it had sped as if to catch up every moment that had been lost. The ambulance crew jostled for position in the already over crowded space that now left no room for manners and even less for requests. She was pulled firmly from where she crouched and forced down into a corner. Afraid and confused she looked at the deep crimson streak that trailed from where she now cowered right the way over to the perfect, bloody foot prints of where she had stood. The spattering had become a pool and it was being trod all over the floor leaving the imprints of three different styles of shoe until they overlapped so many times their form was completely lost.

High pitched electronic sounds surrounded her and whilst they held no defined meaning as far as she was concerned, they had a tone and pace that spelt out the urgency they encouraged. In all the confusion she tried to figure out whether the alarm had just been raised or if it had always been there to be heard, just she'd not been listening. She hoped for the latter as that would mean Noel's condition had not deteriorated but the reaction of the crew suggested otherwise.

'What?' she whispered, then screamed it realising how weak her first attempt had been. 'What? What's happening?' No answer came. She was ignored completely as she was the last person that needed information at the moment. It wasn't that nobody had heard her the first time; they just didn't have the chance to reply and knew that she was unlikely to understand if they did. She watched them circle Noel with equipment that she could only glance at before it disappeared from sight as she was shut out of the gathering circle.

'What's happening, tell me what's happening!' Her voice cracked with desperation so obvious it at last provoked a response, however abrupt.

'He's gone into shock, now please, give us space!'

It was almost barked with frustration but it needed saying; if a brief explanation could keep her quiet it was worth the few seconds it took for the sake of their concentration. With the benefit of a more rational state of mind she might have done just that, but she was a long way from making sense as pure emotion took over completely. She begged for more information but eventually fell silent as the one tone she recognised cut through everything else and straight into her. It's monotone incessancy shredding the hope that until now had been easy to grasp. She didn't need to hear the words 'we're losing him' but still they came as if it wasn't painfully obvious.

Evelyn scrambled to her feet, scared to see what was happening but unable to stop herself from staring. The view between the medics shoulder was a nightmare vision as Noel's body was blasted with a voltage so powerful his whole body convoluted. Then again and again the pulse was sent through him in an attempt to restart his own. His spasms showed the suspected breaks in his arms all too clearly as his flailing limbs bent and twisted in places they were never meant to like some broken doll in a storm. It was nothing less than horrific and made all the more harsh in contrast to the almost eerie sense of serenity that had preceded it.

Nobody was talking in full sentences anymore, just spitting the essential words as each second mattered more than they ever had done before. It may well have been a different language as far as Evelyn was concerned but it wasn't important, she could see everything and it didn't need explaining. The scene ripped away at her, exposing every nerve and making the very air painful to breathe as her skin prickled all over with a sensation of helplessness that was a year old today.

She wanted to close her eyes, to run away from what was increasingly likely to happen; but surely all the time the crew were panicking it at least meant there was a chance they could bring him back; didn't it happen all the time? But one by one, those that surrounded Noel busied themselves elsewhere with whatever excuse they could find to look away as the dreamlike world they were so certain was too good to be true looked to be exactly that. Having injected him with everything they could, they gradually left Noel's side until only one remained, still insisting that his colleagues should clear the area despite the fact they had all now deserted him. Before tonight he'd have joined them already but after what he'd witnessed, the impossible seemed a little easier to believe.

CHAPTER FORTY-EIGHT

There were only two things that made Joe think that there was the slightest chance that his girls still believed. There was of course the noticeable change in their behaviour since mid November; they'd both become less mischievous lately which could be entirely coincidental but it could also be a very real fear of finding themselves on the naughty list. He hoped that it was the latter, partly for his own sake but more so for his wife's. The other possibility was that their wish list continued to contain the impossible. They still insisted on filling those stables despite him being made redundant from the job that had paid for them to be built almost two years ago. Regardless of their age, the twins were both capable of deducing that he was a long way from fulfilling that particular dream for them but he wouldn't accept that either of them were cruel or manipulative enough to deliberately make him feel the guilt that racked him daily; and that must mean that they still held onto the hope that someone else could make it happen for them.

He could understand their frustration though. He felt it himself. To have moved for the sole purpose of gaining the land and space that they needed seemed premature but he'd learnt to take his opportunities when and where he found them. The property's seclusion and the expanse of its grounds normally came with a price to match but most who could truly afford it were looking for somewhere in the heart of the country and not within half a mile of the High Street but for Joe and his family it was the perfect compromise. At the time he had a career that paid just about enough to meet the mortgage but when that came to an abrupt halt, the chauffeuring that was meant to be temporary had become permanent. Whilst the fares subsidised the essentials there was never enough money left to save towards everything he'd promised his girls, least of all the horses. The expensive creatures were all he could think about as he'd abandoned his pulverised cab tonight and walked the short distance home.

It was all his girls could think about too as they pulled their covers up tight around them as if they were cold but it was only to obscure their faces, already partially buried into their pillows in case their eyes flickered and gave them away. They'd also learnt that keeping silent and perfectly still was what Mum and Dad would expect them to do and so, at five years old they double bluffed their parents; breathing in staggered bursts and stirring every now and then in the name of realism. This tended to work for them on two levels; and not only did this convince their parents that they weren't faking, it also gave the impression that they could wake at the faintest disturbance and so deterred too much investigation. Tonight was no different as Joe came into their room and stood perfectly still, analysing both beds for the slightest hint of consciousness before advancing any further.

The twins began their subtle double act, now so well rehearsed that they sometimes fooled each other. Joe alternately sat on each of their beds longer than he usually would, unsure whether it was through remorse at having again missed their bedtime, the dread of seeing their faces in the morning when all their presents were the kind that could be wrapped, or if he was simply delaying the lecture that lay coiled in wait across the hall. His wife was a good woman but could be incredibly unfair; not through malice, but through a complete inability to see things objectively. She wanted the best for them but that meant wanting everything, however contradictory it might be. She wanted the house they lived in and to get their daughters whatever they asked for yet he was about to get the third degree for working so late. It'd be easier to accept tonight though; after everything that had happened, and more importantly what *could* have happened it'd be good just to hear her voice whether it was raised or not. There was nothing like being the catalyst of such grand destruction to get things in perspective and he tucked the covers a little more tightly around his girls tonight.

The only doubt he had that they were asleep was the same as every other night; the fact that they *always* were. He never had to quiet them down, send them back to bed or do anything other than be careful not to rouse them. It was unnatural for children of their age; of that he was sure but he was never quite certain enough to question them about it and he still visited their beds in reverse order every night just in case. He'd been accused of having a favourite once before and never wanted to face the same interrogation again, especially when they continued to work together, even on such a dividing issue.

He kissed them both gently and headed back towards the door, stopping mid tread as Faith let out a sudden sigh and turned in her bed panicking him so much he daren't place his foot down until she'd settled again. The girls struggled not to laugh, hiding their beaming smiles in their pillows; they did it to him every single night but it never became any less funny. He eventually made his way to the plateful of mince pies and glass of milk that awaited him. He sighed quietly, loathing himself for bolstering the legend; dishonesty couldn't be more premeditated than this and under the circumstances he had lost his appetite. He crushed the pastry in his hands making sure he created the crumbs that would be expected and swallowed the rest whole to get it over and done with as quickly as he could.

He left the room and returned less than a minute later with stockings, identical to those that already lay at the foot of their beds except these were full to the brim. He'd learnt a long time ago about the logistical nightmare of doing it any other way and simply exchanged them. With his mission complete he pulled the door to its frame and left to face his trial.

'I told you' whispered Faith as soon as the coast was clear.

'No you didn't, I told *you*' came the near identical retort, their voices as similar as their faces. Joy was already half lost in her stocking, carefully judging the weight and shape of each of its contents. When this gave no clues she switched on her bedside lamp, holding each present up to the light trying to see through the wrapping. She felt relatively unaffected; it wasn't that she didn't care Santa wasn't coming; it was just that she wasn't surprised. The science of it never really added up... all those houses in one night? For Faith it was different. To everyone else she insisted that she agreed with her sister but privately hadn't been so sure and now sat at the window, staring blankly out into their driveway with her illusions shattered. The family tree remained as intricately decorated and still lit the pathway beside it but it suddenly didn't seem to shine quite as brightly. Joy coerced her away and beckoned her over to what she thought might well be the present they'd placed second on their list but they both froze in unison to listen more carefully to what should be virtual silence.

Even with their very different preoccupations, neither could fail to hear the commotion outside. They looked at each other with opposing suspicions; Joy was as scared as Faith was hopeful. They each crept towards their door and eased their tiny bodies through without even having to touch it. With exaggerated steps they reached the top of the stairs in near total darkness but they'd done this enough times before. They knew which floorboards would give them away and which steps they should avoid to evade detection and reached the lower landing without a single sound.

Joy had been trying to encourage her sister back towards their parents' room but Faith knew what she was looking for and that there was no need to be afraid. Gradually, they started to grow in confidence and the silence made them doubt whether they'd actually heard anything at all. Perhaps they'd just wanted to; but then they heard it again. This time they couldn't be more certain and it was coming from the direction of the living room.

'Should we get Dad?' questioned Joy.

'Come on' Faith insisted, not really answering the question but stating her intentions clearly enough. She had no doubt now what or who was responsible for the disruption and she took her sister's hand to reassure her and to lead the way, the sound growing with every step they took towards it. For twins they seemed to disagree on most things and turned out to be right almost alternately. Faith couldn't be happier that it was obviously her turn tonight but Joy remained unconvinced, needing to be dragged onward but belief is infectious and her resistance gradually eased until they ran together down the hall and into the front room.

It wasn't just the glow the string of bulbs that crisscrossed their garden shining through the patio doors that lit their faces as they turned the corner. Through the glass a dozen reindeer were illuminated by fairy light; some galloped in small circles, unsure why, but just glad to be able to after a day spent in a trailer. Others rummaged through the families rubbish for food which was plentiful enough. The fruit peel and vegetable excess from their mother's ridiculously over the top and premature dinner preparations combined with the first clearing of open space the herd could find proved an attractive combination and having been raised together they didn't separate now freedom was theirs. The twins looked at each other wide eyed and open mouthed.

'I told you!' squealed Faith.

'No, I told *you*!' Joy's insistence was even louder, but it didn't matter. Neither child cared who heard anymore; they slid the door open so hard it slammed and the pair of them ran barefoot onto the paving slabs towards the backyard gate that blew in the breeze not caring how cold it was.

'Come back!' pleaded Joy, thankful for such unbelievable presents; they were better than those she'd listed and she needed to apologise for ever doubting him. 'I'm sorry!' she gasped as she struggled for breath but he was nowhere to be seen; she must have missed him by seconds. She understood his hurry though as she again considered what he had to achieve in just one single night so she gave up her chase and shouted just one more apology as loud as she could, hoping that he'd hear.

'He knows he's just busy' smiled Faith. Her sister's face raised until their expressions matched; they looked at each other for a few moments before they at last agreed on something; and they did it without a word being spoken. Together they raided the cupboards making as much noise as the reindeer themselves, stopping only to hug each other so excitedly they jumped up and down on the spot, unsure of what else to do until one of them stopped having detected a more human approach. She scanned the garden again to check that this hadn't been a scene from which she was waking and sighed with relief when it remained the same.

Joe thundered down the stairs, woken by the commotion and panicked by their screams only to find them tossing whatever food they could find into the garden. Most of it barely landed before it was swallowed almost instantly. Grateful and eager for more, the reindeer approached the girls; they'd grown used to humans but not to kindness and hardly flinched as the twins threw their arms around them.

Joe stood behind his daughters absolutely stunned, unable to take it all in before yelling at them.

'Get away from there!' he ordered but as he ran towards them he could see they were in no danger at all. The girls called for their mother and to his surprise Joe joined them, almost as excited. He didn't even turn around as his wife careered down the stairs still wrestling with her dressing gown.

'What on earth…' was all she could muster as the first of the deer dared to enter her immaculately ornamented living room.

Her girls didn't know what to do with themselves. Their faces beamed in a way she hadn't seen in sometime as they believed in everything that defied logic once more… that in itself was the best present she could have wished for. She looked at her husband guiltily; she was thankful that all this had happened before she launched into the tirade that she'd rehearsed over and over as she'd awaited his return home; it was no wonder he was late. But however impressed she was, it had to be shown subtly as to be openly appreciative in front of the twins would only raise their suspicions again and that was the last thing she wanted. She could relax now; at least until next year. She gently wrapped her arm around her husband's and leaned into him, confident she wouldn't be heard over the chaos that surrounded them.

'How did you manage this? Can we afford it? Why didn't you tell me?' she whispered. Joe didn't answer. It wasn't what he'd expected to hear as it hadn't even crossed his exhausted mind that she'd assume he was responsible. And had he have done, he'd never imagine that she'd actually be *pleased* as hoof prints were stamped into the carpet but the look on her face was unmistakable. He shook his head in disbelief realising that she obviously held him in higher regard than he thought; perhaps higher than she should. In turn, she misread his response and assumed he was disappointed that she'd questioned his attempt to surprise her as well as their children and apologised immediately.

'Forgive me' she whispered. 'Thank you.'

Joe remained silent as he pieced together what must have happened and why. He thought about where to start the story that he doubted she'd believe and considered the aspects of it that he'd rather she didn't; should he leave Evelyn and her suggestions out of the evening's events? But then how would he explain the disappearance of his coat or the blood on his trousers? Excuses wouldn't be too difficult to invent but it wasn't something he felt comfortable with. They'd sworn they wanted the truth from each other whether it was what they wanted to hear or not and he drew breath to stand by that promise. As he did he noticed the gratitude in her eyes... she hadn't looked at him like that for far too long and beyond her, he saw Faith and Joy become the innocent, naive little girls they deserved to be. They were happier than he'd ever seen them before; their mother hadn't been wrong to keep the truth from them... it kept the magic alive and he could do the same for her. He said absolutely nothing.

The more he thought about it, the more convinced he became that there was a realistic chance he'd be able to keep his secret; in fact it was more than likely. Whichever event the herd had been destined for would be drawing to a close by now and he felt sure that nobody would be looking too hard for them considering their next appointment; their owners would probably prefer to avoid the cost and negative publicity associated with it. He guessed they'd actually welcome their disappearance but that suited him fine; he had room for them here and by the looks of it they were happy to be fed on just about *anything*.

He turned his attention back to his wife; the right thing to do was to let her continue thinking whatever was bringing a tear to her eye.

CHAPTER FORTY-NINE

It was obvious from the mess she'd left behind that Mary had deserted her flat in a hurry. Having just entered through the open door, Donna was surprised to find the place abandoned. The television remained on and whilst that in itself wasn't unusual when it came to her neighbour, leaving the apartment was and forgetting to lock up was totally out of character. As she stepped over Holly who refused to accept that the floor was now licked clean she wondered if she should be more concerned, but there was no apparent signs of forced entry or any kind of struggle and she allowed herself to relax a little.

She turned to the screen and watched the unbelievable images being re-shown as the newsreaders continued to try and speculate as to what had happened; they were already gradually piecing the events together but for the time being it was pure conjecture. But perhaps this explained things... she'd imagined that Mary would be more interested in where the events were taking place rather than who was involved but she assumed curiosity must have gotten the better of her. That would be no bad thing; at least she'd left the flat and that would make next time slightly easier.

When Donna had been unable to contact her friend by phone she'd called round to see if she was watching what everyone else couldn't take their eyes off; obviously she had been and whilst that remained the most likely reason for her disappearance, a little further consideration made it less convincing. A passing interest alone wouldn't have led a heavily pregnant woman down to the street; especially Mary of all people.

She ambled over to the window, still amused at the sight of the street so completed coated in extinguisher foam that it looked like some Hollywood set. The firefighters had begun to control the jets but not completely as they still sprayed into the air albeit not as violently as before; it remained quite a sight though and she considered joining those below before thinking better of it. She could see everything she needed to from here; she might even see Mary and that would put her concerned mind at rest.

She pulled her mobile phone from her pocket and redialed. After a few seconds she heard her call received, the familiar ring tone coming from the chair from which Mary rarely moved; if she wasn't quite worried before, she was now and looked a little harder out of the window at the scene below.

She sighed and again thumbed through her list of numbers until she arrived at the beginning; the call she made was answered almost instantly.

'Hi, how are you doing? Are you at your parents yet? The answer was brief and to the point but Donna continued undeterred. 'How long have you been there? I wasn't sure if you were coming back?' she asked, still looking through the glass as the situation was explained in full before she stated her reason for phoning. 'Well if that's true and he's really the reason you came back tonight, then there's something I think you should know. I'm not sure if you're going to thank me for this but if it was the other way around, well I'd want you to tell me… switch on your parents' television.' A silence ensued, presumably whilst the request was met. 'If you're quick enough and can pick up the local news you'll see what I mean; they've been showing it over and over for the last hour.'

Donna looked back to the screen herself to see the admittedly stunning footage; it was the third time she'd seen it tonight so could only guess how many times it had actually been shown. She could understand why though; she'd still not tired of it and she could imagine it was the same all over the city. The initial landing still made her flinch each time she saw it despite the fact she knew it was coming and the moments that followed were heartbreaking but in a life affirming way. She'd never seen anything quite like it… she was sure it would make the ideal finale to a novel or film one day and she wished she'd dreamt it up herself but knew not everyone would find it quite as sickenly beautiful.

The phone line went dead as it was disconnected the other end without a word. The combination of disappointment and humiliation had been too much for Angela who'd slammed her phone down, hardly able to believe what she was seeing. Minutes later, she was in her car, heading back out of the city just hours after she'd returned and unsure whether she appreciated the call or not but certain that she'd never seen Noel smile at her like he had done on screen.

Donna had half expected that reaction and wasn't surprised at the apparent ingratitude. She wondered if she'd hear from her again now that Angela didn't need her monthly reports anymore; Donna knew she'd been used, but she also knew not to expect anything else. It was why she'd been the only friend Angela had left; after tonight she'd ceased to be of any use and the fact that they went through school together would mean nothing. It didn't upset her like she thought it would; in fact it actually felt like a freedom she didn't realise she'd ever lost. She'd chosen her friends for their very different qualities these days and that was why she was in Mary's flat rather than chasing after her old class mate the way she had done for a decade or more. She was actually glad to see Noel look at someone else that way even if she was a stranger to her... it was about time. Instead of rushing back to her own flat she waited where she was. The view was better here and through the window she watched the first of the ambulances pull away precariously, unaware of the turmoil within it....

'Leave him be Shephard! I'm ordering you to leave him be!' demanded the willowy man, who didn't even lift his head from his hands as he shouted. He found it just as much of a tragedy and wished for the same result as his colleagues did but his considerable experience told him that the time for hope had passed. 'It's been too long, much too long', he added re-emphasising his simple statement more to justify his outburst than to advise the other medics who already knew what he was saying was very likely to be true, yet they acted like they couldn't hear him at all. That seemed slightly less insubordinate than openly refusing to obey.

Still caught up in the euphoria they persisted trying to revive Noel's body long after they'd usually have pronounced him dead. Whether it was through sheer desperation to keep the disaster's apparent body count to zero or a genuine new found belief in miracles they were not sure, but the harsh reality of the world they lived in was re-establishing its presence, invading their optimism like always. When they were inevitably disciplined they'd argue that to continue striving for resuscitation could do no further harm and that was always difficult to debate against. Even Noel, having survived until now against the odds could only die once and there was nothing they could do to him now that could worsen his condition. That would form the basis of their debriefing when they had chance to talk it through with Weitzman but he was still screaming at them to stop, the authority in his voice having deteriorated into a pleading that was evidence of his genuine belief in his decision. He'd always felt it disrespectful to persevere after the point of no return and all that was being achieved here was the prolonging of Evelyn's obvious agony.

He looked at the state she was in and suddenly felt guilty for mourning his own sense of loss. He took the girl in his arms in an effort to console her; something he'd never done with anyone else, always thinking that physical contact was a step too far in his profession but tonight it seemed different somehow. He attempted to turn her face away and bury her head in his chest as even the most optimistic of the crew began to accept reality. They knew that they were well beyond any known revival limits and there was no point in giving the girl false expectations any longer; there were physical boundaries that could not be breached whatever the time of year but Evelyn wouldn't accept it even if they did. Reason, science and medical history mattered little to her; everyone was giving up on Noel. They were letting him go and to her it was as simple as that.

They didn't know him or what he'd done so they'd have no clue that he deserved better; that their efforts could never be enough. Maybe they owed him nothing, but she did; she owed him life itself and that was nothing less than what he'd earned.

Evelyn wriggled violently within the grip that protected her only for it to tighten in response. She was left little option but to react with strength she was surprised to possess. Even in her usual state, her slight frame would have struggled to escape so it came as a shock to everyone when her now fragile and wounded body erupted, her arms exploding outwards and jettisoned her away but it wasn't far enough. Weitzman reached for her again with the best of intentions but cried out as Evelyn, having thrown her aching neck backwards snapped it forward again to bring her full force against him. She brought her forehead down into his face and he at last gave up trying to restrain her, holding his nose instead as he crumpled to the floor.

She scrambled away and towards the stretcher before anyone else had managed to react to what had just happened. They'd had their backs turned so were slow in their attempts to stop her and she reached Shephard before he'd even turned. She threw her arms around him from behind and down onto his, pushing them lower until the pads he held were again in contact with Noel's body, her face contorting with effort just to hold them in place. She'd have been unable to compete physically but the element of surprise helped her initially and once in position, physics was on her side too. She held her ground whilst virtually hanging off of him, using every ounce of her weight to compensate for her lack of strength.

'Again! Try it again!' She kept screaming so loud that it hurt Shephard's ears as she remained locked onto him. 'Just one more time... now do it!' Her feet kept sliding across the blood soaked floor as she wrestled to maintain her control for as long as she could, praying it would buy the time that was needed and that everyone now understood that she didn't want them to stop trying for her sake. As she whimpered her one last desperate plea it descended into a sobbing which caused an indecision that shouldn't exist.

The weaker minded of the crew shook her head in anticipation of the disciplinary she now knew she'd get as she struggled to hold her hand steady over the button that could administer the final powerful shock for which Evelyn was begging. She couldn't afford her loyalty to her superiors to be questioned at this early stage in her career but she could see that the breaking heart in front of her would forever hold her responsible for what happened if she continued to ignore her own.

Evelyn's voice competed with that of the man who'd taught her most of what she knew but they were no louder or clearer than each other and still she hovered in painful hesitancy. She tried to secure herself as the ambulance gained pace over the difficult terrain and was steered carefully through the labyrinth before them. Its driver had to choose between two possible exits and weighed the merits of each. The first was the clearest but it was hard to anticipate whether the gap was quite wide enough for them to pass through. If she'd guessed correctly it was likely to be the safest route but she opted for the other as she predicted it would be quickest. The foam was thickest there but it thinned the further to the left she drove. It was still slippery, more so than the ice beneath it but it remained the most direct passage and her approach was careful enough. But in avoiding the more difficult surface she'd given herself little room for manoeuvre as a Labrador charged awkwardly but determined towards the vehicle. Instinctively she swerved to avoid it taking the ambulance over the very area she'd struggled to evade. Its wheels spewed the strange, slippery sludge beneath them as she attempted to accelerate out of a collision but it took time for the front tyres to find their grip; when they did, the back of the ambulance span out wildly and suddenly. It's potentially dangerous slide was cut mercifully short by a car, previously undamaged but now crushed between the full weight of the ambulance and the lorry to its opposing side. Only a colour coordinated bumper and its limited edition production badge escaped complete ruin and Mary watched it all.

Even under such extreme circumstances she found time to

appreciate the scene as the father of her child mouthed words of disbelief, most of which didn't bear repeating having just been forced to witness the dream car he'd left her for destroyed before his eyes but she didn't dwell on it for long. She couldn't be happier to find that it didn't please her as much as she'd have imagined; he belonged in the past and as her water broke, the future and all its endless possibilities filled her mind.

She was hurried in the same direction as her father; both of them now needing medical attention as much as they needed each other. But with the hospital so close and its staff already aware of the patients coming their way, preparations were already being made for Nick. Mary knew she'd done the right thing and despite being asked to make a decision on his behalf it had been the easiest she'd ever made; she'd pointed absolutely everyone who might need to know towards the empty containers and made them all aware of what the bottles used to contain. The information had already been put to use and had enabled the paramedics to begin stabilising Nick and he seemed to be improving by the minute. Father and daughter lay there looking at each other; everything said without a single syllable spoken. Their loss was about to be replaced with a new life that couldn't be in better hands and whilst that didn't make everything right, it did make it easier to bear. They'd never stop missing Grace and the sadness they both felt now wouldn't ever vanish completely, but in that way she'd live on and neither of them would have it any other way. They had to look ahead now and Mary concentrated on that alone as her first contraction took hold. With that glorious agony any thought to look back towards the man still analysing the irreparable damage to his beloved, customised sports car completely disappeared and she instead looked to the man that would never leave her; he'd be just fine given time and so would she.

CHAPTER FIFTY

The unexpected collision sent everyone and everything in the ambulance off balance including Noel who'd been lying absolutely motionless until the effect of the impact re-animated him if only for a second. Had Evelyn not been keeping constant pressure on his body by continuing to force Sheppard to maintain his position; effectively holding the corpse in place he'd have been thrown from the stretcher. They were reliant on each other to retain their awkward and uneasy stance, each providing the other with someone to cling on to but the rest of the crew were in a very different situation. Unaided and unable to steady themselves, they lost their stability completely despite their cramped conditions.

Weitzman had still been recovering from his injuries when he was catapulted from one side of the vehicle to the other. He contorted his body, bending it into almost inhuman shapes to avoid Peter making the extremely violent landing all the more painful; it did nothing to dislodge his outrage at being so blatantly ignored but as he reassessed the situation he realised that he may not have lost his authority entirely. If the young medic who stood at those vital controls had any real intentions of administering the increased voltage in defiance, surely she'd have already done so. He convinced himself of that as she too suffered the effects of the impact and was thrown sideways, her tiny frame rebounding off the stacks of monitors that surrounded her. She attempted to regain her poise but as the sliding rear of the ambulance bit into the road again and straightened, she was hurled into the equipment over which she'd hesitated. Instinct provoked her to break the fall anyway she could and she reached out to protect herself. In doing so, her open palm didn't merely depress the very button she been ordered to stay away from, she slammed into it with her full weight.

The resulting surge of electricity was massive and found its way down the leads unnoticed in the mayhem until it reached Noel's body which erupted, reacting to the wattage so suddenly and powerfully that the resulting spasm was enough to send those who'd loomed over him reeling.

Still intertwined, Evelyn and Sheppard dragged each other down as they fought to gain a grip against the slippery surface on which they stood. Out of reflex they'd grappled with each other, neither wanting the other to win the race back to their feet. Evelyn almost managed it, helping herself up by pressing Sheppard further into the blood soaked floor but she slipped again. Peter just shook his head in disbelief as he watched the two of them pushing and pulling each others arms and legs from under one another, repeatedly landing them flat against the crimson washed floor as they both failed to realise it couldn't matter less anymore; if it hadn't already been too late to revive Noel, it would be by now. The voice of reason could be heard again, still shouting and demanding in no uncertain terms that they come to their senses and calm down. Almost instantly their aggression subsided as they accepted he was right and the pointlessness of any further struggle set in. Embarrassed to have turned on each other, they both fell silent, allowing the other to establish some sort of balance, rising in near perfect tandem as Weitzman screamed just one word that was obeyed by all.

He'd made a plea for silence and in that moment nobody had failed to realise why. Hardly daring to breath they listened for what they'd all agree would be the most glorious sound possible; the simple, rhythmic, electronic representation of a pulse that couldn't possibly mean more. They looked at each other for confirmation, each doubting their own ability to hear as the deafening metallic clash still rang within them. Having both accepted the truce, Evelyn looked intently at the man she'd somehow overpowered and he stared straight back. There was no hint of hostility on either side anymore but for both of them it was still a nightmare vision. As they'd tussled on the ground, desperate for the upper hand, they'd coated themselves in claret except where the contours of their face were deepest; it emphasised their features, making their appearance almost skull like. The horrific vision forced them both to look away; as Evelyn did so she moved suddenly; all three medics flinched, unsure of her next intentions but they needn't worry. All she'd wanted to do was everything and anything that she could; she'd had to go one stage further for Noel than they would have but she'd done that now. Despite her efforts, it hadn't been enough and hope suffered a lingering death in the near silence; they could hear nothing but the engine and the street outside and she knew exactly what that meant.

She tried to quell everything she was feeling by reminding herself that he was technically little more than a stranger to her. Approaching him calmly she almost squinted, half closing her eyes as if that would make it easier to bear his; they were unnaturally wide as if he'd been aware of what was happening to him and that the realisation had lead him to take in as much as he could during that last, unforgiving moment. The very thought of it destroyed any consolation she'd attempted to comfort herself with and she passed her trembling hand over his face. Reluctant tears ensured that she failed to notice his pupils dilate, reacting involuntarily to the shifting light as she brought her finger lightly to his eyelids and closed them gently.

That was the last thing Noel wanted and he only just found the strength to open them again; it was a simple pleasure he'd never really appreciated before. He'd didn't want to even take the risk of blinking, let alone look around but he didn't have to... he could feel Evelyn's hand on his face and so knew exactly where she was. He dare not talk in case that shifted the delicate balance in which he found himself; he'd lay as motionless as possible and didn't doubt whilst staring straight up that everyone to his sides were busy doing whatever they could to stabalise him and that his vital signs were being monitored with unfaltering attention.

Evelyn remained rooted to the spot, unable to leave him but she looked away, at last accepting what she'd been told was inevitable whilst the others focused on her alone. There was little they could do to comfort her but they all felt that they should do *something*; only Weitzman retained the ability to think clearly. It was true that they couldn't hear anything; but that didn't make sense… surely they should be able to hear the haunting tone of the flat line? He pushed himself forcefully past the others and towards the equipment; they virtually ignored him as he held the monitor against his own chest. According to modern technology he was as lifeless as Noel; feeling nauseous with suspicion he instead tried the old fashioned method and reached for Noel's wrist… the pulse was faint, but it was undoubtedly there.

He began giving orders so fast he'd barely finished one before he'd started another. He didn't need to explain himself as his colleagues at last paid him the attention he demanded and began doing everything they could to keep up with the list of commands.

Noel did his best to remain composed and tried not to listen to what sounded very much like panic but would probably be termed as urgency. But through it all he could hear Evelyn, unable to answer a single question she was being asked; it had never been more important to discover who he was and it was the last problem they expected to have. Sheppard was used to interpreting body language and translating gestures but despite his initial assumption, he'd now noticed the absent rings. It surprised him that he wasn't dealing with a married couple but it also meant that he needed to establish the next of kin; should the worst happen he was sure they'd want to be there and he sounded both confused and suspicious as he continued to press Evelyn for information.

'I don't need you to know the number, just their names will be enough' Sheppard assured her as he readied himself to make the necessary call. Evelyn just shook her head.

'Their surname then, you must know that?' continued the exasperated medic but when she simply looked away he wondered with regret if he'd been less than tactful under such extreme circumstances. Peter was sighing with frustration, unable to understand why she wasn't helping in everyway possible and he urged her to do so but as a professional, Sheppard knew he should be more patient so he adopted an apologetic tone.

'Forgive me', he said quietly. 'Have they passed away?'

He was met with a shrug of her shoulders that he took to mean she'd rather not talk about it. He'd begun with the worst case scenario as time couldn't be more valuable but there was a possibility that there could also be a confusing family history that she may not be aware of, yet even a more sensitive line of questioning lead to a similar response. It was infuriating but he accepted that she may be in shock; he'd take on the additional work tracing the contact details would involve but he needed to start somewhere and so asked for nothing more than the name of the man she'd effectively brought back to life. Realising he wasn't going to stop talking until she started, Evelyn answered as honestly as she could.

'I really don't know.' Evelyn looked up at him as she said it; she struggled to believe it was the truth herself and so couldn't reasonably expect anyone else to. She imagined that he'd make his own assumptions and would judge both her and Noel by their clothes… or lack of in her case. She was sure that he'd come to the obvious conclusion however wrong it was but she'd underestimated just how emotive her display of commitment had been; the degrading thought that her company had been paid for never even crossed Sheppard's mind. But he was at a complete loss as to why she appeared to know nothing about someone she obviously cared so desperately about and he continued to stare at her for signs of a possible motive but gave up, the time it would take was a luxury he didn't have. He forgot about his horrific, crimson coated skeletal features and the effect they could have on Noel as they suddenly entered his sphere of vision and reached into his inside pockets. Sheppard found nothing but tried again; on his second attempt he discovered exactly what he'd suspected he might; that kind of suit usually contained plenty of them. He pulled a fistful of business cards from within the tailored jacket and began thumbing through them. Nobody noticed Noel's expression change but had he dared take a deep breath he would have done so as he remembered the note he'd written that was contained within them; he'd never be able to explain it and even if he could find words that could be believed, surely she wouldn't stay around long enough to hear them; she'd be gone before she'd read the last simple sentence he'd scribbled so hastily. But he was saved, for now at least by a ringing phone. Evelyn raised her hands to indicate that it wasn't hers which in turn made the medics look accusingly at each other; they should all know better than to have their mobiles switched on around such sensitive equipment but they all denied their guilt.

In near perfect synchronization they looked towards Noel; perhaps he hadn't been alone in surviving the fall? Quickly but carefully they searched his pockets for the source of the ringing until they found it; Sheppard held it aloft triumphantly knowing he needed to question Evelyn no more. The caller display showed him that it was Noel's parents on the line and whether it was coincidence alone or simply that they'd been alerted by the news didn't matter... they could tell him everything he needed to know from medical history to allergies. He answered and explained the situation as gently as he could whilst remaining economical with the truth and getting to point as quickly as possible. The ensuing conversation was a comfort to Noel as he could guess what was being said based solely on Sheppard's responses; it sounded like his family were already on their way and would probably arrive at the hospital before he did. It was just as well; he had a lot to say to them and he hoped to be able to do so before he was rushed into surgery as it couldn't and shouldn't wait any longer. With a little luck, Caroline would be there too; knowing her so much better now, he was sure she would be.

As the call ended he turned his attention to the list of readings and figures being quoted above and around him; they meant little to anyone but the medics who continued to speak in what might his face was still hidden but that was what made it familiar so she must have imagined the lazy smile. It was the relaxed expression of a rich man; and from his point of view he was... he'd won his bet against the odds just like he'd promised he would but Evelyn spent little time thinking about that; she was far more concerned with everything else he'd said as he'd rushed her away from that alleyway assuring her she had somewhere she needed to be.

It sent a chill through her that wasn't due to the weather as she remembered their conversation; his words were so much more poignant now. Everyone said the odd sentence that could be interpreted several ways and hidden meanings could be found everywhere if somebody was prepared to look hard enough but this seemed so much more than just coincidence; could everything that had followed be no more than a chain reaction? She contemplated the enormity of the question but not for long. If she was ever going to answer it, it wouldn't be now, hanging out the back of a moving vehicle about to turn a particularly sharp corner. She'd do as she was told soon and retreat back inside as she'd rather not be taking any chances at all; but somehow it didn't seem like a risk tonight. She felt invincible and she had just one more thing to do... she raised her hand and waved ever so subtly just in case she'd been wrong in guessing the figure in the distance wasn't quite a stranger but her gesture was returned reassuringly. His image was fading as she left him behind and the ferocity of the snowfall increased. Evelyn reached for the change he'd offered her thinking she'd return it when she saw him next but began to doubt herself; even having searched the deepest corner of Joe's coat pocket the coins were no longer there. She glanced up again but he'd disappeared completely.

She would have expected the uninviting conditions to have cleared the street but an incredible amount of people had stayed to make the most of an atmosphere they'd probably never be part of again. The carol singers were sheltered by the building and remained largely unaffected except for being covered in a thick coating of concrete dust but it had taken them a while to accept that they'd escaped unharmed. They counted their blessings as they brushed the debris from their clothes. The hymns they'd sung had never seemed more appropriate and with the passing of the last ambulance to leave the scene they saw Evelyn, smiling and waving between its swinging doors. They had no idea that she was looking beyond them and that her attention was directed elsewhere so they responded enthusiastically. Taking it as confirmation that there was nobody to mourn, they saw no need to hang onto the respectful silence they'd maintained any longer but somebody had to break it first and it was the eldest amongst them. Uncertain of the words when singing alone, those she remembered rang out with a conviction she'd lacked before… she believed in the lyrics as they held a resonance she'd missed until now. Her sons were more than a little surprised as she'd struggled to find the confidence to come along at all tonight, let alone give a solo performance so having looked at each other they gave her the support she deserved. They were hesitant at first, embarrassed to be leading the somewhat amateur group when they'd only arrived through compassion for their mother and her insistence on tradition but when they saw the look on her face they stopped holding back; it didn't matter if they were in time or even in key as that reaction in itself was more than worth it. And as their apprehension vanished, they found a voice that inspired others to join them; to do what they'd set out to achieve tonight and spread a little Christmas spirit but they couldn't have imagined the success they'd have. As they moved from the verse and into the chorus they reached the part that everyone knew and found themselves at the centre of a choir, the density of sound far fuller and greater than their humble gathering could ever create by themselves. They were slow to realise and the last to hear it over their own semi-trained voices, but their private celebration had spread outwards and was making its way to the other side of the road as the surrounding crowd begun to join in. Some disguised it, little more than humming under their breath whilst others embraced it, overacting in exaggerated theatrics to compensate for any failures they made in hitting the right note but however they contributed; everybody was infected. Like a lit fuse it recruited new voices regardless of age or gender; it chased in and around the carnage, hunting down every last person until they either joined in willingly or were coerced into doing so by insistent partners, keen not to miss the opportunity to be part of something so spontaneous.

The mass hysteria was being recorded and when viewed in a different frame of mind it would be revealed for what it was; out of sync and out of tune, but to those that were there, nothing had ever sounded quite so perfect. It surrounded them and continued to rise until it drowned out the sirens and engines and became all that could be heard.

Evelyn reprimanded herself. The girl who hated to cry was in floods of tears again. It was all too much, even for her as the ambulance cut a swathe through the mass of people that had gathered together, this time through choice rather than necessity. The dividing wall of sound made their parting just as evident as their physical movement. Evelyn looked above them at yet more people who'd leant awkwardly out of their apartment windows having seen what David and Declan were still beaming live into their living rooms. They'd wanted to see if it looked just as surreal as it had on screen suspecting clever camera angles had been used to exaggerate what was happening, but for once real life was more amazing than what they'd seen on television.

With the crowds having compacted and unknowingly centred themselves, David's point of focus at last stood still. He dared to take his eye away from the view finder for long enough to look to his anchorman for confirmation that everything had really just happened the way he'd seen it through his lense. They didn't speak at all knowing that whatever they said would be broadcast miles beyond where it was intended. Instead, Declan just raised his eyebrows in a manner that indicated he always knew this would happen. David raised his open hand imitating he was about the give him the slap he deserved but as their mocking expressions dissolved into knowing smiles they'd only just had chance to raise, he lowered and extended his arm. The pair shook hands firmly, both having fulfilled their half of a partnership that so nearly never worked. It was a brief moment as both men were eager not to release their grasp on the chance they'd latched onto so fiercely. Their microphones continued to pick up the crescendo that was being sung yet again, but louder this time yet their camera began to move slowly out of frame. David had lost his train of thought but pointed across the street to justify himself before he received the reprimand he knew he should expect from his career minded colleague. He was ignored so he physically turned Declan's face until they shared exactly the same view and stared towards what was left of the Wainsbridge entrance as its owner emerged, stepping over the rumble that surrounded it. His wife continued to walk awkwardly, her injuries still apparent but she was gently guided by his hand.

Both David and Declan were unsure of what they were seeing and so used their camera to zoom in for confirmation; amidst every unbelievable sight they'd seen tonight this was the most difficult to digest; Ivy looked… happy. She clung to Richard's hand as if it was power and influence but carried an expression that suggested she cared little about either anymore. She saw the young men that had perhaps single handedly saved the immediate future of Wainsbridge Media but knew even if that remained to be seen; they'd undoubtedly saved their own careers. She'd be forced to take back everything she'd said to them but would be only too pleased to do so. In case they doubted it, she fixed them with a look that indicated they had nothing to worry about other than how they'd handle their sudden celebrity status. Richard had been made aware of their actions the second the elevator doors eventually opened and he acknowledged his appreciation. The pair smiled back until they noticed Ivy's over exaggerated gestures, silently demanding that they concentrate on the scene behind them rather than on her rekindled marriage. Both men shook their heads in disbelief but did as she wanted; it had been too much to expect that she'd change completely and they had accepted that they'd have to learn to work with her less than perfect manners… or at least meet her half way. It'd be easier from now on knowing that whichever way they looked at it, they actually had her to thank for the promising careers that now awaited them.

They continued to film the crowd as the ambulance made its way through; in such poor visibility it would soon be out of sight but within it, Weitzman had run out of patience and had every intention of pulling Evelyn away by force if necessary. He'd do whatever he had to so long as that meant he could lock the rear doors; there'd been enough oversights already tonight and he could see that by craning her head out the back for a better view she was ensuring another accident waiting to happen. He'd eventually given up waiting for anyone else to intervene but they'd seen what could happen should Evelyn be approached in the wrong way and so busied themselves elsewhere in an effort to steer well clear of her. Weitzman sighed and accepted the responsibility was his, he'd rather run the risk of being attacked rather than be disobeyed again. But when he stood directly behind and could see what she was witnessing he joined her in watching just for a moment before coming to his senses. Reaching out further than he felt comfortable with, he gripped the handle intending to slam the door shut harder than he needed to; partly to be sure it struck the latch this time and partly to make his point. As he did so, it halved the entrance to the ambulance just before it was turned into the corner that Evelyn had predicted and it was slowed down considerably in preparation. Even so, it still swayed them slightly off balance and they both had to steady each other before he eased Evelyn aside; but this time she let him. It should have been easier than he expected but he found himself with another difficult decision to make.

He'd let protocol rule over compassion already once tonight and it had turned out to be the wrong choice; almost fatally so. If he closed the last half of the door now he doubted anyone would ever know what they'd left behind but he found himself hesitating. He knew what he *should* do and that if he failed to, he'd be breaking every rule he'd ever known as far as hygiene and safety was concerned but still he delayed. As he felt the brakes applied he started to speculate as to whether he was the only one who'd noticed they were being followed as the vehicle was slowed way beyond necessity by a driver who'd never admit to having done so through choice. Weitzman knew better than to question her; he almost understood her actions as the Labrador, clearly exhausted from the chase leapt with the last of her energy, her front paws gripping surprisingly well but her single hind leg repeatedly attempting to help her establish a balance that would keep her onboard. When she was just at the point of falling backwards she was grabbed and helped onboard by a man who couldn't believe what he was doing; Weitzman rolled his eyes as the others watched him carry the exhausted and ageing animal over to Peter who already had his arms outstretched in anticipation of the ecstatic reunion.

It assured Noel that he'd been right to make his offer of a loan and he was glad to see that the decision made fourteen years ago couldn't have been a better one, but his thoughts were cut short as he noticed Evelyn. She'd at last calmed down but it seemed as though her mind needed to be constantly occupied. Crouched in the corner she rummaged through the business cards abandoned by Sheppard who no longer needed to search for clues but he had neglected to share his knowledge. For a moment she considered pressing him for information but the role reversal was inappropriate right now and she knew it. He needed to stay committed to his job and it was in her interest to let him so she remained none the wiser yet eager to learn whatever she could.

Most of the cards informed her of nothing she hadn't already known or worked out for herself; that Noel had an enviable career with professional contacts but was surprised when she came across something more personal. She glanced at him and then back to the words she'd begun to read; it was the first time he'd seen her face since slipping from this world and his shocked expression ensured she was reminded of how it had changed; she could only imagine how the hideous mixture of grime, dried blood and tears looked and what a shock it would be for him to see her like this, especially as most of it was *his* blood. But her appearance was the last thing on his mind as he was more concerned with what was in her hand. He was all too aware of the message he'd written and just how specific it was; she'd never believe his explanation and the future he'd hoped for began changing shape and slipping away. He watched her lips move; she was digesting every letter and exactly what it meant. He accepted defeat as she stood before approaching him, stony faced and ignoring the fact that the ambulance had at last begun picking up speed. Below it, a card soaked in foam remained stuck to the front tyre; less than an hour ago it had been separated from the others and replaced carelessly by shaking hands so it was the only one to break free as it plummeted earthwards at such colossal speed that it was virtually ripped from its shelter. Carried on the breeze that was tunnelled between the buildings it came to rest amid the pedestrian mass below, seemingly insignificant and unnoticed. But it had been kicked from one side of the pavement to the other before being walked up and down the street during the frantic stampede that followed only to be picked up again as the ambulance pulled away and rolled over it. The weight of its wheels and everything they carried bore down, squeezing the moisture it had gathered in its cheap fibres and rendering its scrawled message almost illegible as the ink bled outwards but it could still be deciphered by anyone who'd take the time. It was turned over and over as the tyres were slowly rotated and the traffic ahead cleared as if it was chasing its passengers and it actually *wanted* to be read. Every revolution only pressed it harder against the rubber to which it clung and if it wasn't for the vehicle being steered through the water now streaming down the roadside it would still be there. Whilst the flames that had engulfed it had been dealt with, what was left of the delivery bike remained hot enough to melt the surrounding snow which had gathered and now flowed downhill, carrying the message over the tarmac until it reached a drain and became stuck on the grating; for a moment it balanced, clinging onto the chance of discovery until the next car passed. In a particular hurry to leave the city behind, its driver sped faster than she should, not even realising she was about to overtake the one person she came here to see, but the resulting draught made a small but very significant difference, sending the confession down into the sewers where its secret would be kept.

Unaware it ever existed; Evelyn couldn't keep up her playful pretence any longer and knelt beside Noel. Her face was a picture of all the opposites he'd expected; in fact it was everything he'd wished for. She revealed what she'd kept hidden and raised an eyebrow; it was an advertisement for a dating agency. The discovery had been as much of a relief for her as it was an embarrassment to Noel despite the fact he'd never looked at it twice; but having prepared himself for so much worse he laughed out loud without thinking, instantly trying to stop himself as he was again ordered not to exert himself. Evelyn held her finger to his lips before slowly and symbolically tearing the card up in front of him. When he wasn't being watched he reached out his hand, at last in no doubt that it would be taken by another; both were severely grazed and would bear permanent scars as a constant reminder of how they met but they intertwined perfectly.

Even breathing was easier like this and despite his condition, Noel had never felt more completely alive but he concentrated fully on the moment... just in case. Outside the snow still fell as the entire city gradually changed colour; those within it considered the events on a far grander scale than Noel who remained largely unaware of everything that happened but he had enough to come to terms with already. At just twenty four years old he already possessed a knowledge that few could speak of and he'd gained it in a matter of seconds; he wondered if he'd share it or deal with it alone the way he always had. If he could convince people of what he'd experienced it could change the way they lived their lives but the realist in him doubted they'd be anything other than cynical; in their position he'd be of the same opinion. Most would be polite if only out of sympathy and they'd probably even accept that he genuinely believed it himself but that didn't mean that they'd see it as the truth; but one day they would. With the last breath they took they'd know he spoke no word of a lie... and he could live with that.

DISCOVER MORE...

For further information on the author, this novel, book signings and appearances visit **www.rossfriday.com** where you can discuss related topics, find contact details and discover how you could win signed merchandise.

You'll also be able to access free downloads, register for the mailing list, learn more about forthcoming stories and vote for which you would like to see published next.

MIRACLES CAN EXIST...

EVERYTHING HAPPENS FOR A REASON...

WHATEVER LIFE'S WORTH... IT'S AT LEAST WORTH LIVING

ISBN 1412086333-7